A Duchess's Dilemma

Silence. And then the faintest crackle in the brush outside—a mouse, she thought dismissively, then stiffened as dry branches crunched under what must be a full-sized human foot. She held her breath but couldn't hear anything except the whine of wind across the sand above and behind her, the pounding her heart made in her ears. And then the whisper that cut through everything: ''One of the women has betrayed you. Flee or die.''

Lialla swallowed, clenched her hands into fists, and dove back through the opening. . . .

Praise for Ru Emerson's NIGHT-THREADS

RU EMERSON

NIGHT-THREADS

THE CRAFT OF LIGHT

ACE BOOKS, NEW YORK

This book is an Ace original edition,
and has never been previously published.

THE CRAFT OF LIGHT

An Ace Book / published by arrangement with
the author

PRINTING HISTORY
Ace edition/May 1993

All rights reserved.
Copyright © 1993 by Ru Emerson.
Cover art by Angus McBride.
This book may not be reproduced in whole or in part,
by mimeograph or any other means, without permission.
For information address: The Berkley Publishing Group,
200 Madison Avenue, New York, NY 10016.

ISBN: 0-441-58088-2

Ace Books are published by The Berkley Publishing Group,
200 Madison Avenue, New York, NY 10016.
The name "ACE" and the "A" logo
are trademarks belonging to Charter Communications, Inc.

PRINTED IN THE UNITED STATES OF AMERICA

10 9 8 7 6 5 4 3 2 1

FOR DOUG

And for Jerry Thompson
Best buddy—darn you, anyway
1944–1991

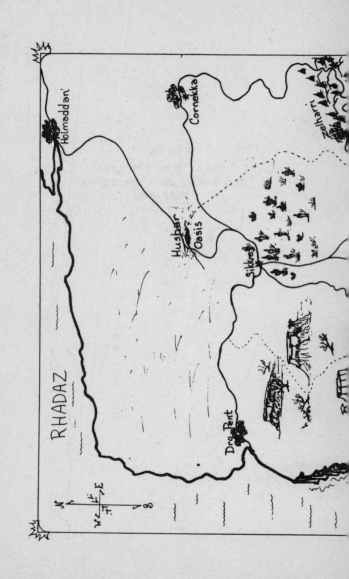

i

THE celebration of Midsummer was just past, but along the northern Holmadd coast, fog swathed sand, low crumbling cliffs and rocky bays, tidepools. The air was chill, utterly still; the shriek of unseen gulls rose to a clamor and died away, leaving only the faint hiss of retreating water pulling at hard-packed, wet sand.

And then, the soft, rhythmic squeak of bare feet on coarse, wet sand.

Five women clad in heavy, dull black moved with purpose along the water's edge. Two carried between them a large basket piled with coarse-woven empty sacks; the remaining three each bore smaller baskets and all walked briskly to counter the damp and chill of the morning air. Other than the squeaking shuffle of feet on wet sand, the hiss of waves, the shrilling of a band of shore birds, there was no sound—though the village was only a short distance off, across a wide expanse of soft, yellowish sand and through a dry, narrow cleft that was a treacherously deep and swift stream in winter months. With such a fog, there might not be a village within miles, but set as it was hard against the inland side of a tall, rocky spine of land, the cries of small village children and dogs seldom carried seaward anyway. Today, the younger children would be indoors, the older ones huddled with their herds or around fires near the pens. On a day such as this, every man from the three elders to the boys initiated into adulthood at Midwinter would be inside the long house, drinking, laughing, sharing tales and cups of a sour, hot wine

the women made from sand berries—or packed like boxed
smelt in the sweat-bath.

The women moved with familiar purpose along the water-
line, then turned to cross a shelf of scoured, flat rock and
work carefully down a short, rugged drop to a small bay.
Here, even the sound of the receding tide was faint; barnacles
and tide-pocked stones stood wet and treacherous everywhere—in deep pools where small fish darted among faintly
swaying grasses, shallow puddles edged in yellow froth,
weed-slicked peaks between such pools. Now and again fingers of water edged lazily into sight, swirled through the pools
and slid away.

The large basket was carried back to dry ground, filled
partway with sand to anchor it should the fog shift and the
afternoon winds rise as they so often did. The women tucked
black skirts into the intricately woven green and yellow sashes
that served to identify them by village, took sacks from the
pile next to the basket and went seaward, picking a cautious,
barefoot way over sharp stone and into the midst of the great
tidepool.

They worked in silence for some time, gathering mussels
and a few small crabs, filling the sacks and dragging them
back to the basket. The sand was poured out, damp bulging
bags went in. Each woman took a second bag. This time,
however, they moved farther west, along the sand, before
turning and walking toward still receding tide. There was a
ledge here: yellow rock and dirt pinned here and there by
gray-green scrub and long, reedy grasses. The woman who
had led the way held up a hand, edged down a shallow cleft
and onto smooth stone. She sat, waited until the other four
women were seated so near that knees touched, then drew
scarves away from her face. Her companions copied her action and one, with an impatient little sound, dragged the cloth
back to bare thick, coppery hair square-cut to just below her
ears. She turned away from the others to gaze toward land,
though there was still little to see.

"There is no need for you to watch, Ryselle," the first
woman said. Her voice was soft and low; her face a pale,
lined oval under straight brows. "No man of North Bay will
move ten paces from his cup of *bratha* and his brothers on
such a day—"

"When the city woman came among us, she warned us not to trust to habit among men," Ryselle broke in sharply.

"That is true. Because the women in the cities have themselves broken with habit and so the men are now suspicious of anything their women do. But *our* men have as yet no least hint of the change we intend will come."

"No. One day they will begin to suspect us, Sretha—if only on the day when we ourselves break the pattern. Since we will one day need to guard our words and actions as though a husband or a father scrutinized the least of them for revolt, why not begin as we must go on?" Sretha opened her mouth, closed it again; Ryselle had turned away without waiting for a response, and one of the other young women spread her hands in a wide, impatient shrug.

"Do as you choose, Ryselle, so long as you do not call suspicion upon yourself and the rest of us by these actions. There is no time to argue such a trifle, not today. Sretha, what of the oversea foreigners? The city woman said they might be of use to us."

The older woman was already shaking her head. "No. Not by this newest message. The city women misunderstood the foreigners, judging them by their words and not by their lives. They call Holmaddi ways disgraceful and shortsighted, and yet, we now are told that while their own women live better than we, most still count as possessions. The foreigners are no answer."

"They seek to divide Rhadaz, pitting the Dukes one against the other, they wish to start war and once Rhadazi eyes are turned inward they will come from without and take all," Ryselle said flatly. "Did you not hear what the woman said concerning that?"

"Whispers and rumor only, even in this new message," another of the women said sourly. "But I am of your mind in this much, Ryselle. To trust ourselves to *men* would be folly."

Sretha shifted on the hard stone bench. "To trust *these* men would indeed be foolishness. There, set that also aside; safe time such as this is too precious to waste in rechewing words and rewording old arguments."

One of the women pressed scarves back to bare hair as short and red as Ryselle's, shot with silver. "What else have we to do, Sretha? We cannot simply declare an end to the life our men have decreed to be ours. We gather support, yes; we speak to those women we dare trust and so our numbers daily increase, we have means and places of meeting, means to pass messages—and what does it all mean? Nothing! We dare not act, or speak aloud! We wait, and wait, and wait! And chance with every day discovery and—'' She shook her head. ''You know the penalty if we are caught, even today. City women might fear the block and the axe; you and I would greet the next rising tide buried to the breast in sand.'' Ryselle made an impatient, wordless sound; the woman ignored her. ''If the foreigners are useless, then we fall back upon our own strengths and our own desperation. And what use is that, if even all Holmaddi women were to speak together?''

Sretha shrugged. ''It is more than half, already. And no one of us ever believed it would be simple, or painless. But you forget the other message.''

Ryselle laughed sourly. ''The outlanders? Why not a message also from the sea witches, offering to swallow the boats of our men whole?''

''Don't speak foolishly,'' Sretha said. ''One is legend and myth. The other—the city women believe the outlanders exist; they have met people who have spoken with one of the outland women. Yes,'' she added quickly, as the younger woman turned to look at her in wry disbelief. ''I know; I have not seen an outlander myself; I know no *Holmaddi* woman who has. What beyond that can be trusted? And yet, if they are any of what is said—from a place that cannot be reached save by magic; where women say and do as they choose, even live apart from men if they wish, standing with them as equals if they wish it—'' She sighed faintly. ''Who would not remain doubtful of such women and such a place? And yet—well, there is no time to speak of this, either; if there are such women and such a place, they do not touch our lives.

''But other things will, and soon. This past night I wove a net of Night-Thread and slept within it, and so brought down a vision. Three things there were and all presage change: a circle, a triangle, a line. I touched the first and it filled me with a certainty of death; the second, Light. The third—the third, I touched and on touching it, woke." She let her eyes close, and for a moment looked old indeed. She blinked and roused herself as one of the other women lay cool fingers on the back of her hand.

"Then, Sretha, what shall our course be? If our Wielder does not know, how shall the rest of us choose?"

"In one particular thing, there is no choice," the woman to her left said flatly. "I have some years left to me, if the gods are gracious and my husband in his drunken wrath does not slay me for bearing him daughters only. I will not see the hell that is my life remain the birthright of my daughters."

"On that," Ryselle said dryly, "we are all agreed. As we are against these foreigners, who are after all every one male. Oh," she added as one of the others cleared her throat, "I know. I have more quarrel with all men than the rest of you. Still: What have they in common, those squatting drunken in the lodge"—she waved a hand toward the village—"the Emperor, our Duke, the foreigners?" She snorted and turned away from them again. "That they are all *men*."

There was an uncomfortable little silence; another of the women broke it with a rustle of stiff fabric and cracking knee-joints as she shifted so she could look down onto the tide-pools. The water was drained from all but the deep pools now. "The hour is growing late—" she began timidly.

Sretha held up a hand, silencing all of them. "Aye. I will do what I can tonight and the nights that follow, to make clear the vision. And do not forget, the city woman told us Red Hawk caravan will come through the village on its way back to Zelharri. The message we send must be complete; we may have no chance to send another for some time to come."

One of the younger women frowned. "This Zelharri noblewoman you will send the message to—is she not powerful and wealthy? Why should she come to our aid?"

"Ask that of her, if you meet," Ryselle said evenly.

"You know that I spoke with the elder caravaner women this spring, when Red Hawk went east to the city; it was then I sent word to the city woman, and then the Red Hawk grandmother first spoke to me of the sin-Duchess. Ryselle was there also."

"And I argued against it, the idea that we chance discovery

by sending for a foreign woman. Still, I would trust her before any outlander. The grandmother says that she is of an age to be long since wed and mother of many children, and yet she has held to her own choice, not to marry—and though the men of the south do not own their women and cannot force marriage upon them, this is still no easy or common choice. If we choose to bring in an alien to aid us, then I say, let us find such a strong one.''

"But, is this not the woman, Sretha, who twists Thread in some dangerous fashion, the one you spoke against so harshly?''

"Sin-Duchess Lialla of Zelharri has done a thing which surely should have blasted her for the mere thinking of it,'' Sretha replied softly. "But she has blended Night-Thread and Hell-Light and gone unscathed; *I* shall ask her of that myself, does she come here. Unless there is a true reason not to do so, I will send out that message, asking her to help us. A man thrown into the waves will grasp whatever comes to his hand; are we less desperate?'' She pushed slowly and carefully to her feet, let one of the younger women hand her the mussel sack, and turned to lead the way back toward shore.

I

THERE might be fog and chill along the Holmadd coast; in Sikkre it was barely midday and already hot—unseasonably hot and unnaturally windless. Banners and canvas awnings hung limp in the still air; sandy yellowish dust, kicked up by heavy foot traffic in the narrow aisles between shops and stalls, lay thickly everywhere.

It was somewhat cooler inside the main hall of the weaver's guild—the guildmasters had had the sense to lay the floor several steps below street level. Ordinarily there was good cross-ventilation, with windows on all sides to catch whatever wind blew. On a day such as this, Jennifer Cray thought wearily, the guild hall was merely a massive, gloomily dark and airless box. The Sikkreni Thukara blotted her forehead on her sleeve and sipped the orange drink that had been placed at her elbow. *I'd kill for ice,* she thought tiredly. The orange was barely above room temperature, and it had been sweetened with honey. After four years, she still hadn't adjusted to the flavor of honey instead of white sugar. She slid a hand along her chin and pinched her earlobe. What she really needed at the moment was coffee; this was the third day she'd spent between the Sikkreni weavers and American traders, trying to finalize a deal, and it was putting her to sleep.

She let her eyes slide left: two local merchants, one of whom had so nearly duplicated the weave of her blue jeans, the other who'd come up with a blue dye that didn't rub out of the fabric and onto skin. One elderly woman to represent those who did the actual spinning and weaving; an even older man who looked simple-minded, but was in fact head of the guild.

On her other side, Americans—or, as the Rhadazi called them, Mer Khani. Jennifer studied the man nearest her as he leaned forward to finger one of the pile of fabric samples on the table in front of him; he turned to speak in an undertone to the man at his right. *She* might as well think of them as Mer Khani herself; they were nothing like Americans from her own, twentieth-century world. Late nineteenth-century, these men were, and they spoke American with a broad English accent—not surprisingly, really, since their America had only separated from England within the past ten years. Peacefully, yet.

She shrugged that all aside; her nephew Chris had given up trying to sort out the differences between the world they'd left and this alternate one and it had never really mattered to her, where and when the two had split. What mattered was that an arrogant old Night-Thread Wielder had accidentally yanked her, her sister Robyn and Robyn's son into this world, and she'd survived it for nearly four years. *Four years exactly, as of tonight*, she reminded herself, and cleared her throat. The American pushed the samples aside and nodded. "We'll make the deal, then. Our cotton, your—your denim. Price as agreed yesterday, raw materials and finished product transported via Dro Pent. Provided the road—?" he hesitated. Jennifer drew the thick writing pad over and made a note.

"It's my understanding the road will be graded and resurfaced by late summer. That's between the Thukar and the Emperor's people; if there's any change, you'll be advised of it."

The middle American planted both elbows on the table and rested his chin on his palms. "It's a legitimate concern, ma'am; we came stright north from the Bez port and my partners here haven't seen that east-west road. I have. The pass was tough enough to cross in dry, early spring weather. In summer heat or under a heavy rain, it would be dire. Even once it's graded and resurfaced—a tunnel there would be a mite more sensible, wouldn't you agree?"

Jennifer shrugged. "If there comes a time when the business between the northern duchies and your people warrants it. In any event, the roads aren't my business, I have enough to worry about without that. I'll pass on your comment."

"No insult intended, ma'am—"

"None taken."

The third man along the table toyed with his orange drink, pushed it away finally. "This supposes of course that the New World Gallic government will give us passage through the Nicaraguan lake—"

Jennifer nodded and bit back a sigh. "Yes, well, we've had that out also, haven't we? Extensively. That's your matter, or rather, for the representatives your government sent down into Central America. If it's necessary to ship everything around the Horn, then we can renegotiate timing, quantities, and price—both for the raw materials and for the finished cloth." She slid the pad across to the man on her right. "If you'll initial each of the points, I'll see the contract is printed and bring it back tomorrow for signature."

She half-expected more argument; there'd been enough of that over the past three days. The American handed the pad to his neighbor so all three men could read down her hand-printed list; after a brief, whispered conversation, he took the pen she held out to him, dipped it in ink and scribbled in half a dozen places. Jennifer blotted the paper and passed it the other way. The Sikkreni went into a huddle—none of them could have read the points even if they'd been written in Rhadazi, but like most non-reading members of the local merchant class they had near-perfect memories—and finally pushed them back across to Jennifer, who initialed the sheet on their behalf. With a loud scraping of chairs, all eight rose at once, and Jennifer fitted the pad, the ink and the pens into her leather case. The four Sikkreni bowed deeply and vanished through a curtain in the rear of the hall. Jennifer blotted her forehead, shoved the wide, padded strap over her shoulder and held out a hand. The lead American blinked, then took it and gave it a gentle pump. "You'll be here tomorrow, about this hour?" she asked.

He drew a fat silver case from an inner pocket and flipped open the cover. "One-thirty?" Jennifer pulled out her own pocket watch, a gift from Chris after the battery on her digital finally gave out, and nodded. "Suits us fine." He stepped aside to let her precede them. "You know, ma'am, we do appreciate what you've done here. This fabric trade. It's not our chief business in your Duchy, after all, but it's a little extra money for everyone. Never hurts, does it? And once we get cleared by your central government to set up a local genuinely mechanized mill, bring in men to organize the work force—why, just think how much fabric these people will be able to turn out.'' He stopped just short of the pool of hot sun at the open door and the dusty courtyard beyond it. ''Now, ma'am, I know you'll say this isn't your concern either, but if we had a better way of transporting things from us to your cities, something that didn't depend on sea power and the conditions out there—say, if we were able to convince your Emperor on the subject of cross-continent transport. That young man, Mr. Cray, he's kin of yours, isn't he? Well, he's certainly in favor of it, and if you were to put your oar with his, so to speak, on the subject of steam engines—''

''That really is out of my hands,'' Jennifer said firmly, but she smiled to take the sting out of the words.

The American smiled back, and nodded. ''So you've said.'' He clearly didn't believe her; a Duke's wife, after all, and a woman with direct access to the Emperor's brother who was himself head of the vast civil service and largely responsible for increased trade with the outside world. ''Still, if you'd keep in mind, one steam engine can pull a number of large cars of materials, and they'd be limited to where they could go by the track system. It's all so much more efficient and faster than carts and horses, safer than ships, you know—''

She smiled again, shook her head gently. ''I know all about railroads.''

''Well, then. And if we could bring track across the mountains; we already have settlements across the plain from the Great Silt River—young Mr. Cray says you call it the Missi-? Can't say it, but that one. Well, we could run track north and south on this side and there'd be direct transport eastward for Sikkre, rather than having to send things around the Horn or portage across the isthmus and through that big lake the New Gallics hold and dragging things overland. The profits would—''

''I understand that. I understand how my nephew's thinking runs on the subject, and I also understand the concerns they're voicing in Podhru. And elsewhere. Gentlemen, frankly

I'm not certain my word would be much use; you must be aware there are those in Rhadaz who worry that because I speak the same language you do, it's possible I'm somehow conspiring with you folks.''

''I—well—''

''Oh, so far as I know it's not a serious concern. If it were, I doubt I would have ever been allowed to deal directly with any of you. Until tomorrow afternoon, gentlemen.'' She tucked the leather case under her left arm, shaded her eyes with her right hand and stepped into the open.

Hot. Fortunately, she was dressed for it: The royal blue caftanlike garment looked formal enough but was made of a practical gauzy cotton and hung loose from a high pleated yoke almost to her ankles; the sleeves were flared and stopped just below her elbows. The flat, open sandals in a darker blue weren't as comfortable as sneakers would have been but the high-tops were pretty disreputable-looking after four years of heavy wear—and Jennifer was using the running shoes only for her courtyard runs, hoping to get another year out of them before they fell apart. There wouldn't be any way to replace them, once they did.

She had walked here from the Thukar's palace early in the day; she could make it back just fine. She glanced up, drew hot, dry air into her lungs. Well, maybe a little slower than she'd come. There wouldn't be any shade to speak of, between here and the gates.

Just outside the courtyard, she turned left, and stopped. Next to the rectangular fountain in the center of the street stood four of the inner household guard and just behind them, her two-wheeled, covered litter and the young man who pulled it. The guards came to attention and one, the captain of the household guard himself, hurried over. ''Lady Thukara—''

Jennifer held up a hand, silencing him. ''Grelt, where did you men come from? I told the Thukar when I left that I would walk back, and I'm certain I left word at the gate.'' She frowned as the other three came across, moving efficiently to surround her. ''It's not that all hot,'' she added.

He shook his head, raised a hand and beckoned sharply; the boy slid into the harness, caught hold of the wooden poles and edged the rickshawlike litter away from the fountain. ''The Thukar sent us, Lady; there's been a threat.''

"Threat?" Jennifer laughed shortly. "Again? What now?"

He shook his head again. "From the lower market, a death threat against yourself."

Jennifer scowled up at him, ignored the hand someone held out to assist her into the litter. "This is ridiculous," she said finally. "If I had a silver ceri for every threat that's rumored to come from the flesh and death peddlers down there, I'd be wealthier than the Emperor himself. I'm walking. If you want to escort something, take this." She held out the leather bag.

Grelt took it, but also took her arm. "Lady Thukara—"

"I don't want to make a scene," Jennifer said ominously.

His eyes were unhappy. "Then, please, Lady; I have my orders. The Thukar—" He hesitated. Jennifer sighed heavily.

"Oh—all right. Before everyone out here begins to stare." She let him hand her into the little cart, pulled her feet in and adjusted the cushions behind her back as the boy took off at a trot. The guardsmen took up positions around the litter and jogged along, one to each side, one behind, one just ahead of the boy and to his left.

My own private secret service, Jennifer thought dryly. But a glance at the man on her left was sobering. His face was grim, his eyes watchful, and for the first time she could re-member, all of them carried long, still-sheathed knives loosely in one hand, ready to pull out of the case and use if anyone came at her. Dahven must have put a genuine scare into them, and she wondered what he had heard—Dahven had been with her for most of her first month or so in Rhadaz, he *knew* she was well able to take care of herself. *Something I can't han-dle—weapons or sheer numbers?* She wondered. She hadn't gone armed, not on a cross-market walk to finalize a trade agreement. But Night-Thread would respond when she needed it—night *or* day, even as seldom as she used it any more. She slewed around on the uncomfortable flat platform and turned to the guard on her right. *Thought so.* He was tall and broad-shouldered—greatly changed in that respect from the first time she'd met him; his face was still too thin, non-descript and gave him the look of a teenage boy.

"Vey? I thought you would be halfway to Sehfi at this hour. Weren't you heading the escort to meet my sister?"

He glanced at her very briefly and the corner of his mouth turned up, before he went back to his study of the surrounding market. "Dahven—I mean, the Thukar—thought I'd be better here. With the rumors." His color was suddenly high. Chris's friend and business partner Edrith had the same difficulty—remembering to speak of his long-time friend Dahven as Thukar, at least in public. After all, both Edrith and Vey had known Dahven for years; Jennifer tried not to know what kinds of trouble the three had gotten into on the occasions young Dahven had snuck out of the Thukar's palace to run wild with two equally young market thieves. The little she *had* heard made her wonder how any of the three lived long enough to grow beards.

"Who's cutting up rough," she asked finally, "that Dahven decided to have me brought home in this uncomfortable box?"

The litter shifted and she clutched at the sides as it rounded a corner. The lane was narrower here, there were people everywhere and the smell of food, dust and heat near overpowering. The boy slowed of necessity. Jennifer's nose wrinkled involuntarily as a man edged past them, going the other way with four huge, foul-smelling camels. Vey shifted his hold on the dagger sheath. His eyes darted from one person to another, never still, and except for that initial glance he didn't look at her again. "Mahjrek."

"Mahj—oh. Again?"

"You've disrupted his business four times, Thukara," Vey said. "And now his building's been razed; certain people passed on the word that he was displeased."

"Serves him right," Jennifer said grimly. "He had enough warning that the anti-slave laws would be enforced; he can't say otherwise." She snorted. "Selling young women! And then, when we begin strict enforcement of the law—!" She drew a deep breath and let it out in a loud huff. "I admit he served a purpose, showing us where the loopholes were as quickly as he did. We might have been years tightening the law otherwise. All the same—"

"Thukara, you needn't convince me," Vey said gravely. "Thukar Dahmec knew the Emperor's law; he made himself wealthy by ignoring it and taking graft from men like Mahjrek. Mahjrek underestimated Dahmec's son—and yourself; no doubt he thought himself clever, changing the name of his shop and calling it a contracting service."

"Contracting service." Jennifer bit off the words. "If I could get my hands on him—" She let the sentence die away as the litter turned into one of the broader avenues heading away from the main part of the market and the boy picked up the pace again.

Vey shook his head. "Word in the lower market has it he feels very much the same about you, Thukara. Enough so, it's said, to warrant caution."

"He hasn't the nerve," Jennifer began.

"I agree," said Vey. "But he knows or can buy any number of men who have nerve—and weapons."

"Hah," Jennifer said sharply. Vey merely shook his head; he was beginning to sound a little winded.

They were near the southern gates now; once they passed the gates, they would turn right once more and take the broad, tree-lined boulevard to the Thukar's Tower. Jennifer rubbed her shoulders against the cushions and gazed moodily beyond Vey. Rickshaws like hers weren't *that* uncommon, but the guard was; people stared as they trotted by, and she could almost hear the remarks. By evening, the fabled Sikkreni gossip mill would be throwing out all manner of wild speculation. She shifted her weight as the boy slowed for the turn.

Just inside the gates, men—mostly foreigners, Americans wearing trousers and shirts unsuitable to a desert climate— stood around an open hole. A telegraph pole lay at the edge of the hole; one of the men leaned on a pick, others on shovels, two held a thick coil of wire between them. Just outside the gate, a lone pole stood, sunlight glinting on glass reflectors and a snarl of dangling wire. This morning, when she'd walked past the men, the near hole had been a shallow scrape, while the men had been in the process of standing the outer pole upright. As she watched, a man began to work his way up it, while two others watched from the base. A small crowd of Sikkreni stood a short distance away. It was going faster than she'd thought; another day or so at most and there'd be a line between the Thukar's palace and the nearest village on the Bez highway—first test of the system. Their end of it, at least; other Americans and a handful of Rhadazi trainees and plain hard laborers had several miles of line installed from Bez toward Podhru, along the old road.

Chalk one up for Chris, whose CEE-Tech Trading Com-

pany put most of its effort into finding things like the telegraph—and then convincing the foreigners to import them,
and the Rhadazi to accept them. He'd had his hands full with
this: The Emperor was growing mentally erratic in his old
age and while he'd put a good deal of power into the hands
of his brother and heir, Afronsan still needed Shesseran's
approval for any outside trade. Particularly for something like
the telegraph, which needed foreign engineers to set up and—
at least for the present—to run and repair. Fortunately, Afronsan had seen the point at once of such swift and accurate
communication; Shesseran didn't understand it, and he openly
loathed the brash and arrogant Mer Khani.

Jennifer wondered again how Afronsan had convinced his
brother to permit the new technology, and the foreign engineers. Probably bribed the emperor's astrologers. She grinned
and leaned forward to watch as the men began to straighten
the pole so half a dozen Sikkreni could shovel dirt around it.

Sharp movement caught her eye; another thing held it.
''Wait.'' She held out a hand to the guard on her left, who
gave her a quick glance, then turned to look where she was
staring. ''Behind the pole—what's *he* doing in Sikkre?'' She
scrambled onto one knee and caught at the guard's shoulder.
''Tell the boy to stop, now!'' The loud, flat crack of a gun
cut across her words and something whistled past her cheek,
splintering into the wooden upright behind the cushions. Jennifer yelped, as much from surprise as fear, and threw herself
flat. Half a breath later, something large and heavy landed
across her, and the rickshaw took off as though it had grown
wings. Her guard didn't know what a gun was; Rhadaz didn't
have them. That something had hit the litter had been enough,
and her reaction sealed it: Vey lay sideways across her, clinging desperately to the far side of the jolting and swaying litter,
covering her body with his own. He was heavy; she couldn't
breathe.

''Lie still, Thukara.'' His words came out in choppy little
bursts of sound as the litter bounced the wind out of him.

''No! We have to go back—!'' But she couldn't shove him
aside, and she wasn't certain she'd get enough sound out for
him to hear her. Behind them people were screaming, and
someone was bellowing, swearing in broadly accented American. She shifted her head what little she could. The point

guard was no longer at the head of the procession. Off chasing an assassin—an assassin with a gun. He wouldn't stand a chance.

Somebody shot at me! Suddenly she was trembling. Rhadazi weaponry was like nearly everything else in the country: a product of five hundred years of isolation behind tightly closed borders. Blade steel was impressive stuff, high in tensile strength. But blades had to be thrust; if thrown, they were like arrows in that it took a lot of skill and practice to hit someone with one. Most often a would-be killer made actual contact with his target; Jennifer was fairly safe in counting on Thread-sense to warn her if someone with murder in mind was near.

But a gun! She fought for calm. This time at least, the shot had missed, and she didn't want to face Dahven in her present state. According to Chris, guns in this world weren't very advanced and none too accurate and most were single-shot. Whether because of that, the moving target or lack of skill, that man had missed her. But there was a very strong law against smuggling guns into Rhadaz; all foreigners understood they and their ships could be searched and if guns were found, they'd be heavily fined, ordered out and permanently banned. Any Rhadazi caught with a gun would be executed, but so far as Jennifer knew, no one had been impressed enough by the notion of foreign weapons to risk death for them; the foreigners certainly weren't about to risk good trade and high profits to defy the law.

The rickshaw plunged into deep shade; they had reached the tunnel leading from the city to the outer palace courtyard. The litter slowed and Vey slid off her as they came into lighter shadow. Jennifer fought air into her lungs and sat slowly, let Vey lift her out and hold her upright until she caught her breath.

Voices echoed in the tunnel and off the high stone walls. Jennifer nodded to Vey, who let her go, and she ducked back under the canopy to peer at the cushions. Guardsmen and servants were staring; Jennifer straightened up and yelled, "One of you get these men water before they collapse! Vey, hand me your knife, will you?" She took it, pulled the cushion aside and dug into the frame behind it. A lead pellet about the size of a marble, partly flattened, popped out of the hole.

She returned the dagger to its owner, beckoned for him to follow her inside.

It was quieter here, though she still had to raise her voice to top the noise outside. "Did you see the man who did this?" Vey shook his head. "Did anyone?"

He shook it again. "Don't know, Thukara. The point man and the rear guard were running toward that post, last I saw of them."

"You didn't see him, though?"

"No. Why?"

"Because," Jennifer said flatly, "I did. And I think I know him." She closed her fingers around the lead shot and started down the long, shaded hallway. "Come with me, down to the family dining room. Dahven was working in there when I left. We'd better assure him I'm still alive; there's enough noise out there, he'll think—come on."

THE outer chambers of the Thukar's palace were hot and stuffy, but the family dining hall was always pleasantly cool. Jennifer led the way, Vey right on her heels. By the time she reached the vine-shaded corridor that led to the family apartments, one of the sandals was rubbing her heel and the gauze dress was clinging to her back. She stopped long enough to ease her feet from the shoes and scooped them up by the straps. The stone floors in this part of the palace were cool and they were slightly damp near the doorway to the dining room. She paused just inside the room to let her eyes adjust.

It was a long room and a dark one, the outside windows covered in latticework and flowering vine. The air was deliciously cool: Water spilled down the walls on both sides of the doorway and fell into low pools, was carried in pottery pipes and troughs to deeper pools that flanked the dining table. Dahven was there, half buried behind books and papers; lamplight picked out red strands in thick, sunbleached brown hair. He glanced up; dark eyes warmed as they found her and he shoved back the chair, came around the table and down the room between the long pools to catch at her hands. He frowned as his fingers touched her right fist, and then the pellet clutched in her fingers. "Jen? You—something went wrong after all, didn't it?" He turned to include Vey in the question, touched the shot in Jennifer's hand and closed her fingers around it again. "Come, sit down, you both look awful. Here, there's chilled tea." He tugged at Vey's sleeve and shoved the young guard onto a chair, led Jennifer around the table and let her down in her own chair. When she would have spoken, he laid fingers on her lips and shook his head. "Just wait. You're unharmed, take a moment, drink something." He felt around the nearest stack of books and came up with a tall pottery mug, filled it from an opaque glass pitcher and put it in front of her.

Jennifer dropped the pellet onto the table between them, took the cup and drank deeply. The mug was cool, beaded with moisture, and the tea had been sweetened the right way, with sugar. *Oh, bless you, Chris,* she thought as she swallowed. He'd gone out of his way to find the stuff for her on his very first trading foray, but it had never tasted better.

"Vey, you'd better have some as well—"

"I had water below; I'm fine." Vey was slumped against the back of the chair and he didn't look fine, Jennifer thought critically. Much too pale. *Probably as white as I feel.* Dahven shoved books, papers and documents down toward the end of the table and came back, picked up the piece of lead and held it under the light, turning it over thoughtfully in his long fingers while Jennifer told him what had happened. When she got to the sound of the gun and the shot slamming into the wood frame, Vey took over. "A foreign gun?" Dahven asked finally.

"As opposed to one from my world?" Jennifer nodded. "I think so; somehow, it got past the Bez docks, or maybe the port guard in Dro Pent got careless. Guns where I came from use bullets—they don't look like that thing."

"I don't like the notion of such things here."

Jennifer laughed shortly. "*You* don't! I'm just glad it wasn't an Uzi; there'd have been a dozen people dead." Dahven waved the unfamiliar word aside with the ease of nearly four years' practice. "I'm not quite as concerned with how it got here as I am with who fired it, though. I saw him. I recognized him—and you would, too; you will, if they catch him."

"I will?"

She nodded. "I don't know if I ever heard his name. But remember the Bez-Podhru road, when those men of your brothers' came after us?" Dahven's face went still; after a moment, he nodded. "Remember—not Firsi, the one the Spectral Host took out—the man who kept trying to hold him back? You talked to him after Firsi vanished—"

"Let me—not Eprian?" Dahven glanced across the table. "Vey, did *you* see Eprian out there?"

Vey shrugged. "Thukar, I—"

"Don't be silly, it's just the three of us in here." Dahven grinned and after a moment, Vey smiled back. Some of the tension went from his shoulders and he relaxed back into the padded chair.

"I didn't see him, Dahven, but I was on the far side of the litter. Yvoric had the left. When the—when you shouted, Jen, I didn't look, I just reacted the way I was trained to."

"Right," Jennifer said ruefully. "If I hadn't yelled, I might have seen where he went after he fired. It startled me." Dahven laughed; she spread her hands in a wide shrug. "But I got a good look at him before the shot. I was watching the work on the telegraph and suddenly, there was this familiar face in with the Americans."

Dahven nodded; the laughter had been brief and his eyes were grave. He leaned back and rubbed his nose with a forefinger. "Are you certain it was Eprian? After all, it was four years ago, almost, you saw him twice on the seacoast road and now even more briefly across that boulevard?" She shrugged, met his eyes levelly. "You really *are* certain. This isn't at all good. After all, four years ago he served my beloved younger brothers—" His voice faded.

Beloved younger brothers, Jennifer thought grimly. Who had conspired with Dahmec to sell their brother to the Lasanachi. That he'd escaped death at a long oar was no thanks to Deehar and Dayher, though when the twins had disappeared on their way to the Emperor's court, the only charges they were officially to have answered dealt with mismanagement of Sikkre's market. Nothing regarding illegal dealings with slavers and local black-market flesh peddlers; nothing to do with Dahven's disappearance from the Thukar's palace and subsequent reappearance along the Bez docks, feverish, deathly thin and carrying marks of Lasanachi fetters on wrists and ankles, a Lasanachi whip across his back. Nothing about the sudden death of Sikkre's Thukar and the production of a new Will naming the twins his heirs. Not even, so far as

Jennifer knew, a single question dealing with the Sikkreni guardsmen who'd hounded them from just south of the Thukar's city into Bez and across country nearly to Podhru—though certain of those guards had been sought in connection with an attack in the Emperor's city itself.

She should have been used to it by now—the way Shesseran could turn a blind eye to anything that didn't affect him personally, to anything that might cause more trouble than the Emperor thought it would be worth. It still infuriated her. And so, Dahven's unscrupulous, egocentric, scheming brothers had left Sikkre unescorted, and had never reached Podhru.

She blinked, came back to the present; there wasn't any point in raising her blood pressure over the matter yet again, and Dahven was still speaking. "I've heard nothing at all to indicate the twins have managed to return to Rhadaz; they'd be known in any port. There's been nothing I've heard about ships putting in along the coast. Vey?"

"Odd rumor about Holmaddi, but nothing new," the boy replied after a moment's thought. "And they'd scarcely reenter Rhadaz that way; it's unsafe to travel other than the roads from Holmaddi south, and they'd be known. They could be anywhere, though; there are enough of our ships out there, of late; I'd wager a man could take passage on one of them, or sign on as crew. They say the port guard in Bez harbor searches only one in so many of the foreign ships and not all of those men coming ashore."

Jennifer sighed, shook her head. "Well, we won't sort it out sitting here and talking about it. If they come back with Eprian, we'll know for certain. Of course, maybe someone else saw him." She got to her feet. "In the meantime, I'm going to go wash and change, so I can get the cotton contract printed out before morning."

AN hour later, clad now in a locally made version of buttonfront jeans and a loose shirt, her long dark hair reworked by her maid into half a dozen braids and fastened high with a pair of combs and tied in bright ribbons, her face still slightly damp, she carried the leather document case over to the long, sunlit room where her clerical staff worked and left them the draft contract; someone would spend the next hour or so handwriting out the initialed articles while another clerk pulled the individual sheets of standard form paragraphs to cut and glue into place. Sometime after that, probably late in the afternoon, the document would be brought to her for approval and then sent down to the lower level and the ancient, painfully slow presses.

It was slow; for a woman used to word processors, fax machines and telephones, it was agonizingly slow. The Rhadazi printing press hadn't changed much in nearly five hundred years. She was fortunate that Sikkre's Thukar had a press; Dahmec had been one of the few Dukes to own one, though he seldom used it. Eventually, Jennifer promised herself, she'd be able to replace it with an up-to-date American or English press. Genuine typing machines, if Chris could ever find such things. In the meantime, she'd applied law-office word-processing methods to the problem of contracts and cut down the time required to typeset them by creating separate formula paragraphs for the sections that were in every contract. That had been easy; the hard part had been convincing both the clerks and the press operators to use them.

SHE went back down the hall that separated business quarters from the suite of private apartments she and Dahven kept, on down to the main gate to find a message waiting: Robyn had left Duke's Fort later than intended and according to the mirror telegraph had decided to spend the heat of this afternoon at Hushar Oasis. Possibly she'd finish the journey after the sun went down, which meant she wouldn't arrive until midnight at the earliest. Maybe even the day after. The message didn't say if she was bringing either of the children— nera-Duke Amarni or baby Iana; messages sent by mirror-flash or at night by lantern were notoriously uncertain, though. Jennifer sometimes thought every operator misinterpreted what he received and garbled what he sent on; by the time a message went through the ten or so operators it took to pass a message from Duke's Fort to the Thukar's Palace . . . Well, it wouldn't be for much longer; with any luck there could be telegraph between them by next spring, and in the meantime there was always the post.

She stopped by the dining hall but the room was dark, the table cleared of books and documents. No doubt they'd been piled up somewhere else, and Dahven was buried behind them once more. She shook her head; the poor man was having an awful time handling the additional paperwork the new roads were making. He did better with people than with paper anyway.

One of the household women came looking for her. "Madam, the Thukar's compliments, he'd like you to join him and some of the foreign men in the blue hall."

Jennifer tucked in her shirt tails. "Thanks. Am I reasonably neat?" The woman nodded, smiled faintly as Jennifer added, "Thanks for the warning. I'd probably have shocked everyone if I'd gone in with my shirt slopping over my belt."

The blue hall was the smaller of the formal hearings chambers, part of the public rooms, near the entrance she and Vey had used earlier. Dahven often used it for criminal hearings. Had the guard returned, possibly with a would-be assassin in tow? She smiled grimly and lengthened her stride.

2

SHE could hear loud discussion as she neared the door; it ceased as she came into the room, and a dozen or more men turned. All five of the guards who'd escorted her, including Vey and the boy who'd pulled the rickshaw; several of the Americans who were working on the telegraph; against the far wall, a Sikkreni woman and a boy. The men who flanked the door, her guard and the woman bowed deeply as she stepped onto a glaringly turquoise carpet; the Americans glanced at each other, at the tall young Thukar who slouched in one of the two blue-enameled chairs on the low platform between tall, narrow windows. One nodded; they inclined their heads. Jennifer bit back a smile; obviously, she didn't look much like the Americans expected nobility to look. *Deliberately, if you only knew,* she thought, and nodded on her way to join Dahven. The Sikkreni had expected more of her, originally, which she thought extremely silly of them— Dahven had probably spent half his youth exploring the market and frequenting disreputable taverns; it had never been likely he'd bring home a stiffly formal wife.

The guard who'd protected her left flank came forward, a cloth bundle in his hands. He knelt by her feet and shoved fabric aside; Jennifer gazed thoughtfully down at a long-barreled pistol. It was unmistakably a pistol, but didn't otherwise bear much resemblance to any historical gun she'd ever seen in her own world, and it was nothing like, say, a Colt or a .38 special. The stock was ornately carved and looked as though it was designed to be held with both hands, rather than to fit against the palm of one; the metal was brass, or more likely steel coated in brass.

Her hand hovered above it for a moment; then she shrugged and picked it up. Fingerprints didn't count here. There was a brief shock, something—she frowned, ran her fingers along the barrel, but the sensation of static electricity didn't repeat itself. *Odd,* she thought, then filed the thought for later.

"They found it," Dahven said quietly, indicating the tight little clutch of Americans, "on the ground, behind the pole they were readying."

She set the pistol down, looked down the room and spoke in English. Most of the traders, like those she'd dealt with this morning, spoke some Rhadazi; men who did the physical work, like these, seldom knew more than a few very basic words. "I presume you men all heard the shot. Did any of you see who fired it?" The Americans warily eyed each other, the pistol, the Thukar and his outland, outlandishly trouser-clad Thukara. "Understand," she added, "that I don't for a moment believe any of you were stupid enough to smuggle that thing into Sikkre—and then to fire it from across a crowded street at a well-guarded, fast-moving litter. I know a little about guns, enough to know that whoever fired this was extremely lucky to hit the litter at all. I'd wager any of you knows that. And anyway, you all know the penalty for bringing guns into this country; there'd be no reason to risk a good job, good pay *and* your life to do something so foolish." The foreigners eyed each other again, and finally one of them—a broad-shouldered, blackly bearded fellow in dusty rust-colored corduroy—took a step away from them and nodded cautiously. "So—why don't you simply tell me what happened out there? You can get back to your work, and we can go on with our business—which is finding the man who dropped this, and tried to leave you all in a very uncomfortable situation. Agreed?"

The American glanced back at his companions and cleared his throat. "Well, lady—uh, ma'am—"

"Ma'am is fine," Jennifer said gravely. "Go ahead, I'll translate for the others."

"I'm John Carrey, foreman for this section of the line. Well, there was a crowd, like always; people watching everything we did. After a while, you don't notice it much, and it

was blessed hot out there, ma'am. Close to midday, folks
started drifting off, or heading for shade. But there was this
one fellow, kept getting in the way. We're told not to yell at
'em, or push 'em out of the way—we work around 'em as
much as possible. But this fellow—big fellow he was, too,
taller'n me by near a head—well, he kept walking back and
forth a little too close to the back edge of the new posthole.
Seems to me, thinking back, he wasn't so much watching us,
more like he was waiting for someone.''

Jennifer held up a hand. ''Dressed how?''

''Mmmm—oh, local-style, some kind of long loose thing,
dark. Britches and boots under, I think.''

''Near enough,'' one of the others offered. ''The shirt thing
might have been dark blue.''

''Might,'' Carrey conceded. ''It was so dusty, a man
couldn't rightly tell, and I wasn't paying much attention anyway; we were getting ready to right the pole and drop it in
place, and the dirt kept collapsing back in—well, you aren't
concerned with that. Anyway, I got Malloy, here—he speaks
a few more words of the local talk than the rest of us do—
got him to tell the feller to back up, something like the pole
could come down on him. So he mumbled something and
backed off, and I figured he'd gone, but no time later at all,
Malloy and I were checking the wire for kinks and breaks
when I suddenly see him coming running alongside the pole
and then he pulls out *that* thing.'' He stabbed a square finger
at the pistol, then snatched his hand back and shoved it in his
pocket. ''Well, ma'am, it would give you nightmares, the
talk they give you about what would happen to the man who
got caught on your ground with a gun, beheading with a dull
sword's the best I've heard. And they told us the way magic's
used here, it isn't like what we have—that your practitioners
could smell the powder or maybe the shot, and from halfway
across that great big southern harbor, too. We don't get to
bring guns into port just on the chance that's true; we surely
wouldn't dare try to take 'em off ship.''

''Very sensible of you.''

''Um, well. Yes, ma'am. I was thinking, though: Maybe
one of those people could tell that piece don't belong to any
of us. None of us even *touched* it, when that fellow dropped

it and ran. One of your magic users could tell that, couldn't
he?''

''*I* can tell,'' Jennifer replied mildly. The American stared
at her, mouth sagging, as her meaning registered; several of
his companions went pale. That pale mauve, twisted with the
thinnest blue: It showed a yellowish *something*, like dust, on
the butt and trigger areas of the pistol. Gunpowder, perhaps,
or maybe residue from the shot. Whatever it was, it transferred, for the same yellow stuff dusted the cloth it rested on;
her fingers, the hands of her bodyguard nearly glowed with
it. Another man—one of Dahven's, near the door—had handled it also: the fingers of his left, apparently where he'd
rather gingerly picked it up. The American work crew bore
no trace of the stuff. She regained the normal world only with
a good deal of difficulty. Her eyes went from the pistol to the
men who'd handled it, back to the Americans who eyed her
warily indeed now. ''You're right, none of you touched it.
Never mind that. Is there anything at all else you can tell me
about this man? Wait a moment,'' she added, and turning to
Dahven, gave him a swift, terse synopsis of what the big
American had told her. ''All right, go on.''

The fellow had taken the time while she translated to go
into a huddle with his fellows. ''I truly didn't pay much attention, ma'am, save he was big and foreign—I mean, a
Rhadazi, not one of us, excuse it, ma'am. Dark brown hair,
a very dark beard, his face and hands were pretty dark, too.
Probably brown eyes, I'd have remembered blue. And, you
know, something about his face, there was a line down the
side of his beard, like a bad knife cut, maybe so the hair
wouldn't grow there any more.''

''Was a scar,'' the man Malloy broke in, and ran a black-
nailed finger from the bridge of his nose nearly to the nostril,
then down past the corner of his mouth. ''I talked to him,
got a better look at him than you did; it must've been a bad
cut, once. Took in the whole side of his face, and then later,
when Carrey here yelled because he had the gun up, like
this?'' He demonstrated, both hands just in front of his chest
in an over-and-under grip.''Had a scar down the back of his
hand, too, fat, white puckery thing. Maybe like he'd seen a
saber coming and tried to block it.''

Dahven spoke little English but he understood it fairly well;

in any event, Malloy's gestures had painted a graphic picture. "Eprian," he said softly. He nodded as Jennifer translated for him. "That scar—it was made by a dagger, actually, at guards' practice years ago. With the beard, it's barely noticeable. I'll wager you didn't notice it yourself, that afternoon on the old south highway." She shook her head. "All the same, there are enough men in Sikkre who'd know him, and know he's a fugitive—well, we can talk about all that later. Why don't you assure them there's no dull sword in their immediate futures and send them away?"

She scooped up the pistol and crossed the room. "You're free to go, all of you. A last question, though, for whatever it's worth: Do any of you have any idea where a man could obtain a weapon like this?" John Carrey frowned. "Is it American, English—whose? And obviously, he didn't purchase it in Sikkre or Bez. How far south or east would he need to go to purchase a gun? Surely not all the way into New London, would he?"

Malloy scratched his head thoughtfully. "No farther south and east than the portage from the Pacific into the Gallic Sea." Jennifer ran this down her own mental map and translated: Lake of Nicaragua. Not very far away at all. "There's a good-sized city on the inner edge of the lake these days; it's pretty much a crossroads between us and you, points on south, the Gauls and those coming across the Atlantic. People know pretty well what's permitted where and what's not, but that wouldn't stop anyone selling, say, rings of the drug Zero to the Portuguese—or guns to your folk or anyone else who had the coin to buy 'em." Jennifer nodded, stood back to let them pass and signaled the men at the doors to let the Americans leave. She spoke briefly with the Sikkreni woman, who had brought her son to watch the Americans work and so had been nearby when the gun was fired; but the woman had actually seen very little, just a large man in a long dark shirt who vanished into the crowd almost immediately. The boy had had eyes only for the telegraph pole and the foreigners.

Dahven was speaking with the guardsmen and the rickshaw boy when she came back to the low dais. "I know you've all signed into Tower service since my brothers left Sikkre; none of you would have served with Eprian. Vey, you once knew him by sight, though, didn't you?"

"With cause, sir," Vey replied gravely. Dahven tipped him a wink.

"Yes. I was with you that night, remember? The rest of you—he was originally part of the outer wall watch, before my—before the old Thukar brought him inside to help guard his pack of Ducal sorcerers. So far as I know, Eprian went on to serve my brothers as part of the personal guard, as you now all do for me and the Thukara. It's been—what?—just over three years, and there will be people in the city and men still serving here who knew him. Get a description of him from Vey. He's older and perhaps changed a little from that. But his scar is unmistakable. He must have planned for the Americans to be blamed, otherwise he'd have used a knife." He reached for Jennifer's fingers. "Throwing knives; he was very good with them."

She managed a smile. "How nice. But he hasn't changed much; not from the man I saw on the coastal road. *I* recognized him."

"Just so. Now, he may have left Sikkre already—but perhaps not. He may have gone to ground with family or friends here in the city. It's possible he doesn't realize he's been found out—he may not think the Americans saw the scar, and even if he knows that, he may trust that they'll be afraid to get involved in a matter such as this. Well—never mind. He must know there's both an Emperor's writ and my own still out for him; he certainly vanished from sight quickly enough after he fired that weapon at the Thukara. All the same," Dahven added thoughtfully, "he's arrogant. Even if he realized he was identified, he might think himself proof against capture—might still think he knows the back ways of Sikkre better than I do. We'd better have the street guard keep a close eye on the alehouses and the inns. One of you report back to me at seventh hour; that's all for now." Jennifer did a mental calculation: nine o'clock, or near enough. The guard and the rickshaw boy left; at Dahven's gesture, the door guards went out with them.

"Damn," Dahven said feelingly. "Eprian. The possibilities are enough to give me a headache. *Why Eprian?* Is this a private vendetta or some strange foreign one, or is he still serving my brothers—? There must be a hundred different possible reasons why Eprian should stand on a hot, crowded

boulevard and shoot a very illegal alien weapon at you—
without the least chance of success! It's convoluted and silly
enough to have been thought up by my brothers—oh, blast.''

Jennifer tugged at his hand and pulled him to his feet. ''It's
not Eprian that's giving you a headache, it's this room. Fourteen clashing shades of blue, including the ceiling.'' She
shuddered. ''It's bound to be cooler in our apartments than
it is here. Blue—this room makes my teeth ache.'' She held
the door for him, shuddered again as she pushed it closed.
''I know, I can change it, you've told me. One of these days—
when Afronsan isn't running me back and forth between here,
Bez and Podhru with trade agreements. Once the local merchants get the feel of working up their own deals with the
foreigners so that all I need to do is look them over and figure
out the Thukar's percentage.'' She sighed. ''Once I get the
chance to start us an heir, trust me, I'll cheerfully stay home
for a while and start redecorating this place.'' She stopped.
''Wait a minute, forgot something, wait here.'' She sprinted
back down the hall, came back moments later with the cloth-
wrapped pistol clutched in one hand.

''The guard should have taken it away,'' Dahven said.

''As well they didn't; I want to test something. Tell you
later.'' They walked down a long, stuffy enclosed hall and
across a dry, open courtyard; the sun only touched the upper
walls of the Thukar's tower at this hour and the wind had
picked up, tousling Dahven's hair and billowing Jennifer's
shirt. There were household servants everywhere at this
hour—women preparing rooms for the imminent arrival of
Zelharri's Duchess, men pulling shutters aside to air the
rooms, lighting lamps, stacking wood and kindling on stone
hearths should the night turn as cold as the previous one had.

Jennifer's personal maid Siohan was busy in her dressing
room but the bedroom was empty. Dahven shoved off his
boots with his feet and dropped onto the bed; Jennifer sat
cross-legged next to him and dropped the cloth-wrapped pistol near his feet. ''What were you and Vey doing to turn
Eprian against you—or is this another one of those scenes
from your exciting and varied youth I don't want to hear
about?''

Dahven folded his hands behind his head and grinned. ''It
wasn't so bad, really. Let me think—it was several years ago,

Edrith and Vey were to have met me at one of the taverns in the central market. When they didn't, I went looking for them. Must have been, oh, who knows how much later? I don't remember what Edrith was up to that night, but Vey—he couldn't have reached his fifteenth year and he looked more like ten—he'd been waylaid by a shifter, a dancer down in the lower market—''

"A *dancer*, was she?''

Dahven laughed. "Don't raise those eyebrows at me! Dancer, I said and meant, a shapeshifter. One of the truly talented ones, could take on a handful of different forms. I'd known her for several years but she and I—ah, we no longer— ah-hem.'' He hesitated, apparently to carefully choose his next words. Jennifer laughed.

"It's me, remember? She must have liked them *really* young.''

"She surely did,'' Dahven said. He considered this, grinned, shook his head. "Ah, well. She knew Vey, of course; knew he was old enough to have a right to be where he was. And of course, *he* knew full well Eprian thought he had prior claim on the lady—Eprian's idea, *not* the lady's, by the way— though Vey swore he *didn't* know Eprian was off duty that night. Fortunately, I got there before there was bloodshed, or reason for the city guard to provoke a riot. But Vey was a marked man from that moment on.''

"And you?''

"Me? Oh. Well. Eprian and I never had liked each other much; he spent much of his off-duty time with women like that dancer—or tried to. Unfortunately, he had neither the looks, the manner with women *or* the talent to warrant his belief in himself as a collector of hearts—and on any number of occasions, he claimed I had supplanted him, using the accident of my noble birth.'' His ears had gone rather red.

"That must have been it; after all, what else would a tavern owner's daughter see in you? What would any woman?'' Jennifer ruffled the hair back from his forehead and smiled down at him. "So, that's all it was? You know, I really don't remember any scar, but I do remember Eprian—that thick black beard and the sheer arrogance of him.'' Her gaze shifted, and she looked toward the window without actually seeing it;

the smile vanished. "The louse. Let me get my hands on him, he'll think arrogant."

There was a long silence. "You promised me," Dahven said mildly enough, finally, "that you were done with violence. The night Aletto retook Duke's Fort, if I recall correctly."

"I did." Jennifer's voice was grim, her eyes dark. "And I meant it, too. I didn't foresee someone trying to take me out with a handgun. Damnit, Dahven, do you have any idea how lucky we are that shot didn't kill someone? Not me, not at that distance—but someone nearer? A harmless passerby, a child? Hell, anyone on the boulevard? I said it then, violence isn't what I do, I'm an advocate, not a fighter. I meant it then, and I still do mean it, but that doesn't mean I'm going to be a fool on the subject. I absolutely will not sit on my hands and let things like this afternoon happen—!"

"It's not as though you haven't a husband *and* a city guard to deal with Eprian, you know. And, I trust it has occurred to you that either Eprian or my brothers—or all three of them—might have taken your temperament into account, and my own?" Dahven sat up and caught hold of her hand, kissed the fingers, then worked his way around behind her and began to massage her shoulders and the base of her neck. "That he, or they, might have sought such a reaction from you? By all the little brown sand gods at once, you're made of sword steel this evening. Sit still, let me." He worked long fingers down the muscles along the sides of her throat, out toward both shoulders. She let her head fall forward, closed her eyes, concentrated on breathing, on fighting some of the sudden anger out of her blood. Dahven finally pulled her toward him and wrapped both arms around her. "I know what you're thinking; that we don't have any way of being certain who's involved besides Eprian. Or that it was anything but what it appears: a chance he took with an illegal foreign weapon to murder you."

"You're right," she mumbled. "Maybe he isn't bright enough to work out anything more complex than that. Besides, think it through—even if I'd squirmed out from under Vey and chased the man down, if I'd actually caught him— what could he have possibly done with me? At midday on the widest and busiest road in all Sikkre?"

"Stabbed you and run? Thrown a knife from a dark doorway? Remember that he was probably the best thrower Sikkre had, will you, please? Also that this may have been a trial run—left to your own devices, you'd chase him down if you saw him again, wouldn't you?" Jennifer sighed faintly; Dahven's hands went still against her shoulders until she nodded, and he resumed his massage. "I'm not the only one who knows your temper, who realizes that's what you'd do, given the opportunity. Maybe he used this chance to raise your anger, hoping for the opportunity to lure you away from your bodyguards and murder you in a doorway."

"I'll keep it in mind."

"Do. Another thing, before you say: I won't try to convince you not to participate in meetings like today's."

"Thank you. I appreciate that."

"All the same, you walked from here to the weaver's guildhall and intended to walk back, and unarmed."

"Not exactly unarmed." She held out one hand and after a moment's concentration, made just visible a pale, multicolored mass of Night-Thread.

Dahven snorted, pulled her close and laid his cheek against her hair. "Very pretty. Even so, there's all sorts of magic that can counter Thread, and we both know the stuff doesn't always respond when you most need it—say, when you're in a full fury, or worn out?"

She sighed, leaned her cheek into his arms briefly and slid out of his grasp to scoot farther down the bed and pick up the bundle containing the Mer Khani pistol. "All right, point taken. I'll be careful, all right? And I'll do my level best to think before I jump. You really aren't," she added ominously, "going to suggest I stay inside the palace walls, are you?"

Dahven sighed in turn. "I said no, and I meant it. And I wouldn't dare, would I?" He edged down onto his side and propped his head on one hand as she unwrapped the pistol and tossed the cloth aside. She balanced it in one hand, ran the fingers of the other along the barrel, touched the trigger gingerly.

"Nothing." She touched one finger to her tongue, tapped the end of the barrel. "Odd."

"What?" He held out a hand. "May I?" Jennifer passed

it to him, grip first; he turned it over thoughtfully, peered into the barrel, turned it the right way around and sat up to position his hands around the butt the way the American had held his hands. "Heavy and awkward," he said finally. "How could you be certain of hitting what you aimed for?"

"They're for close range," Jennifer replied absently. "Where I used to live, they could shoot more than once and more accurately than this thing—but people used them mostly to kill each other face to face. Disgusting." She blinked, shook her head. "Not at all accurate, no," she said. "But what if someone used a spell on the shot—or magic of some kind? I know of half a dozen things that could improve the accuracy of local weaponry; any of them might work on a round of lead shot."

Dahven held the pistol out and eyed it worriedly. "But, it didn't—"

"It didn't hit me; I don't really think it *was* bespelled. Still, it came awfully darned close, particularly when you consider the speed that litter was moving and the way that boy had just taken the corner. The thing was rocking on its wheels; I wouldn't have thought it possible to hit." She shrugged. "I thought—well, I can't sense any spell on the weapon. Must've had good luck on my side. Maybe if I'd walked back like I intended, it would've been Eprian's good luck. Did I remember to thank you for sending that litter, by the way?"

Dahven grimaced and handed the pistol back to her. "No. And I heard how you tore into those poor men when you found it waiting! You're still alive, that's thanks enough, but next time don't try to override one of my orders, you only made everyone uncomfortable, you know. It's not as though I issue such orders very often, or without a good reason. It was your life at stake, after all."

"I'll keep that in mind. I know, you were right, about the threat and about the guard." She edged down off the bed, picked up the cloth that had fallen to the floor and rewrapped the pistol, then laid the bundle on the edge of her small work table next to a stack of notepads. "We're eating alone tonight, aren't we? Unless Robyn arrives in the next little while?" She fished the watch out of her shirt pocket and turned away from the window to let what was left of the afternoon light touch its face. "You have just about enough

time to wash the smell of Mer Khani handgun off your fingers
before they call us.''

THE family dining hall was almost too cool for comfort when
she first sat down: A stiff breeze whined across the open
corridor through small openings in the lattice and vines; it
blew water from the fountains in fine droplets across the floor.
When a hard gust sent spray over the table, a man was sent
to locate the shutters that had been removed from the doorway for the warm season, and two of the women for more
candles. The room was darker than Jennifer liked it, with the
shutters hooked into place; candleflames still fluttered as air
edged around the base of the shutters or slid through the
upper lattice and vine-covered window openings behind them.

Dahven shoved his plate aside. ''I don't believe that water
did the rice any good, and I'll swear there's sand in the stuff.
I'm not very hungry tonight anyway.''

Jennifer ate a last rolled-up bite of sliced, cold meat and
drained her tall water glass. The serving woman hurried down
the table with a pitcher, refilled the glass and retired to wait
by the door that led down to the kitchens. ''I'm not, either.
Too much to think about, I guess. By the way, what was the
panic-making rumor you heard this morning? Vey said something about one of the slavers—ex-slavers—being a little
angry.''

''Mahjrek. He was,'' Dahven said. ''Probably still is, what
with his business reduced to splinters and shattered brick.''

''Serves him right. All the same, it's an interesting coin-
cidence.''

''Mmmm? Oh. I suppose it might have been just that,
Eprian *and* a very graphic threat from the lower market, all
in the same day. I can't think of a reason for Eprian to have
such a rumor circulated and it would have been better for him
if I hadn't heard any threats; Mahjrek's threat was rather
graphic but not precisely a death threat.''

''Oh?''

Dahven glanced up, shook his head. Jennifer waited. ''In-
volving a sleep spell and a large bag, a journey into the Holmaddi interior; is that enough?''

''It'll do.'' Jennifer thought she could sort it out and it
wasn't pleasant, but rather than frightening her as it clearly

had Dahven, she found herself picking up the water glass, drinking slowly and counting until the anger was under control. So the filthy little monster planned on selling her to one of those backward, barefoot-and-pregnant northern throwbacks, did he? *Let it go,* she urged herself. *Wait until Dahven's not around. Then you can think of fifteen different things to do to him, once you get hold of him.* It had clearly been a mistake to destroy the man's slave business and leave the man himself free; one she wouldn't make a second time.

She drank the last of the water and set the glass to one side for refilling; Dahven picked up his own glass—a clear, heavy piece of Bez stemware filled with a dark liquid—and sniffed cautiously. He finally shrugged, took a very small sip, but immediately spit it onto his plate. "That last shipment of Cornekkan red was sour, and this is utterly undrinkable. They must have kept back all the best in hopes of selling it to the Mer Khani."

"I didn't like the Cornekkan red at all."

"It's not the best available, of course, but it's ordinarily all right for a plain meal. This particular bottle, though—it's the worst of the entire lot." Dahven scowled into the glass once again and set it firmly on the table, then shoved it to arm's length. Jennifer handed him her water glass and a cube of bread.

"Here, take the taste out of your mouth." She leaned across him to take hold of the wine glass and sniffed it even more cautiously than he had. "That *is* awful. You don't suppose someone—put something in it, do you?"

"Of course not!" Dahven began indignantly. He stopped short and shifted in his chair to look at her. "Of course not," he repeated, but he didn't sound nearly as certain. He popped the bread in his mouth, chewed vigorously and washed it down with the rest of her water, waited until the serving woman refilled the water glass and moved out of hearing.

Jennifer's eyes followed her. "I do wish she'd just leave the darned pitcher; I either have to drink slow or feel as though I'm wearing the feet off the woman."

"At least they bring you the water," Dahven said. "Remember how long it took you to convince them that was what you wanted with your food?" He got partway to his feet. "Ihlani, bring the Thukara's water and then leave us, will you? No, leave everything where it is, we'll ring when we need you.'' He took the pitcher, set it between them, smiled at the woman and waited until she'd gone out by the kitchen door and shut it behind her. He chuckled and resumed his seat. ''Wager what she'll tell the rest of the kitchen staff?''

''God,'' Jennifer said feelingly. ''No.'' She picked up the wine glass once again and this time touched her finger to the liquid and then to the tip of her tongue. ''Though I'd rather they thought I was rolling around with you under the table than that we might be discussing one of them doctoring your wine. I think it's just badly bottled, it tastes like soured to me. Here, though; let me try something else.'' But though Thread finally responded, once within it, she couldn't think of any way to prove the wine. At least there seemed to be no grossly obvious tampering—no Light, no spell, no sense of even a tenuous link between this liquid and a person who might have intended harm. She finally withdrew and shook her head. Dahven sat with his chin in his hand, the question in his eyes. ''Nothing. Maybe the casks weren't good oak; or there might have been mold in the batch, they could have just scraped the green fuzzy stuff off the top. *You* know how cheap the Cornekkans can be, I can't picture them dumping iffy wine if there was a chance to sell it instead. Of course, we can always send this down to Rebbe. He's no more a chemist than I am, but he could tell if someone had added ratsbane to your Cornekkan rotgut.''

Dahven laughed, and reached for the glass; Jennifer shoved it across the table. ''Don't,'' he said. ''You're probably right, it's only gone bad. Come to think, it tasted rather like mold.'' He leaned across to fill her water glass, drank and refilled it before handing it back to her. ''Here's to overactive imagination—on both our parts.'' She nodded, smiled and took a sip of water. Her sister Robyn's favorite quotation floated into her mind: *It isn't paranoia if they're really out to get you.* She repressed it firmly and brought her thoughts back to the moment as someone tapped on the door to the outside corridor. ''Come!'' Dahven called out. A moment later, a tall blond man in blue jeans and boots pushed past the hovering servant and came down the darkened room and around the table, bringing chill air and a gust of wind and fountain-spray with him.

Jennifer jumped to her feet. "Chris! I thought you weren't coming!"

Her nephew leaned across the table and hauled her easily off her feet, hugged her hard, gripped Dahven's hand, then settled on the edge of the table. "Hey, dudes. Didn't plan on being here; the day's only worth celebrating if I get to strangle old Merrida, and she's long dead, you know? Mom get here yet?"

"Not yet."

Chris nodded and expelled a deep breath in a loud, long gust. "Good, that gives us a chance to talk. Which is why I'm here." He ran a hand across sunbleached hair that was cut short, except for a long skinny tail at the base of his neck. "God, I think I killed myself, this trip; seems like only day before yesterday I was trying to cut a deal for sneakers down around what ought to be Peru." He tugged on the tail, blinked.

"Peru," Jennifer prompted finally. "So what are you doing back here?"

"Peru," Chris echoed, and shook himself. "Yeah. Because I thought I better tell you guys that we have got serious, *genuine* trouble."

3

JENNIFER and Dahven looked at each other; he shook his head finally and she shrugged—it was a typically terse and dramatic Chris-type comment; she had long since given up trying to second-guess him, and Dahven was rapidly learning. Chris caught hold of a high-backed, deeply cushioned chair, snaked it across the floor and collapsed into it. Jennifer winced as the slender legs squawked across the polished stone floor. "Anything left of dinner?" Chris demanded.

"Probably," Jennifer said. She added mildly, "I had a hard enough fight getting decent chairs made for in here, kiddo; they won't survive that kind of treatment."

"Yeah, sorry," Chris mumbled. Dahven leaned back to catch hold of the bell-rope.

"You have enough strength to explain this genuine trouble before you start shoveling in cold meat, bread and rice," Jennifer asked finally, "or are you going to try to drive us nuts?"

"Which I don't recommend," Dahven said, "because it's been a rather—involved—day here, for both of us." The door to the kitchens opened and he turned to call, "Would you bring food for merchant Cray?"

Chris made a noise that sounded suspiciously like a giggle. " 'Merchant Cray,' " he muttered. "Rully."

"And more water, please?" Jennifer asked. "I hope a cold meal's all right, Chris—" She stopped short as she turned back to him. Chris had snagged Dahven's winecup from in front of her place. She grabbed for it; Chris merely grinned and leaned back in his chair, holding it well out of her reach.

"Hey, you can share, lady, I haven't picked up any weird communicable diseases this trip out, all right?" He ignored her furious "Chris!" "I think I'm half dust, especially the inside of my nose; that was a gruesome ride." He tipped his head back and drank deeply. "All the way up from—AKKK!" He doubled over abruptly and noisily spat wine back into the cup. When he sat up his eyes were narrowed little slits; a trickle of deep red ran down the three-days'-growth beard he cultivated with such care. He rubbed at it with his sleeve and transferred the glare to his aunt. "That was really rude!"

"I tried to tell you," Jennifer said. "You were too busy playing keep-away and generally being a smart-aleck. Serve you right for talking over me."

"Oh, sure, blame it on me. *Really* rude. And since when did you start drinking rotgut wine, Jen?"

"I don't—I didn't—oh, hell," Jennifer said finally. "Never mind! Here," she added as Chris began to cough dramatically. "Have some bread and what's left of my water—"

"That's what I thought I was getting in the first place, your water." Chris gasped. "I think I've killed my taste buds."

"If you hadn't been running your mouth, maybe you'd have noticed what it was before you chugged," Jennifer said. "Or doesn't your nose work?"

"Of course it does," he snapped indignantly; he tore the bread in half and shoved a large bite into his mouth. "Yeah. Well, all right, so I *am* plugged up from all the dust between Bez and here, it's still a dirty trick, leaving that where you did and then trying to make out it's *my* fault. Whoa," Chris added as he rapidly chewed a large bite of bread and swallowed. "That was righteously *bad*. You guys actually had that with dinner? Pass!"

"It seems the last shipment from Cornekka went bad in the barrel," Jennifer said. "And no, *we* didn't drink it, we left it there to see if we could palm it off on you when you came in."

"Too, too sweet of you." Chris glanced up as the serving woman came in with a tray for him. "Hey, this is great, seriously, thanks." He turned back to Jennifer. "You would not *believe* some of the stuff I've eaten lately."

"Spare me any description, please," Jennifer said. "Look,

I know you can eat and talk at the same time; start, or I'll force-feed you the rest of that wine.''

Chris shuddered. He tucked the rest of the bread into his cheek and began to talk around it. ''My latest venture, think I told you before I left here the last time, didn't I? Anyway, sneakers, right? They—the Incans—they have rubber, we have access to decent canvas from the English, and they'll trade the Incans for some other stuff, anyway, I thought, molded rubber soles, canvas tops, so they aren't Air Jordans, they're still one up on the local sandals *or* the fifty-pound boots without arch supports. Probably only sell to guys my age, locally, but maybe they'd go over good for on board ships. We figured, do a few dozen, I can afford that kind of outlay, see how the market looks.''

He shifted bread, chewed and swallowed, washing it down with a deep drink of water. ''With me so far? Okay, so we—Eddie and I—we were down in—well, *I* can barely pronounce the name of the place, it's an Incan word, about a mile long and ninety percent consonants. But the town is about where Lima would be, major coastal city actually and the only place foreign traders get access into the empire. Even then, it's a little like our China used to be, they don't let foreigners have access to the entire town, just the portside and the taverns and stuff around the docks. And everybody in the world hangs out there, I swear—well, anyway, there's always a huge mixed crowd, ten different languages, fun place.''

He scooped up another piece of bread and broke it into quarters. ''So I'm out eating with a bunch of the locals, trying to figure what's the best way to work out the soles part of the deal—you know, work up the mold for the soles without totally sacrificing what's left of one of my high-tops, get it to them, export the rubber and import finished bottoms—well, anyway, I can see you don't care about that part,'' he added hastily as Jennifer cleared her throat ominously. He bit the bread in half, chewed at it half-heartedly, drained his water cup and shoved it across for Dahven to refill. ''So, while I'm running the bargain, Eddie is doing what he does best, kind of cruising the night spots, fading into the woodwork, listening—*you* know.'' Jennifer glanced at Dahven, who cast his eyes up slightly. They knew. Edrith *was* very good at that kind of thing, but it got him into strange waters as

often as not. ''And he's down in this one corner of the docks—
don't look like that, Jen, it was well lit, very busy, lots of
people—and that's the whole problem 'cause there's no way
he could figure out who said what they said, and—'' He leaned
back in the chair suddenly, blotted his forehead on the back
of his shirt sleeve, drank deeply and only set the cup down
when it was empty once more. ''Warm in here, isn't it? Don't
you usually have the doors off by now?'' Jennifer refilled his
water cup and handed it to him. He looked at it as though
uncertain what it was; he was wadding bread into a hard ball
and seemed to have forgotten the plate of rice and cold meats
entirely. ''So, yeah, like, anyway—'' His voice faded; he
blinked, shook his head very slightly, picked up the water
and drank thirstily. ''So, right, where was I?''

''Edrith, overhearing someone in a busy street,'' Dahven
said.

Jennifer got to her feet and looked at him, suddenly anxious. ''Chris, are you all right?''

He blinked up at her indignantly. ''What'd'you think, I got
smashed on just a hit of that junk wine? I'm sh—I'm awright,
fine!'' The words were slow, slurred. ''Um—so what—? Oh,
yeah, Eddie, over—yeah, so—um—'' Water beaded on his
forehead and he swayed forward, then suddenly sagged. Dahven threw himself across the table, scattering crockery, plates
and food in all directions as Chris went utterly limp; he was
only just in time to keep the younger man's head from striking
the stone floor.

It felt like forever before his eyes opened once again and
Jennifer was able to breathe: In actual fact, he was uncon-
scious for less than a minute. He blinked, looked up at Dahven, then at Jennifer who knelt at his other side, and closed
his eyes again. ''Ohhh, man?'' he mumbled. ''I feel really
gross. Kinda like when I was real little and one of Mom's
boyfriends slipped pot in the chocolate cake, all of a sudden,
'Woooo, everything's gone utterly weird.' Oooh.'' He was
silent for a long moment. ''It was that garbage wine, wasn't
it? Hey, that was truly a dirty trick, I thought you guys liked
me.'' He winced as she blotted his forehead with her sleeve.
''All right, Jen, what'd you put in it—that puke-stuff you keep

around if you have little kids?'' Dahven frowned in confusion and glanced at Jennifer, who shook her head.

"Never mind, tell you later.'' She turned back to Chris. "*We* didn't put anything in the wine.'' Chris shifted against Dahven's knee so he could look at her but his eyelids fluttered and closed almost at once. "Chris, are you going to be sick? Because if you're going to urf, I'd rather you didn't urf in the pond *or* on the floor in here where we eat; the smell will never come out of the tile.''

"Mom always said you were a hard woman,'' Chris mumbled. "I don't think I'll try for a gold in cookie-toss but maybe you'd better leave me down here on the nice cool tiles for a while. Just in case.''

"Leave him down there, on the nice cool tiles,'' Jennifer told Dahven expressionlessly. Dahven let Chris down flat. Chris opened one eye and eyed her with speculation.

"Boy, do you look weird upside down. Yuck.'' The eye closed. "Wait. *You* didn't dose the wine. So, who's out to get you?''

Jennifer shrugged, then added aloud: "We don't know the stuff was dosed, or that anyone's out to get us—not with Cornekkan red, anyway. Maybe it just went sour.''

"*Not*. Vinegar's one thing, this was something else. You taste that junk?''

"No—and all things considered, I don't believe I will. Could be you're just the ultimate cheap drunk, kid.''

"No way,'' Chris protested. "I *don't* drink the stuff; doesn't mean I *can't*, you know? Guy goes out and makes trade deals like I do, he usually winds up sealing the bargain with a mug of something or a shot of something else. I don't do a lot of it, but one big glug wouldn't flatten anyone. Except—you know,'' he added suddenly, "what I really think this reminds me of? Back when my buddy Carlos finally passed his first martial arts test and got his green belt, he wasn't really into the whole concept yet, so he still thought 'celebrate,' and that meant cheap wine—like I say, didn't exactly have the spiritual end of it pegged back then. So, he gets this *rully* cheapo-crud white wine, says 'sulphites added' in big letters right on the label? I had one little glass of the stuff and I thought I was gonna *die*. Passed out and puked and everything.'' He fixed her with one darkly accusing eye.

"Which was not 'cause I drank a lot of it. 'Cause, remember me and the salad bar in that restaurant? The night I lost it in the parking lot, big time?"

"Forgot about your tender tummy," Jennifer replied, and, to Dahven, who'd listened to all of this with little or no comprehension, "There's a substance that's sometimes added to food, to keep it from spoiling. It makes some people very ill, and Chris is one of them." Chris snorted and closed his eyes again. "You going to live, kiddo?"

"To my sorrow," he growled.

"Can't be sulphites, Chris."

"I didn't say it was. I just said it *hit* me like sulphites. I think someone put that puke-stuff in your dinner wine." He lay still for a long moment, shook his head. "Or something nastier. Are we back to poison? God, my head aches!"

Jennifer glanced at Dahven and sighed faintly. "How do you suggest we find out?"

"How should I know? But why poison?" Chris groaned. "You two are so cute and loveable, who'd wanna off either of you? You will notice, I'm going with the assumption that one of you set that crud aside because it tasted so rotten, not because you wanted to try and off someone yourselves."

"Who would grab my glass and drink from it?" Jennifer demanded and added dryly, "Other than someone I didn't know was coming in the first place?" Chris waved an impatient hand.

"This is all too much for me right now. Speaking of trying to off people," he groaned again and held up a hand, "give me some water, will you? Get the taste out of my mouth, so maybe I can finish what I was trying to tell you, *God*, I feel awful." He let Dahven drag him back partly upright and drank deeply, then took a chunk of dry bread from Jennifer and let Dahven lay him down flat once more. He closed his eyes, took a small bite and chewed cautiously.

Dahven got to his feet. "I'm going down to the kitchens."

Jennifer looked up. "I'm going with you—"

"No," Dahven said flatly as he snagged the winecup. Jennifer's eyes widened as he loosened the silver belt knife in its sheath. His eyes followed hers and he managed a slightly abashed smile. "In case, that's all. You stay here." And before she could form an argument, Chris caught hold of her sleeve and tugged urgently.

"No, please," he said, and swallowed hard as she came back down to peer at him. "Um, lookit, I feel totally stupid for even asking, but I'd really rather not be alone for a few minutes, all right? I mean—in case?"

She wrapped fingers around his wrist, glanced at Dahven and nodded. "I can't fight both of you; all right, Dahven, go." She watched him, waiting until the door to the kitchens closed behind him, then settled cross-legged on the floor next to Chris, who was watching her warily.

"Hey. You don't think one of the *kitchen* staff dosed that stuff—!"

"I frankly don't know what to think just now. And if you don't mind, let it drop. And lie still, damnit, kid! I'm trying to get a pulse!"

"Hey, don't take it out on me, scream at the noble boy wonder when he gets back. And I've got a pulse; it's doing a slam-dance on my temples, all right? You still fix headaches?"

"Ordinary ones, now and again." Her lips moved in a silent count. "Pulse is all right, a little fast maybe. Headache brought on by something nasty, I don't know."

"Well, try," Chris said peevishly. He lay back flat and closed his eyes. Jennifer eyed him worriedly, closed her own eyes and shifted into Thread-awareness.

THERE was a wash of gray just under Chris's ribs but it was impervious to Thread and muffled her attempts to work around or through it to soothe her nephew's stomach. It didn't seem to be spreading, though. His headache was a throbbing mass of muddy dull red—rather as though the usual red of a normal headache had been overlaid by that same gray film, and either it was stubborn or she'd lost more of her touch than she'd thought. It eventually gave way when she remembered how to thin the heavy yellow. She finally came back to the rather unpleasant sensations of hard floor against unprotected knees and a chill spray on her shoulders. Chris mumbled something.

"What'd you say?" she asked as she got to her feet.

He rubbed the back of his neck thoughtfully, then slowly and cautiously sat up. "Nothing real. Thanks."

"My pleasure." Jennifer went back around the table and dropped into the chair once more. "You notice I didn't say, 'any time.' "

"Appreciate that." He moved with slow care, to his knees and, a few minutes later, to his feet. "Wooo, too fast." He bent over at the waist, hands brushing the floor and head dangling. For several more moments, he stayed there, breathing slowly and deeply. Finally he raised his head and, when nothing unpleasant happened, sighed deeply and settled in the chair once more. He eyed the plate with misgivings. "Think I dare?"

Jennifer shrugged. "It's what we both had—"

"Ugh. I didn't think about more funny stuff in the comestibles, I was just worried about my stomach not wanting anything coming down to visit. Thanks a *whole* lot. You don't think—?"

"Kid, I honestly don't know." Jennifer spread her hands in a wide shrug. "I—here, all right, let me try something." It was starting to wear on her, moving in and out of Thread so much; it was getting harder to get in and nearly impossible to remember how to leave it and regain the real world. She stood, planted her hands on either side of his plate. There was no visible or aural difference in the Thread around and across his plate—no sign of that filmy gray. "I think it's safe. And I think it was only the wine. Every murder mystery I ever read, if you want to do someone in fast you dissolve poison in liquid. I can't sense anything wrong."

"Is this supposed to reassure me?" Chris asked sourly. "Don't answer that," he added and fetched a deep sigh. "Yeah, well. You're probably right, that wine was so gross, it had to be something lethal." He scooped up a very small chunk of rice and chewed cautiously; once he'd swallowed, he simply sat for several long moments, eyes closed. When nothing unpleasant happened, he picked up another chunk, folded this in a strip of meat, and popped it in his mouth.

He jumped and Jennifer turned as the door from the kitchens opened and Dahven reappeared, cup still in his hand. A distant noise, as if many people were all shouting wildly at once, echoed up the hallway, then faded to near nothing as

the door shut. He came across and dropped into his chair,
set the cup in front of him. "I've sent for one of the guard
to take this down to Rebbe. The bottle's disappeared."

"Say what?" Chris shook his head.

"Who took it?" Jennifer asked at the same moment. Dahven looked at her sidelong and his mouth quirked.

"It's funny *you* should ask just that question. It went via
the same person who brought the bottle—your new winemaster, I'm told, Thukara."

"I—my new—my *what*?"

"The new winemaster you brought in, Thukara." Dahven
gave her a positively evil grin. "To make certain the Thukar's
wine was properly chosen and correctly decanted—"

"I never—" But Jennifer stopped short as Dahven laughed.

"Of course you never. Nor did I. Nor did anyone. The
kitchen staff is properly horrified, under the circumstances—
that they allowed a total stranger access to a bottle of my
wine and to my favorite cup, however innocently. The man
only presented himself and his credentials an hour before the
meal tonight; it was chaos of course, and none of them can
remember him, only a rather bright shirt and breeches—and
that, of course, he'll have changed by now. A very short time
ago, one of the undercooks said she was carrying clean plates
over to the cupboard and she saw him pick up the bottle and
walk out the door into the long passage." Dahven paused a
moment. "Which, as we both know, leads in short order past
the fish ponds and across the low wall into the mid market.
He could be anywhere in Sikkre by now."

Chris planted both elbows on the table and leaned forward.
"Hold it. You're saying, someone really *did* try and poison
you?" Dahven nodded. "In that stuff?" He nodded again.
"Whoa, man. That's really cold."

"Dirty," Jennifer agreed grimly. She turned back to Dahven. "No massive beard, no scar running from the bridge of
his nose off his chin and onto his fingers?"

Dahven shrugged. "Nothing of the sort. The guard is talking to everyone who was downstairs, preparing the meal or
in the cellars; there may be someone who can identify him.
Myself, I doubt there is; anyone with so much nerve no doubt
has matching luck, the two seem to run together. But from
now on, there'll be a guard in the kitchens at all times—the

senior cook suggested it. It *had* already occurred to me, of course.''

"Everyone who works in or around the kitchens has been with us two years or more," Jennifer said. "And they all know each other. There shouldn't be any need for a guard."

"No. And every man, woman and boy down there knows that from now on, no one—new winemasters or other personnel—will be hired into the kitchens without a *personal* introduction from myself or from you. No exceptions.'' Dahven let his eyes close a moment and he sighed heavily. "One more untoward thing this day, and I'll—little green sand gods, I forgot.'' Accusing eyes fixed on Chris, who was mopping up the last of his rice with a bit of mustard-coated bread. "You. And this major trouble. Explain, please.''

Chris nodded, shoved the bread into his cheek and nodded again. "Okay. We did the bit about where, and about the sneakers, didn't we? So I'm doing the wheeling and dealing with the local money boys in this coastal Incan city for who gets what, who puts out what, and how we turn local rubber and imported canvas into killer footgear. And Eddie is off in the down-and-dirty section of the market. With me so far? So he's in the middle of a mob scene, a zillion people everywhere, dozen different nationalities and like that. Just walking around and listening, and what he heard, in *English*, mind you, was this:

"Some guy with a deep voice says, 'They'll only pay in silver or gold for a very few, certain items, they don't care to part with real coin, and there's little we have they want badly enough to do a straight purchase.'

"Another voice, a little higher and reedy: 'Everyone winds up paying silver *and* gold for a drug like Zero. Eventually. It's a matter of working out ways around their watched ports, and you say your contact men can find such ways.'

"First voice: 'Yes, well. You know what they want—my superiors—in exchange for your usual cut, of course.'

"Second voice breaks out laughing, like it's a real joke, and finally, guy says, 'That's a ripe 'un. Your superiors!'

" 'It's only words, their choice of 'em, not anything that matters to me. Those paying me, if you prefer.'

" 'Nearer the truth. Silly fools. Do they think we'll hand 'em the whole backward little land on a tray, once all's done?'

"First voice again, and they're getting far enough away Eddie's gotta push his way through the crowd to keep up and hear 'em. 'They do: All of it, so far as I can gather.'

" 'Won't ever happen, can't they see as much? Our people get in there, we won't be turning loose of so much as a square mile of sand. But your fellows're greedy—maybe greedy enough that coin will settle them where land won't.'

"Second voice, fading all the time: 'Coin—or they might trade for product, themselves. They're fool enough, both of 'em.' And the last thing Eddie heard before he lost them both for good: 'Within a year, wager you fair, Rhadaz will be ours and we won't have to do anything else to get it.' "

There was a deadly little silence. Chris shoved his plate aside and planted his elbows on the table so he could brace his chin against his hands. Dahven sat back in his chair and the two men looked at each other for several minutes. "They?" Dahven asked finally. "We?"

Chris shrugged. "Well—that's a problem. See, if we were in the world I grew up in, I could tell an American from an Englishman, but here, it's not the same thing: Americans *were* English right up until a few years ago. Sometimes I can tell 'em apart but not always; Eddie can follow English, but that's about it. I mean, he can just barely figure out what they're saying, and he's got a rotten ear for accent anyway." He moved his head cautiously and resettled his chin against his hands. "Anyway, Eddie found me and told me about it; I spent two nights crawling around the low-life end of the wharves with him, hoping to pick out the same guys, but no such luck. Finally, we decided best thing to do was to come back home, fast, and warn you."

Jennifer shook her head. "You should've gone straight to Podhru, Chris."

"What—and told the Emperor's brother that there's this real vague threat overheard by a guy whose English is only so-so, and we don't know what the threat is or who made it?" Chris laughed briefly and humorlessly. "Look, most of the guys working for Afronsan are middle-aged pen-pushers; *you* figure how long I might cool my heels in the hall, just trying to get word in to the guy. And even if I did get through to him right away—" He spread his hands and began to shake his head, winced and stopped. "Ouch. Damn. Look, he's an all right guy, but I'm not either one of you. The few times I've talked to him, I get the feeling Afronsan is all too well aware that I'm barely twenty, outlander, and that I'm not exactly your average conservative merchant type. That's fine, but you can't tell me it wouldn't work against me if I went to him with a story like this. Jen—you know me real well, at least as well as Dahven here knows Eddie. And Afronsan trusts both of you. *You* tell him, all right?'' He leaned back in his chair abruptly and let his eyes close once more. ''Look, I hate to spoil the happy fizzy party here, but I'm *dying*. Anybody mind if I go crater—sorry, Dahven, I need some sleep.''

''Let me get a couple of the housemen to help you,'' Dahven began. Chris snorted.

''Oh, sure. Let the whole place see me staggering around like a bad week on booze!''

''You think it'll be any better if they find you passed out in the hall?'' Jennifer asked dryly. ''Get him some help, Dahven. Stuff the pride back in your shirt pocket, kid. The kitchen staff already knows what's happened, if the rest of the household doesn't yet, it will within the hour. Sleep late, if you want; we'll figure on seeing you when we see you.''

DAHVEN went with the man who'd been stationed outside the door, to help Chris to the room set aside for his use when he came to Sikkre; she picked up the wine cup then, and set off for the lower level, where Dahven's father had once housed his dozen or so sorcerers. The sole Light Shaper had gone by the time Dahven regained his birthright—quite possibly with Dahven's brothers. Dahven had pared down the members of the magicians's quarters since his return, and now there was only an elderly maker of charms who was too old to find herself another noble household to support her—and a magician/alchemist of middle years and a reasonably clever turn of mind.

Rebbe shook his head and made tching noises over the cup as Jennifer handed it to him. ''Ah, what things are coming to! To dare attack a ruling Duke in his own household! Frankly, dear Lady, the poison may be foreign and I don't know how to track such things or what name to put to any I do find. All the same, I'll do my best.'' He was still shaking his head and cluck-ing unhappily when she left.

THE hour was still early when she and Dahven retired for the night, but Jennifer found it difficult to hold her eyes open long enough for her woman to brush out her hair and put it into the tiny braids that created the waves once made by per-manents. She pulled on a short, silky blue nightshirt and crawled into the great bed, fetching a little sigh as Dahven sat up to tuck covers around her shoulders and turn down the lamp. She snuggled into his warmth gratefully and sighed again as his lips brushed her forehead. ''Long day,'' she mumbled.

''Long day,'' Dahven agreed. He was silent for some mo-ments. Jennifer shifted so she could wrap an arm across his waist and laid her cheek against his chest. For several long, warm moments she listened to the deep, slow beat of his heart.

''You still awake?'' she asked softly.

''Not really sleepy,'' he said. ''You?''

''Deathly tired but too tired to sleep,'' she said. ''Too wor-ried.''

''And what could you possibly have to worry about?'' he asked lightly; his arms tightened briefly.

''This is me, remember?'' She pushed away from him and pried her eyes open. There was light beyond the windows of their bedroom, lamps in the corridor and a blue-light in her dressing room, more lamps outside in the courtyard. Enough that she could see him and the grave eyes watching her. ''You think your brothers are behind this—what? call it a conspir-acy?—Chris told us about, don't you?''

Dahven rolled partly away from her, onto his back, and turned his eyes toward the distant, ornate ceiling. ''Not wholly, no.''

''Not entirely.'' Jennifer levered up onto one elbow and laid a hand on his cheek. ''You want to know what I think?'' She felt the brief nod against her fingers. ''Zero—I've heard about it several times recently now: a drug, highly addictive substance that comes out of the Incan Empire—or via the Empire from somewhere else. We had something similar; it could even be the same stuff.''

"I know, I've talked to Chris about such things, though it's been some time now—before we came back to Sikkre. But it's not the same here, you know. For one thing, the Emperor and his council, Afronsan and his people, would never let such a substance come into Rhadaz. And our people just aren't likely to want such a thing. What's the sense of a thing that costs money and does nothing save addict—and to no purpose other *than* addiction?"

"Mmmm." Jennifer decided to let that one slide; to an Angeleno that sounded painfully naive, but Dahven might like to sleep tonight. No point in correcting his misapprehensions and giving him nightmares. "All the same, it's worked in other lands in this world. And those men Eddie overheard seem confident. It sounds as though they plan to import the stuff in secret, putting ships in somewhere along the coast where there isn't anyone to stop them, then they'll send it inland and sell it to people—they intend to, at least," she added as Dahven stirred. "They seem to think it will be simple to sell the drug to Rhadazi, and that once this happens, once sufficient numbers of people here are hooked on the stuff, that their people will be able to come in and simply take over.

"From what I know of the outside world and from what Chris said, either the English want land and ports on the western side of the continent—or the Americans do. And they're willing to play dirty to get what they want." She smoothed the hair from his forehead. He was still gazing at the ceiling. "Neither the Americans nor the English could know the Rhadazi coast—where it would be safe to put a ship in, how to find Rhadazi men who would meet them in secret and risk bringing this substance into the country. If they had help, though—"

"If they had my brothers," Dahven said softly. "Who have not been heard from in lo, these past three years at least, but who are rumored to have gone south. Who have already proven themselves to care for nothing that stands between them and what they want. Who might well be the men who will aid foreigners to bring in this highly addictive substance in exchange for Sikkre?" He shook his head. "No, it's ridiculous! How could they dare hope to return? Let alone regain Sikkre?"

"Because Afronsan controls trade, but Shesseran is still Emperor," Jennifer said. "And because Afronsan still must deal through his brother. It's an old story, Dahven; knowing Shesseran as they do, why *wouldn't* your brothers believe themselves safe from anything worse than slapped wrists if they did return? You remember the rumors: that when Afronsan put you back here and later sent for your brothers, Shesseran didn't want them harmed in any fashion? And we *do* know Afronsan only planned to levy fines on them. Shesseran's still alive and he gets worse every year, why wouldn't they think they could get away with anything, including Sikkre? Particularly . . ." She swallowed hard. "Particularly if you were dead?"

Dahven laid his hand across hers where it rested on his chest; his fingers tightened briefly. "I wish I could pick holes in your theory, Jennifer."

"I wish you could, too. Keep in mind it *is* only a theory, with nothing but what Eddie with his bad English overheard in a crowded and noisy market. Really, though, it sounded to me less like what you suggest, more as though they don't plan on having Shesseran *or* you *or* Afronsan around to ask for explanations. They want it all." She shook her head. "It *is* only a theory. It could be a lot of different people, almost anyone."

"No. You're forgetting the attack on your litter this morning. That *was* my brother's man."

"Oh, no, I wasn't forgetting. Any more than I was forgetting that it would be easier for your brothers, or one of their followers, to get a man inside the household kitchens than for an outsider. Or a foreigner. They know where things are, how the household works." She let herself back down flat.

Dahven was silent for a long time. Finally he stirred. "Jennifer. You must promise me something. If something happens—to me—" He lay long fingers across her lips. "No, let me finish. If somehow Deehar and Dayher are behind any of what's happened here, and down south—if they find a way through my defenses—*swear* to me you will go at once to Afronsan. No," he added sharply as she shook her head and strove to set his fingers aside, "listen to me! Reach Afronsan and you would be safe—"

"Safe?" Jennifer slipped from his grasp and sat upright. "Why would I want to be safe? And what about Sikkre?"

"*I* want you safe! And Sikkre—how would you stop my brothers, if they still want the Duchy badly enough to kill me for it?" He sat up and caught hold of her shoulders. "You're trembling, I'm sorry; here, lie down, let me cover you—"

Jennifer nodded, not quite daring to trust her voice. *Reaction.* Three years of such mundane, ordinary existence. She'd scarcely used Thread at all since she and Dahven came to Sikkre; to have to use it several times in a day and under such circumstances, to have so much violence spill into their lives in such a short time, and to have so few answers—

They won't kill him, they won't touch him, she promised herself flatly, over and over again. They would have to go through her first. Dahven's arm went limp across her shoulders; his breathing became slow and even. She lay still, pressed against him, chilled despite the thick covers and the warmth of his smooth skin. *They won't touch him.* Bravado. "They" had already proven themselves capable of reaching into the very household. She fetched a little sigh; Dahven murmured something in his sleep and his fingers tightened on hers. She brushed her lips against his shoulder. She was beyond tired, shaking with exhaustion suddenly, but she couldn't simply sleep as he had: They'd found a way into the kitchens that might have proven deadly; the rest of the Thukar's palace could be as open to them.

She finally closed her eyes and fought her way into Thread. A protective sphere should turn a hand or a knife; it might turn heavier weapons. It *would* warn her if anyone tried to breach it. *Probably scare the staff half silly when they come in the morning.* The thought made her smile very briefly, but the smile vanished as she considered Thread.

Fool, to let the Wielding slip away from her fingers, to set it aside as she had. Oh, yes, she'd had plenty to do these past several years, but only a complete fool would have been so complacently certain that they were safe, with Deehar and Dayher still out there, somewhere. *Let it go,* she ordered herself. *Tell yourself later how dumb you are, get the sphere built first, all right, Cray?* The silver stuff—there. It was hard to find, she couldn't remember how it should sound at first: She had forgotten how elusive it was. It came into her fingers, finally, but it remained rather like working with cobweb, slender as it was, and it was slightly tacky to the touch. Jennifer built slowly, weaving a dense, protective form that completely surrounded the bed. Once it was finished she sighed tiredly and returned to the ordinary plane.

Probably it wasn't necessary at all. The household would be very much on its guard, and guardsmen would patrol the halls, alert for anyone not one of their number. (*It could be one of them,* Jennifer thought, then hastily forced her mind away from such a thought. It wasn't conducive to sleep.) No, the sphere probably wasn't necessary, but it would keep anyone from the bed, and she truly did need the practice. It had taken—what, nearly an hour?—by her watch, over forty minutes, to create the sphere; it shouldn't take a reasonably strong Wielder anywhere near that long, and it might be the difference between life and—*Stop it*, she told herself angrily.

She smothered a yawn against a slightly coarse linen sheet. If anyone so much as touched that silvery Thread, it would waken her. She smiled grimly, slid a careful hand under Dahven's pillows. As she'd half suspected, his dagger was there, sheathed but only loosely. ''Try, brothers-in-law,'' she whispered. ''Dare to try anything against him tonight.''

4

𝔷

LIALLA edged off the narrow wooden seat and settled cross-legged on the carpeted floor of the small caravaner's wagon as the wagon groaned and rocked and began to move forward. Finally, with a creak of leather harness and the muffled thud of shod hooves against the hard-packed dirt road, the caravan was on its way, leaving the market of Sehfi on a northward swing that would take it on a double loop journey running from Hushar Oasis to Holmaddan, to Dro Pent, to Sikkre and then to Cornekka and finally back to Zelharri. According to the watch Chris had given her the winter before, it was nearly ten—barely an hour past sundown at this time of year. By her reckoning, the last wagon wouldn't cross the Zelharri-Sikkre border until sometime around four; with good fortune, and if the old back roads had been reworked as well as the caravaners claimed they were, they might actually reach the Hushar Oasis about sunrise.

By the time Aletto realized she was not in her rooms, she'd be well and truly gone—well and truly beyond his borders and beyond his ability to recall.

Lialla felt around the dark interior until she found a net of cushions strung across one corner; she pulled out two, settling one between her shoulder blades and the bench seat, sliding the other under her. She pulled scarves around her shoulders with quick, irritated fingers, settling one across her hair. It had been a long time since she'd worn Wielder Blacks—since Aletto's return to Duke's Fort, she'd come to rely on Chris's taste in colors and styles, and her two elderly sets of loose black breeches, snug-fitting long-sleeved shirts

and loose, sleeveless overshirts had stayed in the bottom of
her clothes chest. She'd had to have new blacks sewn for this
illicit journey: She'd gained weight, mostly breadth in her
shoulders but enough breast that the shirts and sleeveless long
overvests were embarrassingly snug. But then, looking back,
she could see how painfully skinny she'd been, when those
aged Blacks had hung loose from too-thin shoulders and
slopped over nonexistent hips. Nerves, mostly: She'd once
been all nerves and thin skin from living under her uncle's
thumb. Well, the veneer of overlying arrogance had fooled
plenty of people; it hadn't fooled Chris. Whatever else she
owed to the three her old mentor had dragged from their own
world into hers, she owed the most to Chris—for helping her
break through that shell of arrogance, for giving her a first
chance ever to act like a kid. Particularly for pushing her into
cheerful clothing, a young way of wearing her hair—it had
changed her perception of herself as a dull and uninteresting
person, but it had changed other peoples' impressions of her,
too. Very much for the better.

  She smiled faintly, and wondered where Chris might be at
this hour. He was like the younger brother Aletto had never
had the chance to be for her, and she missed him. Chris
always brought her stories from distant lands, told her about
the odd forms of magic he ran across and sometimes brought
back curious charms, bits of fashion—belts, scarves, shoes—
or drew pictures for her of the strange garments women in
other lands wore. She loved listening to his tales of the hard
bargains he drove, found pleasure in the now familiar cadence
of his speech as he spoke of yet another strange invention of
his own time and place, and the possible substitute he'd found
for it in this time and place—of how he planned to present
the thing so it might pass Afronsan's lists of what could be
legitimately imported, and Shesseran's much tighter lists of
what could not enter the country. She sighed. He was supposed to be somewhere on an island in that clear blue-green
ocean south and east of Rhadaz by many days' journeying. At
this hour quite possibly in one of their smoky taverns that
smelled of the oils men used on their sturdy brown bodies,
drink unlike any in Rhadaz—not that Chris would be drinking
any of their strong dark liquids. Very likely he'd be working

another of his close bargains, or plotting the course of the next one with Edrith.

Who would have thought? Lialla remembered her first glimpse of Chris—a tall, blond giant of a boy, but quite obviously still a boy, years younger than she, and possessed of a towering impatience, loud mouth and a bad temper. It had struck her as a terrible combination for a journey that needed secrecy and quiet above all. Of course, he'd proven himself long before they reached the Emperor's city, and now she couldn't imagine having won through without him. The years hadn't added much height to him—as if he weren't big enough!—but he'd proven to have a keen intelligence and a formidable memory. Those assets combined with his outlander past and his knowledge of his own world's history worked to his benefit in the new foreign trade. Usually he was the first to see the benefits of a new thing, and the only one who did until he'd gone through long and tedious explanations. That poles-and-wires thing the Mer Khani were installing, for example: Shesseran was said to disapprove of telegraph still, and Aletto was only just beginning to see the point of it. But Chris was already involved in new projects: The last time he came through Duke's Fort, he'd told her about a portion of Mer Khani that was hotter and damper than Bez—and the machine he'd found there which could make ice, even during high summer.

"But we *have* ice!"

He'd given her the usual long look. "Sure. But even when there's lots of it on the lakes and it's cut up midwinter and stored the right way, it's still all melted or used up by late summer. And how about those poor people down in Bez and Podhru, who have to pay through the nose for what little they can get? Okay, never mind about them, think about having a cold glass of juice, with ice that nobody had to wash straw off, and that doesn't taste green like lake water. Better yet, think about ice in a big box with thick walls, so you could keep meat fresh for longer than a couple nights."

Put so, it had made much better sense to her; Robyn hadn't needed any arguments. She'd lived in a world where there were machines for ice, and she spoke of them wistfully. Aletto still didn't get the idea of the maker of ice, either, but

Aletto . . . Lialla sighed. Aletto could be absolutely devoid
of imagination sometimes. All too often, any more.

And as overbearing, recently, as their uncle—*No.* She shook
her head, hard; the black scarf slid down her hair, tickling
the back of her neck as it slithered to the floor, and the long
plait pinned to the top of her head came loose and slapped
her forehead. She hadn't let herself think about Jadek in a
long time; she wasn't going to begin now. And it was a very
unfair comparison—lousy, as Chris would say. Aletto didn't
want her to leave Duke's Fort. Jadek had flat *refused* to let
her leave the fort unless she agreed to marry his cousin, and
then she'd only have left to move onto Carolan's estates. She
shivered, then shook her head again. *No Carolan, either!* Aletto had never pressed hard when she'd said she wouldn't
marry—he too had grown up under Jadek's thumb, he understood. Probably, she thought, he simply assumed she'd eventually change her mind. *Hah.* He'd never objected when she
traveled around Zelharri or even into Sikkre and down to
Podhru and Bez. He'd been pleased when she began to in-
volve herself in the women's league of shop owners that began in Sehfi and spread to outlying villages, pleased when
she set up the network of younger Night-Thread Wielders so
they could exchange information and practical ideas apart
from the older and more hidebound practitioners of that form
of magic. Because he was normally so easygoing, it had
thrown her badly when he'd tried to forbid her the journey to
Holmaddan. Unfortunately, because he was Aletto, he'd come
across as overbearing and pompous, and then furiously angry
when she'd responded with arrogance and then anger of her
own.

If he'd simply said he was worried for her safety—but he
couldn't unbend so much with anyone except Robyn or possibly Jen, and Lialla couldn't stop the anger, even knowing
they were both reacting as they always had. Pulling each other's chains, as Chris would say.

"All the same," Lialla growled under her breath, "it still
means he doesn't think I can take care of myself. That he
thinks I'm a complete fool. All the risks I took with him when
we ran from Duke's Fort four years ago! All the times a fool
would probably have died, and I came through it all in one
piece!" Well, it wasn't any good getting angry now; she'd

managed the final argument that he couldn't answer. She let her eyes close, massaged at the tension in the back of her neck and her shoulders with hard, capable little fingers. Finally, she expelled a long breath in a loud gust. "So he'll probably discover tomorrow afternoon that I've left, but possibly not until evening meal, when I don't come down. He might send Robyn or Mother to check, but then again, he might think I'm sulking—Robyn wouldn't intrude and Mother might not—I can't count on that, though. So assume tomorrow, around dark." She considered this, sighed quietly this time. "Good. Even so, I'll be well across the border onto Sikkreni soil, miles north of the oasis. Too far for him to send men to bring me back." Too far in a few hours, actually: She'd claim Sikkreni land-right once they were out of Zelharri, if need be. She considered this, smiled grimly at the thought of Aletto, his men, Dahven and Jennifer embroiled in such a dispute—though it surely wouldn't arise. It would be long hours before Aletto put together her disappearance and the caravan leaving for the north—another had headed out for Sikkre hours before and she'd sent her horse with the westbound wagons, a letter for Jen in the old leather bag behind the saddle; Jen at least would know where she'd gone and why, and she thought Jen would understand.

By midday, two days off, she should reach the Holmaddi village. And once there—She didn't continue the thought.

From there, she didn't know. And she wondered if the women who had asked her aid knew, either.

That letter. That desperate, heartbreaking letter had gone right under her skin. Women so downtrodden, hoping for something better for their daughters—not even mention of their own lot. It had been sent to the sin-Duchess Lialla, and signed by every woman in that coastal village.

"Why to me?" She'd wondered about that from the first. False modesty aside, of course. She knew some people looked upon her as a hero, as much a hero as Chris, or Jennifer, or Dahven—or even Aletto, for her part in getting Aletto his father's Dukedom. Gossip must have spread all the way to the north.

Even so: It was one thing to run as they had, to travel Rhadaz in search of their father's men and allies—she'd fled an unholy alliance with Jadek's horrid cousin, the certainty

that neither of them would have survived the year had they
stayed where Jadek could lay hands on them. It hadn't been
so difficult to act, and even later none of it had seemed particularly brave—just necessary. To sneak into a Holmaddi village, to be presented as the Wielder's new novice, to not just
remain unknown but to teach village women how to be strong,
to rebel against men who'd kept them powerless for five hundred years—Lialla rubbed the back of her neck and wondered
for the first time if she hadn't taken on more than she could
possibly handle.

She let her eyes close and mentally ran through the letter
once again. The women of Holmaddan, it said, wanted only
what their southern sisters had: They were tired of being
treated as slaves. Those in the villages wished to be permitted
to own the sheep they herded, or at least a share of the pro-
ceeds of the wool and the cloth they wove from it; a say in
who they would wed, or if they would wed at all. Those in
the cities wanted the right to own property, or to hold stalls
in the marketplace. In all the rest of Rhadaz, the letter said,
a man could be fined or imprisoned for hurting his woman,
but in Holmaddan he could kill her and face at worst a fine
in the city. In the villages, women were beaten for lagging at
their labors, killed outright for disobedience or for looking at
an outsider or speaking to an unwed male from another village—whereupon the husband was praised by his fellows for
having protected his property rights and his personal power.

In the city, the letter said, there were women who had been
in Bezjeriad and in Sikkre, and who were setting up an underground to educate their sisters. In the villages, there was
no such network as yet, and the city women could not go to
them; at best, they dared occasional letters, but even that was
done at rare intervals, lest what they planned come to the
attention of their men before they were ready for confrontation.

And so, they had decided, a disguised outsider was their
best and only hope. The sin-Duchess would need an excuse
to be in the village, and the women had worked this out: The
Wielder had lost her novice; she had obtained permission
from the council to find another. Lialla would be presented
as the new novice, a woman from among the outlying fishers
or the herders. The sin-Duchess would know how to maintain

such a role, the scarves and swathing Wielder Blacks would help her maintain the disguise, and the village men would not care enough to closely examine the story. And since they thought of Thread as women's magic, she would thereafter be doubly beneath notice. Of course, it would be the village Wielder who learned from Lialla, rather than the other way around—who learned to utilize Night-Thread during the day, and possibly even the new and wholly other skills Lialla had honed over the past years.

Whether Holmaddi men used any magic at all—she didn't know anything about Holmaddi men's magic, whether there was such a thing. Perhaps a magic stronger than Night-Thread—''But the magic I use now isn't purely Thread.'' It was stronger, more powerful, it was utterly unique; it *could* potentially help her, it might expose her. Even Merrida had been able to detect the difference between her once barely competent Wielder novice and the magician she had become: deft and skilled with Thread but able to shape Light as well. Able to blend the two, as they had blended themselves when Jadek's Light had invaded her and she'd had to shape it or watch those she loved best die.

Thanks to Jadek, of all people, who had done his best to kill her with Light, and had instead given her this. She gazed down at her fingers, scarcely visible inside the darkened cart, watched as the nails began to glow a soft, deep orange. She smiled faintly, let the color fade. It had proven useful: She could hear distant conversations, see things far away, even move herself short distances—when her concentration was good, at least. It was faster and more efficient for her than mere Thread had ever been. It was the one thing she was counting on to keep her safe in this village, over and above any plans these women had worked out. But—if?

She shrugged finally. If they'd heard enough of the stories to think she was the one to help them, the northern women surely knew she was no longer a plain Wielder; surely they wouldn't ask her for aid if her magic would give her away. The Wielder who'd penned the letter had come across as intelligent and cautious both, *she* would know better. All the same . . .

Why am I here? I'm not that brave, or that strong, Lialla thought gloomily. She adjusted the pillow behind her back and resettled her shoulders. *I'm stubborn, but that isn't the same thing*. But if she had said no, who else could they have asked for help? The Emperor? Shesseran had always taken the path of least resistance with his Duchies, and to his way of thinking Holmaddan was a prosperous, *quiet* land—he'd never lift a finger unless there was open revolt, and quite possibly not even then. His brother and heir Afronsan had only reluctantly taken the time from his other duties to restore Sikkre to Dahven; he'd sent a few clerks when they'd gone north from Podhru to Sehfi but had otherwise stayed out of Aletto's retaking of his own Duchy. He was even more buried in paper now than he had been four years ago. And of course, he was male—surely a very black mark against him in the eyes of many Holmaddi women, Lialla thought. Jennifer was at least as busy as Afronsan, still settling the vast Sikkreni market, working out the finicky details of foreign trade with Afronsan and all the various new foreign merchants. Robyn would never leave Aletto or the children. Lizelle—Lialla bit her lower lip. Her mother had lost weight again recently, and she looked nearly as haggard as she had when Jadek lived. She wouldn't let her daughter send for physicians, wouldn't let Lialla examine her. But Lizelle wouldn't be the person to help a Duchy of downtrodden women find their feet: She had spent her entire adult life completely dependent on one man or another—their father, then Jadek, now her son, Aletto.

She'd set the letter aside at first, hoping to think of someone she could hand it to—and there had been no one.

She shifted again. Somewhere out there in the darkness, someone began a very silly song about rain and camels and the girl he loved, his high, resonant voice breaking on the low notes and jerking as he bounced along; someone on the seat of her wagon tuned an a'lud and began to accompany him with a simple strum. When she sat forward to peer through the gap in the back curtains, Lialla could see lamps swinging from poles on both sides of the wagon-driver's seat, other light to the side that cast shadows across the driver but lit the road. It was pleasant, and light-hearted, and suddenly she felt the tension leave her.

"Maybe they only need me as an example. Well, I can be a figurehead as well as anyone, that doesn't take much courage, or talent—or skill in devising plans. If there's need for

a plan, I'll think of something.'' She edged down onto the
floor and stretched hard. She hadn't slept at all well in the
past several days and she was suddenly tired indeed. Reaction, no doubt—to be finally on her way, following the letter
she'd sent with the last northbound caravan to tell the village
Wielder she'd somehow come, as soon as she could. She'd
find out soon enough what was wanted of her. She settled her
hip against the thick carpet of the floor, one pillow under her
ear, the other under her shoulder, and closed her eyes. The
wagon rocked and creaked, and lulled her to sleep.

THE sun was low in the morning sky, the air still cool when
the caravan reached Hushar Oasis and fourteen wagons settled near the deep pool where Jennifer had once washed her
hair. Lialla climbed down from the back of the wagon and
stretched luxuriously. All around her was hurried but well-
organized activity—mules and horses being unhitched from
wagons, a pair of camels howling furiously as they were
forced to their knees and bags pulled from their backs. All
around small fires were lit and water set to boil; the soothing
odor of mint reached her. An outsider was only in the way
at the moment. She left her boots on the back step and went
barefoot across soft sand and water-smoothed stone to soak
her feet.

THE water was cold; she splashed a little across the back of
her neck, smiled faintly and shook her head as she looked
across the broad pool. Nearly four years ago, she'd lent Jen
her bag of soap so the woman could wash her hair in this
very pool. Lialla couldn't imagine ever being desperate
enough for clean hair as to dip her head in water this cold.
But it had been the first time they'd talked without snipping
at each other. The truce hadn't lasted very long, of course,
but Lialla had seen for that moment, for the first time, how
pleasant it might be having a friend—someone just to talk
with, someone she could trust. And she'd suddenly realized
how very much she wanted that.
    She sighed, stepped onto already warm flat rock as two
boys came barging down the path with several of the horses;
they were laughing and talking very loudly, and she could
hear others coming along behind them. In a few minutes, this

place would be unbearable—and wet. The horses splashed into the shallows; the boys moved into deeper water and began to splash each other. Lialla turned and left. There should be a cup of mint tea for her by now, and quite possibly an oat cake or two.

When she got back to the wagon, its owner was waiting for her. "The grandmother asked to see you, once you've eaten."

"Oh?" Lialla settled on the back step to ease her boots back on. The woman set a thick two-handled pottery cup beside her and a covered wooden dish.

"That's all I know. Here, everyone knows how the sin-Duchess likes oat cakes." The woman fished one from under the cloth for herself and dipped it into her tea. Lialla bit into one and nodded.

"Wonderful things, thank you, Sil. Hard to remember, I actually did get tired of them once." She chewed and washed the bite down with a sip of very hot, too-sweet tea. "She doesn't plan on sending me home, does she?"

Sil shrugged. "The old woman doesn't tell mere drivers like me much, and her son says even less. He needs a wife to settle him, he grows more above himself hourly. But if you want a guess, I'd say not. If that was her thought, she'd simply have refused you passage." She grinned briefly. "Even the head of the Gray Fishers wouldn't hope to get away with abandoning a Rhadazi noblewoman in the middle of the desert."

Lialla finished the granolalike hard cake and took another. "No, I suppose not. But it's bound to be my first thought. After all, I'm—I told you down in the market, before I ever talked to her, my brother wasn't best pleased with my idea of a journey and he all but flatly forbid me to go." She finished the tea, set the cup aside. "Not that he could do so, of course."

"I should hope he couldn't," Sil replied indignantly.

"All the same—" Lialla sighed and got to her feet. "No point in sitting here wondering what she wants, is there? Where's her wagon?" Sil pointed straight across the loose circle of wagons. Lialla tucked the last bite of her second oat cake in one cheek and went.

The headwoman's wagon was set apart from the others only

by the door—a real door instead of the usual curtain across the back. The door was open, the white-haired matriarch of the Gray Fishers seated on the top step, watching her son, a broad-shouldered hulk of a man, himself salt-and-pepper-haired and bearded, who was doing something to one of the rear wheels. He cast the sin-Duchess a dark look and went back to his work. The grandmother stood and gestured with her head, led the way into the wagon and pushed the door closed behind them. ''When I agreed to give you passage, you said only you wished to travel to the coastal Holmaddi village of North Bay. I asked no questions then, fearing so many open ears in the marketplace. But now that it is only ourselves and you and all the desert between us and any un-friendly listeners.'' She indicated a deep pile of cushions strung along the bench; Lialla eased down among them and the older woman sat next to her, so near their knees touched. ''Now that it is safer to speak openly, I would tell you first that I know your purpose—it has been largely through the caravans and women like myself that the village women learn of the outside world.'' She paused; Lialla merely nodded. It was news, if not exactly surprising news. ''All the same, once within the Duchy's boundaries, even we walk with a certain caution. Should the Holmaddi males see us as bad influences, we would lose both the chance to assist their women and a rich trade as well. And so, I can only offer you advice. If you will have it.''

''Advice,'' Lialla whispered. She was silent for several moments, eyes fixed on her hands. She nodded then. ''You know about the letter? About what they've asked me to do?''

''The letter was given to a Red Hawk woman by the Wielder of North Bay—how else could such a written message have reached the Emperor's mails and so come to Sehfi? It's as safe a role as any, the one they've chosen for you. But there are males in any village who seek a wife—men who might think to turn a novice Wielder from her chosen path. Be aware of the males, wary of the attentions of any and yet, do not hold yourself totally shy of them, lest one think your actions to be either threat or challenge. Also, know that not all the women are agreed on a course of action—none would con-tinue as oppressed as they have been for so many years, but there are degrees between a small change and a great one.

Be cautious what you say, and how, and to whom. Until you know who is trustworthy.''

"Trustworthy," Lialla echoed unhappily.

"Aye." The grandmother touched her knee. "Understand: If there were any in the village who would divulge your true identity to the men, the Wielder would not have sent for you. Or if we thought such women lived in that village, we would not have brought you even this far. And do remember you are the sister of Zelharri's Duke; no one would be foolish enough to lure such a one into peril, since even the Emperor would intervene, should a sin-Duchess be in peril of her life.''

"If anyone knew of it," Lialla replied gloomily. She scrubbed suddenly damp hands down her breeches.

"*We* would know," the older woman said calmly. She touched Lialla's knee once again and when the younger woman looked up, she drew a small object from her belt, held it out for the other's inspection. It was a charm, Lialla thought: copper and silver wire, bent in a complex pattern about a very pale blue stone. The stone itself, on closer examination, was not the plain blue she thought; it was made up of a swirled pattern of the near white of snow on a winter's night under full moon, moon white, the blue of distant mountains—it held her eye and it was only with an effort she could look away from it. The grandmother nodded and restored it to her belt. "The Emperor's brother has permitted the Mer Khani to come into Rhadaz and cross the land with wires, to send messages." She patted the belt and smiled complacently. "There are wires and wires," she said, "though anyone might control the Mer Khani magic that sends messages along their wires, while only a caravaner who has the strength of years and who has borne the weight of a man and then born a child can control *this*." She considered this and laughed so suddenly that Lialla jumped, scattering cushions. "There is true women's magic for you, sin-Duchess. Remember it. Other competent Wielders have spoken through a grandmother's stone.

"But do not dwell on the thoughts I fear I have put into your mind! More likely than not, you will be safe and protected. If not, remember your brother knows where you have gone, and we do. Caravans will all know where you are and in what guise, and the Gray Fishers will come back through North Bay just before the full moon. Twenty-three days.''

It wasn't as reassuring as the grandmother intended; a lot could happen in twenty-three days. Lialla's palms were damp again. She nodded; anxiety clamped her throat and she knew the fear would show if she tried to say anything. *What have I done to myself?* But the caravan leader was speaking once more.

''You'll do well; remember, they'll want to hear from you about how women in the southern Duchies live, everything you can tell them about the two outlander women. Mostly, I believe, they want you as proof that there is a life different from—better than—their own. Particularly in the outlying villages such as this one, the men spend most of their time either fishing or in the men's hut and the steam-huts bragging and drinking, they do not stoop to consorting with the women—even their own women, aside from helping them produce sons. A little caution, a little care, you'll do well.'' She let her head fall to one side and thoughtfully regarded her younger companion. ''A thing I pass on to you, as it was told to us in Podhru.

''There may be ships, foreign ships, coming to land along the Holmaddi coast. If you see such ships, or foreign men who may come from such ships, or if you see rings—yellow rings of thick rope, so large,'' she held up her hands, fingers widespread, thumbs and forefingers barely touching, ''about the size of a band of silver to circle a woman's arm just below the elbow, perhaps. Many of them, strung on a length of slender white rope, or along a pole—even a single such ring, or a few of them—do not speak of it to anyone, but store everything in your mind: where you saw it, and under what circumstance. When we next meet, tell me what you saw. Or another mistress of a caravan—but *no other person.*''

Lialla shook her head; this conversation was increasingly confusing and more than a little frightening. ''Rope rings? Why? No, wait.'' She held up a hand. ''Let me think it out: Foreign ships can't put in anywhere but Bez Harbor or Podhru—Bez, really, since Shesseran doesn't want them anywhere in the southern sea, or in his bay. If they were—they'd be smuggling, wouldn't they? But what?'' She frowned. ''What use would little rings of rope be?''

"Foreign ships have landed along the coast between Dro Pent and Holmaddan, and I am told one was seen near the cliffs a day south of Dro Pent, heading back out to sea. The rope itself is ordinary foreign rope until it is soaked in a substance called Zero, which gives it the yellow coloring. Once the rings have been brought safely to land, they can be moved about as they are or soaked again, the substance removed and given another carrier." Lialla's frown deepened. "The substance itself is a narcotic, a drug said to give certain of the southern foreigners much pleasure. It controls the lives of those who take it, and does not let them go this side of death."

"A drug?" Lialla said faintly. "Wait—Chris, the outlander merchant Chris told me about drugs in his world. But we don't have them here."

"We did not," the older woman said. "With care, we will not."

"Why would they?"

"Because they are foreign and their minds are not like ours? Who knows? We need not worry about the why, only who and where. Remember: If you should see such a ship, or such men, or such goods, do nothing. Watch and remember what you see."

"I'll remember."

"Good. Go now, rest. We shall leave here when the sun is low, so as to reach North Bay and the Wielder's hut while the men still sleep." And as Lialla stood up, the older woman stood also, laid both hands on her shoulders, and placed a kiss on her cheek. "I may have no later chance to speak to you in private. Go in peace and return to us safely."

Lialla nodded and left the caravan without speaking. The grandmother's son was now under the wagon, working on the axle; nothing could be seen of him but two large boots, but Lialla could sense the black mood that emanated from the man in those boots. *Peace and safety,* she thought gloomily. It hadn't even seemed likely before this meeting.

SOMEHOW, she managed to sleep, waking late in the afternoon as the caravaners began to hitch up and reload for the journey north. Sil brought her a cup of soup and offered her a place on the driver's seat. Lialla drank soup; listened to the caravaner woman's rambling talk and her conversation with the boy who rode next to her wagon—Sil's eldest nephew, she gathered. It was nearly an hour before they reached the main road which ran from Sikkre to the Holmaddi border, and though the road itself was deserted, Lialla climbed into the back of the wagon. She felt increasingly tense, embarrassed that Sil might realize it; and even though there was no one visible along the road but Gray Fishers now, they weren't moving very quickly and the terrain was changing. A fast horse could come up behind them, or one could appear around one of the turns in the road and over a ridge, heading south. She didn't want to be seen by anyone, just now.

For some time she simply sat, bolt upright, on the long bench. But as daylight faded, she edged down onto the floor once again, and somehow, fell asleep once more. Siohan woke her long hours later when the wagons stopped at a river crossing. There was a faint line of dark blue pre-dawn above the eastern mountains when they went on again. By the time it had spread to the entire visible eastern range and all but the brightest stars had faded, the wagons had stopped again. And this time, Lialla could smell the sea.

THE caravan stayed where it was, half a mile or so from the edge of the village; Sil's nephew took Lialla on the back of his horse and rode her to the wielder's small hut, waiting only until a very short, squarely built woman holding a blue light in one hand opened the door. She gave the young horseman a brief glance only before stepping back into the room. Lialla fought down strong misgivings and followed.

5

JENNIFER slept poorly; the sphere of silvery Thread might serve as protection, but she could *hear* it, and the sound— oddly reminiscent of a minor-keyed Chopin prelude she had once played on her cello—haunted her dreams. She woke at first light, short-tempered from the bad combination of short sleep, too early an hour—everything that had gone wrong the previous day. Slightly depressed from Thread-music and the memories she'd thought carefully buried. *My cello. My own music, real classical stuff I could play, listen to on the radio, my collection of opera tapes and videos*—She finally bit down hard on the side of her hand, swore as her teeth hit a sore spot—splinter from the litter, apparently. Already red and swollen, the way her cuts got any more, thanks to the climate and the wood. Whatever wood it was, she'd picked up splinters of it before, and they went septic fast. *Ouch.* But by the time it was out, she'd effectively broken the miserable thought pattern.

"Up. Out," she mumbled to herself. "There's enough going on today, you'd better at least be awake when it all falls down around your ears." She dissolved the sphere so she could sit up properly. *That* had been a large part of why she'd wakened so early—what Dahven would say if he woke to find himself trapped. Her woman's reaction, or that of the man who took care of Dahven's wardrobe, if they came into the room early and found the bed and its occupants behind an invisible, impassable barrier.

She scowled at her still very peacefully sleeping husband. *He* didn't seem to have suffered any ill effects of so much violence and intrigue. "Probably thriving on it," she growled. But she couldn't stay angry with Dahven at the worst of times; just now, he was sprawled across two-thirds of the huge bed, a hand tucked under his ear, the other clutching the covers, face slightly flushed and his hair rumpled. She sighed, shook her head and slid her bare feet from under the linens and onto a very cool floor.

The room temperature at this early hour was an incentive to dress quickly, if she'd needed it. She pulled on pants before doffing the nightshirt, hurried into a loose, thick shirt that came nearly to her knees and shoved her feet into fur-lined slippers. Her woman would be appalled to see her wandering the halls so clad, and no doubt she'd hear about it later. Jennifer squinted at her reflection in the small mirror, fished a wide blue ribbon out of one of the tabletop boxes and tied the tiny braids securely back behind her ears. "One of these days, she'll learn there are more important things than how you look in your own house. Especially at such a grisly hour." Well—maybe. Siohan had very definite ideas about how a Thukara should act and dress; Jennifer figured she disappointed the woman at least half the time. She wrinkled her nose at the reflected too-pale face—pale with lack of sleep, no coffee, no makeup. With luck, though, the printer would have the contracts ready for her to check. If she could get that task out of the way early, it would considerably simplify the rest of the day.

Delivery of those contracts might present a small problem, but Jennifer had already decided no one was going to keep her from delivering them personally. The negotiations had been tortuous enough; there was still enough chance one side or the other would break off before the papers were signed. Especially after the fiasco with that Mer Khani handgun. . . . Bad enough, having the black-market merchants out for her blood, without the wealthy and influential Weaver's Guild taking against her for ruining their chance at good foreign trade and money.

The hall was absolutely frigid; a chill draft ran along the floor, making her ankles crack, raising goosebumps on her calves. Only every third lamp was lit at this hour, and there was no one else anywhere in sight. Even the printers' hall was quiet, the doors and windows all closed, the long, high-ceilinged interior illuminated only by ruddy sunlight coming through tall eastern windows. The head printer's desk was covered in boxes, dangerously unstable-looking piles of thick paper, loose bits everywhere, wooden boxes of new type. The deep, document-sized tray marked ''Thukara'' was in its usual place, on the corner against the wall. She fished out the thick stack of finished work—fortunately already wrapped and tied since no one had put one of the thin sheets of wood under it for stability; it flopped across her arm like a sandbag as she went back into the hall. ''Coffee,'' she mumbled, and turned toward the kitchens.

The early cooks were already there, of course, preparing the household breakfasts for staff. One of the older women was stirring a pot of Dahven's invariable hot, honeyed cereal that reminded her unpleasantly of her aunt's gluey, library-pastelike oatmeal. Two middle-aged women and a boy looked up from the main table and a welter of plates, bowls, utensils, loaves and trays as she came in. All three inclined their heads politely, but didn't say anything or suggest helping when she set her bundle on a counter near the far door, opened the cabinet underneath and drew out her coffee-making supplies. She set about grinding beans, and the only sound was the clatter of wooden plates being set on wooden trays, the noise of the grinder. It was one of the first things any new staff learned: not to talk to the Thukara (cheerfully or otherwise) before sunrise, and never to get between her and coffee, if she came down early to make it herself.

She knelt to retrieve a tall, heavy mug and a matching, handled pottery jug with a thick cork for a lid, set both on the counter and felt around for the cloth filters she'd had made and the colanderlike basket that held them. One of the women came briskly across with a steaming kettle, which she set on the counter before walking briskly back across the room. It irritated them, of course, particularly those people who'd served in the Thukar's palace from the old days. A morning like this, she could almost hear the thought in that woman's head: *Why doesn't she do like the old Thukar did, and like the new one does? If she slept to a proper hour, we'd make the coffee and bring it to her in her bed. The proper way.*

Well, she hadn't managed to become comfortable with be-ing served breakfast in bed, and if three years hadn't acclimated her, it wasn't going to happen. *And*, Jennifer thought grimly, as she closed the cabinet, *I'm damned if I'll wake Siohan at an hour like this so she can come down here and get me badly made, weak coffee the way the staff does it. I'm up this early, there's a reason for it—ah, pfui on it.* Obviously she *needed* that first mug of coffee today; probably the staff was only thinking about getting the early meal done, so they could clear up and get on to the midday one. She felt around for the last item—a box containing sugar—then got back to her feet in a flurry of cracking knees and ankles, threw a double handful of grounds into the filter, balanced the basket atop the pottery jug with a thumb and fingertip, cautiously poured near-boiling water into the filter. It was a far cry from an automatic drip machine, and particularly when she was this tired it could be a hazardous task: The water had gone over the top a few times, spilling grounds into the jug, twice she burned her knuckles; once the basket had tipped over and grounds had gone everywhere. Fortunately today she managed without any disasters; she corked the jug, ran one last spill of water over the grounds, this time dripping coffee directly into her oversized mug. She took one cautious sip of very hot, near-black liquid before putting things away. The roast was still far from perfect, she couldn't get the grind nearly fine enough, and at the same time the filter always managed to let some grounds through, making the resulting liquid gritty and acidic. Still heavenly—especially considering the alternative of none at all. Beans and grinder—back onto shelf; kettle back onto stove; wet grounds into the kitchen bin and a scoop of cold water from the stone cistern poured over the cloth filter, which she left on the counter to dry. By the time she was done, the coffee in the mug was drinkable—or would be, once she'd stirred two heaping spoons of sugar into it. She drank half of it in one long swallow so nothing would slop out on her way to the family dining room, caught up the jug in one hand, the mug in the other. The floppy, awkward bundle of contracts went between her arm and her ribs and threatened to slither free all the way up the long servant's hall and the short flight of steps that led from the kitchens into the dining chamber; somehow, she managed to get it braced against her hipbone and when it finally did fall, it landed on the table.

She was only mildly surprised to find Chris already there, a stack of dry toast and two large oranges in front of him. He was spooning dark apple butter onto one piece of toast, chewing another. Chris had always shown an annoying tendency toward early hours he hadn't inherited from his aunt *or* his mother. He held up his free hand and waggled it back and forth briefly, but didn't smile or try to speak—Chris knew her better than the kitchen staff did. Jennifer slid the bundle of paper across so it would be at her elbow when she sat down in her usual chair, leaned across the table to snag the piece of apple-buttered toast from Chris's fingers before he could bite into it. He gave her a dark look, shook his head, picked up another piece and spooned more fruit onto it. Jennifer settled into her chair, leaned back to drain the coffee mug, refilled it and sighed deeply.

"Got your fix?" Chris inquired mildly. "Do I dare say anything yet?"

"Why'd your mom raise such a smart-mouthed kid?" Jennifer asked.

"Wanted to keep *you* on your toes, why else?"

"Me and the rest of the world." She sipped, shook her head. The stuff in the jug wasn't anywhere near sweet enough. She pulled the small covered bowl of sugar over, set the lid aside, paused with a mounded spoonful halfway to the cup. *That stays on the table, right in front of my chair, all the time. If someone thought of dosing Dahven's wine—* She turned the spoon sideways, let the grains slide back into the bowl. They didn't seem to move any differently from usual, but that only meant nothing liquid had been added to it. *Rats.* She touched her tongue to one finger, pressed it into the bowl and once again to her tongue.

"I thought *you* were the one with manners," Chris said mildly; he'd set his toast aside and was watching her with great interest. "Isn't that supposed to be everyone's bowl of sugar?"

"Shut it down a minute, kid, okay?"

"Guess I was wrong all around," he began. Jennifer glared at him and he was abruptly silent.

Thread? She sighed faintly; it was hard enough to access Thread these days, damn near impossible at an hour when she was still half asleep. It was sluggish when it finally did respond, but there was no sign of any shift in lines or colors anywhere around the bowl or its contents. She blinked, shook her head to clear it, and scooped more sugar into the spoon, pouring it into the mug this time. Chris cleared his throat.

"Um. I'm presuming you figure someone might've doped the sugar when they did the wine, right? If *you* urf and pass out, what do you want me to do?"

Jennifer paused with the mug halfway to her lip, laughed shortly and without humor. "Don't eat the sugar." She drank, leaned back with her eyes closed, finally sat up and drank more deeply. "Tastes fine. Seems okay."

"Yeah. Don't I remember old Agatha Christies, they used to hide the arsenic in the sugar? And that it takes a while to work?"

"Little of last night's red wine with your toast, kid? What're you doing up at this hour anyway? I thought you'd still be green sick after last night, and I really hoped I'd have this place to myself. I have some trade contracts to go through before I run them down to the weaver's hall later this afternoon."

"Yeah, I'm so sure," Chris retorted. "I heard about *your* little shooting party; you think your old man's gonna let you out of here today?"

"That word isn't in his vocabulary. 'Let.' " Jennifer snorted. "It better not be," she added ominously.

"Yeah. Okay, he's not your average macho jerk. But I bet he'd change the rules on that 'let' stuff right now if he could figure out how. I mean—someone smuggled in a pistol just to take a potshot at you?" Jennifer shrugged and drank more coffee. "Hey, you must've really pissed someone off. Was it really that one guy from back then, the night Ernie broke his leg?"

Jennifer bit back a sigh and set her coffee mug aside. Chris wouldn't give up until he got the story out of her, and since it possibly tied into his news, he should know about it anyway. "All right. If you'll sit back and listen for a few minutes, I'll tell you all I know. Which isn't much." She did. Chris ate toast and was silent for a moment or two after she finished.

"That's *all* you know?"

"You don't have much else from down south. And it hasn't been a whole day since it happened."

"Mmmm. True. Let me think about this too, all right? Because, that dude was working for Dahven's cruddy brothers, wasn't he? Back then, at least? And, they aren't anywhere around just now—"

"Left Sikkre for Podhru, to report to Afronsan on exactly what they'd done, just before Dahven and I left Zelharri to come here," Jennifer said.

"And they dropped out of sight, right?"

"We think they left Bezjeriad by ship—remember Casimaffi?"

Chris snorted angrily. "Ernie's dad's old buddy Chuffles, almost got us *killed* waiting for his lousy boat? You think I'd forget that jerk?" He broke a cold piece of toast in half, scattering crumbs, and ate half of it. "You know," he went on once he'd swallowed, "I keep hoping, every time Eddie and I take off on one of our trips, that we'll run across good old Chuffles. He doesn't hang out in popular ports much, though—in fact, not at all. Funny, don't you think?"

"At this hour?" Jennifer growled as she poured herself more coffee and added a generous scoop of sugar to the mug. "Are you crazy?"

"Daring to carry on a conversation with you this early? Probably am. So anyway, what if ol' Chuffles is hanging out with *them*, they wouldn't even need to have gone far, just to Fahlia or someplace along the southern seacoast, there's a bunch of little fishing villages and a couple medium-sized ports on that side of the sea, we went into one that first trip out, when we did the overland through the Gallic—you know, Mexico."

"I don't want to untangle one of your complex plots this early in the day," Jennifer growled. "I can't even handle listening to them, it's going to give me a royal headache, and I'm even less friendly at dawn *with* a headache. If I have to kill you to shut you up—"

"Nice. All right, I get the point."

"Think about it, you come up with anything, let me know, all right? Any time after ten or so," she added flatly.

"Gotcha."

"How'd you find out about the fun and games by the south gate?"

Chris laughed. "You kidding? It's all over the place. I heard rumors when I rode into the city yesterday evening, and the guys who tucked me in last night told me. Somebody actually *shot* at you—whoa, I bet that was strange. I mean, I've *seen* a few rifles and such, but I haven't heard a gun go off since we left L.A."

"You'll find your nerves remember all about them," Jennifer said dryly.

"I'll bet. You know, a few of the big ships, the Gallic ones, have cannons, I've seen those, too. But I talked to some guy, he said the cannon needs some kind of charm or a magic user to make them fire, none of this fuse-and-match stuff."

"Maybe why you don't see too many of them." Jennifer hefted the jug and sloshed it experimentally. About half gone. "I used to wonder why they didn't have any in Rhadaz. What you said, way back in Podhru, about these people splitting off from Spain and Portugal when the Moors overran Ferdinand and Isabella?"

"Something similar."

"There were guns of some kind by then, weren't there?"

"Our world, sure. This one—who knows? I haven't had that much time for this-world history recently, you know, and I've given up trying to figure out all the splits. Way Eddie and I figured the gun thing, though—the Rhadazi put their borders into cold storage for a long, long time, so no one ever got in with stuff like guns. And because magic works so well, even after the borders opened some, a few years back, no one wanted to bother with a mechanical thingie that took five minutes to load—and is about as accurate as mom with a softball. Hey, just break out whatever brand of magic you use, buy a market spell or charm, off someone that way. That's how I figure it, and it does seem to be the same attitude most places I've been—we have this magic so we don't need to create killing machines. Fortunately for me, there doesn't seem to be much magical mental communication at distances, like in some of my old books and games. Because then no one would've bothered to invent the telegraph."

"Yeah. You're getting convoluted again, kid. Look, find me a typewriter, next trip out, why don't you?"

"Oh, sure," Chris grumbled. "Along with a few million other things. It may be nearly the twentieth century out there, but not all the good inventions track from one world to the other."

"Enough do. I heard about the ice-maker."

He brightened. "Yeah. Now, if I can convince that dude to do a deal with me, and convince everyone around here that it's not just a noble's toy for making slushy drinks in high summer. Aletto just looked at me when I told 'em about it at Duke's Fort, just couldn't understand about iceboxes. Which reminds me, I can't stick around here, you know? Mom's supposed to be here today, she doesn't expect me and she'll figure something awful's happened. And you know I can't hardly ever fake her. She's got enough to worry about without worrying that someone tried to off her baby boy."

"I'd rather keep the whole incident from her, which means I'd better get hold of Siohan this morning and have her spread the word to all the staff to keep their mouths shut."

"God," Chris said devoutly, "I forget you have enough people inside this hunk of rock to populate a small middle Eastern kingdom. It'll never work; you know mom, always hanging out with the kitchen people and stuff, it'll come out."

"She won't be here very long, and I'll have Siohan put it that Birdy doesn't need a bad scare, also that I'll strangle the first person who says the wrong thing." She managed a faint, early-morning grin. "It's not like I resort to threats very often, they'll know I mean it."

"I won't hold my breath, if you don't mind. She's got enough to worry about right now, anyway, though; maybe she'll be too busy telling you about everything that's going on right now at the fort, won't even notice anything else."

"Oh?"

"Oh—usual stuff really," Chris said gloomily. "Lialla and Aletto have been sniping at each other, it's been a real damp, cool spring up there so Aletto's walking funny again and Mom is afraid to try and get him working out because she's afraid it's like polio and he'll wind up completely crippled in the next year and a half if he pushes it. And he won't push it unless she gets him to. And I think Lizelle's really sick or drinking or something, she looked pretty bad when I went through last time—the little I saw her. She hardly comes down

to meals or anything, I guess." He shook himself, managed
a smile. "Hey. Let *her* lay all the bad karma on you, why
should you get it twice?"

"If I know Birdy, I won't get any of it; you know how she
feels about bleeding her soap-opera situations all over me. It
would be pretty hard on both of them if Lizelle was drinking,
though."

"Tell *me*. Mom hasn't touched the stuff in what—almost
four years now? And Aletto hasn't either, and both of them
used to be darned good at popping the cork and draining the
bottle in one long shot." He shook his head. "I was never
so glad of anything as when she decided to quit so he'd have
someone to lean on, so *he* could quit—except when Mom ran
out of cigarettes. You would not believe how bad it gets outside, some of these ports where there's tobacco. I mean, people smoking really rank pipes of stuff just everywhere, big
gnarly cigars—suffer city, really."

"Pass," Jennifer said. She spooned apple butter on her last
corner of toast and bit into it. "I'm glad you're up to leaving
today, though. You *are* up to it, aren't you?"

"I still feel junky, but not nearly as gross as last night.
Not up to dealing with Mom, though. Why're *you* glad? I
mean, it's not like I upchucked in the fountain."

"Nothing to do with it. I just think you should make for
Podhru as quickly as possible, let Afronsan know what you
overheard."

"Yeah. I guess I have to, don't I? I'm looking forward to
that—*not*." Chris sighed. "But, right, he needs to know, and
since Eddie's not here to give him a face-to-face on it, I'm
stuck. Too bad Ernie wasn't there, I've let Ernie do most of
the paperwork and stuff; Afronsan knows him pretty well.
But I thought, if you could write up something to get me past
the front desk and his clerks, straight up to the man himself.
You know; say something about how you know me and I'm
not just trying to build gossip into a big thing?"

"I can do that. Though I don't think that would occur to
him. After all, he knows about you via all the deals you've
cut and because of Enardi—all right, Ernie, sorry. And from
me—not that I brag you up," she added. "I've mentioned
you in connection with various products, services and deals,
all right? But keep in mind that Afronsan's no fool. He has a

fair idea of what's what, I don't doubt he'll have a reasonably well-rounded idea of how trustworthy and believable you are. He certainly won't think you're a big-mouthed kid simply out to cause trouble, not after the past four years.''

"Yeah—guess not,'' Chris said doubtfully.

"Trust me. I'll write you an introduction; I need to send him a letter myself, anyway, because he's going to have to hear about that gun and I don't want *any* other versions of the shooting getting to him before mine does. Too darned much work has gone into getting that telegraph into Rhadaz, getting the men in to set it up, convincing Shesseran not to mess with it; I'm not about to have all that work, and our only chance at a decent communication system, sabotaged by rumors.''

"*Or* by someone who has that very thing in mind,'' Chris put in. "You know darned well that for every two people who are wild about stuff like a telegraph, there are three who don't see what the big deal is, and four who want to know why we need it, and three others who think it's gonna send the whole country to hell in a handbasket.'' He folded a thick slice of toast in half and bit into it. "I *really* miss hot buttered toast, you know?''

"I know. Don't remind me.''

"Well, anyway.'' He finished the slice, grabbed an orange and got to his feet. "My stomach's been screaming at me for hours, I finally had to give up and come get something to separate the right wall from the left wall so it would shut up. Think I'll go put my feet up again, make sure what it got stays put, I still feel cruddy. Oh. You know where Vey is? Eddie sent him a message, and I'd like to talk to him anyway before I take off.''

"No idea. Some of the day staff should be moving around by now; ask someone to go find him.''

"I guess.'' Chris ran a hand through his hair. "I still feel funny, doing that. Ordering the servants around.''

"You order about like I do, kid, please and thank you and all the rest of it. But try living with a whole houseful of servants day in and day out.'' She sighed faintly. "I have to keep reminding myself it's what we pay them for, even after all this time, but so far as I know, working in the Thukar's palace is still supposed to be the top job. And no one's quit and griped about being treated like dirt—at least, not since we moved in.''

''I should think not. Listen, couple hours sleep and I'll be ready to roll. Can you draft up some kinda letter for me by then?''

''With Robyn on her way, and probably arriving by noon—is this a trick question? The minute I finish my coffee, I'll go up to the clerks' hall, you know where that is, don't you?'' Chris considered this, finally nodded.

''Later. Um—you feel okay and everything? No mad desire to dive for the floor, no green tummy?''

''Sugar was apparently clean,'' Jennifer said dryly.

''Just checking.''

''Don't sound so wistful; anyone would think you were sorry I didn't get sick.''

''Ha.'' He handed her the plate with its two remaining slices of cold toast, shoved the other orange and the container of apple butter over next to her sugar, then left. Jennifer watched him go. He might feel awful, but he didn't look it. Just as resilient at twenty as he'd been at sixteen; it wasn't fair. She hefted the coffee jug, decided there were almost two more short cups in it and poured out one. It wouldn't stay hot much longer anyway. Better leave a note for Dahven, so when he came down to eat he could order her another jug and have it sent up to the clerks' hall for her. Tell him strong coffee, she thought. It looked like a long morning.

Particularly once Dahven found out she intended to hand-deliver that contract. She drank deeply, then reached for the toast.

DAHVEN brought the coffee himself, arriving just moments after Chris did. By then, Jennifer had had an opportunity to proof the contracts (they were clean enough for signing, though somehow a word had gone in upside down on the bottom of the first page); she'd put up one copy for Afronsan, with notes in the margin explaining why certain of the paragraphs read as they did (stiff necks on both sides of the bargaining table, mostly) and written a brief longhand note for Chris that should get him into the heir's chambers with minimal difficulty—as well as two pages that would let Afronsan know about the shooting and the wine.

That wine. She'd taken a detour down into the apartments the old Thukar had set aside for his motley crew of sorcerers, wizards, Shapers and alchemists. At this point, two wizards and the boy who served both seemed a little lost in the ten or so chambers that opened off a central circular room. Once she found the aged and rather garrulous Rebbe, he confirmed her fears: The wine had been dosed with a narcotic that left a white residue in the bottom of Dahven's cup. "It's not one of those I'm most familiar with, unfortunately, though I've seen it used a very few times. Not often; the taste gives it away, you know. Whoever put it into the cup misjudged the amount necessary, or simply assumed the young Duke still willing to drink whatever is set before him—there are still tales about the market, you know, Thukara, about the young Duke's travels through some of the more questionable wine-seller's tents and the taverns. I think myself it was poor knowledge of the substance used: A very little of this particular powder will kill, and so quickly you would not have been able to save him. So small an amount would, the taste of a tart red wine would likely cover it completely—or nearly so. As much as was used, the taste would stop most from attempting to drink; so much of the substance in one swallow, the stomach would eject it at once." He handed her the cup, empty, washed and dried. "I'm told the merchant Cray took a swallow by accident and was quite ill. Send him to me, I have a liquid which may ease whatever distress he still feels."

An American pistol fired at her, but not by an American; evil-tasting wine poisoned by someone who'd walked right into the kitchens. She made no mention in the letter of Dee-har and Dayher, since there was nothing to connect them with either incident save suspicion. It wouldn't be necessary anyway: Afronsan was intelligent and had trained himself over long years to read what was meant between what was actually stated.

She'd worked out half a dozen different arguments to use on Dahven, should he try to stop her from carrying those contracts down to the Weaver's Guild; somewhat to her surprise, he heard her out without interruption. "The main thing," she finished, "is that there've been so many points at which one side or the other has balked. If I sent these instead of taking them, one side or the other might take that as a reason to pull out.''

''They'd think the threat against your life a poor excuse?'' But Dahven wasn't arguing, merely asking. She shook her head.

''I wasn't even harmed; no one was. I know there are probably a hundred wild rumors circulating the market this morning, but the Sikkreni know all about market rumors and I'd wager the Mer Khani do, too. Besides, the Mer Khani merchants have certainly spoken to the work crew, *they* know I came out without a scratch. And unless you've heard any more death threats from the lower market—'' She paused; he shook his head. ''Well, then. You know how your Sikkreni can be; I can read the Mer Khani pretty well. Both sides are capable of seeing it as an excuse to break the contract—and hold out for better terms at a later time. And then lay the blame at my feet, for not following through. I really don't want that, Dahven; besides, it's bad enough the flesh-peddlers are out for my throat, without having the regular merchants thinking I'm trying to keep them out of the foreign markets.''

He thought about this, finally nodded. ''All right. I accept the possibility, and I'll take your point. When are you expected? Because I'd like to send Vey and some others out now, let them wander along the main street, the way we'll go, see if they recognize anyone.''

''For instance, Eprian?'' She laughed. ''They could get lucky, I guess. I caught that 'we,' by the way.''

''You won't argue it, I hope,'' Dahven said. ''Because—''

''No. I'm always glad of your company, you know that. I'm not taking the litter, though.'' He opened his mouth, shut it again. ''You know how the market gets around midday, streets and alleys absolutely jammed with traffic of all kinds, nothing moving for long minutes on end sometimes. Afoot, even with a guard or two, I could probably edge my way through, but that litter—if it got stuck in traffic, I'd be a sitting duck.''

''I do know how the market gets, and again, I see your point. Although, don't you think it more likely people would stay well clear of the litter, after the violence yesterday?''

''No. Some might, if they actually saw the litter coming, but once some of those streets start filling up, who can see anything but what's right in front of them?''

"Besides," Chris came in on her side suddenly, "people are so weird, I bet you anything they'd close in on you just to check out the bullet hole, or see if they couldn't be right there when the guy took you out."

"Nice," Jennifer said. Dahven gave him a black look. "It's another point, unfortunately. But it doesn't matter, because no way am I riding in that wheeled death-trap today; walking, I *might* be visible but in that thing I'd stand out like a flag."

"This is logic?" Chris demanded. "Thought you were a lawyer."

Jennifer stood up and planted fists on her hips. "Whose side are you on, kid?"

"My own, of course. Just pointing out the holes in your—"

"I thought you were going to grab the paperwork and go play in the traffic before your mother showed up. Which could happen momentarily." Jennifer bent over the table to flip through the thick pile of paper. "While you're out looking for things this next trip, why don't you find me manila envelopes?"

"Why not just ask for a computer and fax?" Chris watched her fold the sheets and slide them into one of the leather cases that went back and forth between the Thukar's palace and the civil service building in Podhru. He took the case. "Jeez. Words like that sound really funny any more, you know?"

"Who's laughing?" Jennifer snapped her fingers. "Just remembered. Go down and see Rebbe, says he's got something for you in case you have any after-effects from last night."

"Hey. I'm fine, all right?"

She scowled up at him. "Just do it. Think how really dumb you're going to feel, halfway to Podhru by the new road and you fall off the horse—"

"—and they find my dead, bloated body two days later and *you* have to identify the gross remains," Chris put in as she paused for breath. "I am so sure. All right, hey, I can take a hint, you know?"

"Did you ever find Vey?"

"Yeah. Reminds *me*." Chris turned to Dahven. "Be all right if I ask for an armed escort for part of the afternoon?"

"Vey? Certainly. You can come down as far as the south gates with us, I'll see he gets word to go back there as soon as he's helped search for Eprian."

"Thanks. Um, listen." Chris shifted from foot to foot. "Look, you two be careful, will you? I'm going to head right back out to sea from Podhru and go south as soon as I can get a ship going the right direction. If there's anything major I need to report, I'll write it down, maybe the heir will stuff it in the pouch here with his own notes. But I gotta get back, find Eddie and see what new gossip he's picked up on. And if I can get a line on who's up to things—"

"Speak of someone who should be careful," Dahven said.

"Oh, hey." Chris spread his hands. "Careful's my middle name out there, it's a rough world and it's like *totally* uncivilized in the dockside end of that place. Besides, if I don't watch my step, I can't come back and warn you guys, maybe earn the next Emperor's undying gratitude, now, can I?"

Jennifer sighed. "Hold that thought, kid. All right, I'm going to change and get Siohan to comb out my hair; I'll meet you both in front of the blue room. Chris," she added flatly, "I'm going to check your pockets for that medication; you don't get out of the palace without it. Got me?"

6

卐

PEOPLE stared; many stood in whispering groups and peered furtively, more gawked openly as Jennifer, Dahven and Chris left the palace gates, half a dozen of the household guard making themselves very visible on both sides of the Thukar's small walking party, behind and before them. After several moments Chris leaned over to Jennifer and mumbled, "Hey. I think you're getting your fifteen minutes of fame. Either that, or one of us has a hole in the back of their pants."

"You'll survive, kiddo," Jennifer said. "It's not like they don't have cause, all the talk."

"Yeah." He scowled as they passed an older man who stood wide-eyed, mouth open. "It's one of the things I *really* hate, I betcha back home these guys would be eyeballing all the blood and live action at a mass murder, and if not they'd catch it on Geraldo later. Any of these people of yours have a *life*?"

"Not nearly as exciting as mine's been the past twenty-four hours," Jennifer said. "Ride with it, kid. After all, people here have always stared at you."

"Yeah. Right. As if that helps. Hey," he added in a clear attempt at a lighter mood, and a definite change of subject, "lookity those guys, dudes're really hauling." The telegraph crew had installed four more poles since the previous day, and now were within another perhaps ten poles of the Thukar's gates. "Maybe I should just wait here; rate they're going, I won't need the horse and the long haul down the road to Podhru."

"If you want to send a message no farther than the first village out, sure. Because that's all that's being hooked up around here just yet, remember? I'm impressed, though. They can't have gotten anything done yesterday afternoon; this must all have gone in since sunrise."

"It did." Dahven spoke for the first time since they'd left the palace; he'd been too busy helping his guardsmen keep an eye out for trouble. "I'm surprised myself that they've accomplished anything today; the guard says there's been an astonishing amount of talk, and there's a delegation of merchants and citizens coming to see me this afternoon—judging from the names I recognized on their list, it's mostly the anti-change coalition and a few hangers-on choosing to make a connection between the Mer Khani and the violence." He shook his head. "I thought of putting out some kind of official notice; perhaps I should have."

"Would it really have helped? Or would they assume you were either lying or downplaying the problem, in order to keep the telegraph on track?" Jennifer sighed. "Anyway, I guess I won't see you until bedtime tonight, if then. Ah, well, I suppose it's just as well, with Robyn coming in. I never seem to have enough time to just talk with her, do I?" They passed the pole crew and its usual large crowd of onlookers. But Jennifer thought the watchers seemed unusually quiet, and she could see only a few children—older ones, those who could wander the streets on their own. Small children who'd still be under the control of their mothers—not one. The crew itself appeared to be concentrating hard on their present task, seemingly unaware of the audience. "It's all right, isn't it?"

Dahven nodded absently; his eyes and most of his attention for the workers and the crowd around them. "City guard is double strength today all across the city, triple in this area. But no one's actually threatened the Mer Khani or the telegraph." He sighed faintly. "You'd know some of the names on that list, too: The usual concerned group of citizens who come out whenever anything goes wrong—which in their minds means, anything which isn't operating as it did in my father's time, or better yet, my grandsire's."

"Ah," Chris said. "The very verbal hell-in-a-handbasket crowd. You can handle them, though—right?"

"I can handle them," Dahven said. "I admit it takes me longer than it did my father—"

"Because you're a lot more careful than he ever was about unnecessarily offending anyone, that's all," Jennifer broke in. "Chris, you're not planning on walking all the way to Podhru, are you?"

"There's supposed to be a horse waiting outside the gates for me, figured it would just hold us all up if I tried to lead it through the streets myself. And . . ." He held up a three-foot staff, just thicker than his thumb, darkened with sweat and dirt. "And besides, I figured, two free hands, just in case, you know?"

Jennifer held out her hand and he slapped the stick across her palm. She turned it over experimentally, held it at arm's length. "Short for a bo, isn't it? What, you washed it and it shrank?" Chris laughed. "Is this supposed to be new and improved?"

"It's as old a method of stick-fighting as the long version, actually; I just find it easier and most of the time less obvious to carry this around than a six-footer. You can do a lot of the same things with it. You'd better be thinking all the time and moving *real* fast, though."

She took a two-handed grip on the short staff, then shook her head and handed it back. "What's this *you* stuff? I don't want a new thing to learn, I haven't got enough time to play with the toys I have. Besides, this thing isn't even as long as a sword *and* I'm very much out of practice—"

"Why doesn't this surprise me, Ms. Flab?" Chris demanded. He grunted as her elbow caught him in the ribs. "Next time I'm in town, I'll work you, okay?"

"With a real bo," Jennifer said warningly. "Not this Tinkertoy version."

"Whatever. Can't have you getting fat and out of shape, after all—will you *watch* it with that sharp elbow, lady? Hey. Gates. How time flies when—"

"Never mind, Chris." Jennifer wrapped an arm around his waist and squeezed. He threw his free arm around her shoulders and hugged back, hard. "Ow, take it easy, you!"

"Remember," Chris said as he let her go, "I wasn't here, right?"

"Who're you?" Jennifer retorted. "Where's your—is that your horse, there in the shade? I don't see any bags on it."

"I didn't bring but one change of shirts and a water bottle. Figured I'd better travel light, even though I traded horses coming north and I'll probably need to do that twice going the other way. That's the longest, most boring road, down to Podhru—Hey, dude!" This as Vey came out of shadow next to the gateway, Chris's reins and his own in one hand, two dark, sturdy-looking desert ponies following. Chris turned to grip Dahven's hand. "So, watch your back, all right? I'll send your guy back before dark."

"Fine. Vey—anything in the southeast sector?"

"No, sir. Rumor everywhere, of course; no one I saw who didn't belong. The Zelharri duchess and her guard was sighted along the east road a while ago, and likely will cross into the city at any moment."

"God," Chris groaned. "I'm gone, or I'm gray meat. Later." He and Vey mounted, turned the horses and set out down the south road at a walk. Jennifer waited; Chris waved from a short distance on and urged the horse to a little more speed—still short of a trot, in deference to the amount of foot traffic, lack of shade and the already warm afternoon. She waved back, then let Dahven take her hand as they walked back into the city. The street was still very broad here, and there weren't very many people out near the gates, but they kept to a leisurely pace: It was also too hot for people to move very fast.

THE meeting was a quick one, the documents signed and both parties at least claiming to be quite pleased with the deal they'd struck. Jennifer kept an eye on the heads of both delegations and decided her original opinion had been right— both parties felt they'd given more concessions, and gotten less gain, than they should have; and the underlying mood was nearer resignation than not. No mention was made of the Thukara's near brush with death the previous afternoon, though Jennifer sensed narrowed, thoughtful eyes on her whenever she turned her back on one faction or other. The Sikkreni weavers seemed uncertain how to handle the surprise visit by their Thukar, but the Americans took the unexpected presence as a personal honor—and perhaps a sign of better things (and contracts) to come. Jennifer sat alone at the table, going through the contracts page by page to make certain both sides had initialed the bottoms of all pages as well as the few minor corrections. They'd all signed everything, of course; she checked that as well. At the other end of the room, Dahven made light conversation with the foreigners. He took, as Jennifer did, a very small cup of cooled, peach-colored local wine to toast the success of the venture; and they left moments later, guard close around them. The narrow way was very congested for the time of day and the heat; Jennifer's shirt and breeches were sticking to her by the time they reached the wider main avenue. Here, there was little traffic and hardly anyone standing about in the sun. The Mer Khani pole crew was nowhere in sight, possibly eating lunch or breaking until the cooler late afternoon. Sun shone down from a clear blue sky, heat waves rose from the paved avenue, and the early breeze blew dust and sand in leg-stinging gusts.

Jennifer pulled at the shirt, tugging it away from her skin, flapping the loose fabric. After that last long stretch, even her teeth felt gritty.

The guard left them in the courtyard and went back into the streets; Dahven parted from her outside the blue room. She scrubbed a sleeve across her forehead, then ran her fingers through the long curled bangs. "Don't get too close to me, I reek. I'll have to sponge off before I even go looking for Birdy."

"I won't have time; I could certainly do with a fresh shirt, for the comfort of my own nose if not theirs." He considered this, smiled. "Well, perhaps it will shorten the meeting."

"Depends on who you're meeting with," Jennifer said dryly. She leaned close to him and sniffed cautiously. "You smell like nice, warm skin, not at all unpleasant. Certainly not like some of these people around here—I swear they haven't bathed since their mothers dunked them in the fountain, back before they could walk. Do you want food sent in to you?"

"Something right away—fruit and bread will be fine." He sighed, dropped a kiss on the top of her head. "If I miss evening meal—well, we'll hope I don't. You have a nice time with Robyn, I'll work out something with the kitchen staff when the bread comes." He leaned against the door, gripped the latch. "Give her my greetings; I'm sure to be done with these people before she leaves."

Jennifer shook a finger at him. "You'd just better; that's a couple of days at least! But I fully intend to come rescue you if those men aren't gone by nine tonight," she went on flatly. "Even a Thukar who used to drink all night in the cheesier local taverns needs his sleep, and I'm not going to let them bully you." Dahven merely laughed and went into the blue room. Jennifer shuddered as she caught a glimpse of bright sun on turquoise carpeting, reflecting off a shiny blue and gold wall. *Disgusting.*

ROBYN was waiting for her in the family apartments, settled down in the Thukara's wardrobe, happily gossiping with Siohan. *If Chris could see this, he'd have a fit.* Jennifer bit back a grin—one of the staff might give Chris away accidentally, but it would never be the close-mouthed and loyal Siohan—and sent the woman into the hall to get her bath filled, to send someone to let the kitchen know about lunch. "Just whatever's easy, and we'll take it in the dining room, easier on the staff and it's a lot cooler in there. All right, Birdy?"

"It's so hot outside, I'm ready to melt. Yeah, food in the room with the pool and the waterfall, I'm for it." And, as Siohan left, "How do you stand it, girl?"

"What—the heat? Same way you handle snow, I guess. It isn't humid here."

"It's a dry heat, yeah, where have I heard that before? I don't recall it made any difference to me, that commune in Arizona. But you're looking good. Your hair's different, isn't it?"

Jennifer shrugged. "A little longer, maybe. Yours looks nice."

"Yeah," Robyn grinned. "Stick in the mud, all the same, huh?" In four years, Robyn actually had changed very little, though she'd made a few outward concessions to the local ways of dressing: She now wore long, loose Rhadazi skirts rather than blue jeans—as much a concession to the pounds put on after two children in the past three years as to her old jeans wearing out in half a dozen strategic places. The skirts were in the same soft chambray blue she'd always loved and

most often worn back in L.A.; the hair was still waist-length,
center parted, no bangs, usually shoved back behind her ears,
though often she'd either pull it back herself or let one of her
women do something up and braided with it. She'd just possibly lost weight since her last trip to Sikkre, but Jennifer
decided she'd let Robyn mention it if she had. Robyn claimed
not to care but the last time Jennifer had been at Duke's Fort,
her sister had made disparaging remarks about looking like
the "before" half of the liquid-diet ads. She'd definitely take
it the wrong way if Jennifer complimented her and she *hadn't*
lost any weight. *Flatter stomach? Or just the cut of this new
skirt?* Either possible. Just now, she was rosy-cheeked from
the exercise of a long ride, bright sun and the excitement of
coming to see her younger sister; the hair that ordinarily made
her face look fuller and dragged down had been pulled across
one shoulder where she'd braided it and tied the end with a
bright blue ribbon. Jennifer grinned at the sight of bare feet
under the nearly ankle-length skirt—its hem deeply embroidered with pink, red and yellow flowers, a vine-tracery of
green connecting them and darker green leaves. Robyn and
her bare feet. Jennifer wondered how far into winter Robyn
managed to go barefoot in Duke's Fort, with those cool stone
floors. She'd certainly done it all that first summer and most
of the fall. Robyn broke her train of thought by wrapping
both arms around her and kissing her right temple resound-
ingly.

"Oh, boy, is it good to see you, kiddo!"

"Same. Did you do the skirt?"

"Me? Sew? This kind of fancy work? Actually, though, I
did do some of the easy parts, just a little of the green vines.
Most of it is thanks to one of Lizelle's new girls—she has a
couple teenyboppers out of Cornekka, really nice kids. Clever
with a needle, and fast, too."

"It's really nice and it looks practical. If Lizelle lets them
take orders, I'd have one of those, looks very cool." Jennifer
stripped out of her long shirt and scowled at the wet patches
front and back, under both arms. "You didn't bring the little
ones?" Silly question; if Robyn had brought either of the
children she'd had by Aletto, they'd be with her right now.
Robyn didn't hold with nannies, or with the notion a noblewoman should only see her kids once or twice a day.

"Too hot." Robyn managed a rather forced laugh. "Besides, this way Aletto knows I'll come back."

Jennifer looked up from shedding her short boots and trousers; Robyn gave her a very small shrug. "He can't have any doubts on that subject, can he, Birdy? Even without the kids?"

"He—oh, look." Robyn shook her head. "Let's wait, okay? I just got in, I'm too hot, tired from all that riding, hungry enough that I hope you don't care if I need a bath myself before I eat because I'm not going to mess with it. Let's eat first, let me grab a short nap, and then—well, I told myself I wasn't going to lay stuff on you but I guess I knew better, really. I hope—I mean, if you don't mind."

"Mind?" Jennifer shook her head, dropped the trousers atop the dirty shirt and went over to the small wash-water bowl Siohan kept ready for her. She fished a cloth from the stack, scrubbed her hands, washed her face vigorously, finished by draping the damp cloth across the back of her neck. She sighed happily. "*Lord,* I needed that! Birdy, you know I never mind when you need to talk. It isn't like you *really* bleed problems all over me all the time, you've never done that."

"I try to not," Robyn said rather anxiously.

"Well, you don't, so quit worrying about it. Hand me that long red thing, will you? You said you were hungry and so'm I, actually; now I can last until after I eat before I dump the whole body in a bucket." She draped the washrag across the edge of the bowl, dragged the loose red gauzy fabric over her head and shook the hem down around her ankles, brushed damp hair away from her forehead and ears and grinned at her elder sister. "I can handle you if you can stand me."

Robyn wrinkled her nose. "Yah. You never did sweat as bad as I do, kiddo."

"You never played tennis with me, that's all." Jennifer fished a pair of sandals from under the table that held the wash basin, shoved her feet into them and indicated the door to the hall with a sweeping wave of her arm. "After you, Duchess."

DAHVEN, as she feared, was still closeted with angry Sikkreni merchants and citizens hours later, and according to his man showed no signs of being able to break free any time soon; he'd ordered jugs of local wine and several loaves of plain bread sent in, then asked the man to check with him in two hours to see if he needed a real meal brought to him. *I might need to go rescue him after all*, Jennifer thought sourly. She uttered a malediction against stubborn city men who needed to be dragged, kicking and screaming, out of the last century, then decided she might as well order an early dinner for herself and Robyn; Birdy might appreciate the chance to get a long night's sleep after the ride from Sikkre; her eyes had been heavy all through lunch and she'd hardly spoken.

It was pleasantly cool in the dining hall, the outer doors had once again been taken off and a very light breeze ran across Jennifer's toes, bared by the scraps of sole and string-thin leather straps that constituted her summer in-house footwear.

Robyn had had her bath and a long nap, and wore a different but equally impressive embroidered skirt; her hair had been pulled back and up in a still-damp braid that one of the women must have plaited for her since it hung straight down her back rather than across one shoulder, and a narrow, turquoise ribbon had been worked into it.

Jennifer waited until food and water had been brought and left. "All right, Birdy, tell. What's hassling you?"

Robyn had picked up her water cup. She set it down, shook her head, finally sighed. "What isn't, is more like it. Thing is, so much of what's happened lately is so damned *fuzzy*, I can't figure if it's them, if it's me—if I'm paranoid or they really are out to get me."

"Your own quote, the last two aren't mutually exclusive."

"I—yeah, what you just said." She picked up the cup, set it down once more. "Well—Aletto, for one thing." She sighed again. "It's not like I didn't know any better, guys like Aletto just don't change, you know? I mean—" She frowned, took a long drink, wrapped both hands around the cup and stared into it. "I don't do the words as well as you do, that's never been my thing. He's insecure, I knew that when I first talked to him, of course. And—not straight possessive, just the kind of possessive you get from a guy who's insecure. You know, though, I really thought he'd get over it when I said I'd marry him—before that, I guess I thought who could blame the guy, for all he knew, I'd split for the bright lights and big city or something, if he didn't have that piece of paper.''

It reminded Jennifer of her old secretary, all those magazine self-help articles Jan used to put on her boss's chair. Mostly on dating, on guys, now and again on things Jan thought she might find interesting. How to read what a guy meant by paying attention to what he said and how he said it; how to help a rape victim—how to deal with battering men, verbally abusive men. Possessive men. *Good old Jan, wonder where she is right now?* Jennifer shook her head to clear it; she'd managed to avoid those kinds of thoughts the past year or so, and when they snuck up on her like this, they got her right under the ribs. She was pleased to note her voice didn't betray the sudden surge of emotion. ''Birdy, men *don't* change because you marry them.''

''Yeah. Like I say, as if I didn't know that, right?'' Robyn replied gloomily. ''All my experience and like that. I guess I was dumb, because I *wanted* it to be different this time— but you know,'' she added, ''there was always that chance. Different world, different situations.'' She shrugged. ''So it wasn't that different.''

''He's not—Birdy, spit it out, what *is* he doing?''

''Doing? Oh, not really much. He gets worried if I'm out of the fort too long at a time, gets a little too stiff and formal if I have to deal with any of the merchant groups or like that, if I look like I'm enjoying myself too much. No, honestly.'' She looked up. ''It really isn't even as much as I've made it sound like, that's why I sometimes wonder if it isn't just me being paranoid. Even me coming here to see you, he didn't *say* anything, really; just put a lot of obstacles in the way of my coming, and then when I made it really clear I was going to go see you no matter what, there were all these nitsy little difficulties about bringing the babies, every time I'd say something, find a way around one argument, he'd have another. And, oh, I don't know, he got real quiet every time I brought the trip up—you know, even just asking little Amarni what he'd like from the city, things like that.

''It's—I can live with that, it's not like he's abusive, or anything.''

''You should sit him down and talk to him, Birdy.''

"Yeah, well." Robyn expelled air in a gust and ran a hand across her hair. "You know how soon *that'll* happen, right?"

"I know you hate to confront people, girl. But this isn't people, this is the man you married, the father of your youngest kids, all right? Anyway, think about it—what if he doesn't realize what he's doing? Or how you see it? Or how it upsets you? That you don't feel cherished and loved when he boxes you in? The Aletto I know is a nice enough guy, I think he'd want to know how you felt; also, I don't remember he ever knew that much about women, maybe it simply doesn't register, that he's giving you a hard time."

"I—yeah. Well. Maybe. Anyway, that was just—it's there, but it's not as bad as some things. I'll tell you, I really was glad to have this chance to get out of the fort for a while, the atmosphere in there is like—God. Remember the first day we hooked up with those two, and Aletto decided to go all noble and not risk any of us, and Lialla blew up and then Chris blew up? I felt like someone had dropped a tornado right between my ears. All the other howling, screeching fights they had, the whole trip? Well, with one thing and another lately, the whole fort has been like that, like someone blew the roof off and the storms just keep hitting. And the worst part is, all this yelling and screaming, it's in my own home; I can't even walk away from it!"

Robyn picked up a piece of bread and broke it into small bites, scattering the bites and loose crumbs all over her plate. "Lizelle looks like—you know, if it was our Los Angeles instead of Duke's Fort, I'd swear the woman was heavy into coke or something, reminds me of people I knew back in the Sixties with all the pills. Just—strange, I don't know. Not right."

Jennifer opened her mouth, hastily turned away to clear her throat. She'd almost given Chris away, that he'd already told her about Lizelle's condition. She folded bread around meat and took a large bite to cover the near goof; Robyn seemed fortunately much too preoccupied to notice at the moment, but she'd better watch herself a little more carefully. "She could be drinking."

"No. I don't spend much time around her any more; she pretty much hangs out in her apartments, sewing with those new girls of hers—she made little Iana the prettiest dress, wish I could show you—anyway, I *think* it was Lizelle's sewing but Aletto goes to visit her every other day at least, he says she's spending way too much of her time just sitting by the window, staring at the walls. That's not booze, and besides, I think he'd say if it was wine. He'd certainly be the first to notice, but I'd probably pick up on something like that pretty fast myself, even if I don't see nearly as much of her. Anyway, if she was that spacey from any of the local stuff, those rooms would just reek, and they don't.

"She's lost a lot of weight, too, all at once, really. In fact, I thought at first, maybe she's got cancer. I had a friend who got really skinny and off-color looking like that, had some kind of girl-parts cancer. But she didn't have that look Lizelle has; Lizelle truly looks like she's toking a bunch of something strong."

"If it can't be cheap wine, it couldn't be pot," Jennifer said. "It would smell at least as much, and *you'd* pick up on that smell. But if she's on something, whatever it is, then how does she get it? It would have to be smuggled into the fort, and you know, I can't see that happening in dead, total secrecy, can you? I can't sneeze around here without the entire staff knowing about it an hour later."

"Yeah—" Robyn said doubtfully.

"Hold that thought, though," Jennifer said, as her mind made a sudden connection. Drug. *Zero.* In landlocked Zelharri? But Robyn would be a very useful ally in finding out it had actually made it into Sehfi; all those drugs she'd taken back in the Sixties, all the people she'd known who did, she had an excellent eye for spotting users. Which made the matter of Lizelle even more worrying. *It would have to be someone the family trusted. A member of the fort's staff, or a guardsman, smuggling lethal chemicals in to the Duke's mother?* "We'll come back to it. But if that's all that's worrying you—"

"Well, no." Robyn was tearing at her bread again; she looked down at her hands, sighed faintly and scooped half a dozen bits onto meat. She eyed the meat doubtfully.

"Chicken," Jennifer said. "Dark meat. There's breast on the platter over here also, but the kitchen remembers your eating habits."

"Oh. Good." Robyn took a bite, chewed and swallowed before going on. "Don't know how you and Chris can do that, talk with food in your cheek and make it look like acceptable manners."

"Practice at eating in polite company and wanting to run your mouth all the time," Jennifer replied gravely. Robyn chuckled.

"Yeah. Where'd Chris ever find any polite company? That's another thing," she added as she held up the meat and bread, "that's driving me nuts. The meat thing. *You* know how tough it's been for me, all these years, sticking to a modified veg diet, no red meat. Aletto doesn't give me any hassle about it, Lialla—well, you know her, she doesn't care what anyone else eats. Lizelle, though—until she dove back into her rooms, any time I didn't keep a close eye on things, she'd go ahead and take over, order up the meals, and I'd find all this red meat on the table, no chicken or fish or beans or anything for a substitute, and if I said anything she'd just laugh that irritated laugh of hers and say, "Oh, go on and try it, it won't kill you.""

"Maddening," Jennifer said as Robyn paused to take another bite. "Lucky she has you to deal with and not me; I'd have beaned her with the platter."

Robyn grinned, chewed and swallowed, washed down the bite with a long drink of water. "I can just see it. Good thing she's playing recluse, I'd get back home after this, look across the table at her and start giggling. Not good for local relations with Amarni's and Iana's grandmama." She sighed; the grin faded. "The thing that really has me uptight is Iana."

"Iana? What could she possibly be up to at—what—all of two years?"

"Two and a half. Looks like you did at that age, really cute, super smart—"

"Looks like I did? Poor baby. Wish you could've brought at least her even if Aletto decided to keep the heir hostage," Jennifer said rather wistfully. "God knows when I'll be able to get to Sehfi next, she'll probably be half grown."

"Yah. Listen to you, whimpering over my babies. That's new. Why don't you get over your fear of local midwives and have your own? I know," Robyn said, holding up a hand, "it's this running around you're doing, too. I think it's high time you told Afronsan to come visit you if he needs personal consultations—or get himself a decent rep who can hit the roads for him. Or—"

"Once the telegraph's in place, the travel part won't be a factor," Jennifer said. "We'll have a station and an operator right in the clerks' offices, just like he will, it'll be just like having a dedicated fax line. And—look, I realize you've managed just fine with your local midwives, but you already had one kid before we came here—"

"What, sixteen-some years before? That pretty much cancels out the womb-already-broken-in effect, or so I was always told."

"Doesn't matter," Jennifer said firmly. "Until that line's in place, there's always the chance I'll have to make a fast trip to Podhru, and it's bad enough bouncing around on a horse or in one of those ghastly, shock-absorberless wagons. I absolutely refuse to do it with morning sickness or a huge belly." She frowned. "How *did* we get off on this tangent? We weren't talking about me—"

"I was," Robyn said, as firmly. "I just want to remind you, you aren't getting any younger. Maybe career women start having babies at thirty-eight and forty back home, but this isn't the same thing."

"I know. *Really*. Can we let it go now, please? Tell me about Iana."

Robyn sighed, shook her head, but obediently let it drop. "Well, she's got another thing you had at that age—the Cray temper. Except she's also got the Aletto-Lialla temper from the other side of the family."

"You're raising a firecracker, in other words."

"Cherry bomb. Well, I can handle that, though it sends Lizelle into a full-scale wailing tizzy when the kid goes off the Richter scale. I think Aletto's kind of proud of the kid, being that little, and standing up for herself; I know Lialla is. But a few days ago, Iana was supposed to be down for a nap, I was out weeding and I caught her sneaking across and into the fountain garden. Had to chase her down, and when I got an arm on her, she rounded on me—wow! If I'd have been *our* mom, I'd have walloped her good right then. Anyway, I had hold of her arm, and she was pulling, trying to get away from me—and I swear to you, I could see the line

of feathers coming up along the back of her upper arm.''
Robyn drew a deep, shaky breath.

Jennifer stared at her for a very long moment. ''She's—
Iana's a shapeshifter? *At her age?* Good Lord, Birdy, I'd be
absolutely terrified if I were you.''

''You think I'm not? And then having to leave her at home—
I remind myself, her daddy and her grandmama and her aunt
don't stifle her baby creativity the way I do, as the parenting
crowd back in LaLa Land would put it. They aren't going to
get her in such a howling rage; and she *was* short on nap
time that day.'' She shook her head. ''I could've strangled
Aletto for being such a hard-necked booger over keeping her
home after that, but the only way I might have budged him
was to tell him what was up. If I'd stayed home, he'd have—
I don't know what he'd have.''

''You aren't not telling him? Robyn—!''

''She didn't really shift,'' Robyn said weakly. ''Not yet.
Not entirely. Though I'm afraid she will.'' Robyn made a
visible effort, picked up the roll and took another bite. ''Thing
is, *I* just fell into it, here, and I never really learned anything
about it except I had to get pissed off or royally scared to
shift, it was horribly hard work, and it only worked at night.
The last time I shifted was when Jadek made me, south of
Duke's Fort, all those years ago—remember?''

''During the day. As if I'd ever forget.''

''Yeah, me too.'' Robyn nodded, let her eyes close briefly.
''I don't think I was ever so scared, being that high up and
knowing the shift was coming apart on me. I—since then,
I've kept away from *anything* that might get me pissed enough
to do a shift.''

''And you haven't asked anyone about it, either, have you?
Talked to anyone?''

''Why? I wasn't ever going to use it again, I figured I
could control it so long as I stayed away from the situations
that forced it on me. Besides, the way Aletto feels about
shapeshifters, it was a lot easier to forget about it. Oh, I
know; he said it didn't matter that I did because it was me,
and I don't think he was just saying that to be nice. But
shapeshifters in general—he still gets this *really* disgusted
look on his face if they ever come up in conversation. But

now—well, now I have to be able to do it, to use it, so that I can talk to Iana about it. Some kids, you could probably scare into cooling the anger by convincing them they'll turn into a monstrous bird and fly away, but not Iana. Kid's got hair.''

"Sounds it." Jennifer picked up the last of her bread and meat and ate thoughtfully. Robyn wasn't saying about little Amarni; she remembered him as a very easygoing toddler the last time she'd seen him, so even if he had inherited the gene from Robyn he might never show it. Whatever, it definitely wasn't the right time to remind Robyn she might have two little flyers on her hands. "Well. I suppose the best thing to do would be to send for someone from down in the market; there are a few shapeshifters who practice some sort of magic—other than the exotic dancers,'' Jennifer put in quickly.

"I—well, yeah," Robyn said. Her color was rather high, suddenly. "But I'd really rather not, I've done my best to keep anyone new from knowing about it—me and shifting. There was some gossip after we first got to Duke's Fort, but it died out when I didn't circle the city at night, and once I got visibly pregnant and then had Amarni—well, as far's I know, nothing's been said since. I really don't want to get any gossip going about it. And from what I hear, shifters are all pretty different anyway. So, I thought, you've got all this open area between the palace and the outer walls, like that pond where the guys found us, that night we got out of the tower?''

"You mean the fish pool. What about it?"

Robyn shrugged. "Well, if maybe just the two of us could go out there, just after dark, I could try and get it to work once more, see if I can't learn a little more about what it is, how it works, where it comes from. You do Thread, I know you can track me; and maybe you could come up with some suggestions, way you did back the first few times I used it." She sighed. "If we have to go to an expert, then, all right. But I think about the kind of gossip that could start going around, and—I'd hate that at least as bad as Aletto would. It's—well, it's tacky.''

"Front-page tabloid stuff?" Jennifer leaned back in her

chair. "I certainly see your point. And I'm willing to do whatever I can, of course, though I'm fairly rusty myself. But why didn't you ask Lialla? I'd have thought—"

"Lialla," Robyn said darkly. "Lialla's decided to go on a one-woman crusade to bring the Holmaddi women out of the Dark Ages; that's what all the howling with Aletto's been about."

"Come again?"

"Oh. She got a letter, little while back, some local bunch of village feminists up north, they want her to come help them set up a support group or an underground or something. She wants to, Aletto figures she's got a snowball's chance of not getting caught and strangled on the spot. From what I've heard, those men up there make my Greek look like a charter member of NOW."

"Probably not far off. What does Lialla think?"

"Who ever knows what she thinks? Except, apparently, she's all jazzed about it and really wants to do it—and honestly, not for the fame and glory if she made headway for them, I have to admit she's a better practicing feminist than I am. Well, a better militant feminist, anyway. Yeah, I know, that's not hard at all. But it's sure been the icing on the cake, those two going hammer and tongs again. Lialla seems to have decided I must be on Aletto's side 'cause I'm his wife, so she hardly talks to me at all any more. I said something to her about shifting after Iana threw that tantrum, just asked a simple question, and she gave me one of her uppity, snotty answers, which tells me she doesn't know a thing about it and's trying to bluff."

"Sounds like a real fun place to live; remind me again how lucky I am being here," Jennifer said lightly. She checked her pocket watch. "I don't see why we couldn't. I've been feeling guilty lately because I haven't had any time for either my Wielding or my bo, and if I'm that rusty, I'd really rather no one was there to watch when I held my first practice session."

"Know the feeling."

"The pond's a good idea, too: It's quiet, inside the walls but secluded. We should have it all to ourselves. Call it an hour from now, I want to change, and you'd better, too.

That whole area is very rough stonework where it isn't prickly ground cover, so I hope you brought boots.''

"Rode in them. And I brought heavy pants.''

"Good. Come to my room when you're ready; I'll leave a note so Dahven knows where we are.''

7

≈

THE sun was down and the evening sky a darkening but still starless blue when the two women came down the broad, short flight of stairs just past the dining room and started across the open, deserted courtyard. "Dahven says his great-grandfather used to use this as a parade ground, but after he died no one could justify the cost of keeping up a yard this size just for a bunch of armed men to practice formations on—couldn't see the point of so many men, as a matter of fact. I keep thinking it should be planted, but it would take a ton of water to keep things green, and this dirt is a disaster."

"I thought it was all rock," Robyn said. "It's hard enough. Save your money, use it to redo a suite for the nursery."

Jennifer pressed a hand against her sister's ear and shoved, sending Robyn staggering. "You made your point earlier, cut it out."

Robyn laughed quietly. "Yes'm. Yeah, I remember this place," she added as they stepped into the grove surrounding the fish pond. "All these neat, tall trees, the water. Bet this is cool during the day."

"I come out here now and again, since I got the pond cleaned up. When Dahven and I first got here, no one had touched it in months and one of the two water-in pipes had quit, you could smell the algae halfway to the family dining hall. The other one was even worse, tons of some kind of weed strangling the pond flowers. I had it drained and it's just sitting over there." She gestured.

Robyn sniffed cautiously. "This doesn't smell bad now."

"Not very. A little fishy. There are some darned big fish in there, too—fat black things rather like those bug-eyed gold-fish I used to have in the bowl back in Wyoming, except a hundred times bigger."

"Darn. Have to come back out tomorrow," Robyn said. "Can't see anything right now. Well." She sighed and felt around for the stone lip of the pond and sat. "Guess I can't put it off any longer, can I?" She let her head fall forward onto her hands.

"Not if you're serious about doing this, Robyn."

"Serious, yeah," Robyn mumbled. "Eager and willing to take up flying again? As Chris would say, *not*. I promise you, I wouldn't be out here for anything less than my kids' sake."

Jennifer leaned her six-foot ash fighting staff against the wall and sat down next to her sister. "I'm right here if you need help." *Though what could I possibly do*, she thought glumly. She had to admit Robyn had a good point, though: A shapeshifter from the lower market would probably find it impossible to keep such a story to herself—any rumors about the Zelharri Duchess that had gone fallow over the past three years would spring to life again. Aletto would hate it, and Robyn would feel horrible for him, having to put up with everyone knowing he'd married a shapeshifter. Surely people in Sehfi wouldn't have forgotten his outspoken distaste for that form of magic. Poor Robyn: She'd hate people staring at her, but she'd hate it worse for the children. Jennifer found a more comfortable spot on the rough and uneven wall for her backside, braced her hands behind her and leaned back to stare up into the trees at the darkening blue of sky far over-head. *Think, damnit*, she told herself. *You helped her with this thing before, and you didn't know anything about it then, either. Think back!* It wasn't easy concentrating, though: all this still, dark wood around them, the occasional soft splash of a fish far across the pool, the gentle tinkle of water running down a smooth sheet of sandstone to form a waterfall at one end, and the gurgle of water spilling over at the opposite end, running down a trough filled with river cobbles and into a clay pipe, where it would be brought back to the fall by a clockwork-and-magic mechanism Jennifer had long since given up trying to understand.

Robyn broke her disjointed train of thought with a mumbled "Oh, dear," as she brought her head up and shook it. The motion was just visible in the under-tree gloom. "I think it might be a little early yet tonight; I *think* I can tell the change place is where I remember it, you know, somewhere around the pit of my stomach. It doesn't feel awfully strong, though." She edged around and pulled her feet up under her so she could sit cross-legged. "Except, I guess it could be just—not working? Like, maybe because I didn't use it so long, it got lost or something?"

"I suppose that's possible—the old 'Use it or lose it' theory of things? Like you say, though, it's been a long time since you've tried it, and you did your best only after it got good and dark, remember? Both times you tried daytime it didn't work very well—"

"God. Tell *me*."

"And now I think about it, the few times you tried to push it early, out there when you were looking for Chris, it didn't cooperate very well, did it?"

"I—" Robyn was quiet for a long minute or two. "Well, maybe that *was* why. I don't remember thinking that at the time, but I guess I had enough on my mind." She laughed sourly. "Not like I was taking notes so I could use it later."

"Yeah. Think how fast you could get between Duke's Fort and the palace," Jennifer said gravely. She felt her sister's start of surprise and added, "Hey, you could come visit once a week, we'll even make you a landing pad on one of the flat roofs—"

"You!" Robyn swung a hand and clipped her ear. "I was taking you seriously! As if I didn't know better by now!" She considered this and giggled. "Do I get a wind sock and all the lights?"

"First class helio-Birdy pad," Jennifer replied, and they both laughed. "You're doing all right, lady; give it a few minutes, you can still distinguish trees from sky up there, and there aren't any stars in sight yet. This is not the time to rush it, all right?"

"Fine with me. Helio-Birdy," Robyn repeated, and giggled again. "You're a rotten broad—but I'm not half as nervy as I was a few minutes ago. Still good at it, aren't you?"

"Glad it still works," Jennifer said. "Listen, though, I wanted to talk to you about Lizelle; this is probably as good a time and place as any. Something I heard about recently, couple of different sources.'' She made a short and reasonably concise story of the foreign drug possibly already being smuggled onto the coastline north of Bez, what she'd heard about its appearance and its effects. When she finished, she could feel Robyn staring at her.

''My God. I thought we'd left all that kind of stuff behind! But—you said it hasn't hit *here*; how would this Zero stuff get into the fort before it came through Sikkre?''

''Don't know. It's a foreign thing, and it's only an outdated saying that everything comes to Sikkre first. Anyway, that's not the point; thing is for you to keep your eyes open once you go home. Watch Lizelle as much as you dare, keep an eye out for these rope rings, keep an ear open for the word 'Zero.' ''

''Damned right I will,'' Robyn said grimly. ''Something I've really liked about this place, no major drug problem. Not that there's so much reason for one in Rhadaz as there was in L.A., not much real poverty, hardly any of the hopelessness you used to see.'' She sighed faintly. ''No Sixties revolution to make them seem like no big deal, yeah. But once something gets in, once people get hold of it—oh, Lord,'' Robyn finished unhappily.

Jennifer patted her knee. ''Well, don't let it get to you, Birdy, what I've heard is still half to two-thirds rumor, and there may not be as much of a threat as we've been told around here. The stuff may not be as bad as they say, and you're right, there's no saying there'd be addicts all over the streets if the stuff did come in, it's a different culture entirely. If we can catch the smugglers early and often, make it tough on them, they may never get up the momentum to make a big deal out of it anyway.''

''Maybe,'' Robyn said doubtfully. ''Didn't I hear a bunch of Republicans say that once?'' She snorted. ''You know, it's so dumb, all the magic there is around here, all the fun you could have working magic, why would you want something like this junk? Except,'' she sighed, ''except that's not logical; you could probably have made a case back home for just about anything being better than dope, and it obviously wasn't for a lot of people. Of course, magic isn't at all what I used to think it would be. You know, all the stuff I tried back home, the Tarots, the I Ching coins, even that dumb Ouija board—there was this sense of wonder, you know? The thought that—all right, sure it's just something somebody made up, but—maybe it isn't, and what *if* it isn't? There was still that feeling, it could be something exciting if you could tap into it, something really neat. Maybe, all along, I was hoping to plug into something that would wind up being like elf-magic in *The Lord of the Rings*. Don't you dare laugh,'' she added.

"I wouldn't dream of it," Jennifer said sincerely. "That was one of the few things you ever shoved at me that I read, after *you* read me *The Hobbit*. It's been years, and I still remember a lot of it, made me cry. Maybe that was why *I* was so surprised at magic, when I finally got my hands into it: You do think it should be exciting and wondrous, and it turns out to be more like knitting or typing—do this, and that happens. Do it long enough, you get tired.''

"Yeah, I guess. I envied you so bad, when we first got dragged here and *you* got the magic. Until I saw what a hassle it was to make it work, how it didn't always do what you wanted, or couldn't. For a while I wondered if it wasn't a bad joke old Merrida pulled on me, knowing I wanted magic and making me into a shifter.''

"She worked pretty strong magic that night but I gathered she didn't usually operate at that level," Jennifer said. "I think the drawing spell, the use of language we all got, my temporary healing for Aletto—I'd swear that totally wiped her out. She couldn't ever have managed something like *making* you a shapeshifter; she wasn't that good. Besides, I use Thread myself, remember? I can't think of a single way to bind up a form of magic and put it on someone.''

"Yeah," Robyn said. "So it really was my rotten temper, huh?''

"Rotten *repressed* temper," Jennifer reminded her.

"Right. Let me tell you, Iana's isn't repressed at *all*." She sighed faintly. "Anyway, magic just wasn't what I thought; still isn't. Lialla's so nuts-and bolts about everything she does, Thread *and* that Light she has. You're so darned practical. Most of the charm stuff you can buy in the markets is—it's like buying one of those throw-away flashlights at the grocery store checkout; use it for a while, dump it when it wears out, go get another. Mine just flat scares me. Where's the joy in any of it?''

''There's a little fun in it, now and again,'' Jennifer said. ''Remind me later, I'll show you something I learned from an old guy down in the brewers' pavilion.''

''Yeah.'' Robyn let her head fall back so she could look up and groaned faintly. ''I'm stalling, I guess.'' She felt for and gripped her sister's wrist. ''If I get this to work, don't you *dare* sing any of that mushy Italian opera to get me back down!''

Jennifer grinned. ''That was pretty darned embarrassing at the time, I'll have you know; my first gruesome crush on a gorgeous man and my subsconscious feeds me lyrics to a song that says, 'Daddy, if I can't have this boy, I'll just simply die.' And then he practically falls over my feet a minute later.''

''Well, it's not like he knew Italian, is it? Besides, you did get him, didn't you?''

''I think that's a safe call. Speak of safe, you are. I can't remember half the words to *O, Mio Babbino Caro* any more.''

''Well, there's *one* good thing already tonight.''

''Knock it off, woman. You get lost, I'll guide you back with something from *Little Shop of Horrors*. I *do* remember plenty of that.''

''Oh, great,'' Robyn mumbled sourly, but spoiled it by giggling. ''Hey,'' she said a moment later, ''helped out again, making me laugh. I can—yeah, is that it?'' Jennifer had no chance to answer her, though; Robyn had already shifted and, with a swift bound, an enormous, sootily black bird was already back in the open and rising rapidly between the trees and the buildings. Jennifer ran the few paces along the path and gazed up; Robyn had passed the palace and blended into the night sky, and was gone.

SHE only thinks there's no wonder in magic; that floors me every time, watching her. It took a long, slightly dazed moment to remember Thread, another very long moment to shift into awareness of the stuff so she could track the bird. *Red— not that one, you idiot, the thicker one—* She sighed with relief, then; there was Robyn, definitely Robyn. She was higher than Jennifer would have thought she'd dare go—probably making certain she stayed well up and out of anyone's sight. She was soaring swiftly away when Jennifer first found her, but now she was making a smooth, tight turn. *Staying close, probably only going to make a circle.* Reassuring. She wasn't certain what she could do to help if Robyn needed it, but it would be harder to do anything at all, even track her, if she went too far.

Well, she could still think like her human self inside those feathers, and she'd surely have enough sense to stay within the city walls—though that was still a very large area. Jennifer swore mildly as she tried to disengage; she finally had to use Lialla's novice word. "If you'd quit thinking of a half-dozen things while you're trying to access or separate," she told herself firmly, as the reassuringly normal dark night closed around her once again. "No wonder it doesn't want to play with you when it has to fight for a small portion of your attention."

She went back to the edge of the pond, sat next to her bo and dipped her fingers in the water, squawking breathily as fish nibbled at her wrist and knuckles; but it was just the soft, slight sucking sensation of skin against skin. Fish kisses, Robyn had called it way back in Wyoming, when those black Moors of hers had mistaken her tiny fingers for food. These critters had much bigger mouths and a much harder nibble, but at least they didn't have teeth. *Fish kisses.* Jennifer grinned and mouthed a faintly smacking "smooch" at the water, wiped her fingers on her pants and wrapped them around the bo.

After a moment's thought, she set it aside; with Robyn working her own rather dangerous brand of magic for the first time in several years, it might be a better idea to hold off Chris's novice exercises until the woman was back on the ground. "I know me, I'd get wrapped up in what I was doing and forget all about her, she could be down for hours and I'd still be here whacking tree trunks. And *I* need to practice getting in and out of Thread, I never used to have this much trouble." She leaned the bo back against the wall and closed her eyes.

This way, too, she'd have a better chance of knowing if anyone had followed them out. There didn't *seem* to be anyone in the immediate vicinity, when she finally accessed

Thread and took hold of the locate-red once more. A little hard to tell, with Thukar's guard all over the grounds, the household servants moving around inside the palace—people everywhere. She found it easier to access Thread than the last time, though. It was still much too difficult to simply step out of it, making Lialla's word necessary once more.

Well. No one in the woods with her, at least. She had really felt a little uncomfortable when she and Robyn first got here, had wondered if it was foolish to come out without a couple of her personal guard. Robyn would have been curious as to why Jennifer wanted armed men in her own back yard, though she thought she could have come up with a reason, if she'd had to. "Yah. Birdy would have flat refused to come out here and try to shift with anybody around but me or Chris." She sighed, shook her head. "Access, do it."

She worked at it for several more minutes, until she could feel the jangling along the red that heralded Robyn's approach; she slipped back into reality as a once-again human Robyn came back along the path from deeper in the trees, and sank down onto the stone wall. "Wow. You know what? That wasn't nearly as awful as I'd thought it would be, all this time."

"Maybe because of how you went into it, laughing instead of scared half to death?"

"Mmmm-maybe," Robyn allowed. She sounded only a little winded. "I just went around the outside of the palace and over the south wall a ways, not too far, had to find a place to come down, though, because the trees are thicker in here than they were last time and no way I'd come down on that empty parking lot out there!" She drew a deep breath and let it out in a gust. "Boy. Bet my shoulders and my belly muscles tell me about *this* tomorrow!" She moved her arms cautiously, rotating them slowly and letting her head roll from side to side. Jennifer looked straight up: There were stars everywhere. Which meant they'd been out here an hour anyway. She figured even if Dahven had finished with his meeting not long after they came outside, he wouldn't be worried about them yet; he'd probably be eating, buried in the most urgent of the paperwork that had been waiting for him all day. She blinked, brought herself back to the moment; Robyn was talking once more. "So, anyway, unless you'd rather go

in or you have something else to do tonight, I'd like to try it
again, check a couple of things. Because it's a sure bet I won't
even want to tomorrow night. And with twice under my belt,
maybe I'll be all right; I know I can get Lialla to watch my
back at the fort while I practice.''

"Fine with me; all I had planned for this evening was time
with you. Sure you're all right?"

"Not even breathing hard. You know what? It's a little like
swimming, you can go so fast and so hard you kill yourself,
or you can sort of scooch along slow, not make waves, it's
not nearly as tough and you can swim for hours without even
getting a little tired. Of course,'' she added and Jennifer could
see the flash of teeth in the gloom, "I was always the swim-
mer who had to go fast because I just knew otherwise I'd sink
to the bottom of the pool and drown. Anyway, couple of
things I want to try, and I just can't believe it's supposed to
be this easy. . . .''

Her voice faded again and huge wings furled with a *fwump!*
of displaced air. Apparently it was just that easy. Jennifer
shook her head in mild, amused disbelief. Robyn had been
chattering away like a little kid at Disneyland, she had practically been throwing sparks. "Yeah, no wonder in magic
around here,'' Jennifer mumbled, and edged off the wall. Her
backside was going to sleep from sitting on that cold, rough
rock. The bo had slid to the ground twice now while she was
working Thread, and again as the wind from Robyn's wings
hit it. She went onto one knee to feel around for it, finally
found it and laid it along the wall. The stone was smooth
along the outside of the wall and at the edge, but unfin-
ished along the top, except the two or three places up by the
waterfall that wood planks had been inset for sitting. The raw
rock made for rough sitting but the bo wasn't going to go
anywhere now unless she shoved it off. She leaned into the
knee-high wall, stared off across the pond toward the sound
of the waterfall, and concentrated on Night-Thread.

SHE'D forgotten plenty of things, but not as many as she
would have thought: The healing Thread was the only one
she bothered with any more, but with a little work it began
to come back. The way Merrida had first explained it, the
way Lialla had taught her—well, yes, she could still find

Thread by the different colors, but it required actually thinking each through. *This isn't how you do it*, she reminded herself. *You're a musician; stop trying to do it by rote and let it come.* After that, it was suddenly much easier; she could almost relax, sensing most strongly the New Age-like Thread that presaged the presence of water; the near-Baroque sound of the red healing Thread, first she had ever used; that Russian processional black stuff old Neri had used for transport— *which I still have no intention of ever using*, she told herself firmly. The way out, now—she slid from Thread awareness, into reality, back again. Easier. Much. Now, the one she wanted to show Robyn, that twist of red/yellow that could actually be made visible and played with: twisted into rings and juggled, poured from hand to hand like a Slinky or a waterfall. The one Brinhe had taught her last year during the market-wide Fall Festival. "Wow!" she whispered as the stuff came to life and curled around her widespread fingers. The single syllable set up a jangly discord all around her, and she hastily closed her mouth. *Ooh. Forgot how weird it feels, trying to talk* inside *Thread. Don't do that!*

It sounded like—more Handel than Bach, different tune from the finding-red, deeper instrumentation but not cello. Her fingers were dark, unclear shapes, lost in a length of rainbow colors that wrapped in and out of them before curling tightly into her upturned palms; bassoon and flute filled her ears, breathily deep, reedy. *Odd. Is this the same stuff? Because I swear the first time I tried it, it wasn't like that blurring-Thread, sort of musical but not a real tune.* But she'd had no problem taking hold of this stuff the first time and the several times she used it after that; the blurring Thread had been awful to keep hold of the few times she'd used it.

She shifted both bundles of shimmering light into one hand, spilled it to the other, and the sound changed. *Ah.* Well. A different shape, a different pattern—the Thread was the same but the sound of it changed. *Ah*, she thought again, this time in deep satisfaction. If Robyn wanted something nifty, this wouldn't qualify as elf-magic, but it was definitely not nuts and bolts. *Now, Brinhe did something that—he held one end and tossed the other, and it did—yeah.* The music changed again as the bright Thread wrapped around itself and created a tight, long bicolored twist.

The music shifted suddenly and alarmingly; locate-red jangled in a loud, sour discord, and her grip slipped off the twist. It simply vanished; but she was already reaching for the red, which was vibrating so hard her fingertips were numbed and her mind a momentary blank. *Robyn?* Robyn shouldn't have made it back so quickly and not without her sister being aware of her before she got this close. But, if it wasn't Robyn—she tightened her hold on the red, gripping it two-handed. Not Robyn, unless she'd grown much larger—and turned into two people. A second Thread, silvery gray to cross-check. The two were much closer than they had any right to be, and the gray revealed an ugly, grimly determined emotional aura that didn't bode well for the woman they were trying to sneak up on. "Oh, damn," she whispered; Thread swayed alarmingly, stilled as she bit her lower lip and fought her way back into the night.

It was all she had time for. A hand clamped onto the back of her neck as her mind came back into the real world; it was very large, the fingers strong, and the arm behind it must have belonged to a big man. The fingers tightened on the hair at the nape of her neck and shoved, propelling her head forward and down. Her shins cracked against the stone wall and her feet came off the ground as her head went into the pool.

It couldn't possibly have been as cold as it felt, though it was shocking enough to momentarily paralyze her. At least there had been enough warning that she'd had the sense to take a deep breath and not let it go when she went under. *It won't last very long. Move!* She flailed around with her left hand for the wall or the bottom—*anything* for purchase to push herself back upright, help her fight against the pressure that was holding her down. The right clawed uselessly at a large, bare, hairy wrist, then felt along the top of the wall for the bo. *No, it sure didn't go anywhere, did it?* she thought, and for the first time she could feel fear tightening her stomach. The bo was directly under her, part of the hard surface digging into her lower ribs and hip bones. Her lungs hurt, and now the fish were nipping at her hair, at one ear. *Git!* She flailed out with her left and felt the scrape of scales and a fat, slick belly across her lower neck and one shoulder. She sensed a shock of surprise through the hand tangled in her hair as her attacker felt it, too and his grip eased. Not much, but she'd never get another chance. She kicked wildly, and what now seemed a mile above her someone yelped as her heel connected with bone. She brought her right hand up, across her right shoulder and more by luck than intent her right thumb located the nerve-filled, sensitive hollow at the base of the assassin's thumb. A little pressure should be enough, just now—and it was. His fingers relaxed one very brief instant, and before he could yank her hand away or tighten down on her hair again, she flattened her other hand against the inside of the wall and pushed desperately, throwing herself forward and toward the muddy bottom of the pond. The hand clawed at her hair and then slapped at her leg; she rolled into a ball as she came off the top of the wall. Her hips hit the water with a loud splash.

She let herself go all the way down. *Please, God, tell me I threw myself out far enough from the edge that he can't just reach down and hold me here!* Not a very nice thought. Her boots were full of cold water and a sludgy mud. *God. Got to breathe.* She gathered her feet and hands under her and slowly pressed herself up, still crouching, until she could feel the top of her head break the surface. *Cold out here, all of a sudden,* she told herself. Her head certainly was, with a very light breeze skimming across soaked hair and scalp.

It was dark in here; she'd just have to hope it was dark enough they couldn't see across the water any better than she'd been able to, or that her hair covered enough of her face for it not to stand out. Didn't matter. Air did. She eased up a little more, until her nose and mouth were out, and let out what was left of that held breath and drew in another. It was one of the hardest things she'd done in a long time, remembering to keep absolutely quiet.

To her right, the waterfall, and way off to her left, the exit pipe. She was facing the way she'd come, then—good; she'd come up completely disoriented. She took another deep breath and felt suddenly less panicked, brought one hand very cautiously out of the water to pull hair away from her eyes enough that she could properly see. She had to blink furiously, finally scooped up a palmful of water and bent her head down to rinse the silt off her lashes and out of her eyes. *Burns.* She wondered very briefly if there was anything in the water that would permanently hurt her vision, but let it go. Unless she got very lucky in the next few moments, she'd never live long enough to find out.

There. She drew a deep breath and let herself back down into the water as someone—at the moment only a burly shadow against the darker tree shadow—started and seemed to lean forward. *Can't stay here.* She considered very briefly, then dug her toes into the silt and slowly pushed off, hands outstretched so she wouldn't slam head-first into the inside base of that stone wall, then even more slowly edged herself around to get her feet back under her and one shoulder against the wall. She brought her head up slowly, still holding her breath until she was certain where that man was.

Off to the side; she'd finally had a little bit of luck and had landed about where she'd hoped to. And now she could make him out once again, at least his head and shoulders as he leaned across the wall to look for her. Somewhere behind him, someone else whispered, "Outland bitch. Where'd she go?"

The reply whisper was nearer but even softer; the man who'd grabbed her and tried to drown her was trying to listen and probably hoping not to give away his position. "In."

"Hope she doesn't ever come up, I think she broke my knee."

The head snapped briefly out of sight and the assassin hissed, "*Shut up!* I'm trying to listen!"

"Try looking, why don't you?" The second man was apparently hurting too much to care if she heard *him*.

"I can't even see *you* from here! Now will you shut up?"

There was a long silence, broken only by the controlled breathing of the man at the wall, and the slight whimper as the other man nursed his knee. Jennifer smiled grimly. *One down.*

If she stayed where she was, maybe they'd think she'd gone out the other side of the pool and run for help. A sensible woman would do that. Of course, a scared woman would have made enough noise on such a still night that they'd know where she'd gone. These two weren't moving; she had a feeling they knew she was somewhere close by, and still in the water.

That man leaning on the edge had made only one mistake—*thank God*. Unfortunately, he didn't seem like the type to make two in a row.

Of course, if he'd heard any of the stories that still circulated about the outland advocate and how tough she was in a fight—if he believed any of them, or had talked to any of the men she'd gone after—he'd know damn well she was close by, keeping utterly still, nursing a towering fury and waiting for a crack at him. In that case, he surely wasn't going anywhere.

This was no place to be, with two men out for blood. At least it was *very* dark in the pool glade tonight; if there'd been an early moon, he'd have had her the moment she came up. As it was, they'd need Robyn's night vision in her bird form to see anything, let alone their intended victim crouched as she was right against the inside of the wall, only her eyes and nose above water.

The second man emitted a faint squawk—trying to get back on his feet, maybe. He whispered peevishly: "I thought you said you were going to take her before she had a chance to do anything about it, and here you let her go!"

"Shut up!"

"Why? You think she doesn't know we're here?"

"Because I'll hold *you* in if you don't shut up!" It was suddenly very quiet on the other side of the wall. Jennifer bit back a grin; it really wasn't very funny. Suddenly she remembered, and the grin was gone for good: Robyn. Robyn would be coming back any moment; she'd walk right into them! *I can't let her,* Jennifer thought desperately. One of the fish slid past her shoulder and tugged at her hair. It hurt, light as the touch was; that brute had almost pulled it out by the roots.

I wonder how he'd like a mouthful of pond water? she thought and fury filled her, heating her face, curling her fingers into the wall. It cleared her mind and for the first time in several long, frightened minutes she remembered something else: *The bo. If it's still on the wall, where he is*—Well, if so, it was out of reach but there were a few loose rocks on the bottom, and Thread wasn't out of reach. Probably most of it wouldn't respond, shaken as she was, but a three-strand rope would plait together almost any time. Braid one, splash a little water to get his attention and throw a loop across the back of *his* neck. Brace her feet against the rock wall and push off, hard; he'd come right in, she'd wind up out of reach—*And he won't come up again, not alive. And once he's down, that other rotten louse won't be any trouble at all.*

But it would take a few precious minutes to braid a Thread rope, especially with nothing but a few reedy grasses nearby to work into it. *Try to find the bo first; you may not have any time left.*

Above her head, the argument went on, both men now hissing at each other. "Something grabbed your *hand*? And you let *go* of her?"

"Will you shut up? You want her to get out the other side and run for help while we're standing here?"

She put one hand flat against the wall and edged cautiously toward the voices, feeling around her knees with the other. If it went in with her, it should have just rolled down the wall. It might have gone a little farther out, though. She felt in a wider area, eased one knee forward and then the other. They sank in silt.

"I thought you had it all worked out, I could've run a knife between her ribs, but *you* had to—"

"You want me to break your other knee?"

The first man must have sounded seriously threatening; when the second spoke again, the whisper sounded almost conciliatory. "Look, maybe she's dead; you had her under long enough."

"Not the way she went in. Not the way she was still fighting."

"Then we'll find her, after all, Krilan's on the far side, she can't get out that way without tripping over him."

"Shhh." Momentary silence. Then, vexedly, "I can't hear anything. Something's wrong."

"*I* know that—" She sensed movement above her and just ahead, as though the watcher turned to threaten the injured man, who shut up abruptly. *Come on, chicken*, she thought tauntingly. *You're covering any noise I might make, you gonna let a pissed-off hulking brute scare you?* At that moment, her fingers brushed across, then closed on a length of smooth, hard wood, about the diameter of a quarter. *Got you*, she thought with grim anticipation. *Come to mother.* She eased it out of the silt, pulled it slowly toward her. It was very quiet out there now. Jennifer set one hand on the wall and pushed slowly away from it. An enormous, bulky-shouldered shadow there, still leaning on his hands to peer across the pond; it looked as though he'd just scanned the water toward the falls, and had turned away from her toward the spillway. She got her balance on one knee and the ball of the other foot, eased her hand away from the wall and wrapped it around the mid-point of the long pole. She flexed her knees a little; anger had taken care of the earlier trembling. *Go.* Something splashed down the pond—probably a fish just breaking the surface. The man leaned out a little more.

Thanks, you jerk! She straightened from her low crouch, using her legs to propel the bo. He spun around at the noise; the tip she'd aimed for the side of his head came up under his chin, knocking his teeth together with an audible click and snapping his head back. He staggered backwards a pace or two and fell flat, out of sight. Jennifer pushed the end of the bo into the mud to pole herself all the way to her feet and brought it up again, bracing herself on widespread legs in thigh-deep water.

Air wrapped icily around wet clothing and skin; she flung her head back to throw dripping hair out of her eyes.

She could just see the man she'd hit, a barely visible sprawl of very still arms and legs. The second man scrambled to his feet, yelped as he put his weight on the sore leg and lurched back a pace, flailing for balance. She sloshed forward, sat on the edge of the wall to swing her legs across. He stepped back again; Jennifer brought the bo up and took two long steps forward, her boots squelching loudly.

"Don't—!" He was edging around the bole of a tree, more visible than before against the open of the old parade ground. She wasn't certain she had anything left to catch him if he ran, even if his knee was hurt. *Get him now; move,* she told herself and threw herself after him.

Light—lights and voices everywhere, all at once. With a hiss of pain, the man spun around and skip-and-hop ran back into the trees. A muffled "Don't!" from a short distance away; moments he later came back toward the pool, moving much more slowly. Two men in loose red shirts and black breeches, the casual uniform of the household guard, were holding him by the elbows.

Grelt, a lantern in one hand and a long knife in the other, came up beside her. "Lady Thukara, are you all right?"

Jennifer laughed breathily and sagged into the bo. "Is this a trick question?" She let him lead her back over to the edge of the pond and collapsed gratefully onto the stone. "Not that I'm not glad to see you, but what are you doing out here?"

"Thukar's orders," Grelt said. He sounded rather huffy. "Making certain the Thukara is protected at all times. Your sister was with you—?" His voice trailed off.

Oops, Jennifer thought. Coming up with a workable lie just now might be the proverbial back-breaking straw.

"When those men appeared, I ran." Robyn's voice came from deeper in the trees, and a moment later, she and three other men stepped into sight—two more household guards and a very unhappy-looking man who must be Krilan. Jennifer wondered if Robyn had seen the danger, or if she'd just been very prudent and shifted back to human form where there wasn't the least chance of her being seen. She looked and sounded a little winded and her voice trembled; of course, that would be taken for nerves. "I was afraid to try and run for help, they'd have caught me out there for certain. So I was trying to go the other way around the pool, but there was a man on the other side. I got down behind some bushes, trying to decide if maybe I should just start yelling, when those men grabbed him." She dropped down next to Jennifer and wrapped both arms around her. "Are you all right? I was so scared, I thought they'd drowned you!"

That answered one question, Robyn had come down while the two attackers were distracted. One of the guards brought over a lightweight summer cloak and draped it over Jennifer's shoulders; Robyn pulled her to her feet and wrapped it around her a little better. "Oh, that's nice. Thanks, both of you. I'm fine. Give or take a ton of mud." Her legs were threatening to give way under her, and when Robyn wrapped an arm around her waist she gratefully leaned against her sister for a moment, then eased out of her embrace and stalked over to where men were hauling a barely conscious and dazed-looking would-be drowner to his feet. He stood taller than most of the guard and positively towered over her. *Yow. If I'd had a good look at that before it grabbed me, I think I'd have given up.*

"Grelt?" He glanced at her. "I'm going to get warm and clean. Get this creature—get them both out of here. Send someone ahead to warn Dahven, please; be sure he knows I'm all right. Give me an hour, will you? Then bring these— bring them to the hearing room across from the blue room." She eyed the big man narrowly. "We'll talk."

8

≈

THE Wielder Sretha was up and moving about her small hut before full light; Lialla, who had not slept at all, finally pressed aside the thick, felted wool blanket and eased her stiff, chilled body off the padded, woven reed mat onto cold and even stiffer knees to scowl down at the thing: Sretha had *said* it was padded. Probably the best mattress she had— very likely her own, poor woman. Still highly inadequate— *Admit it,* Lialla challenged herself sourly, *you've gone soft since Aletto took Duke's Fort. Was a time you slept harder, damper and colder, and didn't complain. At least, you survived it,* she added honestly.

And *if* she was going to be honest with herself, it wasn't the bedding that had kept her wakeful, any more than it had been the unaccustomed company in the room where she slept—or the unaccustomed mixture of stuffiness and occasional drafts, the unfamiliar smells left from the evening's cooking. The now-and-again, rafter-rattling snores of Sretha's sister, who occupied an opposite corner of the single room—or the rustlings and odd little noises from the half-loft, where the sister's two small children slept. *I do wish I'd known about these three before I came, though.* Lialla cast a doubtful glance at the sleeping woman, another toward the tiny added-on room that served as kitchen, washing room, and working chamber for the Wielder, where a lantern was lit, casting moving shadows across the far wall of the main room as Sretha walked back and forth.

What she could have done about the extra woman, the small children, even if she'd known in advance they'd be there—not

much, she realized. Sretha, if she'd judged correctly by the few
words the woman spoke the previous night, and by the look
on her face, would have much rather not had the burden of
a recently widowed sister and babes herself, but with Emalya's husband dead, there had been no choice. Sretha was her
only family, and Emalya had refused to stay in Holmaddan
City with *his* kindred.

Several of whom were, like her late husband, members of
the Duke's guards. Lialla swallowed hard, made herself look
away from the peacefully sleeping woman and pushed awk-
wardly to her feet. Such an affiliation didn't mean anything;
it made Emalya no more of a threat than any other village
woman. The husband was dead, the kin still in Holmaddan
City—*Stop it, now,* she ordered herself. From the rather
pleasant smell in the little hut just now, Sretha was brewing
a mint tea. *Go, take some tea, see if you can't speak together
before the children waken.*

The older woman glanced up, nodded once woodenly,
expressionlessly held out a heavy, handleless pottery cup and
indicated a wooden stool at the narrow trestle table. Lialla
nodded in return, wrapped both hands around the warmth
and bent over the cup, letting her eyes briefly close. Well,
there was one good thing: Sretha apparently had no more use
for inane pleasantries at hellishly early hours than she did
herself. A chatterer would have done her in, at this point.

There was a second cup of tea, a lozenge of hardened honey
to drop into it, a thick slice of crusty, hot bread. Finally
Sretha heaved a sigh and set her cup aside, and when Lialla
looked at her, she gestured with her chin toward the main
room, set a finger against her lips and nodded her head toward the opposite side of the hut. Lialla leaned sideways to
look, squinting as level sun hit her full in the face. She muttered under her breath, threw up a shielding hand and was
just able to pick out the door—a dark bulk hardly visible
among the catherine wheels that flamed red and gold across
her outraged eyes and her vision. Unexpected, a second door
in a hut the size of this one. Sretha must be suggesting they
slip out that way. Lialla considered her bare feet, then
shrugged and got up. Sretha was barefoot herself and she
wasn't willing to risk wakening anyone by going back for her
foot-wraps and boots. She blinked rapidly until she could see

a little better, held a sun-warding hand before her as she followed the older woman into the sunrise and onto a very cold drift of sand and grasses. A stiff, brisk wind hit them as soon as they came around the corner of the little building—and went right through everything Lialla had on. She tucked her chin into her chest, pulled one of the black scarves down to serve as a block for most of the dazzling level rays, then hugged herself tightly, tucking suddenly icy hands between her arms and ribs.

Sretha gestured imperiously and turned to the north, led her guest at a brisk pace down a narrow path and into a sheltered dell; the wind fell away at once, which helped. Moments later, the woman stooped and moved into a tall tangle of brush; Lialla crouched down, eyed the mess of dew-laden branches and reluctantly followed. She came out a moment or two later in the very middle of a small sunny clearing, her back damp and a trickle of water running down the side of her neck. Sretha settled down cross-legged and patted the sand next to her. Lialla sat, easing a more comfortable spot for an ill-padded backside, blotted the side of her neck with a sleeve. *Oh, warm,* she thought happily, and let her head fall back to soak up the sun. That wind had been right off the water, reminding her of a winter east wind blowing from the snow-clad foothills into Duke's Fort.

Sretha stayed quiet for some moments, possibly savoring the warmth and quiet herself, or simply letting her guest have a moment's peace. Finally she touched Lialla's hand to gain her attention. "I thought you might feel more comfortable, talking out here instead of before my sister. This dell has nothing the village men want, and they make a great show in any event of avoiding the local Wielder—women's magic," she added by way of explanation; her mouth quirked in a sour smile. "The children avoid it because it is mine. Women come to my house, of course, but to this place only in my company." She hesitated. "I would *like* to say I trust my sister and that we could speak freely around her. But it is not merely my life at stake, and Emalya has lived in the city for so many years, I no longer have any notion of her thoughts. And so—"

"I appreciate your caution," Lialla said as the older woman paused for comment. Her voice was level, no sign of fear there, she thought, except she probably sounded haughty, like always when she was afraid. She kept her hands tucked under her arms: They were trembling; Sretha would notice and worry she'd sent for the wrong outside help. She made herself go on, chatting the way she'd learned from Robyn, so the Wielder wouldn't think she'd brought in a snob. "I'm glad we'll be able to talk freely somewhere. It may be your sister is trustworthy, but children as young as hers—" She shrugged, spread her hands helplessly. Her fingers were still visibly shaking; she hastily tucked them between her knees. "My brother's small children have not yet learned what secrets are, either, or how to keep them."

"Just so." Sretha sighed; she looked rather annoyed. "It is a pity; her husband ought to have died years ago and saved everyone trouble: By all I've heard, he was a particularly poor creature, even for a man—spending most of his off-duty hours and his earnings in the dockside taverns, once he made her a son and then learned there'd likely be no more than one boy. Of course, Emalya *could* have stayed in the city—but that was her choice, and no doubt *he* told his family she'd bear him no more sons—they'd have taken her from duty and made her life a worse hell than our usual lot. And here—once the year of mourning is past, she'll marry again—she's young and after all *has* borne a son; she has a small pension from the Duke since her husband died in service." The old woman smiled wryly. "That would doubtless make her an acceptable prize in any society, but in ours, the men already do everything they dare to attract her notice, so that when the day comes that she is free she may choose among them without delay."

"Ah." Lialla wasn't certain what else to say. Sretha gave her a keen glance.

"Ah, indeed," she replied. "Now," she went on in a more businesslike tone, "there'll have been someone awake to notice the caravan passing by last night—herder, farmer, doesn't matter, someone will have seen. The village has already been told I've chosen a novice from village Gray Haven, it will be assumed that novice was brought by caravan last night from Gray Haven." She paused; Lialla merely nodded and resisted the urge to wipe damp palms down her Blacks. *Look calm, if you can't act it,* she reminded herself—Jennifer's words to her, years ago. *Keep your mouth closed, if your voice will give you away, and if you must speak, make certain there's enough air behind the words to keep them from trembling.* "We'll go into the village at midday, you and I; I'll announce you publicly as the new Night-Thread novice. This will serve to warn the young men away from you—in Holmaddan, a Night-Thread Wielder is left to her studies unless she makes clear she welcomes suitors; a novice is *not* given such a choice." She spread her hands wide.

"Why?"

"Why?" Sretha laughed. "Such a rule saves a Wielder losing novices—after all, what Holmaddi man would wed a Wielder of any color sash and permit her to continue Wielding? The true reason, of course, is that whatever things they say of Night-Thread and its Wielders, they *do* fear it—or, say, fear how it might be turned against them. Before you ask, it hasn't been banned for that same reason—however they jeer Night-Thread and call it pitiful women's magic, they much prefer to keep the magic and the Wielders where they can see them. Outlaw it, drive it underground—any woman might then be a secret practitioner."

"Any woman still might," Lialla replied, "if there is no way your men can detect its use." One question answered; she felt a weight come off her shoulders.

"If they have such a trick, I am certain we'd have heard of it before this," Sretha said dryly. "Few men can hold a secret for long; they spend so much time in that longhouse of theirs and in the sweat-baths—they exchange lies of personal prowess and gossip, all the time ignoring the women who come to bring them food or liquor, or fresh straw for the floors." She considered this, laughed with a high, thin cackle that reminded Lialla sharply and uncomfortably of old Merrida. "I know more of the habits and thoughts of the men who live on the opposite side of the village from me than I do of my own sister's thoughts and habits, thanks to what they themselves say, and what is thereafter told me by the women." She wiped at her eyes with a sleeve, looked at Lialla, and laughed again. "Ah, well. This introduction: The men will stay away from you, one and all, and the women will know you by sight—for the future. There are places in the village you mustn't go, others it would be improper—I'll do as much as I can to warn you of things a born Holmaddi would know."

"Fine," Lialla said; the word came out a little high. She cleared her throat, adjusted a scarf against the back of her neck and tried again. "Better, I won't go anywhere or with anyone unless you say—I know it isn't easy to remember things you yourself have always known."

"True. I warn you, you won't have much opportunity to simply walk about the village. It is usual, though, for me to go out with the women at low tide; certainly the men will find it fitting that my novice earn her keep by helping the women harvesters and shore gleaners. The men have no reason to be on the sand at low tide; they never go that way unless the boats are to be put out. If the weather is cool or wet or the shore fogbound, we have it entirely to ourselves."

"The children?" Lialla asked. Sretha shook her head, not understanding. "In Sehfi," Lialla explained, "the older children are kept busy with learning or household chores and with caring for the younger ones; in Sikkre, the women often keep the small children with them as they go about their own business, and many of the older ones go about as they please."

"Ah. Sikkre is a vast city, is it not? Here, women carry only the smallest babes with them; otherwise, children carry out whatever tasks they are capable of, the elder girls caring for the youngest and those in between in charge of gathering wood, or tending goats." She laughed sourly. "The village children are no danger, believe me; not a girl of any age nor a boy under twelve years would dare approach the village men with rumor against their mothers. To a child in North Bay or any other Holmaddi village, the women represent food, and warmth, and safety from the men who only approach them in anger or when staggering with drink." Lialla's throat closed and a chill ran across her skin; she managed a nod when the Wielder paused for comment. "I don't expect anyone from the outside to understand this," the older woman said finally. "As one who was a child in this village, all too many years ago, I tell you it simply *is*. Children form their own groups, and know nothing of how their elders think and little of what they do—they keep their own counsel and learn at a very early age to avoid the men—particularly fathers, when they come home from the men's house late.''

''Yes.'' Lialla understood better than the older woman would think; she wasn't certain she'd ever be able to tell Sretha or any other village woman why.

''Well. Never mind the children, then. It's unsafe for women to meet within the village, of course, and suspicious if they come to my hut in numbers—this leaving aside my present house guests,'' she added flatly. ''But many women going out to fetch mussels and shore crabs for stew—that is seen as a proper women's task. What we do out there besides gather shellfish and seaweed—who is to know that besides ourselves?''

Lialla considered this in silence for some moments. Sretha might think this all quite safe; her younger companion felt more vulnerable than she had in a long time. *Then again, these women know all too well the danger. You knew it yourself, before you ever agreed to come here, even if you didn't feel it like you do now.* ''Sretha—do you trust all of the women in this village?''

To her relief, Sretha didn't immediately leap to the defense of her fellows, or become angry that Lialla would even dare ask such a question; instead, she gazed into the brush and seemed to give the matter serious consideration. She finally shrugged. ''Trust? I understand why you must ask; you know none of us. I have known most of the women of North Bay all my life, or all of theirs. We have women who came to us from other villages and two women even who left the city when they married North Bay men. One of those has been here ten years or more, another less than a full year.

''Until we began to work against the way things have always been, I would have said, yes, I could trust any woman in North Bay with anything of mine—including my life. Though then, it would not have occurred to me there might be the need for trust beyond the return of a borrowed measure of grain.

''Now, I still believe I could trust any woman here with my life—and yet—well, you will see yourself, when you begin to meet the women and speak to them. However it falls out in the city or the other villages, here we have young women who would put men aside entirely and at the other end of the question, women who dislike how they must live their lives but see any alternative we present as no improvement. There are women who live in such dread of being caught in this conspiracy that we seldom dare ask them to join in the shore groups. After all, even *their* fools of men might begin to wonder what is so terrifying to a woman about a simple walk across the sand for shellfish!''

''They—what, do they think you'll fail?''

''Some do. Others simply fear they'll be somehow discovered and if they are, the penalty—''

''Your letter said.'' Lialla's voice scraped past a very dry throat. ''Death.''

''Not a pleasant one—if any of them indeed are. Some women hold back to see how determined we are, fearing we'll fail because there is no chance of success—or because the men will stop us. Or because women will go only so far before they decide to abandon a dangerous sea in a leaky boat and return to shore.'' She peered at the sin-Duchess. ''You smile? What amuses you?''

''Not the situation, Wielder,'' Lialla replied somberly. ''I was remembering a conversation some time back with one of the outland women.'' Jen had broken down her world's women's movement for her and in just about the same groups. Funny old small world, as Chris would say.

''Ah.'' The older woman glanced at her again, finally shrugged and went on. ''Now. As to this introduction at midday. You'll need to do very little save be present. When I name you, you may then look up, enough that the village can see your face to know you by, no more. Make eye contact with no male, turn once completely around, then look down at once. Remember that! There is always a young man trying to cause trouble, hoping to score off the women, or the other young men—expect noises, a sudden shout, something to make you look up other than that permitted once. Keep your eyes down, your mouth closed, your manner humble and reticent—'' Sretha suddenly turned a very bright red and lowered her eyes to her own feet. It took Lialla a moment to realize the woman was horrified; she'd been ordering a noblewoman around like a wayward child—or a young and untrained novice.

''Sretha—Wielder, please. Don't do that; remember who

I'm supposed to be, not what I am. I'm not offended, anyway; in Zelharri a Duke's daughter isn't usually ordinarily treated like nobility and I certainly never was once my—once Jadek came in. And I *was* a novice to Merrida for a good many years; I got used to being ordered about and shouted at for failure. I'm supposed to be your novice; if you don't order me about, the men will wonder why, won't they?'' She fastened her own eyes on her fingers. ''I admit, I'm quite nervous just now—being here, and not yet properly fit into an acceptable place, it won't be difficult at all for me to pretend to be shy and afraid.''

''Well—I won't say 'good,' '' Sretha said doubtfully. She leaned forward and squeezed Lialla's fingers reassuringly. ''If you've anything to say to me, other than novice-to-Wielder matters—well. You must know Wielder hand signs—?'' she added doubtfully.

''I haven't used them at all the past three years, but I know them—old Merrida insisted on them, and they came in very useful at Duke's Fort.''

Sretha held up a hand, palm up, thumb folded inside, all but the index finger folded over it; she turned it over and opened the loose fist to rub her thumb against the center and ring fingers, then rubbed her right temple as though trying to ease headache. ''So—?''

''Meeting, usual place, immediately,'' Lialla replied readily.

''Just so. I suppose we had better check interpretation before using any other sign, just to be certain you don't have a different meaning from ours. But that much—if you want to talk, sign that much, we'll come out here. If Emalya or the children or anyone else, should come close to this place uninvited while we are here, is it true, what I have heard? That you will be able to sense presence?''

It took a moment to realize what the woman was hinting at. ''You mean, sense them during the day?'' Lialla asked. Sretha nodded sharply. ''I can do that.''

''Well—that *may* prove useful.'' Sretha let the younger woman aid her to her feet. She sounded dubious. *An improvement over my own reaction, when Jen said she could see Thread during the day,* Lialla thought wryly. A wonder Jen had ever spoken to her again, after *that* nasty little confrontation. Sretha wasn't going to bring up Lialla's Light just yet, apparently; she must be willing to deal with it though, since Lialla was here. In her place, Merrida would never have sent for a Wielder who could manage Thread during the day, let alone one "infected" with Light.

Sretha was talking; Lialla brought herself back to the moment. "You'll need another scarf, an extra one for your face, to pull across your chin," she said as they worked back out of the bushes. It was noticeably windier and much cooler back on the path to the hut. "Around the single men in particular; so they don't have the excuse to take any liberties—spoken ones, only!" she added hastily as Lialla stopped in her tracks. "Wives, daughters and betrothed women have no rights of any sort but they're stringently protected against any attentions whatever of other men; women such as you and I are also protected but not as closely. In short, men may utter—impolite things—in your presence and not risk punishment for it. The younger men one and all have a gift for such impolitenesses."

Hey, baby, smooch, smooch, Lialla thought, remembering what Chris had told her about *his* world. Something else Lialla remembered: something Chris had once told her—it had actually struck her as amusing at the time. "Of course, it's property rights," she said. "If you own it, you keep a closer guard over it and tighter laws concerning it; if you don't own it, you don't care quite as much." Suddenly, Chris's remarks didn't seem amusing at all, nor did the notion of being considered property—*again* being considered property, she thought grimly. To Jadek, she'd been a commodity, too. Sretha grinned, then let her head fall back and laughed that Merrida-like old woman's cackle; Lialla only just managed to keep from shuddering.

"Just so," the older woman said; the laughter was still in her words. "Mind, though! Any young Holmaddi woman knows from years before her Change to never be caught staring at any male, and to keep a scarf handy to pull across her lower face should one stare at *her*. One or two of our young women keep the cloth in place at all times."

It would make a statement, Lialla thought. *Hands Off!* And at least as well as she'd ever said it or implied it by icy looks or posture herself.

In such a society as this, icy looks and a stiff bearing would probably be considered challenge or threat. *You keep a scarf around your throat, ready to grab,* she told herself. Lialla followed the older woman back through the rear door and into the dark and slightly stuffy back room. The bread and tea sat like a lump in a suddenly queasy stomach.

BUT the introduction went very smoothly—as far as she could hear; there was a ringing in her ears that must have been nerves, but seemed a fair trade since her hands weren't shaking at the moment. Her knees were trembling, but the long overtunic and baggy black trous covered them. Lialla could see nothing but her sandaled feet, Sretha's bare ones, the bare feet of two women that stuck out of gray skirts the natural color of the wool they'd been spun and woven from, and at some point in the proceedings, a pair of large and grubby man's feet, emerging from long, bright blue trous. Lialla reached for the face scarf, but at that moment, Sretha cleared her throat ominously and a man farther back in the crowd laughed; the feet hastily withdrew. Shortly thereafter, Sretha finished what she had to say and a male voice spoke a few words—so quickly and harshly that Lialla understood nothing of what he said. However, it seemed she had been approved: Sretha touched her hand to get her attention and murmured, "It's all right, look up and turn."

There was a blur of villagers—men, women, children, a few skinny dogs, all staring right at her, it seemed. There must have been a hundred, and from well back in the crowd of men, she heard jeering laughter. It was hard, pretending she hadn't heard it, but not as hard as she'd have thought earlier *not* to put on her usual chill and disapproving face; she was too frightened to do more than let the village see her face and then return her gaze to the ground, just as Sretha had told her.

Silence. The sound of leather-shod and bare feet shuffling over hard ground and retreating men's voices, then Sretha's voice once more: "They're gone, it's all right." Now there were only a few women, perhaps a dozen of them, all sizes and shapes, ages—so far as Lialla could guess by half-seen faces—everywhere from fifteen or so to Sretha's age. Two shared the handles of a large, sand-covered basket filled with sacks, several others held bunched cloths or sacks. "The sea is that way, the tide low at this hour. We'll go for shellfish; you've been granted permission to work with the shore parties, with or without your tutor, so long as one of the elder women is with you."

"Oh." Lialla couldn't think of anything else to say, besides, "Thank you."

"Thank Ryselle's father for that—privilege," one of the other women said dryly. Lialla cast a glance behind her; there were a few men sitting on a low platform before a long building, taking in the sun, but they were paying no heed to the women. Away to the left of them, on the road that led from the Wielder's house into the village and on to the next village, several small children with a number of enormous gray geese. She turned away and walked with the other women out through a narrow cleft and toward the sea.

The women walked quickly and in silence; Lialla, unused to the ocean wind, remained chilled despite the pace. There was a little shelter from the breeze once they reached the distant bay. Lialla glanced over her shoulder frequently; there was no sign of anyone behind them on the sand or on the low cliffs, and she finally made herself stop looking.

The women set the basket in the sand and scooped sand into it for an anchor, while one of the younger women handed out sacks. When she came to Lialla, she hesitated; Lialla held out a hand. "You'll need to show me what to do."

"Of course." No comment in those two words. The woman tucked a strand of very red hair back under a snug scarf, tucked long skirts into a broad sash and stepped onto wet stone. "Test your footing; the rock can be slippery."

"Thank you."

It was the last thing either woman said in some time. Lialla found the smell of tidepool somewhat unpleasant but not nearly as bad as the fish-and-saltwater smells around the docks in Bez and Podhru; the water was cold and the shellfish hard to break free, especially at first. She couldn't bring up the nerve to catch hold of any of the small, fast-moving crabs with their fearsome-looking pincers. Her companion showed her how but didn't force the issue, merely caught several herself and stuffed them in the top of the bag she carried.

She was slightly dizzy suddenly—everything so overwhelmingly different from what she had always known, perhaps, or merely the odd smells, the result of moving around so long bent head down over pools of salt water. Or even that she hadn't eaten since bread and tea quite early. *Hungry*, Lialla thought suddenly, and her stomach growled. Her companion glanced at her and nodded.

"You've enough there, and so have I. We'll take the bags back and rest a little; there's bread, and my mother brought smoked fish and dried fruit." Lialla nodded, followed the other woman up the sand to the basket, where she set her sack and then Lialla's into an already nearly full container. "I know your name, of course." She handed Lialla another empty sack from the pile next to the basket and took one herself. "Ursiu, isn't it?"

"Ursiu," Lialla agreed faintly; for one horrified moment, she'd feared the other would name her truly; the slightly malicious gleam in her eye showed she knew what Lialla thought.

"Ursiu. I am Ryselle—one of the village headman's daughters, and my mother over there"—she gestured toward a group of several women walking out a spit of sand toward the water—"is his second wife. Come, we'll join them, the food is there."

"Good." Lialla followed where led, her stomach tight from hunger and nerves, equally mixed.

The bread was dark, coarse-textured and made of a grain she hadn't tasted before; the fish a pleasant surprise—a smoke-flavored, delicate-textured flesh that would have been considered a luxury even at the Duke's table. The fruit had been mashed and dried in sheets, and she thought it might be a mix of several kinds. Slightly odd in flavor but sweet; the food altogether took some of the edge of strangeness away and eased the mild beginnings of a headache. Hunger pangs assuaged, however, the pinch of nerves gripped her midsection once again, particularly when Sretha cleared her throat and the women turned as one to gaze at her.

It was startling: Until this moment, few of the women had more than glanced her way. She gave herself a mental shake as Sretha began pronouncing names, did her best to attach names to faces. Ryselle, Impere, Lisbet—she'd never manage it, names and persons were difficult enough to match and here, with ten of the twelve similarly clad in the grayish hand-weave, pale faces and pale eyes, hair covered by snug-fitting scarves—it was impossible; Sretha would have to help her sort them later. Ryselle was easy, that flame-red hair and the mocking look in her very blue eyes. Headman's daughter. Ryselle made her nervous indeed.

Sretha had finished her introductions; the silence stretched for a long moment. *Do I simply begin talking?* Lialla caught black fabric in clenched fists; her palms were clammy. Sretha touched her arm. "I thought perhaps you might tell us a little of yourself. One of the city women said that of all the southern women, you might be most willing and able to help us, but most of the rest we know about you is rumor and likely half-truth. We have"—she glanced over her shoulder toward the tide, then overhead to track the sun—"some time."

"I—all right." Lialla drew a deep breath, let it out slowly. It wasn't going to be any easier to begin than she'd feared all along, certainly less easy than she'd hoped. Her voice didn't want to work. *Deep breath, lots of air with the words so they don't tremble,* she ordered herself. "Let me say first, this is—very different from Zelharri." She considered this, shook her head. "Not—not the difference you may think, that I am used to luxury and plenty. I am first a Wielder, then a Duke's daughter. At one time, I lived very rough indeed, four years ago. Let me say also that I intend to do all I can to help you, whatever that may prove to be." She paused. Silence. Every eye was on her, which increased her nervousness. She drew another deep breath, and made a brief story of her journey with Aletto, their return to Duke's Fort, Jadek's death, leaving out only mention of Jadek's Light Shaping, his Triad— the Light she carried as a lasting legacy of her uncle's hatred. There was another silence when she finished speaking. One of the older women stirred finally. Petras, if she remembered aright.

"You've not wed?" Lialla shook her head. "Does your brother not command this?"

Lialla shook her head once again. "He has *suggested* once or twice that I might consider one suitable husband or another; each time I said no, and he no longer makes such suggestions. In Zelharri, women wed or not, as they choose, and only a noble father can command his daughter to marry—

and then only if the succession would be in doubt if she did not. If there was no son, or the son had no children.''

''Why did you choose as you did?'' another of the older women asked bluntly. ''Not to wed?''

Lialla swallowed. Half a dozen of the easy lies and joking half-truths she'd tossed out over the past few years passed over her mind; but none of those, nothing short of the ugly truth, would do here. The words didn't want to come. ''Be-cause—of my uncle, partly; because as a girl, I saw how he treated my mother, as an older girl I saw the men he'd have chosen for me, and they were no better than he and often worse. Because I knew the only way I could remain myself, as poor a creature as that self might be, was to avoid such marriages. Since my uncle's death,'' she said with a shrug, ''I've known men who are friends, others who are comrades because they too Wield—none I'd choose to wed.''

She looked from one woman to the next; the notion of men as friends seemed to be as alien as that of men as Wielders. Ryselle finally shook her head and laughed quietly. ''Well! *Ursiu.* I was one of those who talked to the city woman, when she proposed you might come to us. And I spoke for you, as you must all remember—it seemed to me, a woman who could go beyond her twentieth year and remain manless had at least a certain strength.'' What she now thought, she didn't say, but the grin she gave Lialla seemed friendly enough. Much friendlier than the look two of the other young women ex-changed—a sour twist of lips, slightly up-cast eyes. ''They do not lie then,'' Ryselle went on, ''who say you traveled for a moon-season or more in the company of outland women?''

Lialla nodded. ''One of those women is now my brother's wife and mother of his two children; the other outland woman is Thukara in Sikkre.''

''Wives,'' yet another of the other young women muttered. Ryselle gave her a hard look and she subsided.

''Wives,'' Lialla agreed. ''But not as you mean it. The Thukara in particular—'' She watched growing disbelief, par-ticularly in the eyes of the older women, as she described Jennifer. *Probably wouldn't have believed it myself, if I didn't know Jen,* she decided.

''She fights?'' This seemed to most unsettle one of the gray-haired women. Ryselle laughed sourly.

"You forget, Mother; most village girls learn young how to fight, of necessity. Besides, if these outland women do all *she* says"—a gesture took in Lialla—"then why shouldn't they also fight? For my part, I find it more interesting that she serves as an advocate, and deals with the Emperor's brother in matters which even our *men* would not comprehend."

The older woman shook her head, addressed herself to Lialla. "My daughter is one of the few, I must warn you, who would say this—about the fighting."

"*Says* it," Ryselle agreed dryly. "Which of you has not even once wished to be able to return a blow?" Silence. Several of the women looked uncomfortable. "Never mind. If there is time, I hope you will tell me more of how this outland woman has come to be a companion of men in such a fashion that the merchants and the foreigners will do business with her. If this is a thing *you* understand, or can explain, or possibly teach, Ursiu, I for one will eagerly listen—yes, Sretha, I see the tide from here, and I am aware it is no simple matter for a short discussion. Another day, perhaps."

"Whatever I can tell you, I will," Lialla said. "It's why I came." *Teach any of these women to be Jen?* It was a mind-boggling thought, even without consideration of how the Holmaddi men would react. *Even after so much time around her, I'm still so very little like Jen!* Jen wouldn't feel woefully inadequate out here on this slightly damp sand; Lialla did, and wondered how many of these women realized it. Ryselle must have caught on to her by now. Certainly several of the other women had; those dubious, or downright disbelieving and sour looks, when they thought she wasn't watching. She shrugged that off with an effort and squared her shoulders. "I can certainly tell you about other women in Sikkre and Sehfi; particularly in Sehfi since my brother became Duke, there are more merchant women in Zelharri, though I'm told that in my grandsire's time, women were permitted to sell in the market only as unpaid help to their men. The explanation I was given—partly, at least, it seems that because there are more goods in Rhadaz, and more money to be shared out, this helps allow change in women's status. Without that, tradition would likely hold."

Petras laughed and clapped her hands together once. "But if men do not permit the goods and money into the hands of women, as they apparently have in Zelharri?"

"As ours do not." Ryselle nodded. "And yet, this might be one way, if we can only understand it and perhaps find a way to pressure that permission—yes, Mother, do stop biting at your lip, I can see it is time for us to go back." She leaned forward and held out both hands; Lialla blinked and extended her own. "There are those among us who have wondered from the first what possible use you might be. For my part, I am now glad you have come." Lialla nodded; that *now* hadn't escaped her. Somehow, she'd impressed one of the younger women already—possibly one of the more important ones. Those others—she glanced over in time to see two of them exchanging those looks once again. *Never mind,* she ordered herself, but it was upsetting all the same.

Ryselle let go Lialla's hands and got to her feet. She had apparently caught the look, too; she addressed herself to the two young women. "Remember what the city woman said, Lisbet, Irea. All of you: No one can come to Holmaddan and *think* for us, or *do* for us. *Act* for us. Like a fire, remember what she said? We gather our own sticks and twigs, we ourselves put the pile together so fire will catch in it; if someone else does it all for us, how will we warm ourselves at our own fires once they have gone?" She looked down at Lialla. "We will make the wood ready; now you must show us the better way to light it."

Lialla got to her feet. The last few minutes, despite Ryselle's well-intentioned words, left her feeling more inadequate than ever. She could only hope it didn't show in her face or her reply. "I will." The words sounded brusque, almost unfriendly, she thought in a sudden panic. But the young village woman looked satisfied as she turned away and held out a hand to help her mother to rise.

The women were silent all the way back to the village. Lialla's feet were icy and her shoulders ached from the weight of the bag she'd filled. By the time they reached the narrow cut that led back through the cliff into the village, the smell of raw shellfish was threatening to make her ill. She felt very lost and alone, all at once.

9

JENNIFER strode out of the glade, cloak wrapped around her shoulders, chin high, Robyn right on her heels. She hadn't gone five paces across open ground before her legs began to shake with reaction. She slowed, let her sister catch up with her. Robyn took hold of her arm. "Hey, kiddo, you all right? I mean," Robyn fumbled for a better choice of words, "you gonna make it back inside?"

"All right," Jennifer managed rather breathily. "You?"

"Kind of winded, pretty spooked. That was really *bad*, Jen."

"Yeah. I guess I should've expected something like—"

"Oh?" She could just see Robyn eyeing her curiously in the gloom.

"Tell you after I'm warm and dry, promise."

"I'll hold you to it," Robyn replied flatly.

"Promise," Jennifer repeated. She spun halfway around as painfully sharp Thread-sense alerted her to a rapidly approaching presence; this turned out to be only a pair of household guards to follow them and a third who passed her at a dead run, to sprint up the steps and into the palace. Of course guards; after tonight, she'd probably find herself close-guarded in her bathtub. After a near-drowning, she decided she wouldn't really mind, either: That man's strength had been utterly terrifying. All the same—she bit back a sigh and started forward again; with those two men right behind her, she wasn't going to lean on Robyn *now*. *Yah,* she asked herself, *who's a macho posturer now?* All the same, she had a certain reputation among the guards, one she was rather proud

139

of. *Tough broad.* She grinned, and somehow found enough energy to manage a decent pace.

Household guards and servants stared in shock at their soaking wet, algae-scented Thukara as she passed them. Everyone who worked or lived in the palace must be in the halls right now. *Probably lose half of them, all this upset. And forget about finding replacement help—after all, who'd want to be caught in the crossfire around here right now?* Something to worry about later, she decided; right now she wanted hot, clean water and plenty of it.

As she turned to climb the short staircase to the private apartments, she heard the echo of running footsteps coming fast; half a moment later a very pale Dahven came around the corner, almost cannoning into her. "Little brown sand gods, are you all right?" He wrapped both arms around her and pulled her against him, hugging hard enough to drive the breath from her. *Warm.* She pressed her face into his shoulder and nodded. "You swear?" She nodded again.

"She walked in under her own steam," Robyn offered quietly, "but I think she's about out on her feet."

"Yah," Jennifer mumbled and pressed against Dahven's chest with trembling hands. He kept his arms around her but let her lean back in his grip, eyed her doubtfully. His dark eyes were all pupil; perversely, his obvious fright gave her strength—if only enough to reassure him and sound like she meant it. "I'm all right. Really, Dahven. Well—a little waterlogged," she admitted.

He shook his head, scooped her up and started up the stairs with her. "Hold still, don't try to argue. I'm going to carry you, whether you want it or not."

"Who's arguing?" Jennifer wrapped her arms around his neck. "I know better when you're in one of your moods. But I'm getting you all wet, and it's pond water; you'll smell like fish."

"I needed a good washing anyway," he said.

"You're going to break your back, hauling me around like this."

"Be quiet, woman," he ordered sternly, but dropped a kiss on her upturned face. Beard prickled damp skin. "You're not nearly as heavy as you think. Robyn, can you make the stairs?" he added with a quick glance over his shoulder.

"Don't worry about me," Robyn said. "I wasn't involved in Jen's little party. Jen, if you're certain you're all right—well, okay, I'm going to go change and wash my face and hands."

"Do that." Jennifer hooked her chin over Dahven's shoulder to look down at her sister. "You look awfully white, lady, are you really sure you're okay?" Robyn nodded; she was leaning rather heavily on the wrought-iron railing and breathing noisily and rapidly through her mouth. "Clean up, take your time."

"I'll want you downstairs, if you're able," Dahven said. "Someone will come to bring you."

"Witness?" Robyn said breathily. "Sure. I saw some of it, and I did see that third guy on the other side of the pond." At the top of the stairs, she went off to the left, one hand holding onto the wall. Dahven glanced after her, then turned right.

"Do I want to ask *what* you were doing out there in the first place?"

"No," Jennifer said simply. Dahven sighed heavily, shook his head and pushed open the door to the Thukars' private chambers with his shoulder, shouting for Siohan as he did. It was the last thing either of them said for some time. Jennifer let Siohan and other women fuss over her, peeled off smelly, clammily wet clothes and let herself be thrust into the deep copper bathtub. She sank down until her chin was touching steaming water, let her eyes close. A room away, she could hear Dahven splashing, sponging down quickly rather than bathing, she thought; she could hear him arguing with his man about the need for a shave, over the change of clothing he wanted. She sighed, pried her eyes open and forced herself to sit up straighter. Cool air ran across her shoulders; she hissed in surprise, slid back down. Siohan stood in the doorway, hair-washing basin in her hands, two women with thick drying cloths just behind her. Jennifer reluctantly nodded. "I'm clean enough; let's do my hair and get me dry."

IT had taken over an hour, altogether; Jennifer insisted on enough time to get her hair nearly dry before she stepped into drafty halls. Despite the heat of her bath, she was still chilled. *Reaction.* Not that knowing why helped much. She let Siohan put her in one of the housegowns she usually only wore in late fall or very early spring, a thick, long-sleeved, high-necked and floor-length affair in dark blue with a lighter blue underdress that boasted snug sleeves and a turtleneck. With the long factory-knit American stockings and thin knee-length drawers that Chris had brought her, she began to feel almost warm. The bowl of hot soup one of the women brought helped, too. There'd been a glass of wine with it; she set it aside. *Wait until I'm ready for bed,* she thought. As shaky as she was right now, even a swallow of wine would go right to her head.

Dahven stopped in her dressing room while she was still toweling her hair; he'd changed into unrelieved black, the Thukar's ceremonial tunic and trous he so seldom wore, and he was buckling on a narrow black leather belt. Jennifer blinked; the belt was one he'd bought in Podhru and held a broad-bladed, wicked-looking knife in a sheath at the small of his back. In the black, he looked smaller—he was in fact only an inch or so taller than her five-foot-eight—and almost boyish. There was nothing boyish about his face just now, though, and his expression was extremely grim and daunting. "Jennifer?"

"Better," she said.

"Good. If you can deal with this tonight—"

"I can deal with it."

"Good. I'm on my way; we'll be in the main hearing chamber, not the blue. I'll send guards back for you—don't argue it, please." His mouth softened briefly as he looked at her; he sounded harassed. She bit back the protest she would ordinarily have made and merely nodded. "I'll also have someone sent to collect Robyn, so you needn't worry about her. I don't intend to do anything about those men until you come; I need time to discuss increased security on the palace grounds with the household guard. That's *my* concern, if you recall, just as yours is contract matters." He turned and went.

HE sent three of them for her, which Jennifer privately considered overkill. She kept her opinion to herself; if she'd had a scare tonight, Dahven had certainly had a worse one, he was entitled. *Teach me to sneak out of the house without them,* she thought ruefully. Judging from what she could see of the three faces, the guards were feeling it keenly that she'd slipped away from them and nearly gotten herself murdered—and right in the family gardens. She wouldn't dare do that again, she realized with a sudden pang—it wasn't fair to these men who had a job to do, who took it seriously, and who'd probably just been royally chewed out for not doing it.

Robyn was already there, settled into a deeply cushioned chair not far from the two-step dais where Dahven sat on a padded bench. Guards stood against the whitewashed walls, two men flanking the curtained double door that led into a small, vine-covered arbor. Two others at the heavy, dark doors that led back into the hall. Dahven was talking with two of the guardsmen, but broke off as she scooped up long skirts to mount the steps and settle down next to him on the bench. He caught hold of her fingers, gave them a squeeze. "That's much better; they aren't nearly as cold. I won't even ask if you're ready to deal with these men just now, not with that look in your eye."

"I don't take well to being held face down in a fish pond," Jennifer said crisply.

"Yes, I can see that." He nodded to the two he'd just been talking with; they turned and left the room. "Now. There isn't much time, so listen, please. You haven't previously been involved in a criminal matter—all right, Afronsan's meeting with me, over Father's death in Podhru, if you like. This won't be much like that. Attack on a member of the ruling family is a capital matter; there are certain forms to be followed, there are—well, there are other things which may not fit the patterns of justice from your world."

His fingers tightened on hers; he glanced at the closed doors. "You'll do me, yourself and Sikkreni justice all a great favor if you do as I say tonight, *nothing* more or less." He paused, waited until she met his eyes. "When those three men are brought in, I'll speak to them briefly. You will tell what happened and Robyn will speak. After that"—he shook her fingers, then let them go—"I want your promise to keep silent—your solemn oath on it," he added sharply.

"Why?"

He laughed without humor. " 'Because I say' isn't going to serve as an answer, is it?"

"Between us? No."

"Well, then. Because I must deal with this in my own way. Because for all your experience as an advocate, all the rest of what you've done these past years, this is—this will be different." He smiled grimly, touched her face. "*Very* different."

She studied him for one long silent moment, finally nodded. "I—I don't like this, the way you look, what you're talking around, and it shows, doesn't it?" She glanced at Robyn, who seemed lost in her own thoughts, and leaned close so she could speak quietly. "You're going to have them executed, aren't you?" The voice didn't sound at all like hers.

Dahven took her shoulders. "Don't go soft on me at the wrong moment and for the wrong cause—and the wrong men. You'd have killed any of them beside the pool, given a chance—wouldn't you?" She nodded reluctantly. "Just as you knifed a man dead below the Bez docks. In anger, and to save yourself."

"And you. And, I had to," she began. Dahven gave her a little shake and she stopped.

"You had to. All right. Remember that. Because now *I* have to. I know you; you won't like what happens here. I trust your intelligence and your common sense, that you'll sort out what's necessary, and see what I *have* to do, to protect you, and myself—and all of us."

He kept his hands on her shoulders, watched her closely. Jennifer sighed quietly, then nodded, and Dahven let his hands fall away. "All right, Dahven. I'll do exactly as you ask." She looked up to find him still watching her, clearly waiting. "My sacred oath on it. If you'll do one thing for me."

He laughed quietly. "Only one?"

"Only one. Get Robyn out of here before things get unpleasant."

"That's a promise. I'd intended it anyway," he said and got to his feet. A moment later, the main door swung open and the two guards returned with four more guards—all six carrying swords or spears at the ready. The three prisoners were boxed in between them.

DAHVEN remained on his feet until the men reached the foot of the dais, then resumed his seat next to Jennifer and held up a hand for silence. "The charge against you is entering without permission into the grounds of the Thukar's palace with intent to commit a crime, and with attempting to murder the Thukara of Sikkre by drowning. Do you speak to these charges?''

Silence. Jennifer gazed flatly at the prisoners, anger shoving aside inner cold and rising nerves. They'd have killed her, killed Dahven—Robyn if she'd gotten in the way. She remembered that awful helpless moment, trapped underwater by vastly superior muscle. It was only luck that she wasn't lying on the bottom of the pond right now. And then they'd have gone for Dahven. . . . Blood was heating her cheekbones, probably putting color in her face.

The limping man was looking furtively from side to side as if he hoped to somehow find a way out; the one who'd attacked her returned her look challengingly. The third—only a skinny boy, she thought in distress—looked up once, then buried his face in his hands. Of the three, he alone wasn't bound. *I can see why; he doesn't begin to look like a threat.* Besides, two men had him firmly by the elbows—probably the only reason he was still on his feet.

Dahven was talking once more; Jennifer came back to the moment as he spoke Robyn's name. Robyn, clearly an uncomfortable witness, gave a carefully expurgated but lucid account of what she'd seen in the glade: ''I went down to the end of the pool to look at the stream, and I heard someone coming. My hearing is very acute, better than Jen's, and my night vision is good. I saw an enormous man come up behind her and she went over the edge of the pool. There was a splash. I didn't dare go that way and I was afraid to scream for help, there was another man, too. I turned and ran, across the stream and along the far side of the pool, but I could see a third man, so I hid behind bushes, and would have yelled for help but just then, one of the men shouted like he'd been hurt and I saw the other one fall. The third man moved as though he was going to help them, and just then, before I could start shouting, the household guards came and grabbed him.''

Dahven asked her one or two general questions, then asked, ''And the men—were you near enough any of them to see their faces?''

Robyn nodded reluctantly. ''The—the boy, him, he was the

third. The—I couldn't see the man who held back but the one who had Jen—who held the Thukara—the big one, I saw the size of him and the shape of his head. That's him.'' The big man glared at her. Robyn somehow managed to simply gaze back without expression, then turned to Dahven, who nodded.

"We need nothing further from you, Duchess. Thank you." He waited until Robyn was escorted from the room and the door closed behind her, then shifted on the bench slightly so he faced Jennifer. "The Thukara's testimony next." The big man shifted and opened his mouth as though he would protest; Dahven fixed him with a chill look until he subsided. Jennifer told her own story in a crisp, businesslike voice. "I didn't see the third man until the guards brought him close," she finished. "Though while I was hiding in the water, I heard the others say he was across the pool, waiting there in case I decided to try to escape that way. I identify these two. I saw both men after the attack, and also my mark is on both of them: that man's limp, and on the other, a bruise here." She touched the underside of her own jaw to indicate.

Dahven stood and went down the two steps; the two guards who had stood between the prisoners and the dais moved aside, and at his gesture, the boy was pulled aside with them. At another gesture, two men took hold of the second and drew him limping back.

Jennifer swallowed hard, and under cover of her thick skirts clutched at the padded bench. *Keep your mouth shut,* she ordered herself. The big man was staring across Dahven's head and straight at her once again, but his attention shifted as Dahven stabbed at his breastbone with a hard finger. "You're Sikkreni; I've seen you in the lower market though I never knew your name. As a Sikkreni, you know the penalty for *any* attack on a reigning Thukar or Thukara. The penalty exacted on the men who tried to murder my great-grandsire. There's a block prepared in the inner courtyard, a man with a new-sharpened axe waiting for you." Dahven paused; Jennifer felt the blood drain from her face and only her grip on the bench kept her upright. The big prisoner must have expected this, because he gave no sign of distress other than the sudden sheen of sweat on his forehead. His companion in the glade moaned faintly; the boy choked.

"You won't save yourself, of course," Dahven went on finally. "You can make it an easier death—and save yourself a good deal of pain right now, I might add—if you answer my questions." Silence. Dahven walked all the way around the man, stopped in front of him once again. "More fool you, to have chosen my Thukara for your attack. Or was she chosen for you?" Silence again. "Who paid you?" Dahven snapped. This time he let the silence stretch for some minutes, finally drew the knife from its sheath and brought it into view. The prisoner glanced down as light flashed from the blade, looked away once more. His shoulders and jaw were set, and Jennifer saw his chest heave to pull in a deep breath as Dahven stepped behind him.

Oh, God. Her stomach dropped alarmingly and her hands were nearly too slippery with sweat to hold the bench. Somehow she kept from flinching as the knife ripped through cloth; Dahven had cut the man's shirt from mid-back right through the collar. He came back around to yank, hard, at the front of it, pulling the fabric down from throat and shoulders. He held the knife at the ready, brought it up between them. "I asked a question. Do you answer it, or do I carve a map of the lower market between your shoulder blades?"

She saw the man's Adam's apple go up and down but he gave no other sign of distress. As Dahven moved out of his sight, he spoke: His voice was flat and expressionless. "I never saw the man who hired me; it was dark. Do what you will, you'll get no other answer."

Dahven came back, looked at him thoughtfully. "All right." He looked beyond the man, found Grelt. "Take him out, the small courtyard. Return and tell me when it's done." Jennifer had to compress her lips to keep quiet. Grelt merely nodded grimly and gestured to four of the guards. Two of them took hold of the prisoner, who shook his arms free, turned, and walked out with them. Dahven had already turned his attention to the second man; the knife now hung from his fingers by his leg, but the limper was keenly aware of it and seemed unable to take his eyes from it; he was trembling violently. "And you—did you see no one, speak to no one?" He brought up the knife, touched it almost gently against the other man's chin. "You're going to die this night anyway; do you want to go now, quickly—or would you rather bless the axe as it ends unbearable pain?''

"Don't—don't—I didn't know—"

"You knew," Dahven's harsh voice cut through the high, whimpering stuttered denial. "If at no other time, you knew once that man led you into the palace grounds. But by the Thukara's own words, you knew who was to be attacked— who was to die. *You* wanted to stab her, and argued with your companion over his failed attempt to drown her." Dahven glanced behind the prisoner, nodded. The guard there handed his short-bladed sword to the one next to him, caught hold of the throat of the man's shirt and tore it down the back. The man's legs went limp; he nearly took the guards down with him. Dahven brought the knife up once again, touched the corner of the man's mouth, then drew the tip lightly across a grubby cheekbone, leaving a fine line of blood behind. Jennifer closed her eyes and drew a deep breath. Opened them a moment later. Better to *see*; she could have nightmares for months imagining what was happening. "It's only a small cut," Dahven said conversationally. "You could do worse shaving yourself." He pulled at the torn shirt, laid the knife across the man's bony chest. "The next won't be a shaving cut; I'll bare your ribs from one side to the other. *Talk to me!*"

"I—all right, don't, please, don't—it was—" The prisoner drew a ragged, sobbing breath, shook his head. "Don't, let me—I'll tell you, let me—"

"Tell me," Dahven said flatly. "Where and when was the contract made to kill the Thukara?"

"It—it was either—of you." He was gasping for air and the words were high-pitched, hard for Jennifer to understand. Dahven nodded, gestured with the knife for the man to go on. The prisoner cast a terrified glance at the shining blade and did. "He said—to go in that way, across the rubble, it's easy, everyone knows that. He said—go that way, get into the doorway by the long hall with the vines, that would be the private apartments and the dining hall is just by that entry; he said to go inside the dining hall, under the table or behind the water, to wait an opportunity even if it took until morning for one or both of you to come down to eat. And then—"

"All right, I can see what was to follow," Dahven said flatly. "He. Who was he?"

"A—I can't—"

"Why? Will he kill you if you speak? But you're dead already; he'll have no chance."

The man shook his head wildly. "My—my—he said my mother—"

"Ah. He'll kill your mother? Tell me who she is; we'll see she's safe." He moved the knife blade across the man's heaving chest. "Tell me," Dahven said softly. "You've no time left."

"It was—ah, gods." Tears ran unchecked down the man's face. "*He*, Nebrin, the big man—he and I drink together sometimes, he said there was a chance at money. We went to—to The Camel, to talk to a man there. A Sikkreni, not seen around the market for several years, except—except in the past few days. Man with a blade cut on his face. Said we'd get a hundred silver ceris each, for us to find a third for lookout. Paid—Paid us twenty ceris each then. I—I didn't—I swear I didn't want—but Nebrin convinced me, the man with the ceris said we'd get more from it than simply coin—and then, when I tried once again to back away, he named me, named my mother—" He brought up bound hands to rub a grubby sleeve across his face.

"Your mother's name," Dahven said finally.

"She's Urios, has a stall in the upper market for eggs and oranges—"

"I know it," Jennifer said quietly; to her astonishment, her voice showed none of the distress she was feeling. "I've bought her oranges."

Grelt had come into the room. "I know Urios," he said.

Dahven nodded. "We'll see *her* safe. The man who paid you. Was this his own vendetta or did he name others?"

"No, he said nothing not to the point. But—a hundred silver ceris each, he's not a man to have such money. And he's known; it's known what two men hold *his* loyalty." Silence. The man drew a heaving breath, said in a rush, "Eprian hired us. And Eprian serves your brothers."

Dahven walked slowly around him; the man twisted his head nervously to keep the Thukar and his knife in view as much as possible. Dahven mounted the steps of the dais finally. "Your choice was a poor one; you might have instead gone to the city guard and so averted what might have been a tragedy, and at the same time obtained protection for your mother and yourself. You need not have died tonight." He glanced at a nearby guard. "Small courtyard." The younger guardsman was white and his lips were tightly pressed together but he managed a creditable bow before helping drag the man from the chamber. It took five of them to hold him upright. Dahven was silent, finally gestured with the knife for the third man to be brought forward. The boy's face was in his hands once again, and the guard had to pry them away, to take hold of the hair at the back of his neck to bring his head up.

"You," Dahven said finally. "You heard that man, you heard what the Thukara and Zelharri's Duchess both said. Have you anything to add?"

The words came as a very faint, choked whisper, nearly uncomprehensible. "I—Lord Dahven, I *swear* I knew nothing, Urwen came to me this afternoon, asked if I'd take on a small task for him. He said—said I could earn the price of a few drinks, nothing more. No one spoke of harm to you or the Thukara, and I'd never have wanted any part of that, I swear it, sir, truly."

Silence. "He can't tell us anything," Dahven said finally. "It's a pity; I know who hired these men, who put coin in his hands. My brothers should be here; they'd share the block with this boy for daring such an attack on myself, particularly for such a threat to my Thukara." He shrugged. "Take him, go." The boy was sobbing openly as he was pulled into the hall. Dahven slid the knife back into its sheath, turned and stepped behind Jennifer, who sat frozen with shock and horror. His hands touched her shoulders. "The boy is going to escape, my love. Before you protest his death." Jennifer started, twisted around to gaze up at him. Dahven managed a faint smile; he looked rather ill. "Don't think I enjoyed that; I didn't. Father would have. My brothers certainly would have. For my part, I fear I've more in common with you than my blood kin, that I'd rather kill in anger as I just had to."

"You could have—" Jennifer stopped as Dahven's fingers tightened on her shoulders and he shook his head.

"Could have what, imprisoned them? *Here?* You've seen the cells; they're for market thieves and the like. Or I could have sent them to Podhru? They'd never get there, Eprian would rescue them and guardsmen would die, I know you wouldn't want that. This way—those two won't be a threat to anyone, ever again. Eprian may suspect I let that boy escape, but he'll get the message, too: More, he'll pass it on to my brothers, and I don't think they'll dare another direct attack on *you*." His fingers lightly rubbed at the base of her neck. The rest of the guards had gone out, except for one man on each of the doors. "Jennifer," Dahven said after a moment's silence. "Jennifer, please don't hate me. I did what I had to."

She brought one hand up to cover his. "If it were anyone but you, I would probably have doubted that. I know you." She tilted her head back and looked up at him. "I see it in your eyes, what you did to that man to frighten him will give you bad dreams, never mind the rest. *I* know you aren't your father, or your brothers. And you learned something, more than I would have. That boy—" She shook her head, let her eyes close. "I nearly said something, promise or no, when you sent him out. I'm glad you let him go."

"Someone had to get word out to Eprian, what happened tonight," Dahven said reasonably. "And the boy will learn from this. Of course, the guards will keep an eye on him. If he gets into any kind of trouble another time, he'll be sorry."

"If Eprian doesn't simply kill him for failing," Jennifer said. She sighed, leaned back into Dahven.

"It's a possibility, but not likely. My brothers would murder the messenger out of anger or spite; Eprian is more logical. Likely he'll simply cut his losses and run. If I have any luck at all, the guard may even see which way he goes. There are enough men posted all around the city watching for him."

"Good." Jennifer let him help her up, leaned against him as he came around the bench and wrapped an arm around her shoulders. "I'd like to know myself where the men who hired *him* are. I warn you, if I get a hand on your brothers, you won't have to worry about executing them." She slid a hand around his waist, starting as her forearm came down across the knife sheath. "Dahven, anything else that happens tonight"—she had a momentary vision of the darkened small courtyard and forcibly suppressed it—"happens without me, I'm going to disgrace myself if you don't get me back to our bedroom right now." She cast him a weak, apologetic smile. "Getting soft in my old age."

He smiled back, but his eyes were concerned. "I'm sorry! I should have thought. Can you walk that far?"

"Bah. Not that soft; of course I can. Watch."

"I'll go with you. You don't go *anywhere* alone from now on," Dahven said flatly. "Neither of us does. I told the guards to let the boy hear them discussing the strength of new security for both of us, by the way; something else for him to pass on to Eprian. I hope it'll discourage another night like this. Come on, let's get you to bed. Both of us, in fact. Grelt doesn't want me out there; he said I had no business outside after dark, even with a guard."

"He's right," Jennifer said as firmly as she could manage. The words sounded faint, rather tremulous, hardly like her voice at all. "You already took responsibility, I heard you pronounce sentence. Stay with me, please, Dahven. I need you." It was the right thing to say; his arm tightened around her shoulders.

10

JENNIFER woke in the pre-dawn hour, the music/noise of the silver protect-Thread jangling in her ears as it had in most of her dreams. She blinked groggily, swore under her breath. "If I begin to start waking up early like this, I *swear* I'll . . ." She fell silent as Dahven mumbled something in his sleep and turned toward her. His hand found hers, dragged it under his cheek, and he sighed happily. Jennifer sent her eyes helplessly toward the darkened ceiling and edged closer to him, resettling herself as comfortably as possible. She felt under her pillows, assured herself the dagger was still there, closed her eyes resolutely.

Sleep wouldn't come. She finally lay very still, eyes still closed and resignedly tried to think through the day before. Sort through it. *All that, one day?* Chris at breakfast, herself with the contracts, that visit to Rebbe and his confirmation the wine was poisoned. Chris running for the south gate before Robyn could arrive—so little time ago that Chris would probably still be well north and west of Podhru—in fact, unless he'd had excellent luck with change of horses (and an iron backside), he'd still be this side of the new crossroads over the almost finished Bez-Zelharri highway.

Then Robyn's arrival—an afternoon that was so ordinary in contrast to the rest of the day she could barely recall any of *it*. That gruesome scene in the glade. *I should have insisted Robyn let me send for a shifter from the market.* But it was useless to insist upon things like that with Robyn, who had an unexpectedly deep and hard stubborn streak for someone normally so easygoing.

153

Well, it didn't matter, after all; Jennifer was still alive, the two men taken (*taken and beheaded*, she thought, and fought a shudder). It just didn't seem real, that last; even those moments in the large hearing room when Dahven had turned into a cold-eyed stranger—a younger but no less daunting version of his father—might have been a story told her by someone else. Something seen on television. If she had any sense, she'd leave it at that. She shifted, came partway upright, then went quickly back down onto one elbow. She felt ill, all at once: queasy, rather lightheaded. Dangerously, bile-in-the-throat sick lying flat, worse upright. Not, she decided cautiously, much better at an angle, but not quite as much in danger of immediately losing it. "Oh, great," she muttered sourly. "Just how dirty *is* that pond? And how much did I drink?" What kinds of things grew in pond water, anyway? "Dysentery, cholera—that's back home, girl." Probably worse things here. The water was fairly clean. But cholera water could *look* clean; germs weren't basketball-sized and neon-colored, after all. *Think*. No good. She didn't recall swallowing any, but she'd had to open her eyes underwater, the stuff had gotten inside her nostrils, gotten into the inevitable scratches on her hands and arms—she was probably chock full of *something*. She glanced at the window—there was faint light out there now—and considered going in search of toast and coffee. But that unbalanced sense, that unnerving dizziness wasn't entirely gone: Bad idea, walking anywhere just now, like that. *Think how dumb you'd feel, passing out halfway to the kitchen.*

She'd never hear the end of it.

Besides, she'd have to break the sphere down. She didn't think she could manage it, suddenly, even though the Thread sphere and the movement and sound was *definitely* leaving her feeling green. She swallowed cautiously, edged back down flat and curled into Dahven. It felt very good, closing her eyes. She nudged the pillow into the right configuration with her chin and shoulder, edged herself near enough to feel his breath stirring her hair, and fell back asleep once more.

She woke to full light across the sheets and Dahven's hand pushing gently at her shoulder. "Jennifer? I'm sorry to waken you, but I can't get up—" He gestured rather helplessly. "And no one can get in; I think Siohan's brought you coffee."

"Mmmm? Oh. Coffee?" It took her a moment to pull herself awake enough for his words to make sense, another moment to remember how to dismantle the protective sphere. The smell of coffee and warm bread tickled her nose.

"It's strong," Siohan assured her, before she could ask. "I went for it myself, watched Rhelliu prepare the beans and had her double the number of spoons she'd have put in the straining cloth." Jennifer let Dahven pile pillows behind her back, watched Siohan set the tray across her legs and inhaled deeply. For once, maybe it wouldn't be so bad, being spoiled. Her stomach still felt a little queasy, but a bite or two of the bread took care of that, and the coffee brought her properly awake. *Cholera, my foot,* she thought with mild amusement. *Early-morning paranoia, wine late last night and not enough sleep after, make anyone sick.*

Dahven had vanished into his dressing room, and he now came out, his man trailing after him with his low boots and a plain, wide belt that held an equally plain dagger sheath centered in the back. Jennifer bit her lip to keep comment back. In the full early sunlight, Dahven looked as though he'd barely slept, and his mouth was haggard, lines visible from nose to the corners of his lips that weren't normally there. The last thing he needed just now was Jennifer, who hardly ever fussed, nagging him about that blade, much as she disliked the idea of him walking around the household apartments armed. She reminded herself sternly that a sensible man wouldn't leave his bedroom *without* some kind of weapon, given the events of the past few days. *Woman, either.* She'd pass on knives herself, though. *That man in Bez was enough.* She'd keep her bo with her—raise a few eyebrows, but a belt like Dahven's would send them higher.

She wondered briefly where that boy was this morning. Hiding, probably, poor thing. Dahven managed a smile for her. She beckoned, held out bread. He came over to sprawl across his side of the bed, took a large bite of the piece she held for him, chewed quickly and swallowed, then scooped up her hand and kissed it. "Take things as easy today as you like," he began.

She shook her head. "I've already had my spoiling this morning. Including some coffee that's almost better than my own; thanks, Siohan." Jennifer glanced at the woman, who gave her a gratified smile in reply. "No, I'm swamped, I have regular reports and messages to draft for Podhru—"

Dahven groaned. "Don't remind me! I'll need to send a detailed report to Shesseran about last night. At once, before he hears from anyone else."

"We'll do it together, after lunch. Damn," Jennifer said feelingly. "I forgot Robyn's still here. But I think she said she intended to go to the market and buy presents for the children. Maybe I can talk her into doing that today; she doesn't usually expect me to go with her."

"She won't get you. Not until the city guard has had a chance to do a sweep and either bring in a few persons, or chase them out of Sikkre," Dahven said flatly as he pushed himself off the bed; his man cleared his throat gently and held up boots. Dahven shook his head, dropped back onto the bed to pull them on. "No wonder my feet felt so cold. I don't think I'm functioning very well this morning."

"Hardly surprising. I'm not in very good form either."

He leaned across to touch her face, got to his feet. "You could fool me. But you keep in mind that you, my good woman, aren't going outside the palace, if only so *I* feel safe."

"Trust me; I'm not going anywhere today," Jennifer assured him. "Except the clerks' offices and the printer's hall."

"And the family dining—I'll meet you there at midday and we can decide what to tell Shesseran. It isn't like advising Afronsan, worse luck," he added gloomily.

"As if I didn't know *that*, by now," Jennifer said. "Though I have to send one of those regular reports to Afronsan, so I'll be advising him anyway. Midday, then. We may have Robyn for lunch, too." He merely nodded and went.

ROBYN came in search of Jennifer only an hour later, just as Jennifer was slipping into trousers, shirt and sandals. She was smiling but her eyes were red-rimmed and she kept her hands tucked away out of sight. She dropped onto the edge of the bed as Siohan set out a cushioned chair so she could work on Jennifer's hair—she had bundled it herself into two still slightly damp braids before retiring; it now came out damp, barely waved and horribly tangled. Siohan muttered unpleasant little exclamations under her breath, began working upward through the length with her fingers, separating the worst knots. "You look all right," Robyn said finally.

"Liar. It's still good to hear, but I feel like nothing on earth," Jennifer said. Her eyes closed briefly as Siohan hit a snarl. "There's still a little bread, probably some coffee left—"

"I had mint tea and bread a few minutes ago." Robyn shuddered. "As if I'd drink *your* coffee anyway, even if I used the stuff. I'm off drugs, remember?" Jennifer laughed. "Listen, I'm afraid I'd better go home early."

"Birdy, listen, about last night, I'm so sorry you had to—"

"Shhh, don't," Robyn said urgently. "Please. Just don't, all right? I—I feel like it's all my fault, getting you out there, what almost happened. And then, those men—"

"Don't let yourself think about them," Jennifer broke in.

"No. I—I don't intend to. I *can't*. But if I hadn't asked you to go out there with me—"

"*If* you hadn't got me to go for a walk." Robyn had stopped speaking to swallow, hard. Jennifer made a warning upward cast of her eyes toward Siohan, who was still at her back, working through her hair. "I don't know how much you heard last night, but if we hadn't gone for a walk, if they hadn't seen us and followed us, they were going to break into the palace by that hallway, then ambush me or Dahven. Imagine if they'd gone into the dining room and waited until breakfast. Birdy, I *really* hate to think what would've happened, if that big goon had got hold of me at an hour when I'm as non-functional as they get."

"Someone in your guard would've found them," Robyn said. She'd caught the look, remembered Siohan's presence.

"Maybe. Probably. But what if they hadn't? No, please, don't feel bad, all right? Personally, I'd prefer they hadn't shown up at all, and the whole evening had gone the way you and I planned it, start to finish."

"Yeah."

"It didn't, but it's all right."

"Well—yah. For *some* of us," Robyn replied doubtfully.

"Don't think about it, swear you won't, Robyn. It's ugly and upsetting, but it's over; dwelling on it won't help. I feel rather lucky because I'm having a hard time realizing any of it was real."

"I know. It's—all the ugly things I saw back in L.A., or

heard about, or saw on TV, this was still so fast, and so nasty, and so—all of it, so *grim*. You can't believe it really happened." She sighed. "I just hope you guys don't get backlash from it. From what he—what—from Dahven's sentence."

"Backlash?" Jennifer started to nod, stopped the gesture as the comb caught at her hair and Siohan's hand steadied her head. "You think people might worry he's on his way to becoming a tyrant?"

An indignant snort stopped her. Siohan freed the comb from her hair and came around to face her. "Tyrant? Don't you think that, Thukara! If anything, some people had begun to wonder if he was hard enough!" She folded her arms across her chest. "If you knew how many people like my brothers and my mother thought the old Thukar should have cleaned out some of the parts of the market, *do* something about the Lasanachi coming in and taking people away—well, I could tell you a thing or two I've heard since you closed down the worst of the woman-sellers, Thukara. Believe this: No decent Sikkreni would want a Thukar who'd take such men as those last night and not—" She cast Robyn a quick, sideways glance, plainly altered what she would've said. "And not make certain of them as he did. No decent citizen would care to have men like that wandering the market—whose children would be safe, whose wives?" She let her arms fall to her sides, and after a moment went back to quietly working the snarls out of Jennifer's hair.

"It's a good point," Jennifer said finally. "And I'll keep it in mind."

Robyn sighed, nodded once. "Yeah. That one guy, he looked like the kind that don't sit in a cell for a few years and turn into model citizens, I guess. Well. Anyway, I promised the kids oranges and nuts, and I thought, maybe a little something for Aletto." She hesitated. "It's not personal, or that I'm scared for myself, but I'm really not gonna be able to stay very long."

"It's okay."

"I just hate leaving the kids, *you* know. And if Aletto hears about last night before I can get back, he'll really panic. I thought I'd send a message this morning on the garble-graph, and leave tomorrow evening. Guess I'd better figure out a *real* short message for them to flash back to him."

" 'Coming, Robyn,' " Jennifer said gravely. Robyn gave a snort of laughter. "Speaking of tyrants, my pet tyrant is keeping me on a short leash today, so you're on your own."

"That's fine. You move too fast for me."

"Yah. *You* amble. But I'll send a couple of the guards with you."

"Sure. I'd like that," Robyn said. "I mean, it's fun, just walking around your market with one of my personal women from the fort for show—you know, can't let a Duchess out without window dressing. But I really am a little wobbly after last night, and it would be nice to have real protection. And someone to carry stuff back for me."

"You're getting soft, lady." Jennifer laughed. "Tell you what, why don't you borrow my rickshaw, and the kid to pull it?"

Robyn considered this, shook her head. "Nah. Nobody's that soft. Send me a two-footed packhorse who doesn't mind talking to a chattering old broad of a Duchess, and a—what'd Chris used to call it?—a brute with a broadsword to keep me in one piece."

"You got it. Make it back for lunch, if you can."

"I'd better. I only got in from that long ride yesterday, if you recall, and I'm gonna need a long nap. Especially if I plan on heading out tomorrow night."

Jennifer wiggled fingers at her as she left, then settled back to let Siohan work her hair into one thick braid. "I gather no one's told her about Eprian and that gun," she said finally. "I'm afraid she'll pick up the market gossip, though."

"Worse luck. Inevitable, I'm afraid," Siohan said. "There. It's not particularly pretty but it'll serve."

"It's comfortable and I'd have only half as much hair left if I'd been the one to untangle it," Jennifer said. "Thanks. And for the coffee. There aren't any messages for me from anyone?"

"Nothing yet."

"Good. I'm sorry about those disgusting clothes—"

"Hardly your fault," Siohan said. "The boots may be ruined, I'm afraid."

"Well, at least *I'm* still here." Jennifer took the last cup of coffee—now lukewarm but still strong enough to be drinkable—and headed for the clerks' rooms.

One of the women stopped her before she got out of the family apartments. "Thukara, one of the guards sent me; he says to tell you there's a horse down in the courtyard, a saddle on it but no rider. And something about a message for you."

Jennifer stopped, annoyed to find her heart had speeded up and her palms were damp. A trap—another trap? "One of the guards? Which?"

"The boy Vey, Thukara."

"You saw him yourself—personally talked to him?" The woman nodded, eyed her warily. "Thank you, I'll go." She hesitated. "Go to my rooms, let Siohan know which way I've gone, will you?" *So someone knows where to start looking for the body when I disappear*, she told herself dryly—as she'd told Robyn or Chris often enough that last year in L.A., when she'd had to go out of town for a document inspection or deposition. It didn't seem that all amusing, any more.

But it was indeed Vey waiting for her near the end of the corridor, talking to the guard stationed in front of the blue room doors, and he pushed away from the wall as she came close. "Thukara? I heard—are you all right?"

"I've slept better," Jennifer admitted as he moved to open the outer door for her and preceded her down the stairs to the courtyard. "You don't look like you got much rest last night yourself. When did Chris finally let you go?"

"Around middle night. But my horse went lame a few miles from the south gates and I had to walk him back; I didn't get in until it was nearly light. This horse—" It was a clear change of subject. *Don't baby him*, Jennifer told herself. *I bet no one's babied him in his life; he'd probably just be offended I thought he couldn't handle his job.* "The beast itself is nothing special, but I think the trappings are from Duke's Fort; they look to me as though the same person who made the Duchess's saddle and pads did them." He was just to one side of her, eyes moving constantly. "I hope you aren't offended," he added. "There was a long meeting of the household guard, early this morning. The Thukar sent word down through Grelt and his second that your personal guard is to stay right at your elbow, near enough to touch you, no walking ahead or behind you unless there's enough of us." He sounded and looked uncomfortable. "And we won't bow to either of you; someone with a knife or an arrow could use that moment when a guardsman's head is lowered to—''

''I get the picture,'' Jennifer said hastily. ''But, Vey, you surely know me better than that by now. I'm related to Chris, remember?''

''I know,'' he replied softly. ''I simply wanted to say— well, just that, Thukara. I do know you, but I felt uncomfortable carrying out such new orders and not telling you why.''

''Well, as Chris would say, don't sweat it. Where's this horse?''

The horse was led out of the stables by the stableman who'd taken the animal. One of the younger boys carried the tack, the saddlebag slung over one shoulder. ''It was brought to the gates just after sunrise, Thukara, by a caravaner.'' The stableman hadn't noted which caravan: the man had been visibly a caravaner but plainly dressed. After the previous night's alarms, the stableman's main concern had been that the visitor had been unarmed, that the horse hadn't somehow been a trap. The saddle and bridle had been ordinary, if finely worked; the bag contained only the one piece of paper. The man who led it, so far as the stableman could see, hadn't carried a sword or one of those complicated foreign weapons that threw pellets and killed at a distance. He'd only wanted to leave the horse for the Thukara, to tell her it had been sent to her and would be collected, eventually. ''After he left, I looked the beast over and it seemed to me the trappings were much more costly than any caravaner would own. The guard searched the saddle and pads carefully, rechecked the bag. There was only this.''

He held out thick blue paper, folded over several times to create a square bundle nearly an inch thick, ribboned and sealed so exuberantly that the original color of the paper showed only on the sides; top and bottom were lost in green ribbon and black wax. No name on the outside, but the stamp was a cat's cradle—Lialla's mark.

She thanked the stableman and the boy. ''Keep the horse and its gear in good condition. It appears to belong to sin-Duchess Lialla. No doubt she'll come to claim it, but if there's anything different in her letter, I'll see you hear of it.'' She let Vey escort her back into the palace. He saw her to the door of the clerks' room, hesitated at the doorway.

"I'm on duty in the market this morning, but I'll see someone is in the hall for you."

Jennifer automatically opened her mouth to protest, thought better of it and merely nodded. The guard was ordered to keep a close and continuous eye on her; she'd promised herself *and* Dahven she'd let them. *Remember why.*

The staff eyed her curiously as she came in, but heads were lowered over work again almost at once. "Morning, everyone," she said, and managed to make the words sound cheerful. "Everything's fine, whatever gossip you've heard. We've got some extra reports to send down to Podhru as soon as we can get them out, that's besides the regular financial sheets. I'll try to get draft done this morning so no one gets stuck working late." She went over to the wide, high-piled table at one end of the room that served her as a desk.

A message from Sehfi had been placed on the seat of her chair—the only place it was guaranteed she'd see it, given the state of the desk. An unusually clear message, considering it had been sent by mirror-flash and took up most of the page: Aletto was frantic. Lialla was gone, missing from Duke's Fort for two days, nowhere in Sehfi, not anywhere in Zelharri. Someone had only just remembered saddling her horse late in the afternoon, and after a good deal of questioning, someone else had recalled the caravan headed to Sikkre. Someone in the market recalled a horse that might have been the sin-Duchess's tied to the back of one of the wagons. Had she come into Sikkre? Aletto realized she was angry with him and thought she might have gone to spend some time with Jen, also that she might have asked Jen not to tell him she'd arrived. Would she please tell him anyway? He wouldn't demand she return, he wouldn't even ask; he just wanted to know for certain she was safe. Jennifer sighed, set the message aside, picked up the blue paper packet and broke Lialla's seals.

After a few minutes, she dropped it on the desk and turned to stare out the window, across the small garden that backed the family dining room. Once composed of scraggy shrub roses, it was now all pattern-raked sand, three large rocks, a few drought-hardy little trees against the north wall—her own interpretation of the Japanese gardens she used to visit at the Huntington Museum. This was far from authentic, but nearly as soothing to look at as the Huntington one had been. At the moment, she wasn't feeling particularly soothed, however. *Damn that woman.* Not that she could argue with Lialla's conscience, with her need to help. Jennifer wouldn't mind being able to help the women up north herself. But Lialla had effectively left her holding the notify-Aletto baby, and she didn't need what Robyn had already told her about the screaming fights between brother and sister to know Aletto wouldn't be happy at what she had to tell him.

Lialla wasn't stupid, though: She knew full well that of all the people who might tell Aletto where she was, he was least likely to come down hard on Jennifer. All the same—*Swell. All the other things I have to do, and now I have to frame a message to Aletto. Damn Lialla, anyway.* Well, put it aside; it wouldn't need to be done until Robyn was ready to go. She could take it home with her—Jennifer considered this, finally shook her head. "Right, and wouldn't she love being part of *that*? Do it now, get it out with the mail this morning." She fished under a pile of drafts stacked in the middle of her table, came up with her calendar. Regular mail to Sehfi—the rider would pass through from Dro Pent late this afternoon on his way east. The letter would beat Robyn home by forty-eight hours, with any luck. With more luck, it might be enough time for Aletto to get over it before she got in.

SHE finished a draft of the letter to Aletto and gave it to one of the clerks, went through most of the financial report for Afronsan and okayed it for the printer, and scooped up two pads of paper to take down to lunch. The guard was one of the older men and clearly even more embarrassed than Vey by the new rules. He came into the dining room, making certain there was a man inside the room before he went back to station himself in the hall.

Dahven was already there, mumbling vexedly over the stack of papers at his elbow, his hair rumpled as though he'd repeatedly thrust his hands through it. He shoved everything to one side as she came in. "Robyn just sent a message down, she had something to eat in the market and said she was going to take a long nap. Probably wouldn't wake until dinner time, said she'd see you then."

"Good." Jennifer picked up the tall glass of orange and drained it. "Mmmm, cold. Just as well, we've got a lot to get done. And there's some new excitement." She told him about Aletto's message, Lialla's letter. Dahven tugged at his earlobe and briefly closed his eyes.

"Gods. I had heard about the horse, wondered whose and why but I didn't really have time to concern myself."

"I'll let you look over the letter to Aletto before it goes out, if you like."

He shook his head. "All yours. Besides, you manage Aletto better than anyone else."

"Yah," Jennifer said in disgust. "You and Lialla. I'm on schedule with the market reports for Afronsan—"

"I'm behind, but not very. Not enough to worry about; besides, I think if Afronsan hasn't doubled his staff, he's probably behind schedule himself, going through everything the Dukes send him. Poor man. I wonder how he'll manage after Shesseran dies."

"He probably petitions every god in Podhru's collection of them, to keep the man in good health."

"Good health," Dahven snorted. "He was worthless ten years past and failing four years ago!"

"You know what I mean." A guardsman opened the back entry and two of the kitchen women came through with trays. Jennifer ate quickly, scarcely tasting the food. "Here, let me see what you've been working on." She took papers from Dahven, drank another glass of thin orange, one of plain water and scanned down several sheets of his neat, precise writing. "Looks lucid enough to me; I can't see where I'd add or change anything."

"You don't think I need to put in anything else—here?" He shuffled down through several pages, pointed. She read once again, shrugged.

"You could probably put in more points for justification. I don't think you need them. As you pointed out last night, I don't know Sikkreni criminal law at all, but you do, and if you truly followed that—" She paused, glanced at him; he nodded. "Then leave it as it is; anything else *would* sound as if you needed to justify your actions, which I just don't see. But I would—here.'' She turned over two sheets, ran down the next with a finger. ''Here, I'd move this point to the end. I think it's time Casimaffi was investigated; he's got a lot of money, a lot of power, a lot of ships out there—I've met him, I never did like him, which might only be a personality clash but I think it went deeper than that. Besides, Enardi's sister warned me about him, I gathered then that however much Enardi's father liked him, the man didn't have a pristine reputation elsewhere. We want to make certain Afronsan picks up on all of that.''

Dahven considered this; picked up a pen and took the clean pad of paper she held out to him. ''He might decide Casimaffi's above suspicion.''

''That'll be his decision, then. And he won't be able to come back to us later and ask why we didn't warn him—''

''If it turns out Casimaffi's really dirty,'' Dahven finished. ''Good point. All right.'' He wrote in silence for a while. Jennifer ran down the sheet and nodded, marked it for insertion into the rest of the report.

''I'll take this to the printers, if you like; I should go see how they're doing on the market stuff anyway.''

''Take it.'' Dahven handed it over and sighed. ''I've got enough left here to keep me busy.''

''You'll be here?''

''It's cool.''

''Better than the clerks' hall.'' Jennifer got to her feet. ''My desk is about to collapse from all the weight, though; I'd better go deal with some of it.''

''Delegate.'' Dahven gave her a grin, and she laughed.

''Sounds good right now. See you later.'' She turned at the door, guard hard on her elbow. ''Any personal message to Aletto?''

''Tell him to calm down; Lialla can take care of herself. Look how she got out of marrying *me*.'' Jennifer laughed again; Dahven merely waved a hand and went back to his paperwork.

11

≋

HE days in North Bay were long—often so featureless as
to be indistinguishable one from the next—but the nights,
Lialla decided, were worse. Nights she slept heavily for an
hour or so, to wake sweating, her stomach knotted and her
heart pounding. Her feet blocks of ice, despite the two pairs
of factory-knit English woolen socks she wore. There were
constant drafts in old Sretha's house, particularly on the floor
where she slept; the air itself was fog-chill and damp, and
penetrated even the felted wool blankets.

Her mind raced from one matter to the next, never for a
moment still. Though her pattern of thought could be utterly
shattered at any time by Emalya; the woman snored in an
irregularity of explosive snorts that went through Lialla like
a bolt, and the impending dread of the sudden noise made
the shock increasingly worse as night wore on. She could *stop*
the woman snoring—the Thread she'd used to gain Jennifer's
attention in that deserted hillside village so many years ago
would tug at anyone, Wielder or no, and Emalya'd snort once
more, roll over, be silent awhile. Long enough that Lialla
could get to sleep if sleep were at all possible at that point.
Long enough to let her loop through another series of de-
pressing thoughts otherwise.

How many days now? Lialla counted the fingers of one
hand, the thumb and forefinger of the other, sighed quietly,
rubbed the tip of her icy nose and stuffed the fingers between
her knees, let her eyes close. There had been one or two days
when she'd done nothing but stay inside the old Wielder's
house; Sretha had been interested in Lialla's peculiar use of

magic but they hadn't dared talk much about it, with Emalya and the children underfoot nearly all the time.

The children: Emalya hadn't yet adjusted to letting them run with the village children, and the children themselves were still trying to take in the enormous changes in their lives: the death of their overbearing and harsh-tempered father, the sudden move from the city they'd always known to this village. They didn't want to stray from where they could see Emalya—and while Lialla could scarcely blame them for that, they made *her* nervous. They seldom spoke and never to anyone but Emalya; they moved like a four-footed wraith. She'd look up from what she was doing to find them simply there, staring doubtfully at her. If she smiled, or spoke, or even looked back, they'd go away, but she'd feel eyes on her from someplace else. Emalya made up for the children, constantly chattering to them, or to her sister, or to the new novice—to herself, if no one else was listening to her.

The village—Sretha usually found a reason to go into the village once a day, and took her "novice" with her when she delivered medicines or visited an ill woman or child. Lialla was glad to get out of the hut, but the village itself was a trial: Unless the weather was wet or foggy, there were men, and she found their silent stares unnerving—as they surely meant them. There had been three trips to the shore for shellfish, and by now she'd spoken to most of the women. It didn't get easier, and though Ryselle had enthusiastically endorsed her, she could still see doubt in other eyes; women who were almost too downtrodden and afraid to listen to her, older women who found her single state—and what they saw as her inner strength—to be unfeminine, her words and ideas therefore not anything they could use. Younger women who wanted vast and immediate change, who eyed each other sideways while she spoke, whose twisted lips clearly said, "We risked everything to bring in an outsider to help us, and *this* poor creature is all we could get?"

She tried to ignore the distractions of such women, knowing that they would only lower her belief in herself to the point where she'd begin to stammer and babble, and then none of them would listen to her. Her sense of self-worth was still shaky enough; something she hadn't properly realized until it was so challenged here.

Sixteen days until the caravan came back through, she reminded herself. She could leave then, if she still felt so uncomfortable. In the meantime, she *did* have important things to tell these women—everything she knew about life outside Holmaddan; about Jennifer and Robyn, about her own life in Duke's Fort. About the changes in the Zelharri market, and how some of those had come about. How laziness on the part of some farm men—or a lack of time and outside help in the fields—combined with an appreciation of the additional money brought in by their women had allowed the farm women to eventually set up their own stalls.

It wasn't enough to satisfy some of the younger women, who were even more set on change than Ryselle; it looked to Lialla as though the more conservative women weren't ready for even that much shift, though such women seldom spoke once they'd established that the sin-Duchess was unwed and childless at the dreadfully old age of thirty-two. It was, Lialla tried to remind herself, a start. Reminded herself that the village men were ripe for such a subtle shift in control. The North Bay men were supposedly full-time ocean-going fishermen—a trade held to be exhausting, time-consuming, dangerous work. In actual fact, they and other coastal-village men like them went out to sea very few days a year and ate more shellfish than cod or smelt. Lazy. Ryselle had grasped that at once; all the same, Lialla reminded herself, Ryselle had no better luck selling the notion to the doubtful women than had the Wielder's new novice.

It didn't help. As the days wore on, Lialla found that though she organized her thoughts better and spoke more to the point than she had that first day, she felt less comfortable when she finished speaking. And there were one or two of the women who made her nervous, the conservative ones who seldom protested anything she said but looked increasingly unhappy. If one of them said something at the wrong moment—! *No. They're women; if you can't trust your own sex, especially at a time and place such as this, there's no one you can trust.* She did broach the subject one evening with Sretha, when Emalya and the children had gone to take a walk and visit with her eldest child. Sretha had listened carefully but dismissed Lialla's fears as groundless. "Remember the penalty any of us would pay. Any women who spoke out could face death as well, since the men would know she must have been among the rebellious, if she knew what was said.''

Perhaps. Lialla told herself to maintain as strong a trust as she could but not to be foolish about it. After all, it was her neck, too.

And then, there was Kepron—that boy of Emalya's who, since he had turned fifteen, lived with the other single men in the longhouse at the center of the village. He must have resembled the dead guardsman husband; she'd never have known the tall, dark-skinned, slender boy with the shock of black hair falling over his forehead for kin of Emalya's *or* Sretha's. His face was still boyishly round and beardless, but his pale gray eyes and the hard set of his wide, thin-lipped mouth belied that youth.

When had she first seen him, to be aware of him—yesterday? The day before? Lialla pulled her knees up toward her chest, tucked the innermost blanket around her shins and shrugged the thought aside impatiently; who cared *when* she'd seen him? She had been following just behind Sretha on the way into the village with a packet of raspberry leaf tea for women's complaint when someone with a reedy, treble voice spoke to the older woman. Startled, she'd glanced up, then immediately away once she realized the speaker was a young male whose voice hadn't yet broken. But not quickly enough: The boy had met her eyes challengingly, angrily, and there'd been enough threat in his face that she'd fallen back a pace before Sretha's hand on her arm restrained her.

"Kepron, there's no point to this; you'll only do yourself harm. The matter was decided and there was nothing I could have done to make it different for you.'' Silence. Lialla heard the boy spit. "I'm *sorry*." She sounded more harassed than sorry.

"I wanted—"

"I know what you wanted, boy.''

"Man,'' he said. The word might have been a curse, the way he spoke it. "Man of North Bay.'' And now there was no doubting the sarcasm and anger in his voice.

Sretha sighed heavily and tugged at Lialla's arm to get her moving. "Come to see your mother. You know it's permitted, and she misses you.''

"*She* chose to return here, not I.'' When Lialla risked a

glance to the side, she saw the boy striding rapidly across the open sandy ground, away from the village and toward the water. Fury absolutely radiated from him.

They'd gone about their business, delivered the herb, spoken briefly to Ryselle as they crossed paths—they going back to the Wielder's hut, Ryselle carrying milk home to make into cheese. "Make me up a packet of dried rosemary and sage if you will, Wielder. And if you have them. To pat onto a cheese or two. I'll come and collect them, and bring you a fresh cheese."

Sretha nodded. "I've both, and a cheese would be welcome. The children scarcely seem to eat, but Emalya more than makes up for them—though she claims to be too upset to eat at all."

Ryselle laughed, sent her eyes sideways to check the porch of the longhouse—empty at the moment, scarcely surprising with the north wind blowing straight down the cut from the ocean into the village. Lialla hunched her shoulders against it; Ryselle caught her eyes and gravely closed one of her own. "I'll come—let me see, it won't be until day after tomorrow that I shape them, will that do? I saw," she added quickly and quietly, "the boy accost you. Is everything all right?"

"Fine," Sretha replied in kind. "He's difficult; it's been too much change for him."

"Difficult," Ryselle snorted. She raised her voice to normal once more as one of the older men stepped down from the veranda and began walking slowly toward the street. "It's done, then. If you need a second cheese or more milk for the little ones, send word." She inclined her head as the older man passed them—he ignored all three women and Lialla had to take a hasty step back to avoid being run down. Ryselle made a quick face at his back, then picked up her bucket and hurried toward her home. Lialla swallowed—Ryselle really *was* dangerous—and clamped her eyes on the dusty, sandy little street, on Sretha's bare feet and the hems of her ancient Blacks as they went the other direction.

That night? It must have been the next night; Emalya had been persuaded to go help one of the village women she'd grown up with, to take the children. Ryselle tapped at the rear door only moments after the three left. "Your cheese, Wielder," she said grandly and held out a thick wheel almost as big across as Lialla's forearm and thicker than she could grasp between thumb and forefinger. Sretha shook her head.

"It's much too large for an exchange—"

"It's to make certain you and *Ursiu*"—she put the usual dry emphasis on Lialla's pseudonym—"get some. We know Emalya will! And there was so much extra milk, even with the men taking their usual half to ferment—" She cast her eyes up briefly, grinned and took a seat at the Wielder's table. "Now. What was all that with Kepron? He's a grand young nuisance, always out and around the village by himself—some of the older men like Father are growing impatient with him; Sretha, if you can warn him to settle down and at least seem to follow the way things are done around here, it'll save him a beating. Not that he doesn't deserve one, but Emalya would fuss for*ever*."

"I'll try. As if he listened to me, or your father, or his mother—or anyone else." Sretha sighed. She turned to Lialla. "The boy on the road. Emalya wouldn't let him stay in the city; she insisted he come. Not that he's old enough to have gone for the guard, but he was certainly old enough to have fed and housed himself by running messages, and the guard would have taken him in as the son of one of theirs anyway."

"*He* says," Ryselle reminded her. "He's male, he's young, and he's in a strange state; I don't trust *his* words."

"Ah, but his mother says as much, too. She wouldn't let him stay. I think myself she's sorry now; she had to let him go live with the other young men, so she hasn't got him with her anyway, and she can see how unhappy he is. Of course, this other thing—"

"He's male," Ryselle broke in, and she sounded almost angry.

"Men *can* Wield," Sretha said calmly. "Ask her."

"There are at least as many male Wielders in the south as there are women," Lialla said. "Why?"

"Because the boy apparently saw a good deal of magic in the city—and he was drawn to it. I gather his father would have beaten him senseless for ever saying as much, but his mother knew, and once his father died, he dared hope he could find a Wielder who would take him for an apprentice. It's utterly impossible in a village, of course, but in the city it *could* have been done—very quietly, you understand, but still not out of the question. By his mother's words, he had hopes, once he'd learned enough and earned a little money running errands for his father's garrison, to leave Holmaddan with one of the caravans and seek his fortune, possibly in Sikkre, perhaps even oversea. I don't doubt that was why Emalya insisted he come to North Bay with her, to keep him leaving her for good and all. When he learned I was a Wielder, and that I had no apprentice, he thought it somehow possible that I could secretly tutor him, even if I could not take him into my house.''

"If you did—" Ryselle shook her head.

"If I had, and been caught at it? And I would have been caught eventually. The boy has no sense of how to keep a secret—only look at his behavior around the village; would anyone know how displeased he is with his present way of life? He'd be crippled for life, and I'd have found myself digging my own hole at the low tide mark, so I could be left to drown at high," Sretha said. "Let it go, Ryselle; the whole affair is beyond either of us, and it makes you angry to no point. There are more important matters than young Kepron.''

"Not if he's still fussing, and if he's giving trouble to your apprentice," Ryselle said flatly. She touched Lialla's arm. "Avoid that young male whenever you can; he's gone through their initiation and still doesn't understand how strictly laws and rules are enforced in a village. I don't doubt that if he heard your voice he'd know you aren't Holmaddan-born—and he'd report you to my father. Worse, he might devise some scheme of his own and cause even more trouble.''

"Gods," Lialla mumbled; she'd merely nodded when Ryselle asked what she'd said. An angry boy, hurting and looking for someone to blame for his current placing—it was absolutely all she'd needed, atop everything else.

LIALLA readjusted her blankets, mumbling curses under her breath. It had often seemed knife-blade cold in Duke's Fort, of a snowbound midwinter night or a foggy and fitfully rainy spring afternoon—never, ever anything like this. She simply couldn't get properly warm, even curled in on herself as she ordinarily slept.

It had been three days ago, she decided, that she'd first

encountered Kepron. Because Ryselle had come the day after with the cheese—which meant it was yesterday when she'd heard the warning.

"Beloved Gods of the Warm Silences," she whispered, "if I knew who spoke, and whether it was intended to warn or simply scare me—!" She'd gone down to the circle of shrubbery to wait for Sretha, who had been momentarily detained by her sister's chatter. She'd gotten damper than usual, squeezing through the growth and into the open, and there wasn't much sun; she'd sat for a few minutes, feet drawn under her, arms clutched across her chest, but finally she'd stood again and began to pace the tiny clearing. Three paces, turn; three paces, turn; pause and work out a cramp trying to start in the left toes; three paces, turn. Stop at the point nearest the path back to the Wielder's hut and listen for Sretha. If the woman didn't come pretty quickly, she was going to go back in herself. The tip of her nose was icy and dripping; she couldn't feel her earlobes.

Silence. And then the faintest crackle in the brush outside—a mouse, she thought dismissively, then stiffened as dry branches crunched under what must be a full-sized human foot. She held her breath but couldn't hear anything except the whine of wind across the sand above and behind her, the pounding her heart made in her ears. And then the whisper, a sexless, penetrating whisper that cut through everything: "One of the women has betrayed you. Flee or die."

Lialla swallowed, clenching her hands into fists and dove back through the opening, too frightened and angry at the same time to even think of Thread. It wouldn't, she realized later, have identified the whisperer, but if she'd had enough time to braid rope, she might have snagged the person. As it was, there wasn't even time for her to reach the path and see anything but a shadowy figure that vanished eastward, across the ridge. She threw herself after, but plunged at once into loose dry sand and slid all the way down to the path again.

Sretha came into view a moment later, as she stood mumbling, cursing inventively and shaking as much sand out of damp clothes and her boots as she could.

SHE hadn't wanted to talk about it just then; she would have liked a little time to think. But Sretha had been terribly curious why her supposed novice was standing mid-path, covered in sand and white to the lips; Lialla couldn't really blame her. She followed the older Wielder back into the brush, getting another good soaking. Her fingertips had gone numb.

Sretha sat with her knees drawn up, arms hugging her legs, a frown creasing her forehead. "That's all? Not that it isn't enough, of course, I don't wonder you've gone so pale, but—that's all you heard or saw?" Lialla shrugged. The furrow between the other woman's brows deepened and she finally shook her head. "It could have been anyone, really—not one of the children, of course. Not me or Emalya, since I was trying to get away from her at the back door. Not that you know this other than that I tell you, of course—"

Lialla laughed humorlessly. "You of all people have no cause to sneak up on me that way, Sretha. And honestly, I can't imagine your sister clambering up that bank."

"No." Sretha chuckled. "I can't, either. She wasn't much good at such things even as a child." She sobered abruptly. "It can't have been any of the men, of course."

"Of course." Lialla stopped, stared across the other woman's head for a long moment.

"What? You've remembered something else?"

"What you said. If it were Kepron? No, wait—let me think it through. He's young and he looks muscular enough to have run up that slope, loose sand and all. I'm in reasonably good shape, Sretha, and I couldn't even come close; could any of your women race up such a bank? And—all right, I don't want to think any of our number would betray us, but if she did, found a way to do that so she wouldn't be one of the punished—how would another woman hear of it to warn me? If *you* did that, would you tell anyone else, or would you keep it secret?"

"I'd *have* to keep silent," Sretha said slowly, as though working it out while she spoke. "Because if women I'd known my whole life died because of me, and someone learned what I'd done, I wouldn't survive very long. But, *if* one of us betrayed us, another woman could easily have heard the men talking when she went to feed them. She might come in secret to warn you."

"Perhaps," Lialla said. She shivered down into her Blacks, tucked her fingers into her armpits for warmth. "I wonder that even men as foolish as yours are supposed to be don't notice women in their midst. And if they had learned the women were growing restive, even fools would be aware of the women around them, and watch their tongues. It makes more sense if it was Kepron who'd heard something in the long house—''

''And you think he'd warn you? More likely if he learned or suspected something was happening, he'd tell the men,'' Sretha said. She touched Lialla's cheek. ''No wonder you're white; you must be chilled all the way through. We'd better go in. We can come back out here in the morning.''

Lialla merely nodded and followed her; her shoulder blades, and the vulnerable space between them, itched all the way back inside.

THEY discussed it fully the next morning. Sretha found an excuse, in the form of a packet of grain, to visit the headman's daughter; Ryselle didn't understand Wielder hand signs but she could read the distress in Lialla's face, the wary concern in Sretha's, and she led them out to the goat pens. ''We won't be disturbed here, or overheard. What's wrong?'' Sretha glanced at Lialla, who shrugged, and told her.

To her credit, Ryselle didn't go on the defensive as Lialla had half expected; she stood in the shadow of the goat's pen and thought, hard. Finally shook her head. ''I don't know who it could be, and that's worrying. I evaluated the women, I made certain this was as safe as it could be before we brought in an outsider. I'd have sworn there was no one who'd risk a final saltwater bath to betray us. All the same—'' She fixed Lialla with a very direct stare. ''You'll tell me I say this because I'm a woman and everyone knows I would do without all men, for any purpose, if only I could. I don't know who came to warn you last night, but I think if anyone's betrayed us, it's Kepron. Only look at him! He's not always in with the men, he's out and about the village and down on the shore too much for my liking. So he could have overheard something and spoke of it to my father, or one of the other men. And it still could have been Kepron who hissed at you last night, if he realized the consequences of what he'd done. He's young, after all, and I've heard so much from his mother about how deeply he feels things. It's just possible he's capable of remorse.'' She sighed. ''It's also possible Kepron or someone else was simply playing a joke—''

''A joke?'' Lialla's voice cracked on the word; she clapped a hand over her mouth.

''It's possible. 'All is known, fly,' '' Ryselle said dryly. ''It's from an old story I've heard since I was barely old enough to walk; every Holmaddi knows it, I'd wager. It could be Kepron, hoping to frighten you into going away, so he'd have a chance with Sretha—''

''As if he would,'' Sretha said indignantly. ''As if I could teach him anything without your father having the skin off both of us!''

''Well, yes, I know that and so do you, but Kepron doesn't seem able to understand anything that simple.'' She was quiet again for a moment. ''I truly think that's a more likely answer than any real danger. But it would be stupid to let it go at that; I'll go about the village today and see what I can find out. If there's anything, I'll learn of it.''

They left her mucking smelly straw out of one of the milking stalls. The day was no warmer than the previous one; there were no men on the street or anywhere in sight. Sretha spoke quietly, keeping her face expressionless as she walked. ''She's right, you know; both that it's the most likely answer, and that she'll find out if there's a woman having second thoughts—or if the boy's up to something.''

''Good.'' Lialla's voice still didn't want to stay down where it belonged; she let it go at that.

ANOTHER wakeful night, though this time she hadn't needed Emalya to keep her awake. *Logic it out,* Chris would have said. She lay flat on her back and went at it from every angle she could think of. Unfortunately, she still didn't have a face to go with that chilling whisper. But there was only one answer that finally fit into the odd-shaped puzzle.

Unless it *had* been a bad joke, or simply an attempt to frighten her away. Lialla shifted on hard bedding and swallowed; she wished she could think that, but that didn't fit nearly as well as the unpleasant answer she'd worked out.

IT was, unfortunately, the right one. Sretha rose as usual in the last black moments before dawn, started the fire, brewed her tea and cut bread. Once the scent of tea and the first teasing warmth touched her nose, Lialla shivered out of her blankets and ran barefoot across the main room to join the older woman. She glanced back into the room, mildly surprised at the quiet. Even if she wasn't snoring, Emalya was usually making some kind of odd little noise. It was dark in the corner where the woman had her blankets, though, and Lialla finally shrugged, went into the warmth and light of the tiny back room. Sretha had heard her coming; a large, thick mug of tea awaited her, a lozenge of honey next to it and a triangular chunk of warm bread. Lialla forgot about Emalya and bit into it, dropped the honey into her tea and tried to blink herself awake. *When I get home,* she thought wistfully, *I'll die before I get up this early, ever again!* Home. It seemed a year or more since she'd seen Duke's Fort, and she wondered how Aletto was dealing with her absence. Worried, probably. She found herself hoping he wasn't taking it out on Robyn and realized uncomfortably it was the first time she'd considered *that* possibility. Poor Robyn just hated being in the middle of anyone's fight; this would really upset her. Of course, Aletto knew that, too.

She held out the half-empty mug as Sretha brought the kettle over from the stove. Lialla tensed, turned away to stare out across the main room; Thread was vibrating all around her, grabbing her attention, partly awake as she was. She dove into access, pulled out of it and opened her mouth to warn Sretha. But the older Wielder had felt it, too.

"Men," she hissed. "Many of them. Here—quick, set that down, out the back way, go!" But there was a heavy jangling vibration at the back of the hut, too. Men everywhere. No time. Lialla swallowed hard and gripped Sretha's wrist.

"Don't say *anything* unless you must. Follow my lead!" And, as Sretha hesitated, "Do it!"

The other woman might have nodded; Lialla had already turned away and shoved to her feet as the rear door flew open and slammed against the wall. Men poured through it; a crash from the front of the house and more men came up behind her. Men in armor and proper house colors—*Duke's men,* Lialla thought dazedly. *Not village men. Not a village woman to betray; Emalya.* It had to be Emalya. She glanced down at the older woman, who sat, trembling, at the small rough table. If it was Emalya, it might make Lialla's task somewhat easier. *Easier for everyone but me*, she thought, and was immediately sorry she'd thought it. Her knees wanted to buckle all at once. Sretha looked at her, and Lialla crossed her arms over her chest, laying her right hand against her shoulder in the sign they'd worked out for the Wielder's widowed sister. Sretha's shoulders sagged; she'd understood, all right.

An officer pressed into the room through the back door, through the guardsmen. "Watch them closely and remember they both have magic."

"Night-Thread Magic," someone mumbled, and promptly fell silent as the officer raked them with a chill gaze.

"It's not completely ineffective. Watch them closely." He dismissed Sretha with a glance, jabbed a finger at Lialla. "We were told there was a female in this village who had no business being here—one represented to be a novice Wielder from another village. Yet she speaks with a southern accent, and while her outer clothing might be the usual stuff worn by such novices and Wielders, her inner things are finely wrought, like foreign. Tell me, *novice*, how a village lass gets any coin at all, let alone enough to purchase such garb? Or where she would obtain it?" Lialla swallowed, shook her head. "There are women in the Duke's city preaching sedition, and so we were sent to make a tour of the coastal villages to be certain such sedition didn't spread. Would you be surprised to learn there are *no* young women gone from village Gray Haven? Either of you?"

Lialla swallowed again and drew in a deep breath to keep the quaver out of her voice. Jennifer would surely be proud of her, how calm she sounded. "No. I wouldn't be surprised. The Wielder didn't know, either."

"Impossible!"

"It isn't. I met her on the road near Gray Haven, and like most old women, she chatted without any pressure. I persuaded her I was what she wanted, offered to carry her letter back to my village. Sent her my own, supposedly from the headman of Gray Haven and came at once. How was she to have known? Should she have questioned that headman to make certain he'd sent her a novice?"

She didn't think he was going to accept it; he glared down

at Sretha, back at Lialla, then at Sretha once again, who shrank away from him. "Well?"

"It's true, sir; perhaps I should have—"

"Never mind." *Stupid woman, what else would a man expect?* Lialla could almost read the thought in the set of his mouth. He turned on her so suddenly she jumped. "Why?"

"My own reasons," she said flatly. Sretha caught her breath loudly as the officer drew a thick-bladed dagger and nodded to two of his men; they came up behind Lialla and caught hold of her arms, pinning her motionless between them. The dagger moved across her line of vision and settled at the base of her throat.

"I asked a question. That was no answer." He paused; the tip of the blade broke skin and a thin trickle of blood ran down her breast. "Or, perhaps it was. What village woman would dare speak to a man so? Who are you?"

She was sweating, the sweat stung where he'd cut. "The city women sent me, to see if I couldn't help these." She looked over at Sretha and let her lips twist. "You see how likely *that* is. I've been here a double handful of days and found no one I'd dare speak to—and now it seems it didn't matter whether I spoke or not." *Sretha, keep quiet!* she thought urgently. Whether by intent or the shock of a houseful of armed men sent by her own sister, Sretha seemed unable to say anything, barely able to keep herself sitting upright.

The dagger stayed hard against her throat. Silence; a very long silence. Finally, he stepped back and nodded. "We'll ask in the village, of course. It doesn't matter whether you've spoken to other women or not. They'll see why it would be better if they didn't recall what you told them." He motioned the guards to bring her.

There was a silent crowd on the opposite side of the road; openly curious men, wary-looking women, most of them covered to the eyes. One or two older children who gaped at the horses, the armor, the bared swords. The officer turned toward the village; Lialla's guards brought her right behind him. She could hear the murmur of voices behind: villagers, the rest of the guardsmen, very likely Sretha. The officer beckoned to one of his men, who listened and then ran on ahead.

It hadn't ever seemed to take so long before to reach the main street of the village.

The sun was nearly up by the time they stopped, just in front of the men's longhouse. By the looks of it, every person in the village had been wakened. The officer jumped onto the longhouse veranda and held up his arms for silence. "This woman, as *some* of you may know"—his hard gaze swept across little huddles of frightened women—"is not from Gray Haven! She—well, I will speak to your headman later about her purpose in being here." *Thinking all the time, don't give women ideas, just in case*, Lialla thought, and almost laughed. She bit her lip; it wasn't funny, she was light-headed.

She could make out faces, suddenly; Ryselle, one of the few women who hadn't covered her lower face, her eyes black and wide, her mouth grimly set; Sretha, among guardsmen but not held as she herself was. The older woman looked near collapse; Lialla could only hope she would keep her mouth closed and damaging words unsaid.

The sun came over the hill, blinding her; she turned away, blinking furiously. The guards officer was speaking again. "I *will* say that what she hoped to accomplish counts as sedition and treason! And so, as a warning to you all, and lest you doubt your Duke's feelings about his laws and how he wishes you to obey them—" He sheathed the dagger he'd carried openly all the way from Sretha's house, and drew his sword. Like the dagger, it was long-bladed, very thick, and it had a two-handed hilt. One edge had been freshly honed and looked wickedly sharp. Sunlight hit it and broke into a million blinding shards. A child was crying and now a woman far back in the crowd screamed as the two men holding her thrust Lialla hard forward and down, onto her knees. She fought instinctively but to no avail—the two were much stronger and above her anyway. Her knees stung, there was something hard against the side of her neck. Another woman screamed; Lialla twisted her head sideways and looked up to see the officer standing over her, the sword high above his head.

INSTINCT saved her. The man shifted his stance, cocked his wrists and Lialla shouted above the noise of crying women: "Don't you dare! I'm Duke Aletto's sister, the sin-duchess of Zelharri!" The officer went utterly still, looked down at her in sudden doubt. "I'm the sister of Duke Aletto of Zelharri, I'm noble; you don't *dare* behead me like a common thief!"

"What proof?" The officer hadn't moved; the sword still hung above her.

"You named it yourself—my clothing. Send word to my brother, he'll identify me."

"He knows you came here—he *permitted* this?"

"*No one* governs the actions of a Zelharri noblewoman!" Lialla snarled. "But I left messages in the south before I crossed the border; my brother will know where I've gone if I don't return." She fought air into her lungs, fought not to give in to tears or wild trembling. Kept fury foremost in her thought, her only possible salvation at the moment. "A public execution! Do you think word won't get out, however you terrify these poor people? And how do you think your Duke will feel when he learns you've killed a noblewoman— whatever her actions?"

The sword came down, slowly; it lay across the officer's shoulder. "I wonder how well you'll do, fencing words with my Duke? You've delayed this, nothing more." He didn't sound sure of his words, though. Lialla went limp as the two men dragged her to her feet; the world spun and went black. When she next became aware of her surroundings, she had been bound and thrown into a closed cart which was creaking and bouncing along a rough road. *I'm still alive. Gods. I think I am.* She wedged herself into a corner and let her eyes close.

The next time she opened them, the cart had stopped moving, but she could hear men outside, moving around—setting up camp, she guessed. The air was colder than it had been, perhaps a little less stuffy than earlier. Darker, too. She pressed her face against rough boards and was rewarded with the least glimpse of brush, a long expanse of moonlit sand, distant surf. The men paid no attention to her at all. Someone lit a fire nearby; she could smell meat being cooked and realized with a pang she hadn't even had time to eat Sretha's bread this morning. Thirst was an even greater discomfort. Well, if they didn't dare behead her, they surely wouldn't dare starve her to death, either.

Someone had moved away from the general pack of men; she could make out at least two separate voices near the front

of the cart. One, she thought, was that of the officer who'd
nearly killed her, the other was higher, more resonant—Kepron's? *You're silly from lack of food and water,* she told
herself sternly. But she edged across the cart, wincing at pressure on bruised knees, leaned into the wall so she could hear.

"Sir, I can't tell you how grateful I am."

"Nonsense. The company was sorry when your father died,
lad; they'd have had you right then but your mother still had
the say of you. I'd have sent someone as soon as you turned
man but there's been so much activity around the city. We
can use you."

"Sir, really—"

"There's a whole new trade coming through, foreign ships
and a new cargo, the Duke's sent us to guard a few special
caravans south to the border; with this problem with the
women atop the rest, we're shorthanded, so I don't doubt I
can convince my captain to waive the age requirement for
you."

"Thank you, sir." Momentary silence. "Did my mother
really send word to you that that woman was a fraud? I didn't
think she had that much wit."

"And what female has?" the officer asked dryly. Both
laughed. "Well, I must admit—though I'd never admit it to
her—that I'd not have thought to look at the woman's under-
garments. I'd never have looked at those foreign knitted
stockings and realized it was suspicious for a poor Gray Haven girl to own them." His voice dropped; Lialla tried hard
but could make out none of what he said. Both laughed once
again. "Tell you what; there's a small slide-hatch in the back
door. Take her a little water, in case she's who she claims to
be? I've heard a little of this Zelharri Duke; he's formidable
they say, for one both young and crippled, and he has the ear
of the Emperor's brother *and* the Duke of Sikkre, Thukar
Dahven. No one would cross *him.*"

"I'll do it if you say, sir."

"That's the spirit, boy." It sounded to Lialla as though the
officer clapped the boy on the back. "Take the unpleasant
orders with such good spirit, you'll get more of the better.
I'd better go set the watches, you come eat something once
you're done." The sound of feet crunching off in two separate
directions.

Lialla let her head fall back, closed her eyes and tried to think. Not easy. After a few minutes she gave it up and edged toward the back of the cart. Almost at once, she heard a faint tap against the wood, saw a dim square of light and then a hand. "Here, woman," the boy's reedy voice said loudly and roughly. "It's water. Take it or I'll let it fall." Someone laughed. But the hand that held the cup held it steady until she got her fingers to go around it—no easy task with her wrists so tightly tied together. "Here," the boy added in a low and noncarrying voice, "I'll hold, you drink." Lialla nodded, bent her head. She got most of it inside her, a little down the front, a bit up her nose when the boy tipped the cup too fast. "I don't know if they mean to feed you to-night," he added in that same low voice, and she could have sworn he sounded apologetic.

"Doesn't matter," Lialla replied softly. "Thank you."

"Thank me later. When you're free and safely out of Hol-maddan. I know you have no real cause to, but trust me." Before she could say anything else, or pull her sagging jaw back up and her mouth closed, the hatch slammed shut and the boy strode off. Distantly, she could hear his high voice making some sneering remark, half a dozen men laughing raucously at whatever he'd said.

12

IT had turned cool in Sikkre—there had even been a little rain to dampen the paving the second day after Robyn left for Zelharri. The morning after that, Jennifer watched from one of the windows in the family apartments as the American engineers set the final telegraph pole in place just inside the palace gates. They didn't look happy, and she couldn't blame them: There was a strong wind that blew dirt and then very fine, stinging rain. The windows in the palace weren't that well set in their frames; Jennifer shivered as a damp, chill gust whistled through cracks and across her throat. She pulled the thick robe close and turned away. Siohan was bringing her breakfast and had sent one of the household to build a fire in the bedroom hearth.

"I'm letting them coddle me," Jennifer mumbled. Siohan liked it, of course; the rest of the staff didn't seem to find it out of line and probably the cooks loved not having her underfoot. Jennifer sighed, sank into a cushioned chair near the fire. *She* hated it, but she hadn't yet been able to snap back from the shock of that last attack, everything else that had happened that night. She slept long, hard hours and still woke drained and queasy; just now, the thought of coffee made her feel a little bilious, though she needed the caffeine—without it, she knew she'd fall right back to sleep and not waken until noon. There was too much to accomplish around here for that sort of indulgence. Jennifer let the collar of the robe fall loose and considered—how long *had* it been since she'd slept past ten? All the way back to L.A., before college even.

This morning, she'd have to get moving, however she felt:

She had overdue responses to a consortium of merchants in Bezjeriad, her usual letters and opinions to Afronsan. And Dahven had sent word up that Afronsan's clerk had just arrived—Jennifer hoped the man had come to assure the Thukar he'd acted within bounds. Officially, Dahven said, the man was in Sikkre to take statements from everyone involved—only should Afronsan need to make explanations to the Emperor at a later time. Which sounded reassuring. She wouldn't let herself dwell on the other possibilities; it would interfere with what she had to accomplish by day's end—a sheaf of documents, contracts, trade suggestions, two opinions on new trade rules to send back to Podhru with the clerk. She needed to write to Robyn, to suggest she write out and send Afronsan her own account as soon as possible.

And according to an outline-note from one of her clerks, Afronsan had sent along a new pile of paperwork for her. There were more proposed trade rules, additional documents for exchanges, a long letter that covered everything from his worries over the illegal trade in the foreign drug to the attacks on her and Dahven, to Chris's news, to more positive things: the telegraph lines were being installed much more quickly than they had originally thought; the newly widened and refinished road from Bez to Podhru was nearly done; the cotton seed the Americans had brought in was already showing promise of a good crop on a number of farms in the most northwesterly corner of Andar Perigha, and on the Emperor's estates, the English merino sheep had more than doubled in number. There was still argument between Emperor and heir over the need for Americans to set up the mechanized mills for preparation of cotton thread and cloth, but Afronsan was confident he'd eventually prevail, particularly if the Thukara could send him a list of positive reasons for such mills—and *if* the Thukara had an opportunity, would she mind helping him work out the following list of bargaining points between Rhadaz and the Mer Khani regarding the mills?

The clerk must have been in the offices at first light, to be able to send her down such a detailed summary at such an early hour, Jennifer thought. *Make sure he knows it's appreciated*, she thought, and fished around for one of her few remaining pencils to make herself a note on the bottom of the clerk's missive. She'd feel awful if things got hectic and she forgot.

It would take days to prepare a response to all that, Jennifer realized. Besides, Afronsan would have left things unspoken that she could read between the lines—he was probably hoping she'd travel down to Podhru and spend a week helping him sort things out. *I can't,* she thought in despair. This once Afronsan would have to understand—surely he would, once he knew what she'd been through the past several days.

It sounded as though they'd be able to telegraph messages back and forth before summer's end, though. Jennifer sank back into the cushions and extended her feet to the fire. "Probably just mean I get three times the paperwork from him, and some poor telegraph operator in Podhru gets carpal tunnel syndrome. To say nothing of some poor sap in Sikkre. Oh, for fax, and a telephone, and an IBM . . ."

"Lady?" Siohan had come quietly and unnoticed into the room with her breakfast. Jennifer jumped and caught her breath. "I'm sorry, I didn't mean to startle you."

"Not your fault, Siohan, I'll get over it anyway. And I was just talking to myself." Her stomach twisted alarmingly as the woman set a tray across the arms of the chair, and the mixed odors of hot coffee, fresh fruit bread and a newly cut orange hit her. She clutched at her sleeves, pressing her arms across her abdomen, briefly closed her eyes. She opened them to find Siohan bending over her, her own eyes wide and worried. "All right," she managed and tried a smile. "Just a little—mmmm, yeah. I think some of the bread first, maybe."

Siohan was already reaching for it, cutting a chunk for her, getting the coffee back so the steam wasn't right under her nose. "Let me, Lady. Here. And there's water."

"Good." It took an effort; Jennifer bit into the bread, chewed cautiously for a full minute before daring to swallow. She sat back, waited, finally nodded and took another bite. "I think—I think that's better." She took a small sip of water, another bite of bread, conscious of Siohan watching her closely.

"Lady, if you don't mind, a personal question?"

"As much as you do for me?" Jennifer managed a smile, took another bite of bread. Much, much better, she thought, and picked up her coffee. This time, it just smelled like good, fairly strong brew—stronger than the kitchen staff would make, still not as strong as her own, but probably easier on her stomach the way Siohan did it. "Ask."

"Well, it occurs to me—when was the last time the Thukar's man bought him a new band?"

It took her a minute; Jennifer drank coffee, thought in mild wonder, *band*? It hit, then: the silver arm band Dahven wore about his left elbow, with the market charm worked into it that prevented children. She set the cup down with a clunk, stared wide-eyed at the fire. "I don't know. I have no idea. It's been so crazy around here, I hadn't even thought—Oh, Lord. You don't think?"

"I think I should ask him, or you should ask the Thukar," Siohan said firmly. "Because, frankly, you're looking and acting just the way my wedded sister did last year. And Pila, down in the kitchens, they had to find her work elsewhere, until the smell of food stopped making her ill." She paused; Jennifer met her eyes but seemed incapable of words. "Both were newly pregnant, Lady."

"Oh." It was all she could find to say. She couldn't tell what she felt. Besides stunned. *But Dahven—* "Dahven will be delighted—if it's so."

Siohan nodded. "I think the Thukar will be pleased."

"But it's just a guess—"

"A strong one. I'll find the Thukar's man at once, if you like, see what he can tell me about the band. And perhaps we should call in a midwife, to examine you."

Jennifer felt a qualm, readily identifiable as fear. She tried to put it aside, reminding herself firmly that Robyn had made do with Rhadazi midwives, that other women did all the time. That it wasn't necessary to have Blue Cross, an ob-gyn and a gleamingly sterile hospital. A part of her mind retorted, *Oh, yah*? "If you know of a good one, Siohan."

Siohan considered this. "The woman who took care of my wedded sister, if I recall, she's the daughter of the woman who was midwife to the last two Thukaras. She's prone to gossip, though. The woman who is caring for Pila is said to be a good midwife, and Evari who had her before—she cleans and waits table for banquets—"

"I know Evari."

"Well, Evari had her because she has yet to lose a mother

or a child, young as she is. And since she comes here often anyway, to see Pila, it wouldn't cause the speculation in the market that might be caused should we send for old Min.''

"Gossip." Jennifer made a face.

"Just so." Siohan poured her fresh water, more coffee, and cut up the rest of the bread. "And there's enough gossip about at the moment; why add to it with speculation about such a personal matter?"

More than enough, Jennifer thought sourly. She drank coffee, nodded. "Let's at least find out for certain first. If we can. Ask the woman if she'll come. We'll truly need discretion, though, Siohan. If the Thukar's brothers are behind the attacks on both of us, and they thought I was carrying his heir, they might decide to step up their efforts.''

"Well, it's nothing we can keep quiet forever," the woman reminded her bluntly. "But it may be four moon-seasons or more before you'll have to announce it. Before it's obvious."

If I'm pregnant. She still couldn't decide how she felt, and she wondered suddenly if Dahven really would be pleased. It was just as likely he'd be worried silly. Pregnancy shouldn't slow her at first—*All right, once I managed to choke down breakfast*, she amended sourly. This wasn't Victorian England, after all; the Rhadazi didn't wrap their women in cotton wool, the women themselves didn't turn into fragile, fainting little creatures once pregnant. *Even so, there'll come a time when you're the size of a truck and awkward as a duck on ice.*

She'd be truly vulnerable then. The brothers would know it. Dahven would, and it really would ruin his pleasure. "It's not fair," she mumbled flatly. Siohan paused in the doorway and looked back at her inquiringly; she waved the woman on.

Four months, with luck. Robyn hadn't been visibly pregnant with Iana until nearly six months, but then there was a major difference in the way the two women were built. *My luck, I'll poof up at the end of two, or it'll be all over the market by tomorrow.* She shook herself. "Lousy thought. Cut it out, Cray." She might not be pregnant; she might have those four months, or even more. And that might be enough time to see an end to the whole sorry mess. *An end to Deehar and Dayher,* she thought grimly. Because it was clear by now that nothing else would stop them.

And, she realized suddenly, the twins had a definite time problem of their own. Shesseran had been in failing health for years, but like many creaking gates he'd hung on despite a variety of odd illnesses and increasing mental lapses. Lately, though, there'd been alarming rumors coming from his estates in Andar Perigha: He'd developed a serious tremor in his hands, his face was all tight-stretched skin over bones, he had trouble walking and could not get to his feet without two servants to help him. In another year Afronsan might finally be Emperor. The twins knew by now Afronsan would not let them claim Sikkre, unless the circumstances were extraordinary and their own hands clean. Whatever their hopes of Shesseran, who had let them rule after the suspicious disappearance of their elder brother and the almost immediate, even more suspicious death of their father.

She sipped coffee cautiously, then drained the cup when the liquid seemed to give her stomach no problems. Of course, there was the chance that even if they took Sikkre while Shesseran was still alive, Afronsan would toss them out of the Thukar's palace once he was crowned. She considered this from various angles as she finished the bread and ate her orange. She couldn't decide. She thought he would, but the twins seemed to have the same poor opinion of the heir that Jadek had once held: a paper pusher, no real strength or brain. The twins might think he'd have to leave them in power, since there were no other members of the family to inherit. And Afronsan might have to do just that, though he might keep a close eye on them, even put the city back on the gold standard as he had when the old Thukar died. He might send a permanent delegation of clerks to make certain the brothers didn't make a mess of the city and its market. She wondered if the twins would think such shackles worth the trade, just to rule Sikkre. They might; from what she'd seen and what Dahven had told her, neither man had much imagination and both had always focused so tightly on a goal as not to see any of the pitfalls or dangers surrounding it.

Siohan had said the Sikkreni people were outraged over the attacks on Dahven and herself, and Vey had confirmed as much. Well, it was nice being so appreciated. Jennifer didn't think that outrage would count for much if both of them were assassinated; common people didn't have a lot of clout here.

And obviously not everyone felt that anger, since Eprian managed to remain hidden. The city guards were fairly certain he was still in the city somewhere; they'd gone through various taverns and inns in the lower market. Mahjrek had been tracked down and questioned for a long time; he claimed not to know the man, which was patently untrue. They could get nothing else from him save some rather bitter comments concerning his loss of business and income and his present state of poverty. Since he was wearing a good deal of gold on his forearms, under loose silk sleeves, this wasn't taken very seriously.

Krilan, the boy who'd "escaped" from his guards on the way to the block, had run all the way into the lower market, to his sister's sweet shop. He hadn't come out of shelter since. Vey had been given the full-time assignment of watching the shop and following him if he did emerge, since Vey knew not only the streets and shops, but things most ordinary guards did not: who would allow traffic through his shop without seeming to see it; where the entries to the underground cisterns for the city water were, and where they connected to other entries within buildings; where other underground tunnels lay and how to move from shop to shop without once going into the streets.

The boy had no such access from the low, narrow and rough-built shop. His sister had a clean reputation among her neighbors. She left the shop once a day to purchase food; Vey made certain one of his old street friends or another was nearby to follow her, or to watch the shop while he went after her. She stayed close to the shop, went nowhere but stands and shops where she could buy fruit and bread. Several times she also bought eggs, and twice meat—which meant, Vey reported, that the boy must have been paid a good sum, since no household of that class could afford eggs and meat so often.

The sweets shop was near the area where Mahjrek had until recently dealt in slaves and indentured servants, but so were many other shops, and there was no apparent connection between the two. There was rumor everywhere, of course—hushed talk about the two dead men, speculation about the third. Vey seemed to think there was mostly sympathy for the boy, as having been dragged into something over his head and not of his choosing, and Jennifer had to agree. Even in the heat of the moment, *she'd* felt sorry for the boy.

Well, that was all out of her hands for now. No point chewing on it, with everything else she had to worry about at the moment. And most importantly . . .

She laid a hand on her stomach, thought for some time. Thread *might* tell her something. It would be another life, after all, however tiny, and Thread could detect life, it was one of the very first things she'd learned from Lialla less than forty-eight hours into Rhadaz and her first brush with magic. She closed her eyes, sought Thread: light mauve that Lialla had called pale red, something very like Bach in her ears as she touched it.

She finally shifted back and sat still, eyes fixed half-seeing on the fire. Uncertain. Too small, perhaps—of course it had been nearly impossible to sense anything through the intense vibration set up by her own body. Thread had felt very strange as it slid through her fingers, and as she tried to work past her own presence it began to sound strange, until she began to wonder if what she did was safe. What if Thread could somehow cause an adverse effect on a baby the way aspirin on alcohol did? All the same— "It certainly would explain a lot." She set the breakfast tray aside, got to her feet and suddenly laughed. One thing for sure, whatever her news did to Dahven: Robyn was going to be thrilled. *One biological clock just went from digital to analog*, Jennifer thought, still grinning.

SHE spent most of the morning and half the afternoon at her desk, working through the stack from Afronsan. Halfway down, she found a handwritten note attached to a pair of folded sheets of paper: "I thought you might like this at once and so have put it in the pouch. I hope you are presently well. A." "This" was a scrawled letter, in English, from Chris—the writing unlike his usual neat stuff that was nearer printing than cursive. *Must be the fact of having more paper to spill onto*, she thought. Or, she decided as she read down the first page, that he was in a hurry and trying to get a lot of information onto paper. "Yo. The Chief Dude was cool, surprise. Told him everything, on my way back out tonight, go collect Eddie and see what we can learn. Saw Ernie this afternoon, he's here doing stuff for CEE-Tech and running an errand for his dad. Says he'll keep an ear open. I'll try and keep you in the loop, but no guarantees, and expect some odd letters hidden in funny places, okay? Keep in mind old Chuffles has a *lot* of ships out there, so you figure the chances any mail I send comes into Bez on one of them. Oh. The heir says he's got some English coming for S. 14th with a string quartet and would you like to come see them? He said to tell you (he probably did, he must've signed a hundred things for you in the time I was there) he understands if you can't. Think he might try to get them to head into Sikkre. Whatever. XXX, Chris.'' And, at the bottom, ''P.S. Watch your back. And lay off the bad wine.''

Jennifer shook her head, sighed, set the letter aside. Waded through more of Afronsan's pouchful of papers. Near the bottom, several hours later, she found the invitation—an official one, lettered in gold and bearing Shesseran's crest and seal. She stared at it for some time, thought wistfully of string quartets, her own long-gone cello. Would the instruments be the same, would the music bear any resemblance to such music in her world?

It didn't matter, she simply couldn't travel all the way to Podhru. It *was* too dangerous, she was living on borrowed time after that last attack, and sick as she'd felt the past few mornings, she knew full well she'd never make it. But when she turned the invitation face down on the ''scanned'' stack, she saw writing on the reverse in Afronsan's neat hand. ''I do understand why you may not wish to travel just now. I hope this matter is resolved soon, for your sake and the Thukar's. In the meantime, if the concert in Podhru is a success, we hope to persuade the English to travel to the inner duchies, at the very least to Bezjeriad and Sikkre. More in a letter herewith. A.''

Ah. She smiled briefly, went through more paper. A last letter from the heir, this one fortunately printed on Afronsan's new presses. Her eyes were getting tired after so much reading in one morning. ''The English meet more with my brother's approval than with mine, I find them cool and overbearing; while they know the forms and follow them scrupulously, one still feels they believe themselves to be dealing with barbarians and peasants. Those I have met with thus far—the traders who brought the merino sheep for my brother's estates, and now these musicians and their entourage—are one and all arrogant. This despite the letters they carry from their Queen Victoria, speaking of a desire for trade and mutual benefits and great friendship. I have no doubt such letters go to all barbarian nations they deal with. But they seem to be a reasonably honest people, and their goods are useful to us.

"Your nephew again proved himself lucid and intelligent, and I have great hopes of obtaining more information from him in the near future regarding both the drug Zero and this outside threat he spoke of. It is a pity, of course, that his friend could not have learned more, though I understand the circumstances were scarcely favorable. Any information I receive about the drug or the threat of arms against us will go directly to the Dukes and so to yourself, and I will hope for reciprocation. A.''

More paperwork, in other words. Jennifer rolled her eyes, set the letter face down atop the growing pile and reached for the next sheet. After a moment, she set it down unread and pulled out her watch. Past noon. No wonder she was starting to feel light-headed. *Go, eat, before Dahven comes looking for you.* He'd done that once this last week when she'd lost track of the time, worry furrowing his brow. Part of her had wanted to shake him until his teeth rattled. But she really couldn't blame him.

SHE told him Siohan's suspicions, found he'd already talked to his man, who'd been talking with Siohan. "In short, the usual household gossip circuit,'' he said, and smiled broadly, wrapped a long arm around her shoulders and pulled her close. "I wish I could give you a better answer than perhaps. The silver bands come from one particular shop, the same one I've always used, and they're expensive enough the charm should remain fully effective, even beyond the usual half-year. I've had them do so in the past; I know of one man who wore one for nearly an entire year, without mishap. All the same''—he shoved his sleeve up and ran a finger across the smooth silver—"it is old enough it should have been replaced some days ago. The spell might have gone erratic.'' Jennifer laid her hand across it. The metal was warm from contact with his skin, nothing else. She'd never been able to detect with Thread whatever spell was put on those armbands anyway.

He had pulled back a little so he could look at her. She smiled. "You don't look as though you'd mind."

"I should probably apologize," Dahven said gravely, but his eyes were alight. "If I were another man, you might think I'd done it deliberately." She shook her head. "I didn't, to get that out of the way. No, I don't mind. If you don't." She shook her head again. "Well, then. Why don't we sit down and eat?"

He pulled out her chair as he normally did, but made no effort to hand her down into it. Not that she'd really expected him to act like Aletto had when Robyn was pregnant with his first. Robyn, of course, hadn't minded at all. "Thanks," she said as he dropped into his own chair and poured water for her.

"Thanks?"

"For not acting like I'm suddenly turned into one of those glass-thread statues they have in the market."

He laughed. "I know better; you'd probably bite me. I do remember Aletto, the way *he* carried on that first summer when we had to stay at Duke's Fort. Surely you didn't think I'd be that way? After all, you have to remember how sheltered Aletto was, the sorts of chivalrous garbage his tutors used to read him, and how little he ever knew about real women." He considered this last statement and colored. It was Jennifer's turn to laugh.

"Whereas *you*," she prompted. "Never mind. So long as you don't start fussing over me, everything will be just fine. Birdy was right; it's about time for Afronsan's clerks to hit that awful road for a change, instead of expecting me to pack a bag and jump on a horse or in a cart whenever he needs me. The telegraph's apparently way ahead of schedule, anyway." She turned the conversation to the English and the visiting musicians over food. "I don't know; from what Afronsan said, I can't imagine why they'd travel across Rhadaz to perform for a bunch of aments and barbarians. He says they're one and all insufferably superior. If they would, though, I think I'd put up with any amount of snootiness to hear what passes for music out there."

"We'll have them, then. And," Dahven added thoughtfully, "it might be we could learn something, if we had a chance to talk with them. Since this might be similar to the music and the instruments you used to play, they might accept you, talk with you. After all, if it was Englishmen Edrith overheard?"

Jennifer considered this, finally shrugged. "Possible. They did it in our world, once, forced addictive drugs on China to break down trade barriers and assure they got silver for goods, instead of just an exchange. On the other hand, the Americans would have more use for Rhadaz, after all; it's the other side of land they already own."

"Yes. But remember the English have doubled their already strong trade up and down the coast south of us, and Chris said they practically own cities where once they had only a wharf, or a small embassy. It seems to me they wouldn't mind having control of a port city like Bez. Or there might be bad blood we don't know about, so they'd want Rhadaz simply to keep the Americans from eventually holding all the land between the two seas?" He pushed his empty plate aside. "I would like to ask my brothers about that."

"If Edrith heard right, they'd certainly know." Jennifer pushed her chair back and stood up, drained her water glass and looked down at him. "I'll be up in the clerk's office all afternoon." She leaned down, kissed his hair. "I suppose I won't see you until dinner."

He sighed, got to his feet. "Likely not. They finished the telegraph posts this morning; I'm to meet with my new engineers and the Americans to sort out details I don't understand at all. Which means trying to look intelligent and interested, and hoping what they tell us makes sense to my men and a little of it filters through to me. With luck, we may even be able to test the line before the day's over, and I think you should be there if we do."

"Absolutely. Send someone for me if you get to that stage." She went into the hall just ahead of him, and practically ran into Vey. She jumped, drew a sharp breath; Dahven wrapped both arms around her shoulders and drew her back against him. "Ah!" she gasped. "You startled me, wasn't expecting anyone! Sorry."

Vey shook his head, touched her arm. "No, I'm sorry,

Thukara, I was moving much too fast and I wasn't supposed
to be here anyway. Thukar,'' he said, shifting his gaze,
''about the boy Krilan—his sister's in the blue reception, she
stopped me in the market just now and asked to come back
with me. She wants to tell you something.''

Jennifer twisted her head round to look up at Dahven. ''I'm
coming too; the letters can damned well wait.''

KRILAN'S sister must have been fifteen years older than he,
and had visibly lived a hard life. She was bone-thin, what
could be seen of her hair under sheer red scarves was nearly
as much gray as brown, and there was a permanent, deep
line graven between her brows, heavy lines from her nose to
the corners of her mouth and down into her jaw. She chewed
on her lower lip, her eyes were seldom still and her hands
clenched and unclenched in the shabby stuff of her gown.
Her feet were bare and she shifted from one to the other.

Dahven had to prompt her with questions to get her to
speak. Her name was Holyss, she said in a soft voice that
trembled a little. She'd lived all her life in the rooms behind
the sweet shop and when her mother died ten years before,
she'd inherited it. Her brother wasn't a bad man; he had poor
judgment, acted quickly and out of loyalty to friends, only
sparing thought later for what he'd done. Jennifer bit her own
lip to keep quiet; she'd heard the same argument more times
than she could count and it still sounded stupid. *Good boy,
got in with the wrong crowd.* What happened to his own
brains? she thought tiredly. Or self-preservation? Obviously,
the argument didn't sound stupid to the people who used it,
who believed it as this woman clearly did. Dahven heard her
out patiently.

''These most recent companions. Is that what you came to
tell us?''

She pleated her skirt and the hands shook now. ''He doesn't
talk to me much, any more, but he was terrified. What he'd
done, that he'd nearly died and that the guard was tearing the
market apart looking for him. But there's rumor about, Thukar—very strong rumor that says he was let go, that it was
impossible for those two to be held and executed while a boy
like Krilan broke free. That the Thukar's guard, perhaps the
Thukar himself, hoped Krilan would lead them to those who

paid him to stand by while those two men—'' She swallowed hard, closed her eyes and stood very still for a long moment. Dahven waited her out. Finally she squared her shoulders and went on. "And so, I thought—I thought perhaps—Krilan hasn't heard anything, he doesn't dare leave hiding. I think—I think he'd tell you himself, the things he told me that first night. But I didn't know, how far to trust the rumor. And, and I thought, if I came myself, Thukar, and spoke to you, so you could see he intended no harm, tell you everything he would surely tell you if he dared—''

"And what," Dahven asked quietly, "would he tell me, if he dared? Here, sit," he added, and motioned one of the guards to bring her a bench. The woman was swaying on her feet. She gasped as the guard touched her arm, practically fell onto it. Jennifer sat back in her own padded chair. Holyss cast her a terrified glance and drew a ragged breath.

"Those two men who—who died. Krilan didn't say how he knew them, but I think he had worked with them before. There were times he brought me money, more than a boy like that should have had. I—I needed it desperately, I didn't dare ask. He never said. But this time, he would only say he was in terrible trouble, danger, that if I didn't hide him the night he'd be dead. I didn't know what he meant, only that he meant it, so I said yes.

"In the morning, he looked a little less frightened, more as though—I think he realized he had only put off what must surely come. He was too calm. He wouldn't say what had frightened him at first, he gave me coin to buy food. He—had so much, *I* became frightened, wondering what a boy must do to earn such wealth. I wouldn't go until he told me.

"The two men had met him in one of the taverns, said they had a contract from one of the gambling houses. They offered him all that money, said he only needed to stand guard so the man they sought couldn't escape until they either collected the debt or dealt with the debtor. It's—it's a common thing, sir—''

"I'm very familiar with the lower market gambling houses," Dahven said mildly. The woman gave him an odd look, perhaps just remembering that the current Thukar had once known the lower market very well indeed, and Jennifer thought the idea steadied her.

"Krilan swore to me, many times, that was what they told him, and what he believed when he took the money. They promised more when the—job was completed. But he began to wonder, when the men led him across the market and when they reached the broken wall of the palace and began to cross the fallen stones, he stopped them, demanding to know what they truly intended. Though he already had a growing fear.

"The leader laughed at him, threatened him, and when Krilan still refused to move, told him: They had been hired by a man loyal to the old Thukars' twin sons, a man called Eprian." Her lips trembled and her voice cracked. "They were to enter the palace, to murder both the Thukara and the Thukar, that the heirs would pay well for the deaths of both. And it was too late for Krilan to back out, they said; men in the tavern had seen him take money and leave with the two. Men had seen them crossing the market openly together. Even if he ran now, if the two were caught, they would see Krilan hanged with them. If they won through, they and the man Eprian would track him down and kill him."

Silence. Dahven finally stirred. "You're certain he spoke of the—that he said Eprian had been sent by my brothers?"

"That Eprian was loyal to them, and that they would pay well."

Jennifer stirred, touched the back of Dahven's hand. The woman looked at her timidly and turned her gaze to the floor between them. "Don't," Jennifer said. "I don't blame you. I saw your brother that night. I don't really know how I feel about him. But he wasn't the one who tried to drown me. I *would* like to talk to him."

"I—I don't know—" The woman shook her head. "I'm so long overdue, he'll have run, I don't know where he'd go—"

"Perhaps," Dahven said neutrally.

She looked away from him, found Vey. "Yes. I nearly forgot. I remember you from the old days, boy; you're easier to see these days." She sighed very faintly, fixed her eyes on her hands. "And so, is market rumor true, that you set him free and then set a man to follow him? Or did the boy simply follow me in hopes of finding Krilan?" Her shoulders sagged. "I've brought about his death."

Dahven shook his head. "If his escape was part of a plan,

then why would I want him dead now? But if your brother truly escaped, how is it the guard has not searched your shop for him? They would have done that as a matter of course.''

She shook her head. ''If you knew he was there, because he was followed, however he escaped, perhaps no one searched the shop because they hoped he might lead them to the man who hired him.''

''Perhaps. And a pointed response. However, let us speak plainly, shall we?'' Dahven sat back, planted his elbows on the padded chair arms and made steeples with his fingers. ''I am less interested in one coerced, frightened boy than in those who hired him. Say he used bad judgment—that's small cause for a beheading. I am not my father, and the market once knew and trusted my word. Go. Take this message to your brother. Tell him to come the way he did last night, come into the hallway. Vey will be waiting inside the doorway he was to have entered. Your brother and I will talk. My word of honor he'll be free to leave once he tells me all he knows. If he wishes, he'll have my protection, for himself and for you as well, until Eprian is taken. Tell him that.''

The woman bent forward, gazed down at her clasped hands in silence for a very long time, finally nodded sharply, once. ''I'll tell him. I can't say what his answer will be.''

''If he has any sense, he'll come.''

Holyss nodded again. ''I—I would like to believe you. I don't see any other choice. I'll do what I can, sir.'' She bowed and got to her feet.

Jennifer cleared her throat. ''A last question. Did he say anything to you regarding the man Mahjrek?''

''Mahjrek? The woman-dealer?'' Her mouth twisted. ''No. But everyone knows Mahjrek is furious at the loss of a business that paid so well. There were threats some days back, I think when his shop was razed. What I heard were the things a man says in anger, the kind that mean nothing. Mahjrek hasn't the courage to make real threats. But—something, I think, yes. When I talked to Freja, she sells goat-cheese not far from my shop, someone there made a joke about Mahjrek and his burned stall, and someone else said his coin seemed to be ringing false with the new Thukara, perhaps he should call in the debt from the Thukar's brothers for a deal he made between Lord Dahmec, them and the Lasanachi—as though

it were not a coin debt but the other kind. And Freja laughed
and said that Mahjrek would have a long walk to hell to find
them, which was all to the good, and everyone laughed. And
then the man who made the joke said, perhaps not nearly so
far as that. Unless you thought of a ship's deck as hell.'' She
frowned. ''Not much of a joke, really, and that was the end
of it. You did ask of Mahjrek, though.''

''Anything at all,'' Jennifer agreed. Her gaze softened. ''I
wager you've had almost no sleep at all since your brother
broke into your house. Go, talk to him if you can, get some
rest. My own word on it, he won't die for coming and telling
what he knows.'' The woman looked at her for a very long
moment, turned and went. Jennifer sighed vexedly. ''I can't
even *begin* to decide what she was thinking. Except that she
was afraid.''

''She had reason,'' Dahven said. ''My father would have
had her thrown in prison as a warning against harboring a
fugitive.''

''Do you think he'll come?''

''Don't know. But he won't disappear, either. Vey left a
good man on that house when he followed her—a boy who
learned his way around the market from Edrith, same as Vey
did.''

''Great.'' Jennifer laughed.

''What's so funny?''

''Nothing much—just a Duke's honor guard made up of
former petty thieves.''

''Who else,'' Dahven asked reasonably, ''is going to know
the ways of a market like ours? Anyway, I doubt Krilan's
going anywhere that Bretan won't track him. Wager you a
ceri, though, the boy'll be here tonight, of his own doing.
And he'll talk.''

''As if I'd bet with you,'' Jennifer retorted. ''I learned
better than that years ago. But this is the first I've heard about
you and the gambling halls, and I wonder why I'm not surprised?''

''It's not like I ever lost—well, not very much, and not
often,'' Dahven amended honestly.

13

JENNIFER kept busy; the early-morning queasiness stayed with her, but the suddenly damp palms and racing heart if someone came up behind her, or when she woke from bad dreams, faded, and she managed to forget the two dead men for long stretches of time.

Later, she would find it nearly impossible to separate the fifteen days post-attack, except by specific incidents.

A long letter from Robyn, who had talked to Aletto and with his blessing cornered one of Lizelle's new maids when the girl came down to get tea and rolls for her mistress. "You'd have been proud of me, Jen. I laid the whole sorry mess on the line and didn't back off when the girl started crying.

"But unless I really misread both girls, I don't think they're in it at all. She'd heard of Zero; she didn't pretend not to know what I was talking about. And I'd swear her reaction was genuine when I said I thought Lizelle might be on it. I told you they're Cornekkan, I guess they recently lost their father and a brother to the stuff, and that it's not as common around there as crack in L.A., but it's around. Her father lost the use of his legs when a tree fell on him, the brother left the family farm and went to sea, out of Holmaddan City. They say that's where he got hooked, finally went back home. The father started using it for pain and—well, you can guess, can't you?

"Bottom line, both girls say they hate the stuff. The one I confronted absolutely denied the par-Duchess could be using Zero but the other later told me that's how her sister *would* react, she isn't sane on the subject. And that the stuff doesn't take everyone the same. She also swears they'd never get involved in it, even when I suggested they might have to protect people back home? Like, if someone threatened their family if they didn't? Well, how can you tell, but I don't think they're in it. Both girls say they'll watch Lizelle.

"I can't tell. Aletto won't let me at his mother, and I agree with him that she's not well. I just think it's something else too, and drug fits. Keep me posted, Love, Robyn."

Two separate sessions with the midwife, on either side of the arrival of Robyn's letter: Jennifer liked the young woman at once—Miysa radiated cheer and pragmatic good sense, listened when Jennifer asked questions and didn't try to put her off with "Oh, pooh, don't worry" type answers. The second visit brought results from the charmed powder the woman used, what Jennifer thought of as a low-tech, over-the-counter drugstore Early Test kit. "What I used to call an Early Warning kit," she told herself after the woman went to visit Pila. She laughed. "When babies would have been a *definite* problem. Instead of—well, let's hope a minor inconvenience in the early stages."

Dahven called a full household meeting in the large hearings room, later that day, while the midwife was still in the palace, and before any of the day staff who lived outside could go home. Jennifer, seated next to him, couldn't see anything but pleasure on the faces around her when Dahven broke the news, anything but concern—or in a few cases outright anger—when he asked for a complete silence on the subject and explained why. "Almost all of you have been with us since the day I returned home. I hope I don't insult you by asking you not to speak of the Thukara's condition, I know it would be a normal thing to talk about and a happy one, too. At the moment, though, you all know there is a man somewhere in the market, Eprian, who has tried at least three times to murder the Thukara or me, and we have yet to find him or those who hired him. I haven't enough proof to send to the Emperor, but personally, I am certain it's my brothers. If word gets out, Eprian, or they, might step up their efforts, in hopes of killing both of us before an heir is born. Also, they might believe the Thukara's condition will render her unable to defend herself as she has in the past."

He then shrugged; there was total silence in the large room. "Once Eprian is taken, I hope that will be the end of it, and believe me, I will be the first to say spread the word." A jubilant, boyish grin. "I'll help you."

He stepped back; Jennifer reached up and caught hold of his fingers. There was a low buzz of conversation, and finally the chief cook pushed to the fore. "By your leave, sir, some of us have served here since your father's time. One never knew how he'd be, day to day, and his younger sons were— well, enough of that. I think I speak for all of us when I say the past three years have been a pleasure, and none of the old staff would ever trade what we have for what we had."

One of the younger guards nodded and moved to stand next to her. "Those of us who didn't serve the previous Thukars still lived under their ruling, we're all Sikkreni after all. Lowen speaks for me. We'll keep it silent, sir."

The boy Krilan hadn't been able to tell them much, even without fear of the axe hanging over him: He had been hired by the other two men and had never seen Eprian. He had not seen or heard from Eprian since.

A note, that day or the next, from Mahjrek: a lengthy and, Jennifer thought, frightened disclaimer of any knowledge of the assassination attempt against her. "The man Eprian is known to me but not of my circle; any perceived threats which might have been uttered by myself against any person whatever in the past days were made in anger and under duress, and not intended to be taken seriously. Ask of anyone in the lower market, whether Mahjrek is a man of violence— personal or hired—or whether he has ever been."

Man should've been a lawyer, Jennifer thought sourly as she read the sheet once again. *And maybe he's never killed or hired a hit, but he was in on at least one deal to sell rowers to the Lasanachi. I wouldn't call* that *particularly pacifist.*

The small ceremony when Dahven, Jennifer and the Americans opened the Thukar's telegraph office by sending a message to the first village along the south road: Some of the Americans had been rather subdued by the swift and violent justice Dahven had meted out, though the foreman of the pole crew had quietly congratulated him when the merchants moved over to check something with the operator. "Serve

'em right. Somebody hired me to follow in *their* footsteps,
I'd be thinking twice right now.''

Dahven had been amused. ''We're hoping so.''

A delivery from Dro Pent—the regular Duke's message bag
that went from Duchy to Duchy, taking in the Emperor's heir
on the southern loop. The messenger brought a burlap bag of
coffee beans marked for the Thukara, stamped in English:
''Jamaica Blue Mountain. Expedite.''

Within, Jennifer found nearly five pounds of green beans
and a letter in Chris's distinctive handwriting. ''Hey, apologies, it *was* grown on what we'd call Jamaica but I don't think
it qualifies as Blue Mountain. They swore it was the best they
grow, and considering what it cost me, it better be. Get back
to me on it, I may need to go hunt down a rebate. Anyway,
I knew *that* on the outside would get you to open the bag
right away, you know? And hey, if the cartels can smuggle
coke in coffee, why not letters? Betcha ol' Chuffles would
NEVER think of opening a bag of beans. (If you did, Chuffs,
shame on you, you jerk!)

''So, anyway. I got passage out of Bez on a French ship, one
of the neat little jobbies cut like a yacht, really hauls, made
a record run back down the coast. Eddie's fine, he got a little
bored waiting. He ran up against those guys again, he thinks,
the night I got in, he'd been hanging out by the docks in case
(I had a slow trip up, spent longer than I'd thought on land,
got back fast—still worked out about the right number of
days). Anyway, he's out there watching the offshore lights and
a boat puts out and coming back over the water these voices.
No flag on the boat, or none he could see, but you know how
good his eyes are, so probably none. There were ships all
over the harbor, the guy who steers that French ship earned
his pay that night, I'll tell you, even after the moon came up.
Three American at least, two English, all kinds of others,
including a few with mixed crews, a couple of Chuffles' and
two of those really distinctive African jobs that come across
from the mouth of the Congo. Hope you get a chance to see
one, there's nothing like 'em where we come from, the carv-
ing is just gnarly. Outstanding.

''This is going across the peninsula by that big lake in New
Gaul (I never *can* remember how much of *this* geography
you've sucked up, Lake Nicaragua and Central America, if

it isn't much. Yeah, okay, I know you're busy, and you're not running around down here like I am.) but it may be one of the last overland trips through there, the Americans have just about finished trips through there, the Americans have just about finished the canal between the lake and the Pacific, which means much easier and shorter trips.

"Hope you can read this; I know I don't usually send such a longie, but I had the time, Eddie's out partying and I wasn't up for local sugary beer, and—all right, maybe I'm a little bored. The local girls are classy-looking, pretty much, but you can't tell by looking who's just out for fun, who's husband-shopping and who's gonna slip something in your yucky beer and clean your pockets while her boyfriend cleans your clock. Don't tell mom, okay? She'd worry about me turning up dead in the harbor (like I didn't have brains or something). I'll make up for it once we get to Cuba (don't tell her THAT, either, but there are some genuine babes up there, and the percentage of just-have-fun party girls is a lot higher).

"Speak of mom, I hope she didn't find out about my in-and-out fast trip.

"There's a LOT of Zero around this end of the world, wherever it actually originates. Plenty of people down around the docks just zero'ed out (I think that's where it gets the name, rather than the O-rings it gets shipped on). I've stayed out of sight most of this trip into Jamaica, and I've had half a dozen people hit on me to buy it, Eddie says he hears that more than the "Hey, G.I." line (local equivalent, okay?). I've told him all the hair-curling stories from back home (including a few old *Miami Vice* plots, how'll he ever know?) and talked him out of buying the stuff and getting chummy with the sellers to see if he can't find out more about it. He'd make a crummy body, I think I've convinced him that's all that's in it for him. Besides that, some greasy little waterfront jerk who's hooked on the stuff himself isn't going to know who's making it OR who's trying to ship it into Rhadaz. Probably that was what sold him on cooling it, rather than the scare. Oh well.

"You better be taking care of yourself, more I think about someone walking in your back door and dosing your wine, more spooked I get. Did you guys change the locks or what-

ever? Yeah, I know. I can hear you now, you can handle it.
All the same, the guy got in, you know?

"Ugh. I just realized, it's getting light out there. And here
comes Eddie. If he has anything to add, I'll put it on the
bottom, otherwise I'll just shove it in the coffee and ship it
off to you.

"Who knows when I'll get another letter off to you? I'll
try and make it soon, so's you know I'm still around, okay?
Oh, for a telephone . . ."

The usual "XXX, C" at the bottom. Apparently Eddie
hadn't had anything else to add.

IT was several days after that before she found an opportunity
to roast the new beans and brew coffee from them—she didn't
allow anyone else, even Siohan, to do the roasting, since no
one else ever managed to do a proper job of it. Unfortunately,
Chris was right—it was excellent coffee, but not true, unmistakable Blue Mountain.

That night, or possibly the next, a brief and secret meeting
with Krilan and his sister, who had been given funds to cover
the price of the sweet shop and passage to Dro Pent with the
Red Hawks. "The only condition I put on you," Dahven told
them both, after he had introduced the two to the grandmother of the caravan and had handed a wallet to the sister.
"If you hear anything in Dro Pent regarding a foreign drug
called Zero, or anything about ships stopping along the coast
to either side of the city and its harbor, or men coming in
secret to the city; anything concerning my brothers Deehar
and Dayher, or men serving them. I have already sent word
to the Duke of Dro Pent. Wudron does not know your true
names or why you move from here to his Duchy and I do not
intend to tell him. The fewer who hold a secret, the longer it
is held, after all. But he will know what to do with a message
sent to his palace for me from Viper, and he'll see I get it."
Silence. "I don't expect either of you to take risks, I don't
ask it. I don't want it, in fact. Just—should you hear or see
something."

The boy had nodded; he still looked pale and shaken, Jennifer thought. Of course, it might be that was his normal
state, but who would've hired an assassin or even a lookout
who was that wan and that jumpy? Krilan's sister hadn't

looked much better, but she'd been gracious when Dahven gave her the money, and before they left, she'd added, "You'll hear anything we do, sir."

"Might even have meant it," Dahven remarked once they were gone.

An argument with Dahven and Siohan, the day before or the day after that one—she couldn't remember which, save that the midwife had been there also. "Just so you know, I'm going to keep running. Women do, where I come from, and I intend to."

Dahven had shaken his head but before she could come back at him, said only, "Well, you'd know more about these things than I. I just hope you don't intend to go outside the walls for the time being."

A firm shake of her head, and Siohan's comb caught in her hair. "Not on your life."

"All right, then."

Siohan had been more concerned. "It's not as though you are still in that world."

"I'm still the same woman," Jennifer said firmly, adding to herself, *Well, physically I am.* "And I'll frankly go mad if you try to coddle me for the next eight months. I won't be anyone *any* of you want to be around."

"Well . . ." Siohan had finished her hair, shook her head doubtfully, glanced at the midwife, who obligingly put in, "I have seen the Thukara run. If she says other women in her world do this, pregnant—it's nothing more taxing than one of my women who owns an inn has done all the months of *her* pregnancy."

Siohan bit her lip. "A first child, though—"

"As the innkeep's is." Siohan gave up at that, and Jennifer made a note to thank the midwife later, once they were alone.

SHE actually had very little time alone, these days: There was always a guard outside whatever room she was in, one guard at least to lead or follow when she went from one part of the palace to another—always people wherever she came from or went. There was always a full clerical staff now, and she was beginning to think seriously of talking to Dahven about taking over the rooms to either side, currently used for storage and records, and adding more staff. The printers' hall had already

expanded, the staff half again as large, in anticipation of the
new presses which, according to Afronsan, had been ordered
for her and would arrive by the end of summer.

The household women kept a very close eye on her, which
Jennifer found unnerving at first, though after a while she
scarcely noticed—or at least paid little attention. Dahven had
hired additional clerks for his own small offices, men who
could deal with such matters as contracts between Duchies,
who could tell him in a few sentences what a lengthy document meant and what options he had for dealing with it.

The new telegraph came with a new staff of four, in addi-
tion to Dahven's American-trained Sikkreni engineers. These
men lived in housing next to the telegraph office, near the
guards' barracks. Jennifer had hoped to have the telegraph
office situated in or next to the clerks' hall but had to agree
with Dahven that the four men had been carefully screened
but they were still an unknown quantity; it would be foolish
to trust them as yet. Besides, the lines between Sikkre and
Podhru were still at least two months from completion. Once
they were done—well, the problem might be behind them. If
not, Jennifer decided she'd argue long and hard for the shift.
Dahven might not want the equipment and its staff inside
now, but he'd probably like it less if Jennifer was running
back and forth at odd hours to send messages. *Probably thinks
I'll be limited to using it eight-to-five. Hah.* Jennifer knew
better, if only because *Afronsan* certainly wouldn't limit himself to such hours. The first several months were going to be
utter panic.

The diplomatic round-robin pouch that had brought Chris's
coffee and letter had also brought a folder of pre-contract
trade letters from Misarla, Duchess of Cornekka and its *de
facto* ruler—her husband preferred puttering with his various
hobbies to being Duke, and Misarla was more than pleased
to let Jubelo putter. Among the trade letters was a small personal note to the Thukar and Thukara voicing concern over
the increased local use of an addictive substance, one Misarla
had heard had possible foreign roots, and had the Thukars
heard any rumor regarding its port in Rhadaz? There was a
very brief and stiff open letter from Holmaddan's Duke, bris-
tling resentment at the rumors being brought to him, that his
fellow nobles would dare think him capable of importing a

substance such as this Zero, and demanding apology and retraction from anyone who had linked his name with the stuff. A letter from Aletto asking for a joint request to the Emperor and his heir (possible draft attached), to do something about making the roads between Cornekka, Zelharri and Podhru safer for wagons; several merchants had broken wheels this past spring and of those fully half had been set upon by robbers. The roads in question being within the Duchies but linking a major portion of the land together, Aletto said, he would be willing to provide the labor for repair but could not at present afford the cost of materials and of feeding and housing road crews—all of which should really be covered by the Emperor. As a separate note, Aletto added, his own guards were not numerous enough to deal with robbers, and it wasn't likely Shesseran would have enough trained armsmen to spare for such duty. Perhaps the Duchies involved could pool their resources?

A bundle of letters from several major merchants in Dro Pent, Sikkre, Sehfi and two of the growing towns between Bez and Sikkre, petitioning the Emperor to look into the possibility of steam trains. *Gee,* Jennifer thought sarcastically as she skimmed through them, *wonder who spread the word on that one?* Busy, busy Mer Khani merchants. She could pick out half a dozen near-quotes from the man who'd signed the wool-trade contract the day she'd been shot at. The Sikkreni market was probably buzzing with the notion of steam trains. Shesseran would just love it—not, as Chris would say.

When the pouch went on, several days later, it contained an open letter from the Thukara. "Rumor moves so rapidly, I know each of you will have heard that there have been attacks on myself and the Thukar. Evidence in hand points to his brothers, either a coup attempt or vengeance. Evidence in hand also links them to foreigners, who may be behind the recent flood of addictive drug. We ask for any word of their whereabouts—solid proof to rumor, anything at all. We have done what is legal and practical to tighten Sikkre's borders and its market against the substance and suggest those of you who have lengthy barren coastline do what you can to patrol it. Even though Sikkre has only city and market guard, Thukar Dahven has paid watching fees to villagers who already travel the coastline to fish or to graze their herds; he has passed word that substantial reward will be paid to those who sight smugglers and get word to the palace in time to thwart such shipments.

"It is our suggestion you do the same: It is easier to prevent problems if the problems do not land on our shores." *Yeah, me and the CIA,* Jennifer thought sourly. They'd have to be certain who was behind the smuggling, though, before they tried putting the fear of God into them—she could just imagine the chilly English presently visiting Afronsan if wrongly accused. They'd break off relations and it would be years before they were reinstated. The Americans weren't as stand-offish but, like her own Americans, the fact that they sounded so friendly didn't mean much. If *they* were wrongly accused, they'd probably make a lot of angry noises, possibly go in for something like gunboat diplomacy, and *then* break off relations.

Hit either with hard evidence—like a shipment, a ship, a handful of sailors, maybe a couple of the latter willing to talk—well, Jennifer thought, who knew? Probably a few heads would roll in high places (figuratively, she added hastily, and with a shudder), a few impassioned speeches would be made by other high officials, sincere apologies tendered to Shesseran. With some luck, that might be the end of it.

She refused to consider the other possibilities: worst of all, the Chinese Opium War in her own world, where major governments had known what was going on and had done nothing. It was going to be enough of an accomplishment to get to step one and catch an incoming shipment.

She'd grinned as she folded the letter and slid it into the pouch: Actually, it had been her idea, hiring villagers and locals to watch for smugglers—something she'd picked out of that movie about the prim New York romance writer down in Colombia, everywhere they went, all those kids, locals, secret police—everyone reporting everyone to everyone else, it seemed. Credit Dahven, though: He'd liked the idea and had immediately sent riders out to all the villages to pass the word.

Warm weather once again. With Afronsan's latest bundle of paperwork back in his court, and with the Duchy pouch on its way to Bezjeriad, Jennifer allowed herself an afternoon to just walk through the various palace gardens. Dahven set

aside the things on his own high-piled desk to go with her.
"When was the last time we did this?" he asked as they
passed the family dining and went down a narrow flight of
steps to the inner meditation garden Jennifer could see from
her desk in the clerks' hall.

"Don't know," she said after a moment's thought. "I can't
count that high." Dahven laughed, put his arm around her
shoulder and steered her to the bench against the shaded wall,
under the vine-covered dining windows.

"I like what you've done with this. It's a pity I don't see
much of it."

She leaned against his arm. "You would if you blocked up
that sweatbox of your father's and moved your offices upstairs."

"I suppose. I know," he added with a shake of his head,
"it's mere laziness on my part, not wanting to go through the
fuss of dealing with the preparation of new rooms, the fur-
nishings, where to put the clerks—"

"Well, let me do it for you, then."

"In your spare time?" he mocked.

Jennifer grinned up at him. "It's not nice to throw my own
quote in my teeth. Sure, spare time. I'd wager Afronsan halves
the paper load on me, at least for a little while, when he finds
out I'm building you an heir. The only other thing I
have to do in that time is decide where to put the nursery—"

"With us."

"Next door," Jennifer said firmly. "With a good, solid
door between. Haven't been around babies much, have you?"

"My brothers—"

"Weren't born, they were hatched," Jennifer said flatly.
"I can't begin to picture those two as infants."

"They were, I can just remember. Awful ones, too. Of
course, my stepmama had rooms apart from my father and
well away from me, and the twins were a corridor or two
beyond her. They had nurses—a number of them, as I recall."

"I don't doubt it. Probably ate half of them," Jennifer
finished darkly. Dahven laughed. "Anyway, I'm of two minds
about this full-time nurse thing, but I do know that if you
aren't the one who has to be awake half the night with the
baby, you don't want to lie awake listening to it." *And since*

it's not even possibly going to be a Nineties-Guy, yuppy-daddy shared experience, Jennifer told herself, *damned if I'm doing all the two a.m. floorwalking.* Realistically, she had full duties besides raising a baby, and even Robyn had nurses for her two little ones. "Anyway," she added aloud, "we'll decide on where and I'll see what can be done about fixing it up. Same with you and a proper office. Because if I drive the kitchen staff crazy going down to brew my own coffee, what about you, spread out over the table with your work when they're trying to get it ready for a meal?"

"No one complains," Dahven said. He laughed. "As if any of them would, of course, don't bother saying it. Is there anything open on the upper floor that would give me a view of this?"

"Check it later," she said. "Come on, let's go around the far side." Skirting the freshly raked sand, they followed a narrow footpath along the vined wall, ducked under a low-sweeping tree branch, and came to a very small, shallow pool. "This is new," she said. "I don't know if I told you I was putting in the water and the bench. There'll be a heavy pottery lantern here, and another here," she pointed, "to hold candles, so you can come out from the other door over there and sit in the evening. The wind seems to blow this way most of the time, but the tree should break the force."

"Wonderful." Dahven turned to look. "Which door is that?"

"It's walled over on the inside, halfway down the main corridor into the family apartments, just at the base of the stairs."

"Oh." His eyebrows went up. "Never even knew it was there. And I used to spend a lot of time exploring when I was a boy."

Jennifer laughed. "Looking for ways out?"

"Well—well, most of the time. But this palace is only the second, you know; the first burned only two years after the Dukes were created and so it's quite old and—well, I was also looking for places to hide, and one never knew, there might be secret rooms, possibly lost treasure. There were always rumors of such things, though I never found anything except once a tiny passage that had been closed off—it's fallen in since, I think." He gazed down into the shallow pool.

"It's pleasant here, you've done a good job. And I've been distracted, apparently, not to notice."

"Bah. You've been busy."

"And you haven't?"

"All I did," Jennifer said, "was remember fancy gardens I used to want, from a museum near where I grew up, and your gardeners did the rest; *there* are some busy and clever people. If you don't mind, I'll get them to clear that entry right away; with the really hot weather coming it'll be nice having it right there. Especially," she sighed, "since the old water gardens in the glade are off limits at the moment." And, as he looked at her sharply, "Oh, not because you said, or because I need half a dozen guards if I go out there. I just honestly don't feel comfortable around water at the moment. I made myself go out there a few days ago, and I was jittery the whole time. Don't you dare laugh at me!"

"To quote someone," Dahven said mildly, "it hasn't been that long, give yourself time. I'd worry more about you if you hadn't been what—jittery? I'd hate to think I'd married someone that nerveless." He ran light fingers along the back of her neck. Jennifer caught hold of his hand and laughed.

There were half a dozen more gardens scattered around the palace grounds, bequest of Thukaras and sin-Thukaras dating back to Dahven's great-grandmother—as well as the sprawling cactus garden that had been his grandfather's pride and joy. Uncertain how Dahven would take to fiddling with such a family relic, Jennifer had only had the gardeners move a few plants, trim others, put whitewashed rock edging along the several new paths through the garden. She led him into the middle of the garden, stopped next to a newly polished bronze sundial. "I was careful with my instructions; they didn't get rid of anything. I didn't know what might be rare, or what particular thing you might be fond of."

Dahven looked all around, finally nodded. "I remember I used to be fascinated by how different the plants all were—I used to prick my fingers on them, just touching things to see how sharp the spines were. But there was always so much you couldn't reach without ruining a good set of breeches. I like the paths. And—" He ran his fingers along the writing at the base of the sundial. "I remember this. Mother had it made, from a drawing in an old book she'd once had, when she was a girl. The lettering was foreign, she said, I think she did. So she had this put on instead. 'Only pleasant hours.' '' He sighed faintly. ''I wonder if she ever did have pleasant hours—now and again, the two of us, I think. Or among her roses.'' He shook himself. ''She was quite fond of the old man and his cactuses; I think she'd be glad of this here.''

''I hope so,'' Jennifer said as they went on through the garden and along the outer walls in the direction of the barracks. Somehow, she noticed, in the past few minutes, they'd acquired a very quiet and unobtrusive but very attentive pair of guards. So near the gates, it was probably just as well. ''Considering how much luck the gardeners have keeping roses alive, and how bad I am at growing them.''

''She had a gift,'' Dahven admitted. If he'd noticed the guards, he didn't give any sign of it. Of course, he'd had about thirty years more than she had to get used to the idea of being followed around. ''A genuine talent. One of Father's magicians claimed she'd have been an excellent magic user, which he'd never have allowed any more than her own parents would have. It apparently came out with the flowers.''

Jennifer took his hand. ''She didn't do too badly raising other things.''

''Hah.'' Dahven grinned. ''You weren't around when I was a boy, or you'd never say that. Did my man find you this morning, by the way?''

''Did *you* sic him on me?'' Jennifer demanded, and dropped his fingers.

''It was his idea—''

''He apologized for almost an *hour* over that arm band of yours,'' Jennifer said sourly. ''And—honestly, Dahven, I like the man all right, but he just doesn't listen. I must have told him twenty times it was all right, that I didn't mind, that I'd been thinking maybe it was time for you to let the next one lapse unreplaced—By the time I finally got rid of him, I felt like I'd been beating a dog.''

Dahven laughed. ''Pay attention the next time I'm talking to him. He's got quirks—''

''Quirks, the man says,'' Jennifer exclaimed.

''—but you can manage him; there's a trick to it is all. Look out, here comes the afternoon hot wind, right on schedule. Why don't we go in and you can show me where that door is supposed to be?'' Jennifer nodded vigorously. ''In all that huge letter from your sister, there wasn't anything about Lialla?''

''Nothing. It really hasn't been that long since Robyn went home, you know.''

''Yes, well.'' Dahven nodded to the man who opened the main door for them. Jennifer stopped short of the carpets to shake sand from her hair and from the trailing gauzy scarf she'd thrown over it. ''I warn you,'' he added mildly as they went on, one guard still just behind them, ''that if Aletto doesn't strangle her, I probably will. Sending you that horse, simply to throw him off her scent! That takes nerve!''

''Hah. You can't have that short a memory,'' Jennifer retorted. ''Right from the start, I spent half my time separating those two; Lialla probably thinks of me automatically when she wants to get her brother off her back.''

''Isn't she a little old for that?'' Dahven growled. ''And it isn't as though you're her mother.''

''No and no. I'd wager you, if there comes a day when Aletto turns a hundred, and Lialla's still around, they'll both still be sniping at each other. And you didn't spend as much time in Duke's Fort that summer as I did; I probably mothered Lialla more in those few weeks on the road than Lizelle did in the thirty-odd years before. Lizelle's a little too nervy and anxious to be a very practical mother—and she did have a minor distraction of her own in the form of Jadek, you know. So did Lialla and Aletto, as a matter of fact.''

''All the same,'' Dahven grumbled. ''Let me get my hands on Lialla—that is, if no one else does first. Didn't anyone explain to her that this Holmaddan sortie might be *dangerous*?''

14

⛎

THE prison cart smelled of sweat and fear—and mildew—and was dreadfully uncomfortable: the floor hard and damp in places, the ceiling low enough that Lialla could barely sit upright without bumping her head. The guard had tightened down the shackles on her wrists and ankles so that it was only with difficulty that she could roll onto her knees and crouch for a while, to ease the pain of sitting for so long. While it was moving, it threw her from side to side, chafing her wrists, and they ached fiercely. Even with the coming of full dark, and the company's stop for the night, she could scarcely see Thread and it didn't respond when she plucked at it. *Special charm in the fetters,* she realized gloomily after a while. Even her own personal link with Light was faint and useless. Not that the Light would have aided her much in such a predicament as *this*.

Well, at least they hadn't wreaked wholesale retribution among the village women, and even the old Wielder had been left alone. Probably figured the village men would deal out enough punishment, Lialla decided, and shifted cautiously against the rough, splintery wood. She hoped Sretha's descriptions of death by drowning were an exaggeration used by the men to keep women in line, not a punishment actually carried out. Horrible. She suddenly remembered something Ryselle had said: "They hit us, of course; that's common. But even the stupidest of them seldom hits hard enough to more than bruise—a woman with a broken arm or a cracked head can't cook, after all. They're brutes, but brutes with cunning."

A woman drowned in high tide wouldn't be able to cook or warm a bed, either.

She swallowed with an effort. Her throat ached from so many hours tightened in fear, and the benefits of the water the boy brought were long gone. Just as well, probably. There wasn't a privy in these luxury accommodations, and she didn't like to think what reaction she'd get if she expressed need.

The cooking fire was burning low. A few men still sat around it, talking, drinking and laughing; when Lialla put her face against a rough crack in the wood, she could see the boy, sitting next to the captain, his teeth gleaming in a flushed face. He was almost unrecognizable—she hadn't, she realized, seen him smile ever before; it changed him entirely. From a sullen brat she'd wanted to smack to something attractive. She felt herself blush. *A little young for you, isn't he, Lialla?* she asked herself dryly. If she'd wed Dahven when his father had tried for an alliance, she might have had a son that boy's age. Brrr, there was a thought to pull her mind from her present troubles!

She rubbed her shoulders against wood, made herself as comfortable as possible and closed her eyes. Things could have been worse, she decided, and began a mental list, a trick she often used to put herself to sleep: They might have already killed her on that veranda; they might have beaten her before she'd had a chance to name herself—even after that, if they'd chosen to disbelieve her, or to chance her brother's wrath. They had locked her in this enclosed box and left her alone; that itself was a pleasure compared to the other possibilities such a company might consider—She swallowed, shook her head. Maybe a list wasn't a good idea. She gazed across the interior of the prison cart for some time, blankly watching firelight and shadow shifting on the far wall, then closed her eyes once more. An inventory of Thread, then. Or a mental cat's cradle. The really complex one Chris had helped her work out a year or so back.

Thread: So much of it, still, she didn't really use. So much even the Silver Sash Wielders didn't, either knowledge lost or Thread never properly explored. Something she'd often thought she'd explore herself, add to the sphere of knowledge; even people like old Neri down in Bezjeriad might have to reconsider her strange mix of talents and her skills, and give her that Silver. She didn't want it as badly as she once had, but it would be vindication of a sort. Immediate recognition by the old school of Wielders; most of them didn't accept anything not within the rigid framework of classic, conservative Wielding. Merrida had been that way; her mother, trained by Merrida, wasn't much better. Lizelle would accept her daughter as a proper wielder if she had that silver sash.

Lialla sighed faintly, shifted. *It isn't that important*, she told herself. *I don't need her approval, anyone's approval. All the same—* All right, she still wanted a Silver, they were rare, they gave status. That might be what Robyn called an ego trip; but as Jen said, status wasn't a bad thing to have. Like a reputation, it smoothed the way for you, let you cut through to what was important, saved time.

All right, *not* Thread; it wasn't going to get her out of her present fix and it wasn't going to put her to sleep tonight, either. Light—?

She let her head fall back, closed her eyes once more. It must be an expensive charm, the one built into the shackles, she thought; Light really wouldn't shape for her. Odd, that; charms were usually specific. Something like this would call for a very high-powered magician—therefore an expensive one. The local Duke must have an interesting cross-section of enemies and prisoners, to go to such expense. She thought about that, twisted one hand so she could lay partly numbed fingers on the metal circling the other wrist. They weren't new. *Not made specifically for me, then,* she decided. That hadn't been likely to start with, though; the guardsmen hadn't known who she was, southern gossip about her disappearance wouldn't have had a chance yet to spread beyond Sikkre, let alone into isolated Holmaddan.

Sretha knew who she was, of course, but Sretha hadn't betrayed her, Emalya had. And there wasn't any way Emalya could have known who Lialla was when she went snooping through Lialla's belongings. Unless Ryselle had told her. Lialla grinned; *there* was a thought, Ryselle gossiping with Sretha's sister. Even if Ryselle had been inclined to such a thing, she'd never have been able to get a word of her own in—it took a talent to manage that when Emalya was in full spate. The sudden flash of amusement helped; she suddenly relaxed and drifted into a light doze.

It must have been hours later when she woke: The fire was a faint glimmer of dull red coals, visible only if she pressed her face hard against the gap between boards. She could hear horses shifting, someone snoring, a low, rapid and almost soothing sound, compared to Emalya's.

Emalya. The earlier flash of humor was gone; reality set in. *Stupid woman, she could have gotten half the women in that village killed. Her sister among them. I hope she realizes what she's done,* Lialla thought grimly.

There was a man, walking slowly back and forth beyond the fire, no other movement. Lialla sighed, stretched slowly and cautiously to the extent of her bonds, then slid even more slowly back into a sitting position. No point in calling attention to herself, rattling her chains. Once settled, she sighed again. *Emalya. I ought to hate that woman. All right, probably I'd strangle her if I had her here right now, but she must have thought I'd pulled a fast one on Sretha and the others, just like I said this morning—really, was it* this *morning? Found my English socks and undergarb and thought I was some kind of spy, sent by the Duke to make sure they weren't getting involved with the city women's nasty movement. Or maybe she decided I was sent by the city women, that I'd be found out and get them all in terrible trouble. Saw herself in sand up to her neck and found a way to send word to the guard.*

She sat up a little straighter. There was a faint noise in the vicinity of her right ear, like one of those large wood-nesting ants chewing itself a hole. She shivered and pulled violently away from the wall. Momentary silence, except for the horses, the snorer, a few distant night bugs.

She'd begun to think she'd imagined it, but the sound came again, and this time she realized there was a pattern to it. Three long, a short, a pause. Three long, a short. Silence. Lialla fought for a little slack and shifted, brought her left hand across her shoulder and scratched in turn, three long, a short, pause. Familiar—she knew very little of the sign used by the mirror-signalers but everyone recognized the initial three long, one short that served variously as, ''Hello,'' ''I'm here,'' or ''I'm sending a message now.'' She drew the arm back, pressed her ear to the wood, made her breathing as shallow and quiet as possible, and waited.

Only a moment or two. A faint whisper. "Kepron."

"Yes."

"Alone," he whispered tersely. "Don't dare loose you here, don't know the land."

"Me, neither."

"City. I know it well. Trust."

"Try," Lialla replied honestly, and added quickly, "once we reach the city, can you find Gray Fishers? Any caravan? They'll know me, they'll help."

"Caravan," he whispered. "Yes. Going now, hold." She heard nothing, then his feet crunching across the road a distance away. She stayed where she was, ear next to the wood, heard muttered speech between the man on guard and the boy who was apparently replacing him, then nothing but the ordinary night noises. When she finally moved once more and looked out through the slit between boards, she could see the boy, pale in the light of a newly risen moon, standing just beyond the guttered fire and the ring of sleeping men. He held a long spear in one hand; first weapon, Lialla thought. It caught in brush as he turned to walk across open ground, bounced off his shoulder when he tried to carry it properly.

She continued to watch him, faintly amused by his awkward antics, the similarity between this boy and Aletto, the first day Chris had cut the long ash bo for him. Her own bo, come to think of it, though *she* hadn't wound it between her ankles and nearly tripped over it. She bit back laughter as the boy did just that, only just catching himself in half a dozen long strides.

What, exactly, had he meant by that little conversation, just now? Of course, Lialla thought, she'd have to decide if she believed him, that he intended to help her get away. If he did, if he could, it really might save her a good deal of unpleasantness with Duke Vuhlem, who was at least as stupid and intolerant as any of those village men—and though he really wouldn't dare execute her, he wouldn't see anything wrong with tossing her in a prison cell and making Aletto send for her, like a wayward child. She could put up with Vuhlem yelling at her, so long as she didn't have to deal with Aletto, too. Aletto would be utterly wild if he had to buy her back from Vuhlem, and she'd hear about it forever. She—*I'd be furious, being shuttled around like so much property. I'd have to leave Duke's Fort or I'd strangle Aletto the first time he brought it up*.

Right. Let the boy help her, even though nothing she'd seen of him thus far assured her it was safe: Holmaddi young male, angry with the world, son of a Duke's guard and now one himself—but why should she trust *her* judgment after that fiasco in North Bay? *Trust other women,* she thought sourly. What had Jen said about it? Something about polarity—not all men being wife-beating drunkards, not all women downtrodden saints?

"Right," Lialla mumbled under her breath. "So I was in a world where all the men *were* wife-beating drunkards and I forgot. Would she have done any better?"

All the same, last night Kepron just hadn't looked as though he wanted to join his dead father's company. *Means to another end.* Put together the lost-boy look of him out there with that spear and what Sretha had told her, what the boy himself had said— *Got it,* Lialla thought, grimly pleased to find she could still logic out a problem, tired, hungry, thirsty and miserably stiff as she was. *He figures I'll be grateful enough to teach him to Wield.* She considered this, shrugged. *Well, and why not? If there's time, or any chance.* She grinned faintly. *I've never fit the Wielder's mold anyway; my first novice was an outlander, why not a Holmaddi boy for the second?*

The men were wakened while it was still dark; Lialla, huddled in a corner in a futile attempt to stay warm, would have sworn there was frost on the nearby brush. There *was* fog. Kepron was sent to her with a little water once again, and moments later the wagon jolted down the road. Lialla closed her eyes, braced her shoulders in the corner and her feet as far apart as possible so she wouldn't tip over.

The sun was only beginning to burn off the fog when the company stopped briefly. Lialla could smell sea and the unmistakable reek of fishing docks; she heard the screech of packs of gulls all around. The captain's voice rose briefly above the shrill cries, bringing her to her knees, the side of her face pressed hard against the crack. ". . . you, and you two, wait here, the foreigners are due in port on high tide, there'll be at least two crates marked with the yellow ring on the end. Piero, you take this—it's the Duke's credentials, don't crack the seal, it gives you the right to make them open the crates. Examine the merchandise, it should be plaited hempen rings so large, fifty to a length of rope, four lengths of rope per crate. Mind! They've shorted us before, and the Duke was furious. Once you've checked, see it loaded, there'll be a long wagon to take it away, and for once we won't have to provide escort. Report to me as soon as you're done.'' Three men rode away, toward a distant line of ugly buildings, a few ships' masts visible beyond them. The captain turned his horse and came back across to the main road, passed the prison wagon without a glance and a moment later Lialla was thrown against the rear wall as they went on.

She scarcely noticed the new bruises; her mind spun. Crates, hempen rings, yellow—foreigners! Put it with what the grandmother of the Gray Fishers had told her at Hushar; what that captain had said to Kepron the night before: The Duke himself was personally involved in importing Zero.

Gods of the Warm Silences, she thought reverently. *If Afronsan knew that!* If anyone did, outside Holmaddan City, Duke Vuhlem, and his personal guard. *They'll find out,* she promised herself as the cart slowed and city traffic was suddenly all around them. *Because I'll get out of here and tell them.*

THE Duke's palace was all the way across Holmaddan City and apart from it, by itself on a high peninsula that ran well out into the sheltered bay. She had several glimpses of distant blue, ocean fading into sky, of steep cliffs and once of large houses and walled estates far below, edging the sand and water of the bay itself. Then forbidding gray stone, much of it coated with pale green moss. No growing things to break the mood of granite, dark gravel or pale sand courtyards.

The cart came to an abrupt halt, throwing her forward. Shackles cut into her wrists and she swore, then threw an arm across her eyes as the back wall was pulled aside and hard, capable hands grabbed her arms. Someone released her from the cart-fetters, someone else clamped wide bands over her wrists.

She couldn't stand, could barely see. The courtyard went by in a blur of light and dark as two men hustled her into a musty corridor that smelled of smoke and mold. Somehow she got her feet under her, her legs working, as they came into a wide chamber, dimly lit.

Blue lights hung from brackets on stone pillars, lanterns flanked a low dais. There were deep, narrow windows and a little reflected light came through these. Enough that she could make out the silhouetted massive bulk of a man standing at the foot of the dais. And then, as they brought her close, the man himself, standing with his back to her, staring out one of the windows as though unaware of the treble presence. But the hands clasped together behind him were clenched into hard fists.

Vuhlem was the oldest of the present Dukes, a graying, bearded, hulking bear; his clothing was fine-woven, dark red breeches and a gray shirt, richly embroidered. A heavy gold chain lay against his throat, partly buried in the tuft of white chest hair; a ruby glittered in one ear, nearly hidden under the bushy beard. When he turned and brought his hands forward, Lialla saw rings on several of the thick fingers. His lips were a tight line, eyes black under a solid brush of eyebrow that crossed a fleshy, long nose. He would have made two at least of Aletto. *Intimidating,* Lialla thought nervously; she kept her chin down and schooled her face to flat lack of expression.

No doubt she would have remained intimidated if he'd roared fury at her, as she'd expected. He stood for a long time, simply glaring down at her, then gestured for the guard to release her and leave. He waited, came down from the dais and walked slowly around her, stopped with his toes nearly on hers, eyes boring into hers. Lialla kept damp palms pressed against her trous, and waited. When he spoke, his voice was reedy, deep; it vibrated through her. "They tell me you are Lialla, sin-Duchess of Zelharri. Does the Duke your brother know where you are, or have you come to stir up my women without his permission?"

Lialla drew herself up to full height, squared her shoulders; her chin came up. Her cheekbones were hot with sudden anger. "How *dare* you talk to me that way? I'm not one of your stepped-on women, or a child. Or my brother's slave, to need his permission for *anything* I do!'' His color had risen, but he seemed momentarily incapable of speech; Lialla plunged on, fury sending words tumbling one over another. ''I *am* the sin-Duchess of Zelharri, and my brother knows where I went when I left Duke's Fort. Bear that in mind before you do something you'll regret.''

''I? Regret? Woman, I'm not the one spreading sedition—''

''Sedition?'' Lialla topped him. He caught hold of her shoulders; she twisted to free herself, subsided as the fingers bit into already stiff muscle.

''Treason, if you prefer. I know all about this notion, the city women who seek to turn everything upside down, the trouble they cause here and in the villages. They won't succeed.''

''No?''

''Don't you laugh at me, woman! Unless you want your brother to receive a mourning note, after your *accidental* death of a broken neck.''

''With your finger-marks in my throat? Don't threaten me!'' Lialla shouted. Her voice echoed in the high-ceilinged stone room. ''Do you think I didn't know the risks, coming here? Do you think I didn't weigh what I *chose* to do?''

''Chose to—''

''Chose! And are you stupid enough to figure you could think up any death for me that my brother would accept as accident? A body, no body, any cause at all, he'd have emergency messages to the Emperor, to Afronsan and to the Thukar of Sikkre before you could wash your hands of me!'' She drew a swift, deep breath and went on before he could speak. ''You've one choice—let me go. At once.''

He laughed. ''You're mad.''

''Am I? Two choices, then. Let me go. Let your city women go on as they've started; do you think you can stop them now they see how poorly treated they are compared to free Rhad-azi women?''

''Shut up!'' He let go of her shoulders and brought a hand down across her ear. Lialla screamed, fury and frustration overpowering fear and pain; she fell heavily and stayed where she was. Vuhlem loomed over her. ''You *are* mad, and arrogant as well. And stupid, to think I'd give any women free rein with *you* as an example of what they would become.

Guard!'' he bellowed. Lialla ignored him, remained on the
floor, bracing herself on outstretched, scraped hands, until
the guards hauled her to her feet. ''Your brother can wonder
for a while where you are. *Maybe* I'll tell him, if he asks.
Maybe, if I receive a proper apology from him for what you've
done and said, *maybe* I'll send you back to him.''

''Ransom?'' Lialla snarled. ''The Emperor will love it,
when he hears.''

Vuhlem glared at her, then beyond her. ''Get this woman
out of my reach,'' he ordered. ''Put her below, one of the
protected cells. Go!''

Back down the corridor, into the chill, sunlit grounds,
across and down a long flight of stairs, lit by infrequent blue
lights and an occasional narrow, windowless slit in the stone.
The sound of a heavy key turning in a reluctant lock, a black
hole beyond it. She was flung inside, the door slammed ring-
ingly behind her.

TIME passed—she couldn't be certain how much. The entire
cell was charmed like the fetters in that cart had been, Thread
wouldn't respond and she could barely sense the core of Light
under her ribs.

The little room wasn't totally dark, as it had first seemed:
There was a slit high up, perhaps wide enough to let her hand
pass if she'd been able to reach it. It was open to the outside,
which meant a constant current of chill air. She didn't mind;
so far below ground level she would have felt smothered otherwise. There was also light from the hall that showed all
around the door and through a small opening at waist level.
A blue-light directly across, lanterns or candles or torches
farther down. The lights the guards brought when they came
with food and water at infrequent intervals. The food was
plain, bread and soup, not good but clean and reasonably
fresh; the water that came with it had an odd taste as though
the well it came from had gone sour, or perhaps seawater had
gotten into it. It stayed down and erased hunger and thirst for
a while; nothing else really mattered.

Except that the guards left her strictly alone. Lialla woke
often from nightmares in which they didn't. *Legacy of my
uncle, may you rot in Light forever, Jadek!* Vuhlem must have
warned them not to touch her; either that, or the horror sto-

ries about Holmaddan prisons were just that—stories. Of course, Vuhlem surely realized that he didn't dare kill her; whatever he'd said up there, he'd eventually have to send her back. In reasonably good condition, which in his mind would mean no broken bones, no unpleasant and unasked-for trysts with guardsmen.

Late at night, with the smell of prison and sea in her nostrils, nightmare fresh in her mind, that was hard to keep in mind. Or to assure herself that Vuhlem was smart enough to know all that.

At first, she'd thought about the boy often; as time wore on, she finally began to wonder if he'd meant any of the things he'd said. She hadn't wanted to trust the boy; she had had enough reasons not to. Perhaps the captain had told him to say the things he'd said, to keep her quiet, so she wouldn't try and escape. . . .

But just as she decided to forget about him entirely, he came. He wore guards' colors, the single-striped trous and plain shirt of a first-level. He came alone, at an hour when there was echoing activity up and down the hall, and sunlight from the air-slit touched the opposite wall, where she could hold up a hand and let it warm her fingers if she stood on tiptoe. She turned as the door creaked open; he slid through the opening, pressed something between the edge of the door and the frame to keep it from locking as it closed, held a hand across his lips. Lialla nodded. He came across, reached into the front of his shirt and brought up a pale cord. Four lumpy objects dangled from it. Lialla touched them in turn—market charms, similar to those she'd once bought in Sehfi. Protect-charms, a blurring-charm. He reached into a pocket, drew out another cord and draped it over her head, settled it around her neck. She only just managed not to flinch at his touch.

Lialla fingered the cord cautiously; another protect-charm. The boy glanced behind him. "I had a time," he said softly, finally, "getting these. I didn't dare come without them, though, and I wasn't given free time until the past day or so. I can't get you out yet; it won't be long, though."

"I understand." She had a hard time keeping her voice low; it wanted to crack from lack of use and dryness. She didn't want to understand. And she was angry—with him for making her jump just now, at his touch, with herself for flinching. Because she was dependent on him. *It isn't his fault, don't send him away.*

He looked and sounded irritated himself, she thought; perhaps it was only nerves, sneaking into her cell like this. Vuhlem wouldn't have any reason to be kind to the boy if he was caught. "I'm sorry," he said softly. "For what my mother did. She didn't know—but it wouldn't have mattered. She has the little ones, nothing else matters to her but finding another man as soon as she's permitted one. All the same—"

"It isn't your fault," Lialla began.

He chopped with one hand, silencing her. "I know it isn't!" he hissed. He glanced around again, drew a deep breath and went on more calmly. "I did what I could, when I learned she'd betrayed you and my aunt to the guards." She could feel dark eyes on her. "Why didn't you go? Or—you're a Wielder, they say one of the best Wielders in all Rhadaz. *Why didn't you stop them?* Or you and my aunt together?"

Lialla bit back a sigh. "I couldn't just leave. I didn't know who'd spoken—that *was* you, behind Sretha's house, wasn't it?" He nodded. "I thought as much. Still, I didn't know for certain. And even if I had, why would I have thought you could be trusted? I didn't know you." *You still don't,* an inner voice reminded her. She pushed it aside. He was listening, lips compressed, arms folded across his chest, and though the look was daunting, Lialla would have sworn he was keeping shaking hands from her sight—as she'd done herself, often enough of late. "I had almost no time between then and when the guard came, if you recall. And—" She shook her head. "If I had simply left, women would probably have died in my place. If I saved anyone's life by staying and feeding your captain that lie—"

"You did, unless he's lied to me as well. But why should *you* care?"

"Why shouldn't I?" She was getting angry; not good. "I can hear it in your voice; all right, they're 'just' women. All the same, they're people; they have a right to live as *they* choose, not as someone else chooses for them. Did *you* like the way the men of that village chose for *you?* Even those women who didn't agree with what I said—look, why are we arguing about this? Don't you have anything important to

say? Before the time runs out on these things?" She held up
the cord he'd draped around her neck, then pulled the snarled
plait up and let the cord slip beneath it.

"You could've stopped them—!"

Lialla laughed sourly, stopping him. "And you want to be
a Wielder? Look, boy, it doesn't make you a god, if that's
what you want. It's—you can't stop a dozen armed men with
it by yourself. Two or three, yes, I've done that, with something to plait into a Thread rope." She couldn't tell in the
gloom what he might be thinking; probably thinking that she
wasn't as good as all that. "A bargain, then: You get me out
of here, I'll show you." Silence. She added, "You wanted
to apprentice to Sretha? I'll teach you twice what she could,
in half the time."

Silence. Then: "I'll hold you to that. There's a caravan,
Red Hawk Clan, trading not far from the barracks. If I go
now, I can find them."

"Do it."

"I'll come tomorrow at latest; these charms won't last for
very long."

"*I* know that." Lialla resisted a sudden urge to laugh at
both of them—macho posturing, as Jen called it, apparently
didn't necessarily just belong to men.

"You may not know *this*," he replied coldly. "There's
rumor among the guard that Vuhlem's Triad is coming back
to the city."

"Triad." Lialla clutched at the wall, felt the blood leave
her face.

"They say it was somewhere to the west, his now and
again winter palace. Whether it was coming back anyway, or
whether he means to somehow use it against you, it's said a
Triad is proof against any charm." There was a question in
the words.

"I don't know." *My voice is shaking,* Lialla thought, and
forced air through it. "I know Light from experience—"

"I've heard, the past days." He eyed her in silence for
some moments. "It doesn't bother me, before you ask; there
are men who helped bring you here who've sought the palace
healer to make certain you didn't contaminate them."

Lialla managed a laugh, knowing he intended it, that he

hoped to ease the tension. "Unfortunately, I can't do that. But Triads aren't—I don't know very much about them."

"Does anyone?" the boy asked. He hesitated, glanced at the narrow window and its fading light. "Hold. I'll return tonight, if I can, but it's unlikely. I'll come tomorrow at latest, though." She heard him swallow. "If you haven't seen me by day after, you won't." *Because I'll be dead.*

"Tomorrow, then," Lialla said, and somehow kept the bleak possibility from her own voice, as he hadn't been able to. He simply turned, took his block from the door, pulled it shut with a click behind him. Lialla crossed to test it, sighed faintly when it remained firmly in place. "Had to try," she told herself. The stone wall was cool under her cheek. Her hands were trembling, and she finally pulled herself back over to the mat that served as chair and bedding.

A Triad. She'd be no proof at all against a Triad. She didn't want to think about Vuhlem having a Triad. *Why didn't I ever hear about it before?* she wondered. *Because he kept it more secret than Jadek kept his?* But they'd been legal for years now; even Jadek could have housed his openly if he'd wished to. In the years since Jadek's Triad had deserted him, such magic users had been—not exactly widely accepted, but no one thought it proof of villainy if a noble kept a Triad among his other household magicians and sorcerers. If Vuhlem had one on the quiet—

But there was a lot of secrecy about Vuhlem. Zero, and a hidden Triad. *Oh, Kepron, get me out of here,* she thought wildly, and pounded on the mat until the sides of her hands hurt. Because word had to get out, she told herself. Because the Emperor, the rest of Rhadaz needed to know. *Because of that. Not because I'm afraid.*

SHE didn't sleep, couldn't even make herself lie still through the black hours to rest. The next day stretched forever, and whenever she heard footsteps or voices in the hall, she went dry-mouthed and clammy-handed with fear. *Triad.* Awful, stupid and horrid that one small word could raise so much terror; she hated herself for the fear and because she couldn't seem to do anything to change it. But the boy came for her, only moments after the guard came through with food and water. He glanced at it, shook his head. "Leave it," he whis-

pered, and shoved another charm at her. "I've better outside." Lialla nodded, gasped as he gripped her shoulder.
"Don't *dare* go weak on me now; we'll both die!"

She tore loose from his fingers. "All right. I'm *not*."

"All right," he scoffed. "You showed a man's nerves back
in North Bay; was that all front?"

Sounds just like Chris, the way he bullied me, Lialla
thought—a Chris with male problems, maybe. It steadied her
a little. "*Man's* nerves. Hah. Women have them too, you
know. But what do you care if it's a front, if it works?"

"I *don't* care, make it work. Let's go." He pushed through
the door into the hall, stood listening for a moment, gestured
for her to follow. Lialla glared at his back, and followed.

It took time—unnerving moments when they had to press
against the wall while men walked past them, unaware of the
blurred pair almost within reach. Several more moments while
the boy paused outside an open double doorway; she could
hear Duke Vuhlem in there, bellowing at someone, couldn't
make out the words. *I owe you one for that slap,* she thought
grimly. *And you'll pay.* The boy tugged at her arm, moved
on before she could react, without turning to see if she was
behind him. Her eyes narrowed as she scrambled to her feet
and ran to catch up. *Arrogant little monster.*

The courtyard was dark, pale sand only a little lighter than
the surrounding walls; there were horses somewhere in
shadow along the other side, nothing and no one else in sight.
High up, the sound of an a'lud, and a woman's high voice
singing a sad song.

And then another narrow hallway, a long courtyard, three
tunnels of stone, open gates and a narrow path leading down-
hill from the broad main road. The lights of the city beyond.
Lialla shivered as a night wind from the ocean slammed into
her back.

The boy brought her into the city by dark, unpleasant-
smelling alleys. Lialla didn't mind; the wind didn't catch at
her here, and if she couldn't see, she likely couldn't be seen.
He stopped abruptly at a corner and she cannoned into him.
"Sorry," she whispered.

"Shhh." He kept a hand on her elbow, listened intently
for a moment, finally sighed. "There's a space here, between
buildings; it's known to a few of the city children. No one

else; no grown man could fit it, few would remember it. Will you wait while I go in search of Red Hawk?"

Have I a choice? Lialla thought bleakly. She touched the charms at her throat, grateful for their presence, gratefully suddenly aware she could sense their spell and the remaining strength of them. She nodded. "Tell me how to get in, then go. I'll wait."

He tugged at her arm for answer, led her forward and wrapped her fingers around the upper edge of the opening. It was low enough that she would have to crouch to get inside. A small safety, a cubby— His fingers were briefly warm on hers, and then he was gone.

Lialla crawled past the opening, felt around. Children did play here. There was an elderly scrap of rug, a carved wagon with turning wheels, a small stuffed cloth that might be a toy animal. She picked it up, hugged it as she turned back to wait for Kepron.

It took what seemed forever. And then he was back, suddenly, on his hands and knees, reaching for her. Lialla had the sense of Thread back after so long; she sensed his presence and began working her way out, a hand outheld. He gripped her fingers, pulled her upright and close so he could speak against her ear. "I found them. They aren't to leave the city for another four days; anything sudden would bring suspicion, and guards."

Her stomach dropped sharply and she was glad of his hand on her arm. "But—Vuhlem wouldn't dare stop a caravan— would he?"

"Will you chance that? But a message: The grandmother said to tell you this: 'Remind her of the oasis, Gray Fishers, and women's magic.' Exactly that," he added, as though she thought he was making it up.

"All right, I understand it," Lialla replied.

"She said then to tell you to go outside the city, where the road branches between city and fishing docks." He spoke as though quoting. "To wait there, until the hour before dawn. That there would be three carts, carrying the flag of Gray Fishers, to bring you to Hushar."

"All right."

"It is?" He suddenly sounded very young. Lialla wanted

to hug him as she would Chris, but she knew he'd misunderstand. Poor boy; it wasn't only Holmaddi women who lost.

"It is. Can"—Lialla hesitated—"can you take me there? Stay with me?" Silence. "I can do it alone, if I must. I—I really would prefer company."

"Company." He smiled suddenly. "Who could blame you for that, after these past days? All right. I can take you there, and I'll stay with you; I've no duty with the guard until midday tomorrow. But—a bargain. A trade. I'll guide and guard you, only if you give me a first lesson in Thread."

"Bargain," Lialla replied gravely. "All right. Get me out of Vuhlem's city. Now."

15

JENNIFER had fallen into a pattern, she discovered: Wake at sunrise, green-sick, eat a handful of dry crackerlike flat bread from the small table next to the bed she enclosed within the silver Thread-sphere each night, drink a tiny swallow of unfortunately warm water, fall back to sleep. Wake an hour later, feeling almost human, when Dahven needed to get up. Breakfast in bed, more to please Siohan than because she needed it that way. The rest of the morning divided between her high-piled desk and the printer's hall and a cold midday meal with Dahven. Another hour or so of work, until it became too hot for anyone in the palace to concentrate, at which time she would send the staff away and head for the sheltered little water garden at the end of her Japanese garden; the doorway had been opened, a wide-netting hammock strung between the outer wall and the one tree strong enough to hold it. Occasionally she took work with her, now and again a book from her growing library—most often she simply fell asleep.

Sometimes Dahven napped with her; usually he remained in the family dining room with its water-cooled air, and worked until the kitchen staff came to prepare the table for evening meal.

After evening meal—which Jennifer made certain she shared with him, since some days they saw nothing of each other save in bed early and late, and at meals—he spent long, late hours in the blue room, meeting with merchants, hearing grievances, sorting out matters with the city and palace guard that couldn't be handled by the respective captains.

Or, on the rare occasion there were no grievances or hearings, he went into a huddle with Grelt and the other captains and officers of the household, city and market guard companies, trying to sort out yet another possible way of tracking down Eprian and anyone else he might have persuaded to join him. There were large numbers of guards quartering Sikkre, day and night; thus far, they had covered a goodly portion of the lower market, nearly half the upper market, and most of the north city, with nothing to show for the search but a few unsuspected smugglers, traffickers in illegal charms, and the usual rumors.

Dahven had given Vey leave from the Thukars' personal guard so he could search on his own; Vey went back into the lower market where he'd grown up and dropped from sight, only a daily verbal message or a note written for him by one of the innkeeps to let Grelt know he was still alive. So far, the former market thief had no more solid leads as to Eprian's whereabouts than the rest of the guard—unlike them, however, he had tracked down a man who'd seen Eprian the night before, a woman (who had a cousin working in the Thukars' kitchens) who had been approached by Eprian earlier the same evening with promise of money in exchange for an unspecified task. Unspecified, Vey reported in the note he'd dictated, because the woman said she had flatly refused before he could say any more; she had no desire to become another Nebrin.

While Dahven spent his evenings and often nights "playing Thukar," as he dryly put it, Jennifer went back to her now reasonably cool office and worked with at least part of her staff for another two or three hours. She still longed for good machinery, but once she had streamlined the procedures (and once the staff accepted her changes), work went out quickly, turnover time on contracts was halved. But the desk remained high-piled and the workload never eased, however many hours she put in.

It would get worse, Jennifer thought gloomily, once Afronsan adjusted to the speed of wire communication. She'd have to find the time to hire more staff—staff that at present would also have to be cleared by Grelt, which would slow and complicate matters even more than they presently were. She'd have to pull Chris's chain, hard, get him to at least find a source of fountain pens—and lead pencils. Those would make handwriting considerably faster, at least for her. That new press Afronsan had arranged for her should speed up the far end of document production, at least. *If they have presses, why not typewriters?* Chris must not be looking in the right places, that was all. Of course, just now he was looking at and for entirely different things.

She let that slide; it made her nervous indeed to think of Chris out there somewhere playing undercover vice or CIA.

The telegraph lines were moving toward each other along the Sikkre-Podhru road, and would meet in between somewhere. Sooner than she'd like, Jennifer thought. Though the lack of them didn't slow Afronsan any: His mailsacks went back and forth via Emperor's post, and two of those tough, wiry little riders with a dozen or more changes of horse along the way could make that ride in under two days. *Almost Pony Express, and nearly airmail*, Jennifer thought tiredly as yet another packet was set on her desk, late in the evening. She had just finished reading Vey's latest message—Dahven had them sent up to her once he'd read them—and wondered which of the kitchen staff Eprian had hoped to bribe. It should have made her furious, she thought; at this point, after so many attempts to break through palace security, she found it simply made her tired. *Give it up, you creep*, she thought. *Grelt's redoubled security around here to the point I can't trip without half a dozen armed men there to catch me before I hit the floor.*

She set the note aside as the clerk hovered short of the pool of lamplight, gazed down at the dark, weatherbeaten leather case. Her face must have shown her distaste; the clerk took his fingers away gingerly, as though he thought it might explode, and tiptoed quickly away.

She drew out her watch. It was late; most of the staff was already gone for the night, only two clerks remained at distant desks, one writing busily while the other crouched over a spill of paper, comparing contracts. A member of the household guard hovering in the open doorway, dividing his attention between the hall in both directions and the nearly deserted chamber. *I could just leave this, save it for morning*, Jennifer told herself. She sighed. *I could; I guess I won't.* She glanced at her watch once again, then looked out the open window. It was still too hot and airless to sleep, and

late as it was, it would probably be another hour before Dahven was finished downstairs. He and Vey had put together a
map of the city, considerably updated from the official ones
Dahmec had used, much more accurate as to the locations of
lower market stalls and buildings, alleys and passages not part
of the normal thoroughfare system. He and Grelt probably
had their heads together, a pile of scrawled-on paper littering
the floor between them; she'd found a similar mess the night
before, when she'd gone to fetch him. "Yah," she mumbled
finally, and stuffed the watch back in her pocket. "Break it
open, see what's there."

There wasn't much, for once—a single envelope bound with
red string and sealed with Afronsan's personal seal. She
pulled it out, tested the thickness between thumb and forefinger, shrugged and broke it open. Five sheets of paper and
nothing else; that *had* to be a record all-time low. Jennifer
grinned at the thought, separated the pages and brought the
lamp nearer. Two were set in type, Afronsan's scrawled initial at the end; the other three were refolded, water-stained
along one edge, and in Chris's handwriting. She set them
aside, scanned down the heir's letter.

It was short, even for a two-page letter; Afronsan had his
points set out in neat paragraphs, separated by nearly an inch
of blank paper between, and the margins were unusually
wide—often, especially when he sent documents by Emperor's post, there was print covering the entire page. He'd even
taken time and space to inquire about her health and Dahven's, to ask if there had been any progress on their resolving
the recent spate of troubles, any new information on her part
on any of the matters of concern to the Emperor. Ordinarily,
Afronsan would assume that he'd hear about such matters,
and he hardly ever dealt in polite form. *I bet he wants something*, Jennifer thought. *He's buttering me up, I can tell.*

If he was, though, she didn't see it in this letter: In fact,
had it been from anyone else, she'd have called it chatty.
There was a paragraph about progress on the telegraph—still
ahead of schedule, he said. The English quartet was considering additional appearances; he would let her know as soon
as he had a commitment or a definite refusal. He had a few
individual points of difference with her on a contract she'd
returned to him some time back; his apologies for taking so

long, but it had somehow gotten buried among his other work. ("Gosh. I wonder how *that* could happen," Jennifer mumbled to herself.) She set the first page aside, ran a finger down the second. More bits and pieces. Then, at the bottom: "I received this today via a French skimmer, and am having it copied for myself so I can send you the original. Time of the essence, as you can see; I have already sent the French ship back to Bez with letters to the Duke, so that he will be able to deal with the situation there. A."

If he wanted something, what the something was didn't show in this letter. "Maybe I'm paranoid, maybe he was just using the time while he waited for his copy to be done." She shrugged that aside; if he wanted something, she'd find out what, eventually. And time of the essence—what, exactly, was Chris up to now?

She gathered up the three sheets, warily; maybe they *were* a bomb of sorts. At least they were readable. As many hours as she'd put in today, she didn't think she could have dealt with three pages of his tiny, squeezed printing. But Chris had made a special effort for Afronsan. His writing was large and neat, and the letter itself was Chris at his intelligent best: clear, to the point, utterly devoid of the usual slang. She skipped the first page; it was mostly rehashing what she already knew, the information Chris had taken to Podhru, what the heir had asked of him.

On the second page, he got down to business. "My partner Edrith and I are now on one of the islands below the Mer Khani southern coastline, having just come here from several days on one of the larger islands. Zero is everywhere in this area, and in widespread use. The things I told you about such drugs in my world hold true with this substance. Another thing, however: Against the local magic users, at least, it often kills. This may also hold true in Rhadaz, though the forms of magic are very different here. We have learned nothing about its origin, or who is spreading it. I still suspect it comes out of the Incan Empire, where a similar drug is used by the natives—something that is, unfortunately, apparently the same as in my own world, though there is at least one additional step involved in the creation of Zero. Rumor here has it that foreign magic (not island *or* Incan) is involved.

"So far, we have learned nothing about the foreigners who

deal in it. But those who use it buy from local men. Whoever imports the finished product is careful to only bring it into the country in bulk, and in secret; whoever buys from them is extremely discreet, either because they are well paid, or from fear.

"That said, this past night, I was in an eatery and overheard an odd conversation. The place was crowded, the men didn't see me, or in fact pay attention to anyone but themselves and their own immediate problem. I managed a glimpse of one when I heard voices speaking Rhadazi and later learned from the barkeep they were officers from the merchant ship *New Wind*. As you may know, that ship is owned by the Bezanti merchant Casimaffi. The men were talking about a planned landing *above* Bez, along the western coast where the cliffs drop down to a small bay and the outlet of a river. I couldn't hear all of the conversation, but enough to be certain they had merchandise they would not want discovered by the Bez harbor guard. There was also talk about Dro Pent and Holmaddan, neither of which are on that ship's regular run—at least, the mate was grumbling about having to get the charts from another of Casimaffi's ships.

"I do not have hard proof, but I strongly (underlined three times) suspect the cargo is Zero, that they expect to be met by men in that bay (maybe also farther north).

"The *New Wind* is like all Casimaffi's ships, new sails but the same body, which means it's slow. I found the fastest French ship in the harbor that might be willing to go into Podhru and asked them to take a bale of fine embroidered cloth, two good-sized crates of refined cane sugar, and this letter. If you have no use for the cargo, I can pay for it and sell it myself later. Otherwise, if you can make it worth their while for the special trip, please do so. *You* can visualize how useful it would be, having access to such fast sea transport.

"Perhaps if the French are pleased with this deal, I could try to arrange matters between us and the French so we could purchase Rhadaz a few of the fast ships?"

It was signed with his full name—Christopher Robin Cray. Jennifer grinned. Silly old Robyn, giving that name to a boy who'd have to grow up in the real world.

The grin faded. Chris had been right after all: Chuffles was in the Zero trade—at the very least, one of his captains was.

Dahven had better get those messengers back out to the coastal villages and warn them to double their watch. And they'd better warn Wudron of Dro Pent, in case the *New Wind* should show up.

She wondered if there was any point to writing to Vuhlem in Holmaddan; the man was already bent out of shape on the subject of Zero and he might take it as an affront, or an accusation that he was somehow involved. Well, she'd draft a note to him in the morning. If Vuhlem had any sense, he'd be glad of the warning.

From what she'd heard about the man, and the way he ran his Duchy, Jennifer doubted the man *did* have any sense.

She set Chris's letter aside, got to her feet. It was urgent but not so urgent as to keep her at her desk any longer: Messages wouldn't go out until morning and they'd be short; she could write them then. She turned down the lamp, stretched and yawned, then glanced down the room at the two still-working clerks. "Joppe, Feron, if that'll keep until tomorrow, leave it," she called out. "I'm going."

Her left foot had gone to sleep; she limped over to the door, leaned into the jamb and kicked out of her sandal so she could massage life back into her toes. She could hear the two clerks rustling papers—getting ready to quit for the night. The guards watched her walk down the hall; there was another at the head of the stairs, just where the first guard would lose sight of her. Another at the base of the stairs where the family apartments were, and yet another lounged outside the doorway into the Ducal bedroom talking to Dahven's man Anselm, who sat on the low bench repairing one of Dahven's boots.

Guards everywhere, Jennifer thought tiredly. She supposed it was better than being flanked by two large, armed young men everywhere she went, though she couldn't go outside without at least one armed shadow. And they were everywhere but not every ten feet, like they'd been after her near-drowning. That had been nearly unbearable, once the first case of nerves began to wear off.

Anselm would stay out in the hall unless Dahven came, or Siohan were in the bedroom, a courtesy Jennifer appreciated. At this hour, Siohan would be out—down in the kitchens gossiping with the staff, helping someone with mending or possibly even eating a late dinner. She had left a long, loose cotton sleep shirt on the bed for Jennifer; the comb and pick were laid out on the little table near the box of flat bread. Jennifer looked around the empty bedroom, smiled faintly and dropped into her cushioned chair in front of the blackened and cold fireplace; after a moment, she sat up and pulled the ties from her hair, undid the four-part braid Siohan had done for her before breakfast and massaged her temples. Too snug, once again; no wonder she'd had a headache most of the evening.

Should she go in search of Dahven, or send Anselm—if he'd leave her, with Siohan away. She shrugged, decided it was pleasant having the bedroom completely to herself for once, and ran her fingers through the loosened hair. It was getting long, almost to her waist, something of a nuisance in hot weather. It snagged more, especially where shirt collars rubbed against the base of her neck. But Siohan balked at cutting it and Dahven liked it grown out.

She glanced over at the little table-desk against the wall. Nothing on it but a pad of paper, a handful of pens and two of her remaining, now stubby pencils, and by stretching her spine and craning her neck she could see the top sheet was blank—no one had left any important messages. Maybe she'd just climb out of the loose blue dress and into the night shirt. There was a book of essays in the dressing room, she had traded it from one of the American merchants for a pair of copper ear-wires to take home to his wife. Not Mark Twain, but something dryly, wittily similar, a name she didn't know. She hadn't had the chance to finish the second of them yet. Perhaps—

She didn't complete the thought; there was commotion out in the hall, a woman's thin, pinched voice, the guard's and then "Lady Thukara—?" Anselm spoke from just outside the doorway.

"Come in, I'm clad," she replied. He slid into the room, stopped just inside the frame and nervously cleared his throat. Jennifer shifted so she could look up at him. The look turned to a stare: He was white and his hands twisted together, white-knuckled.

"A message, one of the kitchen girls just brought it. The

Thukar asks you to meet him in the family dining, there's been an incident—''

''Dahven—?'' She was on her feet. Anselm shook his head.

''He's all right, she said to tell you that at once. The man Eprian, somehow he got in and attacked the Thukar, another of the kitchen women was there and was badly injured. The guard came at her cries, and overpowered Eprian. The girl who brought the message said the Thukar wants you to be there when the man regains consciousness, if you don't object.''

''Object? You just bet I'll be there,'' Jennifer said grimly. *In the dining room!* ''Who was hurt?'' she demanded. He shook his head.

''Dija spoke to me; she was shaking and nearly ill, I wonder she remembered anything at all. She did say Lord Dahven wasn't hurt.''

''Dija—'' One of three young sisters who washed dishes and scrubbed vegetables, if she recalled correctly. What was *she* doing upstairs? She put that aside, she'd find out shortly. But Eprian—She could see it now; Dahven bent over his work, oblivious of everything and unarmed except for one hard-to-reach knife against his spine, then that man sneaking up on him—*Eprian! I'll kill him myself.* She pushed past Anselm into the hall. The girl was no longer there, nor was the guard. Anselm was just behind her, clearing his throat.

''Porlo came from the head of the stairs and took the girl back to the kitchens. Heriq said to wait, he's checking the other rooms along the corridor, then he'll escort you to the dining—''

It took an effort not to yell at the little man. ''Wait? Are you mad? With Dahven down there and that—that—fat chance I'll wait.'' She ran back into the room, snatched up her bo, and came back into the hallway.

Anselm was right behind her, stuttering out argument. ''You—Thukara, you promised Lord Dahven you wouldn't go anywhere without a guard!'' He recoiled as she stopped in front of him, her nose practically touching his, the bo in her hands at the ready between them.

''You wear a dagger, don't you?'' she demanded. ''I know you do, I've seen it. You guard my back, and come on.'' She was already around him, on her way; the man made a faint, unhappy protest, but she could hear his feet thudding on the floor right behind her. *Useless*, she thought sourly. Well, he was there for show, so Dahven and Grelt wouldn't come down her throat later for breaking her promise.

Dahven. Her hand was damp against the bo, suddenly, and her mouth dry. He'd *say* he was all right; she couldn't be certain. Eprian and his throwing knives; she was sorry Dahven had ever told her about them. She'd feel a lot better once she saw him. She plunged down the stairs and was running when she hit the corridor that led to the family dining hall.

THERE were no guards between the stairs and the fountain-cooled room. *They'd be with Dahven*, she thought, *guarding Eprian. Eprian. I'll strangle him with my bare hands, if he's hurt Dahven, I'll beat what brains he has in with this stick.* She ran into the dining room, stopped short of the long table. It was quiet and empty: Two blue-lamps glowed brightly near the steps to the old parade ground, and just inside the dining room, set on the edge of the waterfall, another blue-light. Another, turned down to very dim, hung on the wall under the small windows, behind the table, and a lantern placed on the table itself so Dahven could read. There were a few papers stacked neatly next to it, but no Dahven or anyone else.

"I thought you said the dining hall?" Jennifer asked quietly as Anselm came panting up beside her. She eyed him covertly from under her eyelashes, shifted her grip on the bo. If it was a trick—but *Anselm*? She almost laughed aloud at the thought; the man worshiped Dahven and he trembled at the sight of his own shadow.

"*Dija* said. But—Thukara, look." She looked where he pointed; light shone from a partly open door at the opposite end of the table from the kitchens. "Maybe she meant the old storage room. If Eprian had been hiding there—No, please, let me," he added with rather tremulous dignity, and he stepped past her, crossed the empty dining room, skirted the far fountain and pushed the door wide. Jennifer was right on his heels.

The door touched the inside wall with a little click and began to swing closed again. Anselm rocked back on his heels and caught his breath in a shrill, horrified little squeak.

Jennifer reached for his shoulder, then froze as she saw beyond him into the small room.

It was empty, had been empty even in Dahmec's time. Now there was a hole in the floor, near the opposite wall, leading down into blackness; a low-burning lantern set next to it. It cast shadows on two walls: something that swayed gently back and forth on a thick black line that must be rope. A woman's limp body. Jennifer's heart thudded; she couldn't breathe. Somehow she fought air into frozen lungs to scream but there was no scream, only a whimper. Anselm stumbled back into her, and then was jerked away, into the room. *Oh, God, no. Go, run, get out of here!* Someone was out of sight behind the door, in that room next to the body. Shadow moved insanely: dead, hanging woman; large man, small man. Anselm flung his arms wildly, then cried out, a hellish, strangled sound that couldn't have been heard above the bubble of water behind her. Then there was blood everywhere, spraying the opposite wall, pooled on the floor. Dahven's man fell heavily to the floor, his hand across her instep. Blood splashed her skirt.

She jerked away from that horrid contact with an outraged, frightened little squawk that didn't sound at all like hers, and stumbled back from the doorway. *Get away, go, run!* The bo hung forgotten in nerveless fingers, but there would have been no time for her to use it anyway; there was no time for anything. A bulky presence loomed behind her and an arm slammed hard across her chest, driving the air from her and pinning her upper body and arms; the other hand clamped down over her mouth. The bo fell and she clawed at hands and arms, twisted in a panic to free herself. The man who held her lifted her off her feet with no effort at all and stepped over Anselm's body, into the storage chamber. Jennifer's eyes touched on the dead, hanged woman—it *was* one of the kitchen girls, she realized dazedly. One of those sisters, but why dead? And Dahven, oh, God, where was he? She tore at the restraining arms and managed to turn partway around. Dahven was nowhere in the little room—there was nothing save two bodies, the hole, the lantern. Blood.

And then, from behind the door, again movement. Eprian came into the open, wiping his dagger on what looked like one of the kitchen aprons. He dropped the cloth, restored the dried blade to a broad sheath strapped to his thigh, then met her eyes and smiled. It wasn't a nice smile.

Bastard. She'd seen that look in his eyes on the road east of Bez, when he thought he had an easy mark, in her and in Dahven. *Bite*, she thought furiously, and sank her teeth in the unseen man's fingers. He snatched his hand away with an oath, but smacked it down over her lower face again before she could do more than draw breath to scream. Eprian reached into his shirt and drew out a folded dark cloth; a smell like hospitals filled the room. *Drug. He wants to use me to catch Dahven!* She jackknifed desperately, brought her knees up and lashed out at him with both feet. Eprian drew back and the man holding her threw her around sideways. Her forehead hit the door frame with a crack that made her eyes water and was momentarily stunning; the cloth pad came down across her nose and mouth.

She kicked out, felt her foot make contact but feebly. Then Eprian's voice against her ear; words no longer made sense. She felt herself lifted from her feet and carried between the two men. *No.* She flailed out; her legs wouldn't obey her, her arms barely moved. The black opening came nearer, then swallowed everything.

DAHVEN paced around the desk that had been his father's, stopping now and again to study the outer wall, the shelves, the floor with its fine carpets. Jennifer's idea was a good one, move the office. But this was much nearer the presses than hers, and he liked the room itself—at least, during the cool season. It had been his grandfather's before Dahmec took the title. The desk had been Denoti's also. *Cut windows?* It would be considerably easier on everyone, he thought.

There was a degree of sense in pooling the clerks' offices and having his work place near Jennifer's. "Then again, I might never accomplish anything, having her right there." He laughed, wandered over to the near shelf of books and touched heavy leather spines. Denoti's personal favorites were shelved here. Over the years, he'd read a few of them—though Dahmec had objected to the volumes being taken from the shelf, let alone from his office, as though their sole value and purpose was gracing the wall of the office. *Poor, stupid father*, Dahven thought without heat. Perhaps he'd have time, sometime, to read more of these. Jennifer had probably gone through more of them than *he* had, the past year or so, busy as she was.

"Windows," he said thoughtfully, and turned to look at the outside wall behind the desk. There was a faint tap on the open door; he turned.

One of the palace guards stood in the doorway, gazing at him a little nervously. One of the boys taken on the past winter to watch the Thukars' walls. "Sir, I'm sorry to bother you, I went first to the blue room but they told me you'd left early."

"No bother." He put a name to the thin, young face at last. "Sabyn, isn't it?" The boy nodded; he looked pleased at being recognized.

"A message, sir. Given to me at the gates just now, the man said you personally were needed and that it was urgent." He held out a small, flat packet, thick paper folded several times, no seal. Dahven came to take it.

"What man?"

Sabyn shrugged. "From the market, I've seen him somewhere, I think in the western fringes. I don't know his name, and he didn't say." He stepped back a pace and Dahven became aware of another guard hovering just behind the first—another of the first-year guards, a boy only slightly older than Sabyn. Wef, something similar to that, he couldn't recall exactly. Nothing special about either. He turned away to hide a smile and open the note. The guardmaster wouldn't be pleased, two lads coming away from duty to deliver a written note and a simple message; someone was larking. Well, first-year guard duty could be long and boring, and as young as these two looked, he couldn't blame them for using the excuse. At twenty or so, he'd been—well, he wouldn't think about that just now; he wouldn't give them away, either.

The message was short and poorly spelled and the writing uneven, as though the writer didn't do much of it. Dahven glanced to the bottom, saw two names: Vey and Halydd—the inkeep who owned the Purple Fingers. A frown drew his brows together. Something wrong there. He glanced toward the door. The guards were still there, watching him closely. Sabyn brought up a smile as Dahven's eyes met his and asked, "Sir? Is something wrong?"

It wasn't what he'd said, Dahven thought. How he said it, the way he looked. The way they had both looked when his back had been turned. Something *was* wrong. Things came together in his mind all at once. He shook his head, smiled. "Not that I know." He laid the paper on the desk under the lamp and read it quickly. "Sir, Halydd's wife wrote this for me. He knows where Eprian may be; he doesn't dare come to the palace, he's terrified for his family and afraid he won't see morning. He won't speak to anyone but you. If you could see your way to come to the Purple Fingers, perhaps we can take the man tonight. Come quickly, and as secretly as you can; Halydd believes Eprian has men watching the inn and if they see guards, he'll go elsewhere." A signature that might have been the inkeep's wife's, then Vey's name in the same writing. "So," Dahven said softly. Vey's name—but not the sign he always put above it. Vey had not sent this.

Trap. And if a trap, were these two part of it? Had they brought the note in innocence, or as something to let them get near the Thukar, to kill him? He doubted the first. *Wait,* he told himself. *Wait and use caution.* Whatever these two were, they *were* inside the palace, blocking the only way in or out of his offices, and both, he could now see, wore swords, though first-year guards didn't—they carried pikes on guard duty. And the ties that normally slipped through the hand-grips to keep the weapon snugly in place hung limply alongside the scabbard. Say or do anything to show he suspected the note, or the messengers, there was at least one blade ready to run him through. *Two.* With a sinking feeling, he realized there was something dark against his wrist when Sabyn moved his arm. The boy was wearing a sheath up his left sleeve, for a throwing knife. *And I have a belt knife, which just now is fastened into its leather case at the small of my back.*

It had to be a trap. Trap within trip within trap, like everything Eprian had tried thus far. Of course, he had learned convoluted thinking from Dahmec—and later and better from Deehar and Dayher. Dahven went over to the desk and dropped the false message.

"Sir?" Wef asked as Dahven settled behind his desk.

He looked up, managed a smile. "Wait a moment, I may

need you both to come with me,'' he ordered, and to his relief, his voice gave nothing away. He spread the note flat, ran a hand into his hair and gazed unseeing at the paper. His mind raced. These two were to murder him, he decided, if he showed any sign of doubting the note to be genuine. Grelt would have a fine time later, if there was a later, trying to sort out how Eprian had bought these two. A further trap outside the palace, where they might try to murder him. *Weapons. They can't object if you want a sword or two, going into the market, the way things are.* He thought furiously. Dress swords and his favorite set of blades in a case in his dressing room; a pair he used to fence Grelt and some of the other household guard in a chest in the blue room. Several that at least had sharp edges, good points and decent basket grips in the large arms closet under the wide stairs, near that door Jennifer had just had opened.

But there'd be another trap, one at least, at the Purple Fingers—if he accepted the note as truth and went there. It made him faintly ill. *My poor friend Vey, how did they catch you, of all men? And what have they done to you?* Well, he wouldn't think of that now; Vey must be a prisoner. Or more likely, already dead if they dared use his name. Halydd and his wife, his family—well, who knew? *Halydd and I are old friends, he wouldn't harm me of his own will. But Eprian could hold his family as earnest of Halydd's good behavior; if so, he'll murder them all, if he wins against me.*

But first things first: Just now, that meant getting himself out of this room alive. Somehow seeing these guards taken. He looked up to find them watching him closely; as his eyes touched Sabyn's, the boy's expression changed to that of a young, impressionable guardsman in the presence of an admired leader; he touched his companion's arm, a clear warning Dahven gave no sign of seeing. ''How well do you know the outer market, Sabyn? Specifically, the streets between here and an inn called the Purple Fingers?''

''I know it,'' Sabyn replied readily, and Wef added, ''I was raised in the same street as the Purple Fingers, sir.''

''Good. This says come quietly, but I think I should have company at this hour for a quick visit to the Purple Fingers. Of course, Grelt would refuse to let me outside the walls if I told him about this, but it's truly urgent, I don't dare ignore

it.'' His eye went to the sword, back up. "Can you use
those?'' Both nodded. "All right, let's go. I need a plain
cloak to cover this shirt, it stands out and the crest on the
sleeve would mark me for certain. And I had better have a
blade, in case.''

"Oh, Sir, we'd be honored,'' Wef said eagerly. Sabyn
cleared his throat, frowned at him, as though reproving an
embarrassingly overeager friend. It was all so well done,
Dahven wondered if he'd made the whole plot up from whole
cloth. But there was Vey's name, and no mark. And that inner
warning, loud and clear, that had saved him from every awful
chance in his life but the Lasanachi.

"All right.'' He turned the lamp down but not completely
out—*Make no move they might interpret as hostile. Wait your
chance.* He walked past them, the muscles between his shoulder blades tight, felt the two fall in close behind him. One of
the household guard only a few paces away. *Tell him.* But
Dahven merely smiled and nodded at the man as they passed;
Sabyn and his companion were right on his heels. One wrong
word, and these two could stab him, stab a guard who looked
only half alert but certainly had no reason to suspect two of
his own kind, and run. From this hallway, they had half a
chance of being gone before anyone could come to find two
dead men near the Thukar's offices.

*If Grelt had listened to me and let me have the household
guard taught Wielder hand sign!* But there was only Jennifer,
Anselm and within limits, Grelt himself. And it had been
well over an hour since Grelt had left his Duke, saying he
intended to seek out food and bed.

Think. It wasn't easy, with death nipping at his heels. "I
hope you won't mind if we don't alert your captain where
you've gone. I don't want anyone stopping me, and he would
try. I'll square it later, is that all right?''

"We appreciate it, Sir,'' Sabyn said from somewhere just
over his right shoulder.

"Good. Well, I have plain swords just down here, in the
guards' cabinet. I believe I'll borrow a cloak from there, too.
So no one can mark me.'' He went past down a flight of
stairs, turned and walked down the narrow hallway that
backed on the kitchens. The two stayed right with him.
There should be more men along here. The hallway was

deserted; probably Grelt had put most of them on entries and large windows, the halls wouldn't be as important if the entries were watched, after all. And offhand, Dahven couldn't think of anyone who'd be stuck guarding down here who would be useful if a sudden, ugly situation like this was thrust on him.

Get the swords, get them into the open, he decided. If the two intended to let him arm himself. Maybe this corridor hadn't been such a good idea after all. But there was light from the kitchen now, a burst of laughter from beyond the door, two of the cooks in the hall for fresh air. Dahven fought not to sigh with relief, and went on.

He practically ran Grelt down as the head guardsman came out of the kitchens, wiping his mouth with the back of his hand. The man glanced at the guards at Dahven's back, then back at Dahven with a question in his eyes. "They just brought me a message," Dahven explained easily. He felt movement; Sabyn moving his right arm stealthily across his body. The sound of fabric against leather as he slid the hand up his left sleeve. "From the men in the telegraph building." He folded his arms across his body, pressed his right hand against the pale shirt fabric and moved his fingers in a very basic sign; he sent his eyes warningly sideways and tried not to hold his breath. "A message from the heir, he wants an immediate reply. I thought, since they were already here with the message, I'd use them for protection when I went out." He added dryly, "I hope you don't object?"

"Object? Which of us is Thukar here?"

Dahven managed a laugh that sounded almost normal. Sabyn relaxed behind him, though the other boy was stiff with impatience to be gone. "The way you bully me over bodyguards, one might wonder."

"I doubt *that*. Well—you're stopping for a blade, I trust?"

"I came this way for that very purpose."

"Well, then." Grelt folded his arms across his chest and glared at the guards. "You know the problem. You'll stay close to him between here and that office, you will not let anyone close to him, particularly the foreigners. Do not trust anyone. Escort him back when he's done and watch every shadow."

Dahven felt the two nod. A chorused, "Sir."

"Good. I'll see your captain hears of it, if you do well."

Dahven stepped around Grelt and the two came after him.

Sabyn yelped in sudden pain; Dahven spun on one heel, caught Wef by the throat and slammed him into the wall, hard. The boy groaned faintly and went limp. When he dared risk a glance, he saw the other boy on the floor, eyes closed, Grelt kneeling over him. "Had to hit him hard, you said he had a knife."

"Didn't kill him, did you?" Dahven asked breathlessly. "It's in his sleeve."

"I don't know. I hope not, I want to talk to him." Grelt whistled shrilly to bring help, then pulled the knife loose from its sheath and tossed it and the sword against the far wall. "*He* was certainly ready." He looked up at Dahven, eyebrows drawn down over black eyes, his mouth hard with anger. "You're entirely too ready with a lie; I would have taken your word just now."

"I didn't have much choice; he was ready to murder me if I gave you any hint at all. See now why I want you to learn sign?"

"Hah." Grelt only just didn't spit. Half a dozen household guards clattered down the hall a moment later. "Bind them, and bring them," he ordered.

"We haven't the time," Dahven said. "There's more." He drew the man back up the hall, talking rapidly as they went. Grelt shook his head.

"You don't know—"

"I know it's Eprian; *you* saw that boy's dagger, it smells like Eprian! He's there, at the Purple Fingers. I know it."

"It's a trap," Grelt said grimly.

Dahven laughed. "Well, of course it's a trap! A layered trap, with Eprian at the bottom of it, waiting for me."

"He's not so stupid as that."

"Not really. The rest of his trap might kill me first. But if not—if I find a way through, he'll be waiting."

"We'll take him then," Grelt began; Dahven shook his head.

"Send guards and he'll be long gone. Damnit, man, he's evaded us all this time, hasn't he? The only men who might have gotten close to him—well, one's a merchant now, and the other a guardsman. And neither is here."

"Vey is probably dead," the other man said bluntly. Dahven nodded. "This is foolish; you can't even think of it."

"No?" But he was losing the argument, Dahven thought. Grelt would send guardsmen, surround the inn, find only a frightened and possibly ignorant Halydd, perhaps a dead Vey. Nothing else. He fought to marshal his thoughts and tried again. "The note says come; if Vey *had* sent it, he'd know I wouldn't come openly, via the streets. Vey didn't send it, though. Eprian will expect me to use ordinary caution; he doesn't know the back ways Edrith and Vey and I used to use."

Grelt shook his head. "They'll be watching the front gates, the walls—they'll follow you."

"I won't leave that way. They won't see me, *or* follow me. There's a way into the city cisterns from the old parade grounds. I wager *you* didn't know that, did you?" Grelt hesitated; Dahven fought to keep a smile from his face. "Come, let me get my blades from the guards' closet, and a dark cloak, and I'll show you." Grelt sighed loudly, but came with him.

But as they neared the outside steps to the parade ground, Dahven stopped. There were voices and lights in the family dining; guards shouting, a woman sobbing hysterically. Grelt pushed past him and ran down the corridor, loosening his sword and half-drawing it as he vanished into the room. Dahven was right on his heels.

Two of the kitchen women were trying to hold onto a third, who sobbed and flailed out, trying to free herself; four guardsmen stood on the far side of the fountain, staring through the open door that led into the unused storage chamber. Grelt went around the fountain; Dahven jumped it, pushed past the men and stopped. "Oh, no." Someone had cut down the dead woman and laid her on the floor, someone outside was shouting for cloths to cover her.

Anselm lay at his feet, his skin a muddy white, eyes staring blankly. Dahven choked, swore and stepped back, out of the man's blood, and wheeled away, hands clawing at the door frame for balance. Someone called his name; he swallowed, blinked furiously, looked as one of the men inside the room stood. Gripped in his hand, a length of polished hardwood. Jennifer's bo.

16

∾

He lost track of everything for a very long moment, and when he again became aware of the room and the men around him, they had covered both bodies; one of the guards, lantern in hand, was climbing up from the hole in the floor and shaking his head. Dahven watched dully as other men took Anselm and the woman away. Hard to remember how to breathe; he couldn't seem to think clearly. *Even with the Lasanachi, I never saw such horrible death; so much blood.* His eyes strayed back into the storage room, however much he tried to keep from looking at the darkened floor, the stain that had spread beyond the doorway. His ears rang and only a few words now and again reached him. *Jennifer.* He started to rise and the room shifted alarmingly. A hand dug into his biceps, steadied him, pressed him down into a chair, and remained there, holding him upright. He couldn't make himself look to see who it was, to make the sound and the words to voice a thank-you. He sat still and concentrated on not being a nuisance, or ill; on regaining control of his mind, at least the use of his legs. Getting his breathing nearer normal. Grelt's voice then, close to his ear, and the man himself kneeling beside him.

"Thukar. They've gone down to check the opening. It led to the old machinery for the fountains and down to the level of the kitchens. Someone has broken through to the palace cisterns, or from them—and recently, they think." His face was very pale; freckles Dahven had never seen stood out across his forehead and cheekbones. "There is no sign of anyone there."

He had to try twice before the words would come. "They won't be. She's—Eprian has her, the Purple Fingers." He dragged in air, shook off Grelt's arm and staggered to his feet. "I have to go."

Grelt gazed up at him for some moments; he finally got to his feet and nodded. "This changes everything. Are you able, though? Honestly?"

Dahven shook himself. Swallowed. His voice sounded better than he felt. "I am—I have to be."

The guards' captain was silent for a moment, his eyes measuring. "I needn't tell you how dangerous Eprian is—wait, don't look at me like that. You know Eprian won't simply hand over his blades and the Thukara and come with you tamely. Will you be ready to fight him, if you must? Able to? As you look just now, one of the kitchen staff could take you."

"I know. I'm—I feel sick." Dahven shook his head, managed a faint smile. "I know how I must look. By the time I reach that inn, I'll be ready."

Grelt looked dubious; he didn't say anything for several more moments. "The plan you worked out should still serve; I personally would prefer one that does not risk you—well, leave that. I have men picked to go out the main gates, they have the cloaks off those two wall guards, and Broden has one of your long plain wraps; with the hood up, he'll pass."

Details, Dahven thought tiredly. "Fine."

Grelt nodded, as though he followed Dahven's thought. "I won't worry you with the rest, except that we'll need a signal from you or from someone nearby once you get into the inn. At that point—" He hesitated. Dahven managed a weak smile.

"At that point, it's all mine, isn't it? Don't worry, Grelt; he can't have that many men. If he does, they'll be outside, watching for three men on the streets, remember?"

"One with a knife is enough; will *you* remember that?"

"I'll be careful. If I'm not, Jennifer—" His voice cracked alarmingly. He clamped his lips together, fixed his gaze on the far wall. Grelt gripped his shoulder.

"I know, Thukar. I'll let you get ready. One last thing: You won't dare use the cisterns now."

"No." He blinked rapidly. "What you said, signaler, it

reminded me. The boy Vey brought into the guard, last winter.'' Dahven blinked. ''Fedris. I don't see him. I want him.''

A very few minutes later, three men walked openly from the front gates of the Thukar's palace: two tall, thin young men in first-year wall guard's colors, a plainly clad man in a fine-woven, hooded cloak between them. Minutes after, a full company of guards began slipping into the market by twos and threes; they were discreet but made no serious effort to conceal themselves, though only a very close observer would note certain of them appeared to be following the first three. At almost the same moment, two darkly clad figures slid from a vine-covered hole far along one of the old, ruined parts of the palace, slid from shadow to shadow and vanished beyond the rubble of ancient wall, down a silent street and into the market, through the back of a stand piled high with fruit and out the merchant's tiny living quarters behind it. Dahven followed where Fedris led, the same route Vey had used years earlier had he known it, to bring a young nera-Thukar's message to his hidden exiled friend Aletto.

Fedris was older than Vey had been at that time, even smaller and at least as agile—and possessed of all his fingers, but he'd used his for juggling in the mid-market. *I hope Vey is right about this boy's agility, and his worth*, Dahven thought as they slid along the back side of black tents and down into a ravine that in winter rains would be a raging stream. He shifted the slender rope from his left hand to his shoulder, under the lightweight dark cloak. *I've put a lot of trust in that.*

He wondered how far his double and companions had gotten; they were supposed to make a good show of approaching the Purple Fingers by stealth and by misdirection, and to take time at it, so that anyone watching for the Thukar would have his attention focused on those three, which with luck would allow time enough for Dahven and his wiry young companion to get into the rear courtyard of that inn.

If the courtyard was guarded; if the bricks had been shoved back flat to the wall, or if the ledge were no longer there— Dahven shook his head, bit his lip and kept walking. *Eprian.* He couldn't think of anything else at the moment; he'd be sick otherwise, weakened by fear if he thought of Jennifer. *You're mine*, he promised Eprian grimly. *And you're dead*.

He became aware of his surroundings, and forced himself back to awareness of the moment. They were drawing near. If he were taller, he might even be able to see the inn's peaked roof, a street away.

JENNIFER swam back to consciousness slowly. She couldn't breathe, she thought in a panic; her chest was too tight, nothing would move. There was a horrid smell in her nose, something extremely unpleasantly sticky pressed into her cheek, clotting her hair. *Sick*. Someone had been ill—she had, from the taste in her mouth. *Relax, breathe*—One shallow gulp of air, a second. She couldn't move, her eyes wouldn't open. *Did someone break my neck, am I paralyzed?* It should have frightened her; there wasn't room left in her mind for that much fear.

Voices; they'd been talking all along, she thought, but she'd only just begun to hear them. She tried to quiet her breathing, to listen. A word here, a few there—tantalizing, frightening snatches of conversation. And then, with an almost audible snap, she could hear again.

"You had a nerve, bringing her in right away. I *told* you that liquid would make her sick!"

"I forgot. You'd have forgotten, as things were." A pause. "Sir."

Who? Look—She forced her eyes open the least bit, closed them at once: a room, men and dim lights, and Thread everywhere, twisting and shimmering like one of those old light shows Robyn had taken her to once, down on Sunset Strip. She'd lose it again, looking at that. *Shift out*. She tried: Nothing there, no response—she could *hear* it, a cacophony of mixed sound, music, shrill noise that vied with the shrill too-much-aspirin whine in her ears. She couldn't shift out, she suddenly realized, because she *was* out.

The men were still talking; she forced herself to try to concentrate on the voices. It cut through the Thread noise and the other noise, but the words weren't any comfort.

"Forgot!" A high, reedy voice that even under stress had an undercurrent of complacency; a self-satisfied voice. One she knew.

"I set the full trap and sprang my end of it." That was Eprian beyond any doubt. "And I brought you the gift that will give you the rest."

"Give us?" A third voice, a little higher and with more of a whine to it, otherwise a near match for the first. "You are supposed to deal with him when he comes, Eprian. You said you wanted him."

"I do. And he is. *You* wanted to see; isn't that why you're here?"

Her mind wasn't working right, Jennifer thought. It was jumping wildly, her senses were wildly unbalanced. That stuff Eprian had clamped over her mouth—chloroform, it must have been, it smelled like hospital and biology labs. But chloroform would knock someone out, fast; it would make them sick after. It didn't do *this*.

This was as if she'd been—*drugged*. They'd drugged her, and another part of the puzzle snapped into place: Zero. Deehar and Dayher had come to take over the palace once Eprian killed Dahven, once she was dead. They'd taken her as bait and given her Zero to keep her quiet.

The air caught in her throat and for a horrible moment everything faded; she thought she'd be sick again. *Drugged.* All the times she'd seen Robyn and her fellow hippies strung out on acid or pot or whatever else they'd taken—she'd *never*, ever wanted that, never tried any of it. Hardly drank, even.

If they'd given her Zero, they might need to do nothing else. Chris's letter to Afronsan: "It's lethal against magic users." Highly addictive—

She'd lost some of the argument in her terror. Somehow she managed to catch her lip between her teeth and bite down on it, used the sharp pain to break that down-spiral of thought. *Bait; they're using you to kill Dahven!* She forced her eyes to open. Thread everywhere, in motion, but she was ready for it this time; it made her queasy but it could be borne. *Move. You've got to, this time.* She couldn't; her body might have been someone else's, for all the control she could exert over any of it. *All right; start small, one finger, then. Do it!*

Something swung across in front of her and stopped. "Awake," Eprian said tersely from somewhere well above her. "Give her more."

The unmistakable rustle of silk rubbing against itself, and

she was suddenly looking into black eyes, a round, dark face surrounded by thick hair. One of the twins. He stared back at her for a long moment, lifted her arm and let it drop, shrugged. "Her eyes may be open; the rest of her is still well under control." The complacent-sounding one; she had no idea which. "She doesn't need more and won't." *Because I'll be dead before this wears off?* she wondered.

Behind him, his brother's peevish voice. "Bind her, if you think it may wear off. There's no point to wasting the substance, Dayher."

Dayher lifted her other arm and let it fall, spoke without turning. "Why, because it comes from *your* supply, brother?" He glanced up as Eprian made a small sound that might have been muffled laughter. "Have care, Eprian. You may be our choice for captain of the new Thukars' guard, but even a man holding such rank knows when to watch his tongue and to conceal his thoughts."

Silence. Then, "My apologies, my Lords. It has been a long evening, and waiting does bad things to my temper."

Dayher drew a small, jeweled chain from inside his shirt and studied the watch that hung there. "You should not have much longer to wait." His eyes fixed on Jennifer's once again. "I never liked you to begin with, and you caused us a very long wait. Four years of it. Waiting does bad things to my temper also." He stood, brushed soft hands across the knees of his breeches and walked away. "Bind her, Eprian. You'd better gag her as well." He coughed and waved a small, soft hand in front of his nose. "And by all the little brown sand gods, open the windows!"

THE courtyard hadn't changed very much, save it smelled less than it once had: Halydd had gotten rid of his sheep, or he paid someone to muck the pens more often, perhaps. A quick glance at the interior of the stable as they passed it showed only one horse, at the far end; no other beasts. The inn itself was quiet, and at an hour when normally Halydd would have a full, raucous house; he could just see dim light shining on the street beyond. *Light and open shutters, perhaps an open door, to lure in an unwary Thukar*, he thought.

He touched Fedris's shoulder, drew the boy back into shadow and squatted, pulling the string of market charms from inside his shirt. Only one of them was his; he seldom carried them any more, and he'd had to borrow from half a dozen members of the household. By the bit-of-tooth-and-twine one, there was no one else in the courtyard or in the stables—no one nearer than the inn or the street behind them, the street in front of the inn. By the dull yellow stone bound in black metal, armed men in the lower hallway—men to catch an unsuspecting Thukar. And there, the red stone so similar to one he'd once carried regularly—men nearby thought of him, and with no good will. Scarcely surprising, that last. But there was another there; *she* thought of him, too.

He couldn't be certain; he thought them all in that upper room. There were one or two others who held him in their thoughts, but without malice or terror—guards, he thought. *Downstairs*, he thought: *to capture a Thukar or block his exit from the inn.*

Dahven looked at the back wall and then at the charms dangling from one hand, and bit back a sigh. *I'm not the light-hearted boy I was the night I led Aletto up that wall and into the corner room. I've spent too many hours warming a chair and not enough warming my muscles. I'm sick from so much death in that small room, and from knowing Eprian murdered that poor girl and my servant only to show me how much violence he has in him. I was a playboy and now I'm an administrator, a paper-pusher—he was a city armsman for my father and then my brothers, and now he's an assassin in their pay. And death means nothing to him, save a means to some end.*

But he has my Jennifer. If I fail, she dies too. He drove a hand into his hair, caught hold of it and pulled until it hurt.

Fedris was still waiting, dividing his wary attention between the courtyard, the inn's windows, the roof. Dahven touched his arm to gain his attention, held out the rope; the boy took it, nodded once, and went crouching off to the left, vanishing in shadow. He made no sound. Dahven set both hands flat against his thighs and used the pressure of his fingers to count.

EPRIAN had done a good job; the drug had worn off enough that Jennifer could move the fingers of one hand, could feel the tendons in the back of her knees respond. With her hands knotted together at her back with a broad strip of cloth that went around her waist and held her wrists against her spine, her ankles snugged to each other and to the wooden bed frame, she couldn't move much else. She still couldn't see without Thread crossing everything; that combined with the smell of the blanket under her, the unpleasant stickiness in her hair and the thick cloth Eprian had bound across her mouth and chin, nearly made her sick again. *Don't you dare urf, people die like that!* Maybe he had intended just that, another horrible body for Dahven to find?

The surge of anger cleared her thought, and her vision, a little. The brothers sat side by side, backs to her, on a cushioned wooden bench and Eprian, his face blue and yellow with writhing Thread, stood facing them. He met her eyes; she forced herself to look back at him, then away as though disinterested. Beyond Dayher, not far from the open window, someone else: Sleeping companion, perhaps? The lamp was turned up briefly as Deehar stood and bent over the table in front of them. There was a sound, the furtive crackle of paper, Deehar fumbling at it and putting something in his mouth, rather like a child trying to be quiet with candy wrappers. Dayher muttered something, caught his brother's arm and jerked him down onto the bench; Eprian lowered the flame in the lamp and turned away—to hide that look of contempt, no doubt. *Deehar's Zero. The man's hooked.*

Something else. She let her eyes move again, narrowed them as she stared at the motionless man across the room. Perhaps because he would have been familiar if she'd been properly herself; maybe Eprian had not turned the lamp as low as it had been. It was Vey.

She let her eyes close. Vey. She couldn't tell if he was alive; couldn't see if he'd been bound as she was. Just his limp body, and his pale face. His eyes were closed. *Not another person dead because of this—not Vey.*

Sudden pain rolled across her stomach and settled there like sharp ice or an evil omen, and one terrifying thought blocked out everything else: *The baby. I've started Dahven's baby and they've given me drugs.*

DAHVEN finished a slow count of twenty and stood cautiously, stretched out his legs, shook out his arms. The sword

belt hung loose across one shoulder; he now reached under
the dark cloak and unfastened the leather ties on both swords,
loosened the dagger in its back sheath. His gaze moved across
the courtyard, along the two stories of upper windows that
were guest rooms, to the roof. Just at the peak, above the
end where the common room was, he could see Fedris slowly
and quietly getting to his feet. As he watched, the boy ran
crouching along the point of the roof, a bundle of rope
clutched in one hand. He let himself down to straddle the
peak, bent low to fasten one end of the rope, and began
paying out the other end. It slid silently down the tiles, came
out over the eaves, and moved down the back wall in a series
of jerks, finally pooled on the tiny little balcony outside the
corner room. The boy sat back up, waved a low, cautious
hand.

Dahven slid into the same shadows that had covered his
companion's departure from the rear of the courtyard, and
ran lightfooted along the connecting wall of the building's
neighbor, fetching up a half-dozen steps later against the back
of the inn. He stood there a moment, listening, untied the
cloak and let it drop, flexed his hands, shoved the sword belt
higher on his shoulder and felt along the wall.

It might have been four years since he'd been there, but his
hands remembered: They found the bricks readily. The narrow little balcony extended beyond the windows where he
would come up, and no one in that room—if it *was* occupied—would see him unless they came outside. He shifted his
feet to the last two bricks, caught hold of the lowest part of
the wooden rail and brought his face slowly above the narrow
walkway. A light in there, dimmed lantern as opposed to
blue-light. No one in sight but his angle wasn't very good,
either. He shifted his grip, pushed off and raised himself by
his arms, pushed swords aside with one leg and got his knee
on the balcony, shifted his grip again to grab the top rail. He
hung there a moment, getting his breathing back to normal.

His heart pounded, then steadied and slowed. He brought
his legs over the top rail, set his back against the outer wall
and edged toward the window.

Fedris's rope—there, dangling down next to the window, a
long length of it on the floor of the balcony. If Jennifer had
to come out that way, they were prepared. He cast a smile

roofward, gave the rope a slow tug, felt it returned, and moved on, until one more step would take him across the low sill and into the room.

He could see one corner of the room now, light and shadow mostly. But near the far wall, a low bed and at its edge, familiar blue fabric, Jennifer's wildly spilled dark hair creating shadow as she turned her head a little. For one heart-stopping moment, he thought she'd seen him, but her eyes were fixed widely on something else—something near where he stood, he thought, but inside the room, below the window, perhaps.

It took him a moment to realize why her face looked so odd; they'd gagged her. Bound her, too; he could see rope on her ankles, pulling in the waist of her loose blue day gown. He'd take that as a good omen, that she was alert and that Eprian feared violence on her part if she wasn't restrained. *He had good reason for that,* Dahven thought grimly.

Voices: Eprian's. Deehar's. Dayher's.

It momentarily left him reft of sense and breath both. *My brothers. By every god in Rhadaz, it's my brothers.* He took in a deep breath, let it out slowly. He pulled the sword belt from his shoulder and bunched the leather scabbards loosely in his left hand. *Wait. Choose your moment.*

He could hear his brothers clearly now: those horrible, high-pitched, carrying voices. They'd grated on his nerves for years; odd to be grateful for them now, but Eprian's words were muffled. He could hear everything his brothers said.

"You'd better ready yourself, get into the hall—"

"There's a man down by the entry and another at the stairs to warn me when he comes. And I'm ready. Sirs." The honorific came almost as an afterthought. "I've been ready these past four years."

"As we all have." That was Dayher, a smug contrast to the fretful Deehar. "I thought you had more men downstairs. If Dahven brings guards with him—"

"He hasn't. What men I have besides those two have been tracking him through the market. Two are more than enough, and if you recall the men watching his back are mine also. Just as their fathers served your father." Brief silence. "If I cannot take him by myself, let alone with four men, I don't deserve him, and I don't deserve to be your captain of guard."

"Arrogance," Deehar snapped. "Our lives and *our* palace at stake, and you play games? Haven't you learned yet the man leads a charmed life?"

"No longer," Dayher replied flatly. "But, Eprian, I do remind you, this is not a game, or a swordsman's exercise. And I have put too much money in too many hands in Andar Perigha to have to retreat now. I would be—*gravely* displeased, let us say, if it were necessary to retreat at this point. Our allies would be even more distressed, should everything turn and fall on a display of male plumage. Do I make myself clear?"

Silence. Then: "Sir." Eprian's voice. "The man will be within these walls in mere minutes, with no way out. Even he will not be able to charm his way from locked doors and through five men. Nor will he wish to; why do you think he comes here to begin with?"

"Oh. Yes." Footsteps across the bare wood of the floor. Dahven drew his head back a little to risk a brief glance. One of his brothers, back turned to the window, stood gazing down at the bed. "Well, then." Dayher's voice. He let his head back cautiously against the wall as his brother turned to walk back into the room. "The other, over there. Why don't you move him, so we can watch both of them? Yes, I know, scarcely necessary, but I'd prefer both of them in one place, all the same."

Footsteps again, heavier ones, heading for the window. Before Dahven could move, he heard Eprian stop and bend with a slight grunt to catch hold of something and drag it away. He risked one more glance. Vey? It had to be, and bound as he was, it had to be Vey alive. *Dear gods*, he thought and swallowed hard. Drew one deep breath, and then another. Eprian moved back into the room as someone tapped at the door. "Sirs, he's a street away; Sabyn and Wef are still with him."

"Go," Eprian ordered harshly. "I'll come in a moment." The door closed. "Sirs, you'll bar this behind me?"

"Of course," Dayher said calmly. Deehar's, "Are you mad? Of course we'll bar it!" nearly covered his brother's words.

Dahven grinned, turned and stepped over the windowsill.

* * *

EPRIAN'S hearing had always been excellent; as Dahven's feet touched the floor, the man whirled, right hand already in the basket of his sword. "I took a shortcut," Dahven said mildly. His eyes stayed fixed on Eprian's, peripheral vision catching movement of the man's hands, the change in his stance. His brother Deehar stumbling back into the little table and turning to steady it; Dayher's restraining hand on his arm, which Deehar threw off with violence and an ugly oath. "Brothers. I thought you gone forever; how nice to see you again. To find you where I can set hands on you." Silence, except for the clink of metal as Eprian loosened his other sword, for Deehar's panting, for a creak behind him that must be Jennifer shifting on the low bed. He didn't dare look at her, didn't dare take his eyes from Eprian. "What?" Dahven went on conversationally. "Weren't your new friends enough company for you? And who, I wonder, have you found in the Emperor's household to bribe? It must be someone very well placed, to persuade the man to ignore my death, and hers, and accept your return."

"It won't be for long," Dayher said calmly, and added in a sharp hiss, "Shut up, brother, you're in no condition to argue with him!"

"No? Of course." Dahven made a small smile that was no more than a turning of his lips. "Because your new friends will give Shesseran no chance to change his mind, or die and leave Rhadaz to Afronsan, is that it? Since Afronsan is less— shall we say, purchasable?"

"Tell him nothing," Deehar snapped.

"Why?" Eprian demanded. His voice was flat, harsh. "Who will he tell?"

Dahven shifted his stance slightly, took one step sideways to place himself between the brothers and Jennifer; Eprian and Jennifer. Eprian was between him and that door, worse luck, but now that the man couldn't use Jennifer as a shield, the door was a minor inconvenience in comparison. And behind him, he heard the faintest scratching sound, nails on wood: two short, one long. Vey was conscious, letting him know. He shuffled his feet, praying Eprian hadn't heard it, too; but the twins were arguing once more, Eprian was nearer them. Didn't matter. Eprian couldn't do anything about Vey, either. *Eprian.* Dahven bared his teeth. "I can tell anyone I choose, once you're dead and they're taken.'' He gestured with his chin. ''Do you still play with those as you used to in guards' practice? Or are they only for show?''

''Show,'' Eprian snarled and drew his swords. Dahven shifted his grip to the baskets, threw the belt off with a sudden jerk and came up with a blade in each hand.

''I see. Then here comes your final lesson. Look out for your head.'' Eprian brought his arms up, stepped back into position; Dahven closed the distance between them in a single leap. The room rang with the crash of four blades coming together at once.

BEHIND him, Jennifer was uncertain whether she wanted to laugh or cry. Dahven's sudden and unexpected appearance through the back window had given her heart for the first time in hours, but he was alone and the situation was still tipped in *their* favor. She'd had to fight herself not to try to cry out, not to do anything that might distract him. And now this, though she'd heard enough to realize it was what Eprian had intended all along, swords against someone he hated so badly that a quick death by stealth, like Anselm's, would never satisfy him.

And then, Dahven. That line. She really could have laughed, and damn Chris and his old swashbuckler movies anyway, when he had fed Dahven that line? The amusement faded as she brought her attention back to the moment. They were fighting furiously, between her and the brothers, and she would have sworn Dahven was driving Eprian back. *God, I guess he has a right to that line the way he's using those swords. I feel like an ass, this must look like something right out of Prisoner of Zenda!* The laughter was back, suddenly. *Except I don't look any more like Dahven that I do Stewart Granger. And I don't remember any movie damsel in peril looking like I must, right now.*

Movement caught her eye, near her feet. Vey's face raised just high enough so he could peer over the edge of the bed. One eye was hideously swollen and blackened; he closed the other in a slow wink, cautiously edged a hand just into her sight and let it slide away. She winked in response, to let him know she'd seen. He let himself back down, and Jennifer's eyes went anxiously back to Dahven. Now Eprian was attacking furiously, beating with long left-handed, overhand strokes while his right sought an opening; Dahven held his ground, managed a small step forward, backing Eprian toward the table. One of the twins swore and moved hastily away, toward the far wall. The other—it must be Deehar, rescuing his precious dope. *Choke on it*, she thought flatly, and jumped violently as something touched her bare foot.

Vey's fingers, she realized after her heart stopped pounding. Not rats, snakes, spiders—two rather cold fingers slid over her instep, across the ankle bone, and settled against the cloth that bound her feet together and to the bed frame. A tug, another; he was working at the knots.

For all the good it will do; I can't move, she thought angrily. But when she experimented, her toes did wriggle. She subsided when Vey tugged hard at the knot, a clear warning to hold still so he could work.

DAHVEN caught yet another overhand swing on his left-hand blade, a little too near the basket for comfort, and brought the sword sharply down and across as Eprian drew his back for another swing. The man was larger than he'd been four years ago, which had been large enough even in practice against a slightly built nera-Thukar, and he clearly hadn't spent the past four years idle. *He's still an unimaginative fighter, purely by the book*, Dahven realized. That was a point on *his* side; he pressed his attack. Eprian fell back a pace, slammed into the bench and nearly fell. He swore and tried to catch it with his foot, to hurl it at his opponent, jumped sideways when the weight of it threatened his balance. Behind him, Deehar shouted something and threw himself at the table, began scrabbling together something there. Dahven ignored him; ignored Dayher's shouted furious remarks. Eprian crouched, caught up a cushion with his off-hand sword and threw it.

Dahven brushed it aside with an edge; a second followed, caught on the other tip and filled the air with an explosion of feathers. Dahven jumped sideways as Eprian threw the last of the cushions and then leaped forward. Deehar was laughing wildly and now he screeched, "I have a knife, drive him over here, Eprian! I'll kill him, I'll—"

"Shut up!" Dayher bellowed, and Eprian roared over both, "Don't you dare, he's *mine*!"

"Am I?" Dahven laughed. "You can't take me, Eprian, you never could, you aren't that good!" His right blade slammed into Eprian's, slid down the edge with a nasty scree of outraged metal; Eprian twisted away just in time to save the back of his wrist. "You never were that good."

"Let me have him!" Deehar again. Out of the corner of his eye, Dahven saw the man swaying behind the table, a heavy-bladed dagger refracting blue-light from somewhere over his shoulder, and then Deehar pushed off from the table and began to move, toward the window.

Dayher swore and moved to intercept him; Dahven drew a pace sideways and then a second, blocking the window and Deehar's insane stalk. His heel hit the wall; the ledge caught the backs of his knees and he nearly fell. Eprian threw himself forward; Dahven caught himself bruisingly on both elbows and shoved. His shoulders burned but he was upright again, blocking two hard, wild cuts, pushing away from the wall with one foot, pivoting away from the window, backing into the room. Dayher had his brother against the wall, holding him in place with his whole body; on the other side of the room, Jennifer's white face and anxious eyes above the wide gag and Vey, who had edged himself into shadow and now crouched at the foot of the bed, both hands rubbing circulation back into her feet.

And then Eprian was on him again, pressing him toward the door. A moment later, despite his best intentions to find a way to bolt the thing and lock the five of them in, it was open, a glassy-eyed man staring, then turning to run; Dayher shouted something after him, Dahven didn't hear what. A step, two: Eprian pressed him, using his greater strength and mass, and somehow they were both out in the hallway, Eprian backing him toward the stairs.

Jennifer cried out as he vanished; only a faint squeak came through the gag but Vey's hands slipped from her feet. Dayher turned, frowned; Deehar pushed him aside, brought the knife up and started unsteadily across the room. Dayher snatched at his sleeve and missed. "Leave her!" he ordered. Deehar ignored him. "If Eprian loses, we need her, against Dahven."

Deehar giggled. "I won't kill her. Just hurt her a little.

Shut up, brother; I have the same rights you do, I'm Thukar, too." Jennifer lay very still and watched him; his eyes terrified her, more than the knife. *But if he comes within reach—oh, God, I can't, can't move!*

He swayed, stopped just short of the bed. She edged her knees slowly up toward her chest, prayed his attention was so fixed he wouldn't notice.

He didn't; Dayher, who had come up to grab him, did. "Her feet—how did you get loose?" Deehar squawked at the sudden sound where he hadn't expected any, a high-pitched, wordless shout of surprise and horror, and whirled. Jennifer jackknifed, wrapped her legs around his knees and yanked.

She was unbearably weak, her reflexes slowed; she probably wouldn't have stopped a half-grown child just now, but Deehar was soft and high on Zero. He fell forward, into his brother, arms and the forgotten knife out to catch himself. Dayher coughed, swore weakly and staggered back. Deehar tried to right himself; Jennifer yanked again and he went over sideways. Dayher took another step back and fell bonelessly just short of the table, the knife buried high in his chest.

Vey pulled himself upright and crawled onto the bed to work at the knots holding his wrists. A moment later Deehar pushed himself partway up, and Vey's hands went still but the man seemed unaware of them—unaware of the sounds of fighting in the hallway or the shouts from below. Of anything save his fallen brother. His shoulders shook; he clawed at his face and began to weep, a high, horrible wail that left Jennifer trembling. Vey tugged hastily at the cloth, murmured against her ear, "I'm sorry, a knife would make a better job of this but they took mine. Nearly—there." She shifted her weight to bring her arms forward, let him unknot the gag, ignoring the pain in her shoulders, numb fingers, the sharp tugs as he tore individual hairs that had been caught in the gag knot.

She lay still, cautiously flexing things; Vey edged over her and threw a loop of cloth over Deehar's head, down around his elbows, and dragged it tight. The man's voice had sunk to a whimper and now he was suddenly quiet. He fell flat when Vey gave him a shove.

Jennifer sat up; Vey dragged Deehar's hands away from his face and bound them behind him, ran the trailing edge of the cloth strip through the frame of the bed. He got to his feet rather cautiously, stood for a moment as though making certain he'd stay upright, then bent down to take hold of her elbows. "I'm sorry, Vey. You'll have to hold me up, I don't think I can stand otherwise." Her voice had an echo; there was still Thread here and there at unexpected moments but that was beginning to fade. Fortunately; she'd never have been able to walk, weak and through a maze of Thread at the same time. "Not that way!" Vey had her on her feet and was trying to lead her over to the window. "I don't care who's out there. Dahven's that way. I won't leave him."

Vey made a wry face and mumbled, "He'll have my ears and another of my fingers for this," but he shifted directions and helped her across the room, toward the hall.

IT wasn't totally dark in the hallway; there were blue-lights at both ends, Halydd's custom, and a lantern near the head of the stairs. Without that, Dahven thought, he'd have come to grief more than once, with all the loose carpets strewn across ancient board floors.

He'd held his own just outside the door for a long time, but a shout from inside had distracted him dangerously, and Eprian had taken advantage; the man was pressing hard, driving him toward the stairs. *Stairs. I'll break my neck, ruin Eprian's fun.* He bared his teeth, kept his back foot on the floor, shoving little rugs behind him as he felt for the drop-off.

There. There were fifteen or so of the things, he couldn't remember, didn't remember having ever really counted them, and they were steep but the steps themselves were wide. He dropped down to the first one, stepped down again and bounced back up, catching Eprian the least bit off guard. Before the man could go back on the offensive, he'd managed a brief glance behind him, found the stairs deserted, seen a pale face staring up from the entry to the commons room and at least one other from the hallway next to it that led out to the street. He skipped down three steps, moving across the stairs, and attacked. Eprian had the superior position now only in that he could hit harder from where he was than Dahven could, reaching up. *But he never was any good on odd terrain; he's mine.*

A commotion in the hallway, men shouting, and then Grelt's unmistakable voice shouting out, "We have them, Thukar, the back is secured and the upstairs. Stand aside!"

"No," Dahven shouted back. "He's mine!" All at once, beyond Eprian, at the very top of the stairs, he could see Jennifer, leaning against Vey. A thrill ran along his skin, standing the hair on end, and he laughed. "You wanted this, Eprian. What, can't you finish it?"

"I'll finish you!" Eprian shouted, and leaped down the stairs. Dahven retreated, lost count, hit the bottom of the flight hard enough to jar his teeth. Men behind him, gabbling excitedly, then silent as Grelt shouted something; men retreating as he moved out into the street, drawing Eprian on, away from Jennifer. The man was using all his reserves, all his strength; Dahven's arms were beginning to ache, the muscles hot and tightening. He pivoted just outside the inn's main entry, turned sideways and thrust and, more by luck than intent, caught the point of his blade inside the protective open metalwork on one of Eprian's. A moment later, the sword flew high, turned over in the air behind both men, and hit the street with a clang. Eprian froze. Dahven slipped his left hand from the basket and tossed it to one side, and attacked, hard.

Men, women all around them, on the far side of the fountain. Eprian must see them, too; he drew a ragged breath and beat off Dahven's offense, brought up an underhanded blow that hurt all the way into Dahven's shoulder, and backed until his legs were against the fountain. Dahven pressed forward; Eprian edged along the stone wall and suddenly pulled himself onto it. His sword came around and down in a vicious stroke. Dahven jumped back a long pace and then vaulted onto the low wall himself.

There was sweat on Eprian's forehead all at once. *Now. Before he realizes the mistake he's made in getting onto this narrow and uneven thing, and takes me. That would be— embarrassing.* Dahven shook his head, shifted his weight and brought up his lead foot as if he intended to thrust—as if he were tiring and no longer capable of subtle movement. Eprian shifted his weight and took one step back; his foot came down on the wall wrong, twisted under him, throwing him off balance. Dahven took one short step and then thrust. It went in below the ribs, angling up. Eprian hissed, tried to thrust in turn; his eyes went blank and the sword slipped from limp fingers; he sagged and fell, face down in the pool.

Dahven's sword was ripped from his fingers. He spread both arms for balance, went cautiously to one knee. Hands caught at his arms, wrapped around his shoulder; men aided him down from the wall, and then helped him sit on it. He drew a deep breath, nodded. "All right."

"You don't sound it." Grelt's voice close to his ear. Dahven laughed breathily.

"All right, you were right, I needed more time with the guards' practices, less behind a pile of papers. I'm winded, nothing else." He pushed the man's arm aside and got to his feet.

People stood silent and staring; they had been pressed back a distance from the inn and the fountain by city and market guards, but stood several deep beyond. Splashing behind him, as men went into the water to retrieve what was left of Eprian.

And then Jennifer, pale face above the light blue of her dress, standing just outside the entry with Vey, who was holding her, saying something. She shook her head, put his arm aside and walked across the road by herself—a little slowly, not very steadily, wrapped her arms around him and buried her face in his shoulder.

17

𝍫

THE Emperor's personal guard came twelve days later for Deehar, and with them not only Afronsan's clerks but the heir himself, which prompted a wild flurry of activity among the Thukars' household to find a proper set of rooms for him and food suited to royalty. Jennifer decided she was not terribly surprised to see Afronsan in Sikkre, after the official dispatches and all the inevitable wild rumor had reached him. Fortunately it was the heir and not the Emperor—Afronsan still preferred efficiency to pointless ceremony, was not at all dismayed that his chambers had been done up in haste.

An hour after his arrival he came down to the family dining, two of Dahven's guards and one of his own his only company, the dust of the road washed away but his shirt and breeches still plain and dark, to accept cool tea and the cooks' version of muffins. At his request, then, Dahven dismissed everyone but the heir, himself and Jennifer.

Afronsan ate and drank in silence for some time, accepted a second glass of tea and another muffin and set them aside. "My apologies," he said finally. "For not having come sooner. My bother is very unwell at the moment; I disliked leaving him but it seemed matters here might be cleared away more quickly if we met." He rubbed a hand across his forehead. "At least, I have left enough men in Andar Perigha that I know I will return to things as they should be, and not as your brothers wished them."

"You've found the men they bribed?" Dahven asked. Afronsan shook his head.

271

"One or two strong suspects; they'll be weeded out. I've sent good men who know how to ferret out such secrets. Your brother Deehar has not said anything to indicate who provided the money, and the drug?"

Dahven shook his head, swallowed. Jennifer touched his arm and answered for him. "The man has said nothing since Dayher died; all he does is rock back and forth and weep. Whether it's shock still, or because we denied him his drug—" She shrugged.

"And you have no clues otherwise?"

"I—was not precisely in a condition to hear everything they said," Jennifer replied. She broke a muffin in half and nibbled cautiously at one corner. The past two days, the morning sickness had stayed with her well past midday. Worry, perhaps: The midwife was unable to tell whether there was damage because of the drug; Jennifer herself could tell only that the baby still lived.

"Eprian would have known," Dahven said finally. His hand came across to rest on hers. "But he wouldn't have said, and now he can't. The men Eprian hired were local men— lower-market men who only wanted the coin, or those like the two young wall guards whose fathers had been loyal to my father and then to my brothers." He smiled faintly. "Since then, the guard captains and my personal staff have gone through the lists of those working in the household or guarding it, to check for such things."

"Like Dija's sister?" Jennifer shook her head and set the crumbled muffin aside. "Poor thing; the only one of the three girls who kept the old loyalty, and once she'd sent her sister with that message, they murdered her."

Dahven snorted. "You're still convinced Dija knew nothing about it?"

"Convinced," Jennifer said firmly. "Let's not waste Afronsan's valuable time with family matters."

"Speak of such matters," Afronsan said, "I am told the Thukara is pregnant."

Jennifer stared at him. "That was certainly quick work," she said finally.

"Quicker than you know." Afronsan leaned back in his chair and smiled. "The Emperor's astrologer told me; it was in his most recent charts." The smile broadened. "I would wager the Thukara could use some time to herself, perhaps a lighter mail sack for the next few months.''

''Just for a few weeks, until my stomach settles,'' Jennifer said. ''There's too much to do for me to simply sit around and get fat for the better part of a year.'' Dahven laughed. ''I'd hate it anyway; I'd be bored silly, same as you would. Get the telegraph up and the new presses here; that will simplify my life no end. You've heard nothing about Casimaffi's whereabouts, then?''

''Rumor,'' Afronsan said sourly. ''Plenty of that. But we've taken two of his ships along the coast south of Dro Pent and another outside Bezjeriad, at a spot on the inland sea—''

Jennifer rolled her eyes. ''Yes, I think I know just the place. We spent a long night there four years ago, on our way to Podhru.''

''The merchant Enardi said as much, and showed the guard where. He'll have the reward for that ship, though he's already going to be a very wealthy young man, since he is part of your nephew's trading company.''

''How nice,'' Jennifer said. ''And thank you on Chris's behalf.''

''The thanks are mine; your nephew has proven extremely useful to me, and I won't be ungrateful. We're keeping as quiet as possible about taking those ships, in hopes of getting others when they put in. We believe one of those we have brought your brothers here; it's being sent to Podhru so my guard can search it completely. There may be some hard proof against one or another of the foreigners, or at least some clue. I dislike uncertainty, and particularly when the trade is so good with both the English and the Americans. I personally have hopes of this device for creating ice.''

''You aren't alone,'' Jennifer said. ''I never knew what it was like *not* to have ice on demand until I came here. Particularly as hot as Sikkre is.''

''It could be worse,'' Dahven assured her. ''I might have been Duke of Dro Pent, which is hotter in summer, colder and foggier in winter and has a constant wind. I'm reminded,'' he added, and fished through the small pile of papers in front of him, ''this came not long ago, in the Ducal pouch; Wudron sent it. From the boy Krilan.''

Afronsan considered this briefly, then nodded. "The not-quite assassin, isn't he?"

"He promised to keep watch there for me; I frankly expected never to hear from him again, but he says that he's seen yellow hemp rings recently, two men wearing them like wrist bands and exchanging small boxes of powder for coin in a tavern by the docks. He says one of the men approached him, to try and sell it to him, but when he claimed he had no money, they left him alone. He says he saw them late the next night, leaving Dro Pent by the north road, and he says he is nearly willing to swear the man who spoke with him had a northern accent."

"A Holmaddi?" Afronsan considered this. "I'll have my clerk copy that letter to take with me, if I may. You know it's reached Cornekka, and the most likely route would be via Holmaddan. The caravaners send word to Podhru, anything they hear, and they tell me they've someone inside a coastal village watching for it."

"God," Jennifer said feelingly. "You *do* know that's sin-Duchess Lialla, don't you?"

He blinked in obvious surprise, shook his head. "Only that she was missing, and that her brother was extremely concerned."

"She's on a one-woman crusade to liberate Holmaddi women; we know she went, but none of her family or friends have heard from her since. I was beginning to wonder—well, it helps to know the caravaners are keeping an eye on her. I'll have to send a message to Aletto; he's probably half-mad by now."

She picked up the muffin and nibbled at it once again, let Dahven refill her water glass; Afronsan ate and drank quickly and got to his feet, waving them down when they would have stood. "Don't; finish your meal. If your guard is still outside the door, they can guide me down to the telegraph station. My clerks can manage for now, getting down what your guards saw and did, and we can schedule the taking of statements from your guardmaster and the man Vey, and yours at your convenience—perhaps this evening?" He smiled at Jennifer, added, "Take care, Thukara," then turned and strode away.

He and his company left late the next evening, through a

close-packed crowd of curious Sikkreni, most of whom had never been so close to royalty before. Afronsan bowed to the inevitable with good grace; over sensible traveling clothes, he wore the bright red and gold short cloak that was his as chief of Podhru's city guards, and a plain gold band in his hair; he let the enclosed carriage go ahead and walked with the Thukar and Thukara at his side, and waved and smiled. Just beyond the gates, he turned and waved a final time, clasped hands with Dahven, kissed Jennifer's cheek and climbed into the coach with his two chief clerks; it set off at a goodly trot, guardsmen and the extra clerks' coach ahead, a few guards and another coach bringing up the rear.

Jennifer leaned close and tugged at Dahven's sleeve. "I'd wager he's already got that case of contracts open."

"Silly wager," Dahven replied lightly. His eyes were following the heir's party still, fixed on the separate closed and close-guarded coach that held Deehar. He still would not speak, but where he had wept and rocked, he now walked when led, sat when pressed onto a bench, ate and drank when food and water was forced upon him—and otherwise sat unmoving, unblinking, hands loose in his lap, scarcely seeming even to breathe.

Jennifer touched Dahven's hand, glanced up at him in concern; he shook his head and managed a smile for her but his eyes were still dark. Around them, the crowds were dispersing, people returning to the market or hurrying home for the night as the breeze began to pick up. Jennifer shivered; the red gauze dress had been warm enough indoors but it was just barely enough out here. Dahven wrapped an arm around her shoulder, pulled her close.

"I'm sorry," she said finally.

He didn't pretend to misunderstand. "You know I don't blame you. I don't know who to blame—Father, most likely. Their mother, who knows? Poor horrid brother. I never liked him; I still don't. But what he did, how he could ever live with having killed his brother like that—"

"I know." Jennifer sighed. Stupid, awful brothers, and such a stupid, awful accident; she'd meant only to stop the man from cutting her. *If he'd simply fallen, if Dayher had grabbed him—Dayher wasn't any nicer than Deehar but he was practical.*

Dahven touched her cheek, ran a finger down to the corner of her mouth. "I know what you're doing, Jennifer; leave it. It wasn't your fault. And maybe it's for the best; I could never have made myself try to force information out of them the way I did Eprian's hired men."

"Afronsan might have."

"Might. He still might; Deehar's not dead, after all. Anything might have happened, or still may happen. Please, Jennifer, leave it." He glanced over his shoulder at the one guard still with them. "You had better pay attention to what I just said, Vey. No more long faces and chewing at yourself over getting caught."

Vey sighed faintly. "I feel stupid."

Jennifer twisted around to look at him, too. "I don't blame you." *Look at what I did*, she thought sourly. *You think I don't know how you feel?* "Things came out all right, though, and no one's teasing you about it, are they? They won't; you did a good job out there, Vey. For a man who's three times the size he used to be—"

"And four years away from sneaking around the market full-time," Dahven added. "Face it, you're not market-thief material any more, Vey."

"I found out, the hard way," Vey grumbled.

"Think of it this way," Dahven urged. "You were where you were needed when the Thukara needed you. Who cares how you managed it?" Silence. A few people still passed them, most heading out of the gates; a few turned to smile and Jennifer could make out the whispers, at least one word of them: "Baby." The market rumor mill had hold of it.

She let Dahven turn her away from the gates, let him set a slow, ambling pace up the main street toward the palace gates; Vey walked behind them, as much for show as for protection. It felt odd, she decided, not being surrounded by brutes with broadswords. *Maybe I can start running again, soon—by myself and along the streets, like I did what—only a month ago? How time flies when you're having fun.*

She wrapped one arm around Dahven's ribs, tucked the other in her belt. The midwife might be able to tell her something in a few days; old Rebbe thought there might be something he could do to make certain the drug hadn't harmed the child, and was down in his chambers buried under a mound of books. She patted her stomach lightly, smiled at a woman hurrying the other way with an enormous basket of bread tucked under one arm. The woman must be in her ninth month; she looked ready to explode, but it wasn't stopping her. She felt the worst of that knot of worry ease, all at once. *Yeah. We're tough, we Rhadazi women. And us Crays. And look at Chris; he came out pretty good despite everything.*

She came out of her thoughts, glanced up at Dahven; he'd turned his head to gaze wide-eyed after the woman with the bread, and she tickled his ribs. He captured her fingers with his free hand and looked down at her. "Don't say it," she warned. "I probably *will* look like that eight or so moon-seasons from now. Get used to it."

"It doesn't look comfortable—"

"I bet it isn't. *I'll* get used to that part." They entered the tunnel that separated city from palace grounds and Jennifer picked up the pace. "Come on. I think I know where we're going to put this nursery. We'd better take advantage of Afronsan's finer sensibilities, while they last, because I know darned well whatever his present intentions, I won't make it halfway to term before he's got my desk loaded right back to where it is now."

"He wouldn't—" Dahven began as they walked into the hall. He laughed. "I know, consider who it is."

"It's the only way he knows, full bore," Jennifer said. She sighed. "I don't envy the man: all the increased work trying to set up all these trade agreements, Shesseran fading fast—"

"We suspected as much, remember," Dahven said. "The timing of the twins' attacks."

"And that's another thing; whoever was backing them and supplying them—and Casimaffi—with Zero. They might have suffered a temporary setback but that won't stop them, whoever it is that wants Rhadaz. They'll regroup and come at us again." She shook her head, tightened her grip on his waist as they started up the stairs to the family apartments. "I'm going to give myself nightmares and warp this poor child's mind. At least for tonight, let's let it go, act as though it's all right."

"Some things are." Dahven dropped a kiss on her forehead as they reached the hallway. "Who knows, maybe everything will be."

"Hold that thought," Jennifer said lightly. She eased out of his grasp, took hold of his hand and tugged. "Come on, this way."

THE sun was high when the three wagons bearing Red Hawk flags pulled into Hushar Oasis, settling into space left open for them by the caravan already in place under the trees. A middle-aged woman swung down from the lead wagon and strode rapidly across rock and sand to the grandmother's wagon; moments later, she came back, the older woman on her heels.

Lialla woke and cried out as cool fingers touched her forehead. "It is all right, you are back with friends now." A familiar voice; she blinked rapidly and found the grandmother of the Gray Fishers gazing down at her, forehead puckered with concern. "Sil tells me they found you in the city, miles from the village, and in the company of a young Holmaddi male."

"I—" Lialla drew a deep, shuddering breath, shook her head. After a moment, she went on. "I'm sorry; I was fine earlier."

"Reaction," the other woman said. "Take your time; we have plenty." She shifted, drew a packet of folded paper from her pocket. "There are messages, things we have heard or been told, that you should know. Read; we can talk about the Holmaddi when you have finished." Lialla nodded, swallowed, unfolded the packet with trembling hands and fixed her eyes on it. She felt the blood coloring her cheeks. *Ashamed. I know it's foolish, there was nothing I could have done to change matters. But I failed, and badly, whoever was at fault. And now I feel as though she must be watching me, thinking I failed because I lost my nerve.*

Concentrating on reading helped, a little; her hands steadied and the lump left her throat. *It wasn't pleasant, some of it was purely ugly; go easy on yourself, you have a right.* And then the letter claimed her full attention.

It was actually more of a series of notes or short memos, as though the grandmother and other caravaners had written down things for her as they heard them, or were given them to pass on to her. "The Duke is very anxious to locate his sister; rumor has it the Lady Lizelle is not well, and while some suspect a wasting illness the present duchess and the Thukara of Sikkre fear she may be ingesting this new drug.'' *Oh, Mother.* Lizelle wouldn't— But Lialla pushed that thought aside almost at once. Lialla would not, but she was not her mother; Lizelle might well turn to something the way Aletto had to wine. Lizelle— *I can't stop her; she still sees me as a child, or Merrida's novice—Merrida's warped novice. Aletto will want me to deal with it, to help Robyn deal with it, and I can't.*

There was another way; deal with the source, remove that.

It wasn't only reaction that was tightening her stomach with dread. Something else, in the back of her mind, chewing on her. *I can't.* This time there was no conviction to the words.

One thing certain: She wasn't going back to Duke's Fort like this, to listen to Aletto for the next twenty moon-seasons.

In his own way, he was as stiffly male as some of the worst Holmaddi. *Robyn encourages him.* She grinned suddenly. That boy Krilan hadn't been nearly as male-arrogant as Aletto at his worst; and once he'd gotten his hands into Thread, he'd been nearly as fun to be around as Chris was. Well, for the short few hours she'd had to teach him, anyway. He'd learned a surprising amount before the caravaners had come for her, and she didn't doubt he'd learn more, the way he was willing to try things. She could only hope he remembered what the stuff was, what *he* was, where he was using it. Playing with dynamite, as Chris would say. Another of those ''Tell you later'' words of his.

She sighed very faintly, read down the last of the messages; most of them were things she'd already heard from Sil during the journey here, once they'd crossed the Holmaddan border and she'd been free to come out of hiding and sit on the seat. Drugs, and an unknown enemy, and Chris—not surprisingly—right in the middle of it. Jennifer and Dahven, a dead twin and a mad one—an heir to Sikkre. *Casimaffi. Chris was right about him, but I never trusted him either.*

That had not been one of Casimaffi's ships in the harbor up north. It had been foreign, its crew foreign—there had been no flags, no markings of any kind. Lialla let her papers fall; a chill crossing her shoulders. *Kepron. Even if he thinks to be cautious with his new knowledge, he's part of Vuhlem's guard; I couldn't persuade the arrogant young fool from that.*

And Vuhlem will be furious I'm missing, he'll question every-
one who might have aided me. And—and he has a Triad. She
clamped her lips together to stop them from quivering, looked
up to find the grandmother's eyes on her. *He may already be*
dead, poor brash child. As much my fault as his—partly mine,
at least. I owe Vuhlem—but I own Kepron, too. She shook
her head, sighed faintly.

"Sin-Duchess?" the grandmother inquired gently. "Are
you well?"

"I—I guess so. Not ill; a good sleep, a little food, I'll
probably feel fine. I'll have to." She looked up to find the
older woman watching her. "Because it's not done, what I
set out to do. Somehow, some way—I have to go back."